The Hero of Negropont

Tales of Travellers, Turks, Greeks
and a Camel

A Quest

John Mole

f

First published by Fortune in 2016
www.fortunebooks.xyz

ISBN:978-0-9557569-3-1

Cover picture is from *Byron's Dream* 1831
Drawn by J D Harding and engraved by J T Wilmore

For illustrations in colour see fortunebooks.xyz

Printed and bound by CPI Group (UK) Ltd, Croydon, CR0 4YY

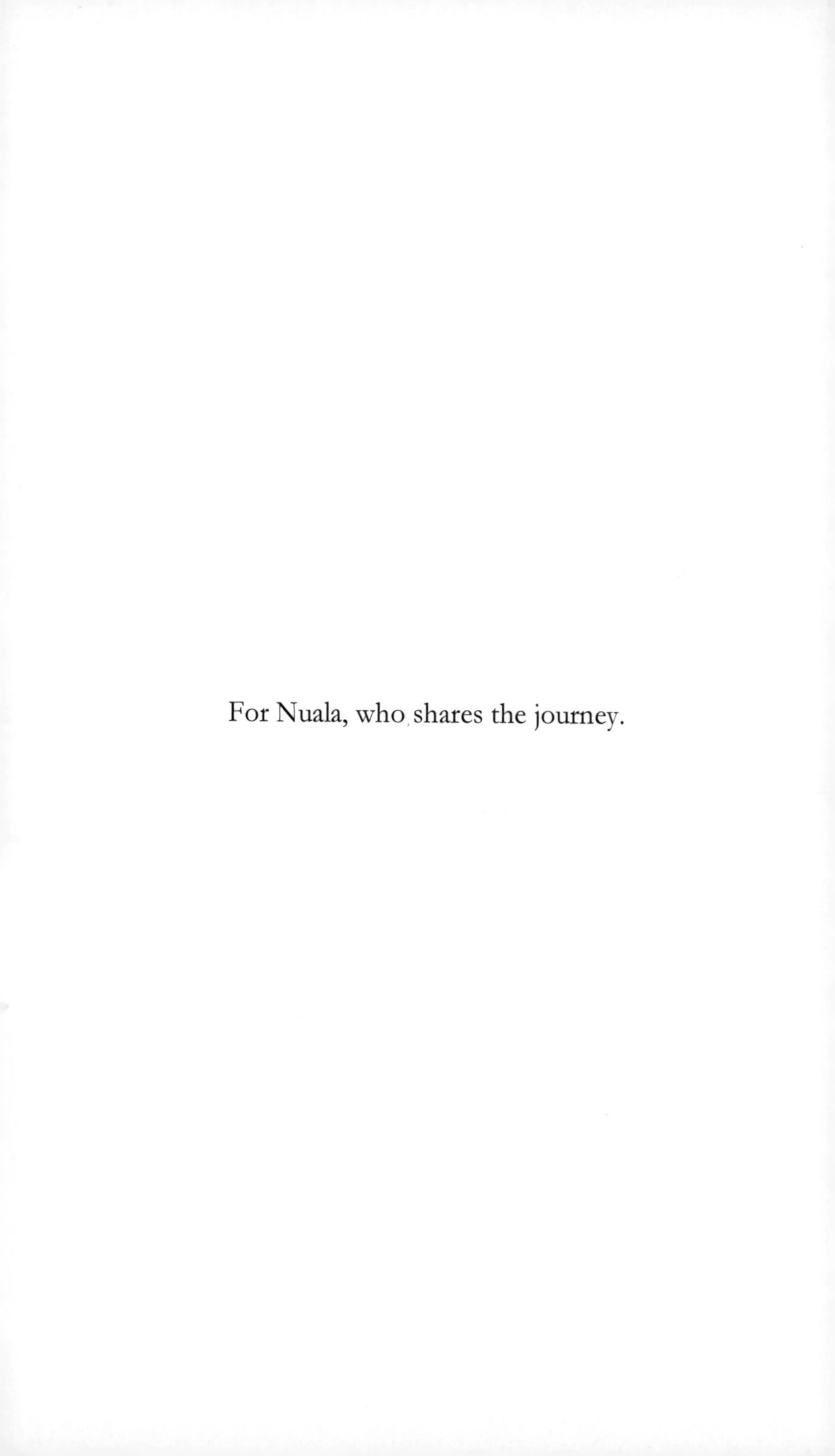

For Nuala, who shares the journey.

Every superficial stripling, who takes a trip, takes notes as he goes along; and, when he returns, puts them into a bookseller's hands to be furbished up and swelled to a marketable size; and then out skips a brace of volumes. This is an ingenious method of making a journey pay its own expenses. With respect to the contents of some books of travels. I cannot help thinking it a species of literary fraud, when their authors fill them with historical accounts, which every man might have collected at his own fire-side.

Vicesimus Knox Essays Moral and Literary. Dublin 1786

Once upon a time, when fleas were barbers and camels worked in public baths and I rocked my mother's cradle

Traditional Turkish

CONTENTS

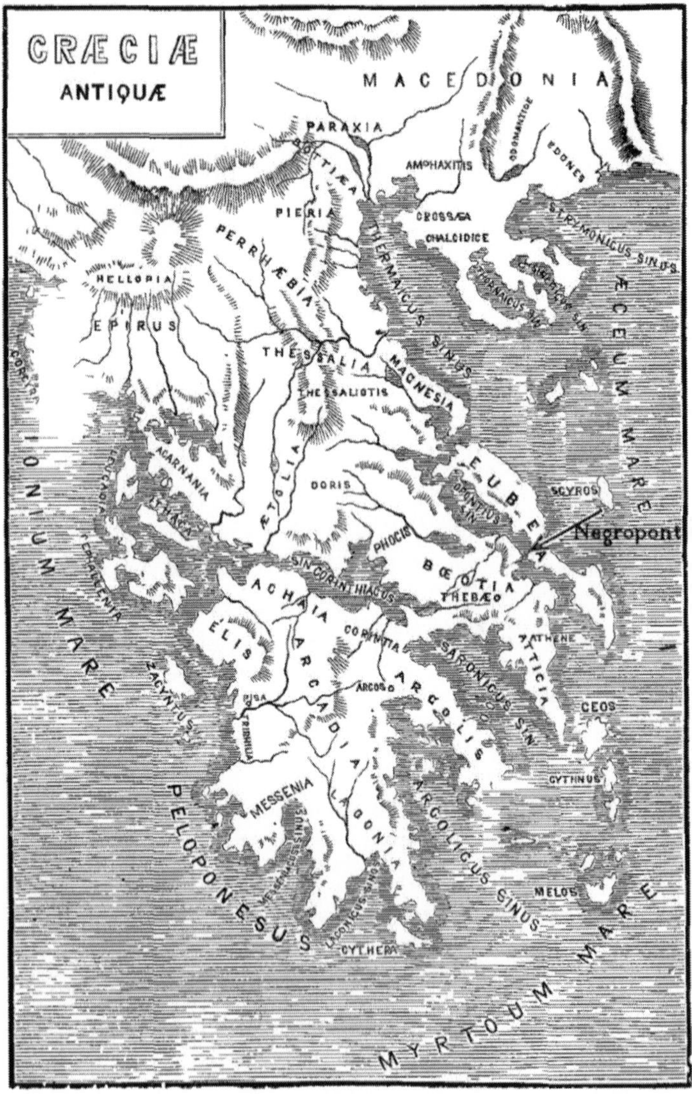

GRÆCIÆ ANTIQUÆ

MACEDONIA
PARAXIA
BOTTIÆA
AMPHAXITIS
EDONES
PIERIA
CROSSÆA
CHALCIDICE
STRYMONICUS SINUS
PERRHÆBIA
THERMAICUS SINUS
HELLOPIA
EPIRUS
THESSALIA
MAGNESIA
THESSALIOTIS
ÆGEUM MARE
IONIUM MARE
ACARNANIA
ITHACA
ÆTOLIA
DORIS
EUBŒA
OPUNTIUS SIN
SCYROS
Negropont
PHOCIS
BŒOTIA
THEBÆ
SIN CORINTHIACUS
ACHAIA
CEPHALLENIA
ELIS
CORINTHIA
ATHENÆ
ATTICA
SARONICUS SIN
ARCADIA
ARGOS
ARGOLIS
ZACYNTHUS
PISA
CEOS
CYTHNUS
MESSENIA
LACONIA
ARGOLICUS SINUS
PELOPONESUS
MELOS
LACONICUS SINUS
CYTHERA
MYRTOUM MARE

Euboea - Negropont - Egripos

FORTUNA

Fortuna!

I looked to where the Captain pointed but saw only a black cloud looming on the horizon. His mate took up the shout. Fortuna! Fortuna! The sailors scurried faster than I had yet seen that mob of Levantine lingerers bestir themselves, pulling on this and tying up that. I concluded that whatever fortune was in store would soon slip from our grasp. The commotion smoked out my companions from our cabin.

"Bigod what's up? Pirates?" growled Higgins.

"God forbid," peeped Winstanley.

We scanned the sullen swell for a Moorish galley or an Albanian brig. There was nothing to see, not even the dolphins and seagulls that had escorted us from Sicily, only the black cloud bearing down upon us. In front of us was blackness and lead. Behind us was brightness and foam. We were on the cusp between two worlds, light and dark, night and day, good and bad. Reason said prefer the first but there was delicious apprehension in the second.

First was lightning, forks of it, tridents of it, two at a time, cracking the sky not top to bottom but side to side, two fathoms above the surface of the sea; then thunder, great gavel blows bringing the world to order before the cataclysm; a canon blast of wind and a dreadful rolling thunder; no horizon but a great tide bearing down on us broadside. The wind began to blow immensely strong and gusty. The waves rose in towering heaps, taking on the lowering black of the clouds and the hollow roar of the thunder. We were assaulted by such torrents from the skies and waves from the sea that it was impossible to distinguish them.

"We are in God's hands" whimpered pious Winstanley.

"We are in God's arse" muttered impious Higgins.

Our Captain paced before the wheel, giving first one order and then another to his helmsman, undecided whether to face or flee our fate. He struck all sail but for a stay on the mizzen and this was soon taken away by the gale. Everything movable on deck was washed away and much that was fixed, including the binnacle and the taffrail and the helmsman, poor devil. The Captain ordered the wheel to be lashed. Our ship ran bare-poled, tossed hither and thither by cross seas; her seams began to open by her labouring; she wallowed like a log; water poured into her hold and our cabin, so it seemed we would drown equally well indoors or out. The Captain bellowed, the seamen bustled, and we were ordered below, accused of conspiring to help the storm by getting in the way of their manoeuvres. We persevered on deck, each praying in his own way for deliverance, Winstanley reasoning with the Lord who had walked upon the water and Higgins cursing the devil and I kneeling with my head in the scuppers to give Neptune his due.

After an hour of this watery hell we heard a new noise dead ahead, a beating, booming crashing din. *Matapan*, went the rumour round the men. This is the name of the great cape of the southern Greek mainland and I felt a surging relief that at last we were near dry land, until I saw the consternation on their faces. The Captain ordered the wheel unlashed. Somehow they rigged a handkerchief on the remaining mast to give us way and we steered to larboard. Half an hour later we heard the same sound again, dead ahead. We tacked away to starboard and soon heard the danger again to larboard. To starboard, to larboard, to starboard again until we heard the ominous din on both sides. There was nothing to do. Helpless, we clung to the rigging and waited for the Clashing Rocks to crush us.

"Like fish in a trap," bellowed Higgins and shook his fist to the sky.

"*Amidst the rocks he heard a hollow roar*
Cliffs and shaggy shores, a dreadful sight!
All rough with rocks, with foamy billows white," piped Winstanley.

As the cliffs closed in on either side the wind blew mightier and seas piled upon seas. I was so disoriented that sometimes I sensed we were flying under the sea, sometimes sailing through the storm clouds; terror was sublimated now into despair, now into elation. After an age of struggling in mind and body against the buffets of the storm I surrendered to the awful power around us. I was immediately wrapped in the sweetness of submission. In a cloak of calm I heard the din, I saw the rampaging waters, but I was in a different place, outside and above it all, at one with an ethereal being. My grip on the rigging weakened, my stance on the bucking deck relaxed.

A goddess rose out of the waves not a chain's length from the ship, rising from the foam, a lovely woman, bathed in her own light, naked as a statue, with only her silken tresses to preserve her modesty. With such grace she extended her hand to me and smiled. Her divine beauty illuminated my true self; she was my saviour; she restored me to life.

"By God I will have you. And a pint of champagne too," I shouted at the vision and was tossed back into the hurly-burly of the tempest.

How did I get into this watery pickle?

EXILE

Look at my parents in the breakfast room: John Bull nourishing the guts of an Englishman with brown stout and offal; Britannia, swathed in Grecian folds and flaunting the shield of righteousness, the helmet of propriety and the spear of pretentiousness, slurping milk slop. Money and breeding! Such a marriage! A line of London merchants, bankers and aldermen, grown rich in the Turkey trade, converged with a line of Lords and Ladies grown poor at the races and the gaming tables. On the stage we know who is New Money, wiping his mouth on his sleeve, slamming his tankard on the table, and who is Old Breeding, dabbing her lips and delicately putting down the crested China cup, but this is not a stage. My father is an Earl. His sister is Lady of the Chamberpot, or some such, to Her Majesty. My mother has an income of fifty thousand a year and her brother has a factory in Constantinople.

Breakfast is the prelude to intimacy. With a belch and a sigh they rise and wish each other a good morning, their first words of the day. Mother leads the way upstairs. At the end of the corridor she waits for Father to open the door. Taking advantage of her déshabille and lack of hoop or horsehair, he slaps her rump, a daily indignity she has suffered in silence since the evening he first ushered her into the bridal chamber.

For over twenty years she has hoped that her indifference will discourage him, while he has hoped for a reaction.

They enter a small room decorated for scholarship. Geography is served by a map of the county, History by a bust of the First Earl, Natural History by a portrait of Excelsior the Derby winner, Natural Philosophy by a diagram showing the correct amounts of gunpowder for different gauges of shot, Fine Art by a silhouette of my mother, Literature by the texts contained in a pile of *The Rambler's Magazine Or The Annals Of Gallantry, Glee, Pleasure And The Bon Ton, Calculated For The Entertainment Of The Polite World*, a long-winded way of saying erotic tales and gossip. My favourites are *The History And Adventures Of A Bedstead* and *The Memoirs Of Lydia Lovemore.* This delightful periodical is aimed at the Man Of Pleasure, a harmless and honourable vocation so long as it consists of both receiving and giving.

And so the philosopher parents take their ease before the window on a velvet-upholstered bench, artfully designed so that its occupants may either look out on the estate or have their backs to the light for reading or sit opposed for the convenience of conversation. Courteously, Father lifts one of the mahogany lids for Mother and the other for himself. They lower what has to be lowered and raise what has to be raised, accommodate themselves on the velvet seat and Hey Ho! Fire Away! I will leave the olfactory and auditory elements of the scene to your imagination, dear Reader. Be generous with them, according to your own experience.

They are privy with each other with unfailing regularity. They have a similar double closet in London and a travelling version for Bath and Droitwich, in case their lodging does not have this convenience. The double throne is the seat, the bottom, the fundament of their marriage. They spend the rest of the day on their own affairs, Father in the hunting fields of the county and Mother in its drawing rooms. Their daily rite is their last remaining intimacy, in which they relieve themselves of their innermost notions, Mother's in dribs and drabs, disconnected little nuggets, squeezed out with sighs; Father's half-baked and blustery, exploding into the world with grunts of satisfaction. They churn and mix together their excretions and, more often than not, dump them on my head, for the issue they most often air is their own, their son and heir.

And so it was that after one of their conflatulations I was summoned into the library; dark leather bindings from floor to ceiling, oaken lecterns, the ladders and galleries of a Newgate scaffold. My disinclination for study derives from this gloomy place of sermon, sentence and chastisement. Father stood at window, back to the light, looming ominous. As soon as I heard the dreaded words 'Yer mother and I have decided...' I feared the worst, but not worst enough. I had been hounded home by some trivial fracas involving a wager, a gallop down Piccadilly, an upset carriage and a summons. I expected a lecture and some vague threat of spending the rest of the season with Mother in Leamington or inspecting our estates in Ireland, serious punishments indeed but not difficult to evade. I failed to anticipate the worst sanction of all.

"Yer mother and I… decided... The Tour."

The Tour! The European Tour! The Grand Tour! The Sword of Damocles hanging over the youth of England! Exile from home, friends, horses, dogs, mistresses. Foreigners with their dreadful languages, food, manners and diseases; the perils of the road with sordid inns and interminable scenery; ruins, museums, galleries, sites and sights, tiresome enough in the smudgy prints and daubs brought home by previous victims and in reality the epitome of tedium.

"Father...but why?"

"Yer Edgy Kayshen, Mibboy."

This was humbug. The only Edgy Kayshen he cared about was whether I could jump the sticks, shoot straight, and use a rapier. He never made the Tour himself. He had done the only decent thing with foreigners: shot them. Now he wanted shot of me.

Oh for the days when the bloods of England cut swathes through Europe in pursuit of Rape and Loot. We descendants of the Black Prince now have to be polite to foreigners in pursuit of Seduction and Shopping. The end result is similar - we come home with cases of bibelots and pox. But where is the glory in spilling guineas not blood? Better to empty a pistol than a purse on foreign Johnnies.

Worse was to come.

"Proceed Italy to Constantinople...yer Uncle accommodate yer."

"But Father, he is in trade."

"Consul's rank…entry to the court.. Sultan… monopoly of walnuts…yer rank uncompromised…Ainslie the Ambassador… me fag at Harrow … introductions yer uncle can't..."

Depending on the good offices of a man regularly flogged by my father was the least of my misgivings. What would I do there? Count walnuts? Buy and sell things is what I should be expected to do. The British ambassador's salary is paid by the tradesmen of the Levant Company. His Excellency is not so much the embodiment of the sovereign power of his Britannic Majesty as Mr. Fortnum soliciting a customer.

And worse. As well enter a monastery as go to Turkey for society - travel no further than Drury Lane to witness the seclusion of women for the sole delight of their tyrannical masters. Add to this the Muslim proscription of wine, dancing and theatrical performance and you are left with a Season which would make Leamington Spa attractive.

There was no point in arguing the toss with Father. My mother was behind this. Appeasement was the best stratagem so I lapsed into his vernacular.

"Very well Father... affairs in order...three months...make preparations…assemble accoutrements… organise passage …find companions… winter… perilous crossing… roads impassable …depart next spring…"

Anything could happen by then: plague, apoplexy, war with the French, and in six months I would be twenty-one and not beholden to their authority. Alas they had anticipated this.

"Leave now…first of the month…companions found…I'll settle yer affairs… creditors … summons..."

I am a scion of the English aristocracy. I am indebted to tailors, boot makers, merchants, publicans, bankers, Shylocks, usurers, and sundry creditors. I was chucked out of school, rusticated from Oxford, ejected from countless bawdy houses, and am generally considered in Town and County the bravest blade. I am valiant in pursuit of foxes, dauntless in the massacre of birds, heroic in a steeplechase, intrepid at the gaming table, spirited at the theatre, gallant in the boudoir, untiring in the bawdy house, gracious at the ball, witty in the coffee house. To my parents I bring pride, expense, summonses for debt and proposals of marriage. In short I am the model son. And how do they reward me? Here is your narrator, your guide, your HERO, for want of a worse word - sent into exile, sacrificed to filial duty and financial obligation. I would enter my majority with a clean slate but at what cost? And with what dreadful company?

I will introduce my fellow Tourists as I was introduced to them.

TOURISTS

When Father pronounced sentence in the library it was only the beginning. There was worse: I was to be denied proper company, good fellows to keep the spirits up, in case we led each other into mischief. I was to be provided with a tutor and an artist. The former was my mother's choosing, the Reverend Arthur Winstanley, late of Christ Church Oxford.

I was summoned to the drawing room. Winstanley sat pallid and prim on the edge of his chair, in tight black clothes, his hair plastered down like a skullcap, his arms to his side and his hands clenched tight, coiled to spring into sycophancy. On his concave belly a watch chain made a thread of silvery slime. He was not many years senior to me but old beyond his years, not in appearance, which was smooth and juvenile, but in the gravity of his demeanour, a maturity derived not from experience of the world but a lifetime spent with dry old books and wet old men. This was to be my companion to the Orient.

"Did you know Mr. Winstanley at the House?"

"I did not have that pleasure, Mama, our paths did not cross."

They may have crossed as he made his way to matins and I to bed. Otherwise my path rarely crossed with anyone outside the clubs, including my tutors, which is why I did not remain long in residence. One especially steered clear of tuft-hunters and biblers like Winstanley, who had been skulking round my mother for months in the hope of obtaining the curacy of the village church, which is in our gift.

"My dear, Mr. Winstanley is an authority on Homer. He will be a precious guide through Greece."

"How do you reconcile the pagan Gods with our true religion?" I asked. He shot a glance at Mama.

"The poets tell of how Jesus Christ redeemed Homer and all the ancient prophets from Hell. They foreshadowed the incarnation of Our Blessed Lord and his Saving of Mankind through his Precious Blood." He bowed his head at our Redeemer's name and my mother dutifully imitated him.

My consolation was that if his company was punishment for me, mine was for him. This pious bookworm must have welcomed the proposal of the Tour with even less enthusiasm than I. All his months of hopes, prayers and ingratiation come to this, a year or more of travel and travail with me. I was his test, his trial, his ordeal. If he came through, his reward would be a living and the curacy of our church. I promised myself that he would earn his sinecure.

The artist was my father's choosing, Cornelius Higgins. I was summoned to the billiard room. Bumpers of brandy were more palatable than Mama's China teas but didn't lessen my foreboding. Father was seated in his great leather chair, a box of cigars at his elbow. Beside the fireplace slouched a menial come to stoke the fire. I selected a cigar and beckoned him to give me a taper to light it with. He had the insolence to ignore me.

"Mibboy…Mr. Higgins…draughtsman…"

Dear Reader, picture to yourself an artist, slender fingered, slight, pale of face, exuding sensibility and good taste, one of the twiddle poops that haunt the Royal Academy. Now picture the opposite and you will begin to picture Higgins, a broad shouldered, bow legged brute of some forty years. His head was different shades of red all over, from beetroot complexion, blood-shot eyes, tracery on the nose, veins on the cheeks to ginger curls and bird's-nest beard. He had boxer's ears, bruiser's lips, wrestler's belly, brawler's arms, bare-knuckler's hands, tug-o-war thighs, and, in startling contrast, dainty fencer's feet.

"Draughtsman, Papa? What will he draw? Our cart?"

"Genius with pencil…"

Higgins selected a cigar, bit off the end and spat it into the fireplace from which he took a taper, lit his own and passed it to me.

"Me valet…the colonies…France…good man with a blade…"

Clearly he was chosen more for his skill with the poniard than the pencil. While Winstanley was to be guardian of my soul, Higgins was to be guardian of my body. But the thought of appearing in the drawing rooms of Europe with this simian in tow…

"Sir!" was all I could say in protestation, which the ape took for a greeting.

"Me pleasure Sorr."

To cap it all the devil was an Irishman.

It soon became apparent that all this was my mother's doing. She wanted me away from scandal; the dames and dowagers of her drawing rooms wanted me away from their daughters; the burghers of her family wanted their lodges and liveries preserved from gossip; their bankers wanted their coffers preserved from my creditors; the magistrates wanted no more inducements and intercessions on my behalf.

And there was worse. Her brother, my uncle, the Turkey merchant in Constantinople, wanted a return for the treasure his family had bestowed on our family name. Whatever my age and whatever reputation that preceded me, I had the rank and title that would ease his path into circles from which he was hitherto precluded, both Turkish and English. It was not I who would benefit from my uncle's patronage - it was he who would benefit from mine.

And there was worse. My brave companions and I were charged with collecting such statues, urns and ornaments we could ship, and drawing those we could not, for the enhancement of our ancient seat. Under my mother's influence the family seat was becoming no more ancient than my own bottom. I was born, like my father and his fathers before him, in a good old English house with chimneys and ghosts from Good Queen Bess, to which each generation added its bit. Since that auspicious day my mother was engaged in pulling the old place down - too dark, too low, too *old,* she said, by which she meant unfashionable. So now we lived in the shell of a Palladian palazzo under Athenian porticos, pediments, arcades, and colonnades. She seized on a harmless bit of plain old English countryside, enough for a decent steeplechase, and was carving out Arcadia: we must have a lake and a grotto and a temple and a grove and a ruin.

Why all this Romery and Greekery? It is absurd to have a Roman villa in a Leicestershire field, a Florentine palazzo on a Kentish hill, a pagan temple in a Surrey wood. The good old English countryside is littered with Grecian trumpery that belongs in Vauxhall Gardens. Do we have no English style, no English castles, no English churches? Why decorate our houses with half naked cherubs and putti, nymphs and satyrs, poor shivering things, exiled from the sun to our misty meadows? We have fairies and hobgoblins of our own who belong in our woods and fields. Even Tudor Christ Church has a Mercury in the middle of its yard - get it out, I say, and put Puck in its place; not to speak of its faux Grecian library all out of scale and out of context in its elegant Peckwater quadrangle, pompous white marble foisted on mellow Cotswold stone.

New Money has no taste of its own so they buy it ready made. Mama wished to see in her house what she wished for herself - taste, refinement, elegance, acceptance of her family in Society for more than her wealth and her husband's breeding line. So she sent me out with a shopping list. She provided us with a list of parts and the most she would pay: a torso, 12 guineas; armless wench, 25 guineas; amphora, 3 guineas, horse head, 15 guineas. Egged on by the Academy, foreigners make copies of their art in cheap stone and plaster and hand them to us with a smirk. They keep the best for themselves and palm us off with bits of old marble they'd as soon burn up for quicklime.

All in all, I was not in the best of spirits to embark on my journey.

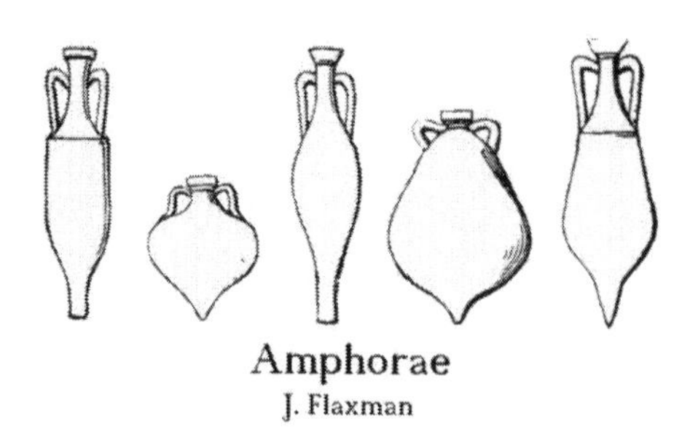

Amphorae
J. Flaxman

A QUEST

My bookseller insists that our journey must have a Quest. There should be some tangible goal to provide a framework for the narrative. The mission must not be easily accomplished but hindered by obstacles that we must overcome for our enlightenment and your entertainment. He says the quest is the spine of novels and travel books.

The quest is more than a literary device: it is an allegory of life. Underlying the quest is the Christian idea that life is a trial, whose sole purpose is reward at the destination. But is this the only way to consider life's journey? For my part, the purpose of a journey is the journey. If it contains any quest at all, it is to find decent lodging, pleasant scenery, good company and to avoid danger and discomfort. A journey is an end in itself and a quest is an unnecessary distraction. Indeed, the committed traveller does not want to reach the goal for it means the entertainment is over.

Substitute the word life for journey and you have a philosophy that was coined by Epicurus. What awaits life's journey is the grave and so we dally and linger and seek pleasure in the byways and put the ultimate end out of our minds. So the Devil take the quest, I say, we shall all get there soon enough. Don't wish your journey away on contemplating what lies at the end.

There is no point to my journey. It is motivated by its origin not its destination, the compulsion to depart rather than the reward of arriving. I am pushed not pulled. I have no goal. Our destination is certainly Constantinople but I have no desire to go there. To lard over our aimless ramblings with a specious quest at the bidding of my bookseller is patronising and unnecessary. I am expelled from England and must arrive in Constantinople, that is the framework of my narrative.

Join us then on an Epicurean journey and let us continue with thunder machine and wind machine and a crack on the cymbals.

A European gentleman by a Turkish artist

EGRIPOS

For how long we laboured in the hollow of the storm I cannot say. It grew no worse and the little light of hope grew stronger. The gale became a wind, the breakers turned to billows, the torrent dissolved into a mist. The clouds above us opened for an instant and we greeted a golden crescent in our various languages, *fengari, luna, selena, moon.* The shores on either side of us took shape and opened from the narrow strait, through which we had shot, into an open bay. We asked our Captain where we were but he ignored us, proof, if it were needed, that he had no idea.

We tossed along the eastern shore, looking for a harbour, and were half a day before we found one. We stood in for the port, steering so close to the land that we were within ten feet of being dashed upon the rocks, and found an anchorage inside the harbour that was scarcely more favourable than the sea outside. The water was so agitated that the Captain would not lower a boat for fear of it being swamped. We gazed with longing at the solid ground so tantalisingly close.

By sunrise it was as if the tempest had never been. The gentle breeze blew away the nightmare and the promises we had made in return for our salvation. We prayed so long as danger lasted and now reverted to ribaldry.

"Didn't I tell you to trust in the Lord?" preached Winstanley.

"Then why did you beshit yourself?" taunted Higgins.

"For the same reason you swore to God's Mother you would not touch another drop of spirit," I scoffed.

"Arrah, we're not saved yet," he grumbled, granting himself a reprieve from sobriety.

So in manly conversation we concealed our true feelings of humility and relief. As for myself, I reflected on my Goddess of the Foam and resolved to honour her at the earliest opportunity. Abstinence since our departure from Italy had given an edge to my appetite for the sex, exacerbated by our near shipwreck. The nearness of death inspires as much regret for the sins one has not committed as repentance for those one has.

On three sides we were dominated by mountains dropping steeply to the sea and penetrated by the bay in which we found shelter. An imposing castle stood sentry on a bluff. A sandy beach was lined with stone hovels and punctuated by a rocky mole. The landscape required the descriptive talents of the brush rather than the pen, as I informed our painter-in-residence.

"Mister Higgins. Surely even your bloodshot eyes will find some pretty sight to massacre. To work."

This was malice. His hand could not hold the charcoal until he had drunk a glass or two of brandy for his breakfast.

"Bigod, how many of your bucolic pictures do I have to draw? I have picturesqued every scene and ruin from London to Leghorn."

"What else can you draw? Other than a cork?"

The truth was that Higgins drew like an old maid. His pictures were competent but lacking spirit, that touch of the daemonic which marks out the nightmares of Harry Fuseli and other modern artists. His bloodless talent was at odds with his boozing, brawly nature. I wished for his sake that he would infuse his pictures with the passion he vented in the tavern.

A crowd of ragged idlers gathered on the beach to gawp at us. We were eager to disembark but our Captain ordered our weapons to be prepared, not that we had anything serviceable but blades and pikes, since every grain of powder was waterlogged. His men jury-rigged the broken masts and tattered sails in case we had to run for it.

"What is the matter? These are God-fearing people," said Winstanley and clutched his ever-present bible. "A false God but a God nevertheless."

"God-fearing or not, if this is a nest of pirates we will make a fight of it," said the Captain. "Unless you prefer to be sold to the galleys."

"We are British subjects, Sir!"

"Then you may be ransomed. But the rest of us will fight."

He pored over his sodden charts but he had little idea where we were. He called to the natives and asked the name of the place. Protimo was the answer, which left him none the wiser, then Egripos, which left him none the happier.

"The Turks of Egripos," he said and glowered. "We must refit as best we can and leave by nightfall."

When I asked the reason for his ill opinion of our hosts he shrugged and said he hoped we would never find out but to keep our purses and our breeches buttoned.

Our companion, tutor, adviser, Mentor and sage, tedious Winstanley, jumped in with the information that Egripos is better known to scholars as the island of Euboea. Egripos is a Turkish corruption of Euripos, the name of a narrow channel, famous in antiquity, in which the tides flow two ways at once. Egripos in turn was corrupted by Venetians to Negropont, as it is known to us and other civilised peoples. Once again his Oxford learning proved admirable but useless.

We were diverted by the sight of a little cavalcade ambling down the road towards the mole. It consisted of a handful of janissaries on broken nags and a platoon of ragged urchins led by a portly gentleman on a mule so short that his feet almost touched the ground. He was of some fifty years of age with hennaed moustaches and a dignified belly. He had put on a fantastical and ancient uniform, like a dancing bear keeper's, to honour us, although his fingers foraged in his nostrils which impaired his dignity. His turban was extravagant and had it slipped further down his waxy face would have extinguished him like a candle-snuffer. We disembarked to greet him.

I had learned on our journey to treat these petty officials with the civility I reserved in London for royalty and my bankers. I said that I was a member of the Great British Aristocracy in such a way that, despite my youthful good looks, he would assume that I was equivalent to his Vizirs and Pashas. I puffed Winstanley as an exalted antiquarian not a two-a-penny Oxford M.A. Higgins I painted as the Gainsborough of Greece, rather than the Dauber of Dublin. In return he introduced himself as Pericles Honorary Consul to the English and whomsoever other infidels had the *fortuna* to alight at this part of the island. His command of our language was passable. He asked to see our *firman*, the passport entitling us to enter the island. We apologised that we had no such document, having flown directly from Italy on the wings of Fortuna.

"But respected Lordos, this is imperative. The Pasha is too stickling in case of Frankish gentlemen."

"We are English, Sir, not Frenchie." I had yet to learn that Franks was their term for all Christians, whatever their nation.

"Also English respected gentlemen."

"Then please provide us with a firman."

"I have not the power. Our Governor, Ali Veri Bey, God preserve him, must write it following a personal audience."

"Then take us to him. Where is he?"

"He is residing in his serai beside the lake, Sir."

"Dammit we'll call on him."

"Sir, I regret you may not leave this shore without a firman."

"Well, we shall make our repairs and leave immediately."

"Sirs, that is not to be possible without a firman of departure to leave the island."

"Which I suppose we have to get from the Bey."

"Oh no, Sir. I am gratified that I am empowered to equip this"

"Excellent news. Please do so."

"How can a person depart before he has arrived? I must not issue a firman of departure until I have seen a firman of arrival. My job is worth more than this."

In the growing heat of the day we tried to resolve the dilemma each in his own way; Winstanley with sweet reason and blandishments; Higgins with hectoring and threat; I with a palmful of silver. I leave you to guess which was most effective. Pericles agreed to escort us to Ali Veri while our captain and crew remained with the ship to carry out repairs and revictualling.

I cut a dash in my scarlet hussar's jacket and Highland cap, a yellow kerchief round my neck; Winstanley minced in black with a white collar like the country parson he aspired to become; Higgins shambled slip-shod in a long plaid jacket, stained with ink and wine. We looked more like a party of strolling actors than English gentlemen.

Consul Pericles led the procession on the mule and we followed behind under the escort of his soldiers. I took offence at being treated as a captive but was soon glad of the protection. Ragamuffins followed us and mocked us and called us Franks and Unbelievers and, I imagine, worse, and tried to tug our clothes and trip us. Their elders stared as we passed, crossing themselves and spitting on the ground. I was uneasy at being displayed like spoils in a Roman triumph; Higgins glowered through his bushy eyebrows; Winstanley blushed and hung his head. We then decided that conquering heroes was the better part to play so we waved and bowed and soon had the lads laughing and cheering us.

We passed through a village of wretched mud and straw cottages. The poverty and squalor turned our stomachs. Animals were slaughtered and fish were cleaned in the street and their entrails thrown into the gutter in the middle, where half-naked children played. Rubbish of all kinds, including the contents of chamber pots, was chucked willy-nilly out of doorways.

"Why, Winstanley, this is no better than the villages on our estates."

I liked to tease my obsequious tutor with such remarks. Relying on subservience to advance his career, he did not know whether to contradict or agree with me.

Our progress was halted by a funeral procession. A score of people followed a bier carried by six men. The women among the mourners wept and moaned and made hideous ululations. The corpse was wrapped in a shroud with the head left exposed. It was a young woman, her eyes sewn shut and her jaw tied up, her blackened face disfigured by ulcers. Pericles made repeated signs of the cross over his breast. Our escorts looked on dispassionately. The Turk believes that *kismet,* or fate, cannot be avoided. Even when plague afflicts the city they go about their business as usual, saying it is the will of Allah if they are stricken.

"*Ti na kanoume*? What can we do?" sighed Pericles. This phrase we were to come across often in our dealings with Greeks.

"Breathe out! Breathe out!" peeped Winstanley, pressing his handkerchief to his mouth.

"Through which orifice shall we breathe in?" inquired Higgins. "The one you speak through?"

We left the harbour and followed a steep path up between steep-sided hills, their rocky faces depilated by goats, devilish black things with corkscrew horns. In half an hour or so our little retinue of Turks, Greeks, Franks, dogs, boys and wastrels reached Ali Veri's serai, or summer house, beside the lake of Distos.

ALI VERI

The serai was beautifully situated on a low headland where the mountains came down to the lake, surrounded on three sides by water and sealed at the neck with a fortified wall. It was a plain and square two-storey building with a tile roof, flanked by stables, to make a courtyard where we dismounted. It appeared more like a barracks than a summer house until we were led out of doors to the lake-side of the building and into the world of a Turkish miniature: an orchard of lemon and walnut trees; a garden of roses; a marble fountain; a cage of songbirds; shimmering water; rippling reeds; the conical hill of ancient Dystos; the mountains beyond. Our host awaited us under a gazebo strewn with cushions and laid with ornate Persian carpets of striking colours and intricate pattern.

Ali Veri was in his forties, of medium height and plumping up nicely. Over plain silk robes he wore a yellow waistcoat decorated with pearl buttons. His moustache was waxed and a black beard came down to his waist. An ornamental belt carried a scimitar and a brace of pistols richly inlaid with gems. I presented him with a Brummagem silver box. He invited us to sit down beside him and we exchanged vacuous courtesies, relayed through Pericles. I was surprised to find such Christian politeness among a people, whom I had been taught to believe were little less than barbarous. Once these formalities were over, Ali came to the meat of the matter.

"May we know what has brought you to our humble island?"

"We are tourists, Effendi."

It was not polite to say that we had blown up by chance and wanted to get away as soon as possible. Earnest Winstanley stuck in his oar.

"Sir, we wish to visit sights, whose fame we have imbibed with our mothers' milk; the seat of Agamemnon Lord of the Greeks; the palace of Achilles; the massive walls of Troy where beautiful Helen was abducted by ill-fated Paris..."

"Thank you Winstanley. We have the picture."

"You are a long way from Troy. All we can offer is the Bay of Aulis where the Greek fleet assembled."

No ruins was good news. I made small talk for the three of us, since Winstanley was ill-at-ease in company, substituting pedantry for politeness. We swore Higgins to silence since his natural argumentativeness soon soured conversation. I welcomed the appearance of servants with a splendid coffee service of rich china cups and gold dishes. Four hookahs followed and were placed before the Bey, Winstanley, Higgins and me. With subtle distinction a *chibouk*, a pipe, four feet long and made of a plain black wood, was offered to Pericles. Winstanley tried to wave the contraption away but I frowned at him. I was less interested in offending the Bey's hospitality than in seeing Winstanley choke and, if the djinn inside the belly of the hookah was kind, turn green. I had no such hopes of Higgins, who was partial to all kinds of narcotic.

The hookahs were made of brass topped with a silver cup containing loose pellets of smouldering tobacco. The hoses that led from the neck were wrapped in red cloth and ended in amber mouthpieces. Winstanley wiped his surreptitiously with his kerchief but I relied on the disinfecting power of smoke. This passes through water in order to cool and clean it so what is breathed in is the only the essence of the weed. It soon reduced us to a pleasantly soporific state. Winstanley, who was not as used to such an enjoyable vice as the rest of us, slumped back on his cushions with a benevolent smile. I imitated him, as a sense of calm combined with heightened awareness pervaded my body.

"I am told that your prophet forbad wine but not tobacco," I said.

"If he had forbidden tobacco he would really have been a prophet," growled Higgins.

"Mister Winstanley, breathe slowly. Don't steam it like your English pipes," advised the Bey.

"Be a man and take a lungful. We'll tell you if you turn green," I said.

"You have no fears for yourself?" asked the Bey.

"My father hardened me against such poisons by letting me taste them from an early age. But this is unusual tobacco. It tastes sweet."

"It is mixed with mastack. You Franks call it bangue. Arabs call it assis."

"Hashish and tobacco? The old world and the new," grunted Higgins.

"Hashish? My dear sir..."

While my tutor's mind protested his body was too drowsy to put down the mouthpiece. He lay back in a reverie and, like us all, drifted in the bluish mist of smoke swirling to the touch of a peacock feather fan wielded by a languorous Negro boy.

"I hope we find other pleasures to entertain you," said the Bey.

As did I. I relied on Sam Johnson's dictionary, whose pithy definition summed up my expectations: *Seraglio – a house of women kept for debauchery*. I hoped to have some sport before we went steeple-chasing over the waves again.

"Effendi, we have a keen interest in the sex. On our travels we look out for all kinds of beauty as well as Classical."

"Please make yourself plain."

"We wish to worship Aphrodite the Goddess of Love. In the practical way."

"This is not London or Athens, we have different manners here."

"And how do your subjects conduct their love affairs, Effendi?"

"With continence, Lordos. With continence."

"However much we try to suppress it with unnatural morality, human nature is the same everywhere."

"The customs here are different from those in Christian countries. Our women are shut away in their own part of the house."

"Gives spice to flirtation, eh Higgins?"

"The women must be good for a tumble if they are so well guarded."

"Three weeks ago, one of the women of my household was found with a Greek of the town. She claimed she had invited him for which I had her flogged. Her confession did not mitigate her lover's crime and he was strangled."

"Ah. Indeed. Consul Pericles, how long does our Captain need for his repairs?"

"Perhaps intercourse will be possible with the English lady on our island," said Pericles.

"What? An Englishwoman? We shall have company yet. Is she young? Is she beautiful? Does her husband keep a horsewhip?"

"Sir, I beg you," peeped Winstanley.

"She is alone but for a Syrian servant. She has a firman from the Pasha of Egripos. She declined lodging in the town and went straight up into the mountains, a month ago. She refused an escort and she is probably dead."

"Why did you allow this, Effendi?"

"She is a foreigner and an unbeliever and a woman and clearly mad. I did not insist."

We had met such women on our travels. They are less of a rarity than is commonly supposed. Past their prime, they roam the world, armed with a watercolour brush in search of views and butterflies, yearning for the romance that escaped them in their fast receding youth. In the end they succumb to brigands or fever or Cheltenham and no more is heard of them.

Fortunately the good mood was restored by an excellent dinner in Turkish style, during which we steered clear of controversy. To our pleasant surprise the Bey gave us wine to drink, although he himself took only rose water. We reclined on the carpet with the dishes on low tables.

The Bey interrogated us about life in England. I painted a rosy picture of the old country with its cultured Nobility and stout-hearted yeomen, quaffing ale and scoffing beef around the village green and altogether superior to the French. Winstanley was inspired to explain the game of cricket, which bemused our host as much as his tobacco did us. He mastered the leg-before-wicket but stumping eluded him.

I asked our host what he found to interest him in Egripos.

"I was tired of the intrigues of Constantinople, jaded with dissipation, harassed with the pursuit of ambition. Here I live a simple life in the midst of beauty."

"I find that the beauty of Nature is counter-balanced by the tedium of having to live in it."

"There are some interesting things here for tourists." He reached to a dish of spit-roast kid, tore off the head and held it up. "On a mountain near the city of Egripos there is is a deep cave. At its mouth, an amazing vine springs from the bare rock. From its size and age they say it was planted by Dionysos himself. Inside the cave are heaps of skulls."

"Human skulls?" asked Higgins, torn from contemplation of his wine cup.

"Goats. Their horns are stuck into the vine and the trees round about."

Our host cracked the skull with his hands and scooped out the brains. Our artist relished the anecdote of the cave more than the delicacy put before him.

"The devil take them. What else, Sir, what else?"

"The Christian saint they worship has the head of a goat."

"Such superstitions have no place in our enlightened age," said Winstanley.

"In that case nor does the goat-headed Devil. Do you want to banish him too, Winstanley? Are you a Methodist?" I said.

"I would banish everything that is not rational."

"There are many spirits at work in the world that influence our actions. Many lurk beneath our understanding," said the Bey.

"Satan," growled Higgins, part question, part answer.

"I plump for Aphrodite," I said.

Our conversation was interrupted by the bringing of pipes again and the ceremony of lighting them, which my tutor watched like a schoolboy before a bag of humbugs. He lay back on his cushion, sighed and closed his eyes. Seeing our appreciation, the Bey promised a pouch of the stuff for our private consumption along with a box of opium pastilles to ease the discomfort of travel.

"Nothing purifies the mind like eating opium. Pythagoras invented it," he said.

"Did you hear that, Winstanley? We can thank the Greeks for something."

"Not the Greeks. Plato and Pythagoras and Aristotle acquired their wisdom from the builders of the pyramids."

"The murky beliefs of the Egyptians have nothing to do with the everlasting brilliance of the Greeks," said Winstanley

"Everlasting? Where is it now? The cradle of the civilised world is now a graveyard of ignorance and superstition. You search for Troy. All you will find is a flat field. Your Greece lives only in your imagination."

At the mention of Troy Winstanley burst like a genie from a bottle. This was a new Winstanley, touched by the muse, the gleam of inspiration in his eye, the eloquence of madness on his tongue. He recitated the beginning of the Trojan war; how Paris visited King Menelaus of Sparta and was besotted with his wife, Helen; how he stole her away to Troy; how King Agamemnon of Mycenae raised an army of all the Greeks to win her back. This was not in his usual sanctimonious drone but in an actor's voice, full of feeling, with gestures and mime that would have done credit to Mr Garrick. He finished with a tableau of the two lovers standing arm in arm on the battlements of Troy and watching the horizon for the vengeful fleet of Agamemnon sweeping down upon them.

We applauded and even the Bey, who probably had understood little, complimented him. Winstanley sat down exhausted, sweating like a horse, gazing about him as if he were only now aware of our presence. He took a large draught of wine and fell fast asleep. The rest of us talked and smoked and drank far into the night until sleep overcame us too and we lay down where we sat, wrapped in woollen blankets, under the stars of an Aegean heaven. Fagged out by our trials at sea we slept soundly until the following day.

East and West
Jean Brindesi

KLEPHTS

In the morning we were left to our own devices. We passed the time with our favourite literature: Higgins in the label on his brandy bottle, Winstanley in his beloved Alexander Pope and I in the stimulating Memoirs of Miss Fanny Hill.

After dinner, we accompanied Ali Veri, who was returning to his main residence in the castle of his town. Our escort, a surly crew of janissaries, was mounted on nags and mules. Their captain, the Chorbaji, which means in Turkish Doler-Out-Of-The-Soup, was from the left side unremarkable. Of middle years, past the flush of youth but still a handsome fellow, he was tall and erect and without the pot belly of those loyal to the standard of the janissaries, the cooking pot. He wore tunic and knee-length trousers and the long greatcoat of his profession, with a dagger and a cudgel tucked into his cummerbund. He was clean-shaven but for a long hennaed moustache and the matching tilde of an eyebrow. His head was shaved but for a braid hanging down behind from under his white felt cap.

And then you saw his right side: a sheep's head in a butcher's window. The skin was raw and red, pocked and wrinkled from the cap to the collar, stretched tight over his cheek bone and his jaw, with no moustache, no eyebrow, no hair at all. His lips strained into a rictus, his eye bulged from its weeping socket, his fleshless ear puckered into a bumhole. The only concession to his monstrosity was the flap of his cap that he made to hang over the side of his face instead of down his back. His right arm was stiff and ended in a hand withered into a fleshless red claw.

Ali Veri mounted a handsome white Arab which I coveted. He was not a man to sell it but perhaps he could be drawn into a game of dice? Unfortunately he was no more a gambler than a libertine. Behind him on a coal-black pony rode his negro boy. Chorbaji Two-Face took the lead with a score of his men, leaving half a dozen or so as a rearguard to swat away the Greek ragamuffins that followed us. Hoping for a coin or two they received kicks and horse droppings and soon abandoned us.

We followed the shore of the lake through fields and orchards into the foothills of mountains rising to our right and ahead of us. After half an hour the Chorbaji called his wobblers to order. The cause was a band of men coming down from the hills on the right. I reached for my pistols but the Bey put a hand on my arm. I hoped his sang froid was based on knowledge of these men and not surrender to our *kismet.*

Their captain rode bareback on a black horse, a small raggedy-coat beast that looked as if it spent its days running wild in the mountains, as did the twenty or so men who plodded after it. Such a band of unkempt ruffians you would send to the barber if not to the gallows. They made Higgins look like a dandy. Each was thatched with tangles of black curls of a piece with untrimmed beards and long moustaches, all glistening and rank with oil. Some wore long tailed caps. They were shod and clad in skins of sheep and goats and smocks of unbleached wool over tight-fitting trousers of the same material. Belts and bandoliers were finely worked with beads and silver ornaments but their sartorial pride was the scabbards and hilts of swords and daggers. Their other weapons were long-barrelled muskets whose ornamentation did not obscure their function.

The captain was a thick-set man of middle years whose authority was concentrated in his black and predatory eyes. He exchanged no more than a cursory nod to Ali Veri and gave the floor to a younger man who stood at his stirrup, or where the stirrup would be if he had one. In addition to his brigandly accoutrements, he sported a secretary's silver ink horn at his belt. He addressed the Bey in a curious mishmash of Romiote dialect and ecclesiastical Greek chanted to a sing-song rhythm. At the climax of his recitation one of the brigands stepped forward with a round parcel wrapped in a cloth like a plum pudding ready for the pot. He laid it ceremoniously on the ground and unwrapped it to reveal the head of a man that might have been cut from any in the band. Delicately he set it upright on the stump of the neck to look at us with half-closed eyes. Winstanley played Salome and turned his own head away while Higgins contemplated it with the indifference of one who has seen such things before. I confess I had to steel myself - I have enjoyed hangings at Newgate after a night's carouse but a bodiless head is unholy and unwholesome. Another ruffian stepped forward and tossed a coil of rope on the ground beside the gruesome relic.

"This is Zarkopoulos? How do I know?" asked the Bey.

"You have the word of the Kapetanos," said the secretary and the brigand on horseback nodded.

"How did he die?"

"He tried to steal a bride on the road to Stira. We were waiting. The price on his head is one hundred piastres."

"It was seventy."

"That was alive. We have saved you the expense of a stake."

"Five piastres for the stake. Seventy five in all."

Without waiting for a counter-offer the Bey took a purse from his sash and counted out some coins. He gave them to Captain Two-Face who handed them to the secretary and went to pick up the head of poor Zarkopoulos. The secretary stepped in his way.

"He was a Christian. We will give him back to his mother."

The brigands formed up on either side of us and we continued on our way. Captain Two-Face and his men aimed nothing more at them than apprehensive glances.

"Who are these men, Effendi?" I asked the Bey.

" Klephts. The vermin infest all Roumeli."

Klephts is Greek for thieves. They live in the mountains and refuse to submit to Ottoman tyranny.

"You do business with them?"

"These are *imeroi*, tame. We pay them and let them carry arms to keep the wild ones at bay. You saw the rope? It is the badge of the wild klepht, the *agrios*, like Zarkopoulos. He carries it to tie his prisoners."

"Why do you tolerate them? Why not send your armies into the mountains? Burn their crops, kill their flocks, evict them from their houses. Starvation and winter will bring them to their knees. This is the English cure for rebellious highlanders."

"It is cheaper this way. And what would empty mountains profit me?"

It is one of the many failings of Ottoman government that officials are appointed for limited terms and that the finances are for their own account. Their aim is therefore to maximise their income and minimise their expenditure.

"By leaving wolves to flourish in their lairs aren't you afraid that one day they will come down to devour you?" asked Winstanley.

"Who will pay them their blood money then? This arrangement suits everyone. I have my peace and they have their piastres."

"And if one day piastres will not be enough? If they declare the independence of their country?"

"The scum lack a sense of common purpose. The region between here and Karistos is divided into two domains each under a hereditary *kapitanos*. I hire those in my district as *armatoli*, to keep in check the klephts of the Karistos district. The Bey of Karistos hires his klephts as *armatoli* against mine.

So we keep them in a constant state of warfare kept alive by blood feud and piastres."

I looked at the lusty band of brigands around us and wondered if they could be managed so easily. It would be the work of a few minutes to dispatch us, as I had little confidence in the martial spirit of our Turkish escort. Those in England who dream that the descendants of Achilles will one day throw off the Ottoman yoke and re-live their ancient glory might as well dream of the revival of the Pictish Empire or the Kingdom of Finn Macool by the sheep-shaggers and bog-trotters of our own country.

The secretary fell back and took hold of my horse's bridle. He reeked of the flocks that clothed him, sour cheese and goat's piss. In a mixture of signs and primitive Greek and with Pericles' help he asked if I was a Frank like the woman who had been their guest in their mountain lair. Her camel, her Arab and her boldness confirmed her identity and I waited for a demand for her ransom.

"Is she alive?"

"Certainly."

Our mutual vocabulary did not allow me to inquire with delicacy whether she had been molested so I resorted to universal sign language, at which he grinned and slapped his chest.

"She is no woman. She sits with the men. She gave me this."

He took from his belt a dog-eared book, no more than a pamphlet. It was an instalment of Pope's Homer published as a weekly periodical by that old rogue Melmoth. Mother subscribed and they lay in her pile with pages uncut. I knew it because the engraving of Homer in the first instalment looked like the man who emptied the privies in our London place. The secretary showed me a picture of Hercules wrestling a lion.

"She said these were our fathers. Is this true, Effendi?"

"Are you Greek, Sir?"

"What is that?"

"Are you Roman?"

He spat on the ground.

"We are Christian, Effendi."

"And what language do you speak at home?"

"Albanian of course."

Far be it from me to contradict a lady, so I resisted the temptation to tell him that he was as much descended from the Ancient Greeks as my spaniel.

The brigands escorted us for a mile or so. In an insolent display, the Kapitanos abruptly left the road, dismounted, and led horse and men straight up a steep mountainside. They gathered on a bluff that dominated us, fired a volley and melted away into the rocks and scrub.

"*Rebets*," muttered the Bey, his face dark with what I assumed to be thoughts of gallows and stakes. "Rebels."

Klepht
François Pouqueville

MISS BURBAGE

After we had rested and the day had lost its heat, we took a tour of the town. The upper part, huddled about the castle, was inhabited by Turks and Greeks with a leavening of Jews. Turkish houses are painted red and the others brown or black. The lower part was inhabited by Albanians, who speak *Arvenitika*, an Albanian language unrelated to Greek.

Winstanley addressed the natives in his Oxford Greek but he was no more comprehensible than Chaucer in Piccadilly. The Greeks call themselves and their language 'Roman', a mongrel of Greek, Turkish and Venetian, far removed from the language of Homer. Between themselves the Turks speak Turkish, the Albanians speak Albanian, and the Jews speak Greek laced with Hebrew. Romans pray in Biblical Greek, Turks pray in Arabic, Jews pray in Hebrew so all of them have no more or less idea of what they are saying to their Creator than a Papist gabbling Latin.

We joined the evening promenade. In the mellow hour before sunset the inhabitants of the upper town, dressed in their best, patrolled the two squares, each to his own religion. Men of all faiths wear cotton drawers and over them a cotton shirt and a long robe like a parson's cassock. They wear a wide belt of cloth wrapped several times round, in which they keep their daggers, money and a tobacco pouch. Over all this they put on a loose coat with wide sleeves. On their heads they wear a tapering crimson velvet cap, like a dunce's cap with the top sliced off, around which they can wind a silk turban, whose size reflects their status.

The word 'turban' means 'tulip' in Turkish and there are more varieties among the artificial flowers than the natural. A Turk wears his biography on his head - race, religion, station, profession, wealth, taste and character. Every trigonometrical shape is represented: cubes, cones, pyramids, spheres, ovoids and a multitude of irregular figures in between, all with mutations of size, colour and fabric.

As ever our attention was focussed on the ladies. Only Christian women join the promenade. Down to the waist they wear nothing but a shift of thin and transparent gauze, through which everything is visible except their breasts which they cover with a sort of handkerchief. They are obliged by the Turks to wear this, which they consider as yet another manifestation of Turkish tyranny. The degree of transparency of a lady's breast cloth indicates her modesty. Their petticoats are so short that they show a lot of leg, which we would not complain about if they did not deliberately thicken their calves by wearing several pairs of woollen stockings. They make great use of face paint to the detriment of their complexions. They shave off their eyebrows and replace them with a continuous line of hair fixed with gum.

We were returning to our lodgings when we saw against the sunset sky an extraordinary silhouette of a man with a musket on his shoulder leading a camel. Before the hump was a figure under a large parasol. We stopped to let this apparition come closer and saw that the person was a lady dressed in a wide-brim straw hat and loose brown riding clothes, skilfully holding herself erect while swaying with the movement of the camel. She was handsome and slender and I judged she was middle-aged, although she might have been younger, since her face was tanned like a peasant's. The saddle was covered with a fancy oriental blanket and hung with rolls and bundles, bags and panniers. The camel was a sorry beast, its coat in tatters, and ignored us with the same disdain as its mistress. The retainer was a swarthy oriental. He wore a red skull cap, short coat, white shirt, baggy pantaloons and much travelled boots.

The lady read aloud from a book on her lap in a language I did not understand but in accents instantly recognisable as English. She ignored me as she passed, although I made an ostentatious bow. I walked alongside her but she continued to ignore me. The servant had the effrontery to level his musket at me but I persisted.

"inna fi iktilafi allayli waal nahari," or some such lingo.

"Madam, I say, good evening."

"Allayu fi alssamawati waal ardi layatin..."

"You're English dammit."

"Sir, molesting a lady in the street in London without a proper introduction is a social misdemeanour by which you stand to lose your reputation. In a Muslim country it is a felony for which you lose much more. Shall I call a constable?"

Her eyes were a penetrating blue, made all the more startling by her tan.

"I am at your service, Madam."

"Then do me one. I need tooth powder. You may bring it to the house of Pericles the tax-collector."

What a Gorgon! But any baggage will do for travellers starved of female company. We collected a box of Dr. Hemet's Patent Pearl Dentifrice and went to Pericles' house in the hope of sweetening the Gorgon's breath with essence of orange flowers and roses and aromatic aracus. Some hope.

AMELIA

Pericles' house was painted red, which showed that he had bought it from a Turk or that his status in society was above his fellow Greeks'. A lackey showed us into his saloon. It was a plain and square room, furnished in the Turkish style with divans and carpets and a copper brazier for coffee and pipes. Pericles sat cross-legged, flanked by two body-guards. Other gentlemen sat about the room, smoking long pipes. Before him stood a man and a boy, who evidently belonged to the lower town. Around the boy's neck was a leather strap, like a dog collar. His head hung low, while the elder man shouted angrily. Pericles shrugged and gestured to one of the guards, who unbuckled the boy's collar. The elder man put his hand on the boy's shoulder and without another word turned and left us, looking with hatred at each of us in turn.

I will interrupt myself with an explanation of this scene. Common Greeks say they labour under three curses: the Turks, the priests, and the *hojabashi*. Pericles was a *hojabasha*, a tax collector, with the privilege of collecting the poll tax from his countrymen. As the tax was payable only by males over fifteen years of age he took a great interest in the births of children and assiduously recorded them. Many escaped his net by baptising their offspring in secret or saying they had died or claiming that a youth was still a child. He decided the age of a boy by measuring his neck with a collar.

Pericles welcomed us and introduced us to his cronies. They were perturbed by the imminent arrival on the island of the Turkish High Admiral, the Captain Pasha. He is charged by the Sultan with keeping the Aegean clear of pirates and ensuring that local governors maintain the system of justice. For the privilege of his protection the inhabitants pay whatever he chooses to extort under pretext of defraying his expenses. This increases the burden of taxation on the islanders and decreases the profit of the *hojabashi.*

I brought out the pretext of our visit, the tooth powder. The box was passed from hand to hand with puzzled curiosity, since they themselves use a kind of twig. Having exhausted the conversational possibilities of dental hygiene, Pericles took us to our compatriot's lodgings. She had a bedroom and a small saloon on the ground floor giving on to an internal courtyard. The upper storey of the house was a *gynaeceum,* or harem, for his women. Our visit caused consternation among them. Through the ceiling boards above our heads we heard them rustling and scuttling as they slaked their curiosity through peepholes and cracks.

She received us in her riding clothes; not for her the stays and hoops of an English drawing room. She wore high brown boots, loose Turkish trousers, a plain cotton shirt and a short plain jacket, all coloured in autumnal browns and greens. Her sun-bleached hair was tied behind. She wore no powder but connoisseurs of the sex would detect a spark of female vanity: her eyebrows were too perfect and her lips too red to be natural, her eyelashes were too dark for her hair, and her ears were adorned with blue sapphires that matched her eyes. Her manners, however, matched her dress.

"Amelia Burbage. Miss, thank God. You may address me as Amelia. I have no truck with ceremony."

"I do however, Miss Burbage. Christian names are for tipstaffs and epitaphs."

Not the most promising of introductions. She was not put out but smiled, with mockery or amusement I could not say.

Winstanley followed my lead, proffering his last name with a parson's sanctimoniousness, Higgins his first with a leveller's truculence.

"Cornelius, the horned one. Do you have horns sir?" asked Amelia.

"If you are as sweet as your honey name, Madam," I countered for Higgins, showing off my classical education.

"Two l's in mellifluous Sir. Amelia has one," said our pedant.

"To 'ell with you too. And you, horny Cornelius."

A girl brought sweet lemonade and saucers of jam. Clothed in a simple tunic, her face unadorned with paint, she was a delectable thing. Although she kept her eyes downcast in maidenly modesty, she allowed herself a darting glance or two at us, as disconcerting as any flashed across the floor at Almack's Assembly Rooms or the stalls at the King's Theatre. I would have loved to know her better but when I treated her to my most engaging smile she ran away.

"A charming girl," I said.

"Eleni. My daughter," said Pericles raising his hands and eyeing the ceiling. "We say worstest things in life are build house and marry daughter. I have four. Four moneys to give to husbands. I am ruined man. And no son. Ai Ai." Lamenting his pecuniary fate he left us to our devices.

We made an odd quartet, the more eccentric in that each of its members would have appeared moderately normal. It was our juxtaposition on an Aegean island which was comical.

Amelia's excursion in the mountains stimulated her appetite for conversation in which we took our habitual parts, Winstanley pontificating on Homer, Higgins as ribald as the presence of a lady would allow, I myself in the exercise of wit. From her interest in our itinerary I deduced that Amelia's pleasure in our company was motivated less by sociability than her desire to leave the island on our ship.

We started a game of Travellers' Whist. This does not need cards and the rules are simple. Each player in turn lays down an anecdote of their journey, trying to trump the previous one. The game begins with the idiocies of customs officers and our little victories over them, followed by descriptions of lodging and transportation, illnesses and accidents. These are the low cards. When the players begin to wonder why ever they left home, they play the court cards, all the triumphs and discoveries which are the reward of travel, if not at the time they are experienced then afterwards, at home, where they are embellished in comfort to the envy of the stay-at-homes. I said as much to Amelia and added that she had more cards at her disposal than we beginners.

"I don't travel in order to glitter in drawing rooms."

"Then tell us why you do travel, Madam." said Winstanley.

"For its own sake; for freedom; for broadening the mind; for deepening sensibility; above all for the study of natural history, and especially botany."

"Do you submit to the Royal Society?"

"The learned societies will only take papers from gentlemen. I refuse to masquerade as one, like others of my sex. My work will find a voice one day, not now."

"Do you return to England?"

"I occasionally return to Dulwich to visit my sister."

"With your, er, man?"

"Ali is my dragoman. He knows Arabic and Roman, Turkish and French. This is his seventh year of service with me. In winter he returns with Rousseau to his family in Sidon."

"Rousseau? You have a Frenchie in tow as well as an A-rab?"

"Rousseau is the camel. Our companion in the wilderness. He goes many days without food or water. He eats more varieties of things than a horse. His distinctiveness minimises the chance of theft. And he can carry as much as a mule train."

"What drives you to such dangerous journeys, apart from the appalling alternative of living in Dulwich?"

"I may be led but not driven. When I exhausted the possibilities of my garden I stepped into the next field and then the next. From the fields of Surrey I strayed to the next county, and so it continued."

It was a credible answer but, while it may have been ungentlemanly to doubt the word of a lady, I was not convinced by it. She may have sat prim and upright on her cushion, dressed in sober colours, her hair done up in a spinsterish bun, her hands folded demurely on her lap but her eyes were bright and touched with kohl and her lips were full and touched with vermilion. My experience of the sex, diligently acquired in practical study, led me to believe that she was one of those women whose sensuality, far from being deficient, needs constantly to be kept in check. She was like a Turkish copper brazier whose hard and polished exterior held burning coals inside.

"And why do you travel in Greece, Lord Exford? Do you have a passion for the classics?"

"Alas!" sighed Winstanley.

"Sure he travels for his digestion. The stews of London were too hot for him."

"For entertainment Madam, for the same reason I go to the theatre. Actors in the artificial theatre are rewarded by our money and our applause. In the theatre of the world the rewards are reciprocated. The traveller entertains those who entertain him, a part in which the English abroad unwittingly excel."

"Get away from the trivialities of society. Go into the mountains where nature lives in flux and tumult and the sights are sublime."

"Yet enjoyment of them may be spoiled for lack of tooth powder."

"Man is born for society," said Winstanley.

"Society is made by man to constrain Nature," she countered.

"Put a man in a wilderness and he will turn wild."

"More ferocious than those in society, who extort and murder for their own benefit?"

I was less interested in this tiresome debate than the debaters. Amelia and Winstanley swapped the fiery looks of duellists and lovers. Unused to either sport, my tutor fell silent. I took up his rapier.

"Everyone pursues his own advantage, which turns out to be the advantage of everyone. Pericles collects taxes for his Turkish masters and gives you a better dinner than a free man in a mountain hovel," I said, parroting the late Adam Smith.

"In return for which he surrenders liberty. That is a high price for a good dinner. There will come a day when his children will claim their freedom."

"Never," interrupted Higgins, "for all they claim to be descended from the ancient Greeks, they are lackeys of a foreign power. They will never be free."

"There speaks an Irishman. He should know."

Amelia's earnest speeches pricked the bubble of conviviality as surely as a Winstanley sermon, seriousness being as detestable a social vice as farting or bringing up the Irish question. Pleading fatigue we rose and took our leave.

"Well now, she is very mannish in her opinions," said Higgins as we made our way through the narrow streets.

"And yet feminine in her appearance," said Winstanley.

"I wonder what caused her to break away from normal society. Was it really an independent spirit? Or was it misfortune? Or disgrace?" I asked.

"Sure, she belongs on Lesbos," said Higgins.

"She compares with any man or woman for enterprise and courage," said Winstanley.

"When women wear the breeches watch out for your own bare arse," said Higgins.

"She is a true Roxalana. Have you seen the play? The women of London love it," I said.

We returned to our rooms in the castle, where our supper was brought for us. A guard was posted at our door. The Bey did not seek our company so we did not have the opportunity to see how a Turk whiles away the evening when gambling, wine-drinking and flirtation are denied to him.

Winstanley devoted himself to the plague. Before we left England he had it from the best medical authorities that the disease is spread by animalcules which nest in the human body. The counter-measures are vinegar and fumigation. Letters should be taken up with a pair of tongs and singed before they can be opened, a precaution which I extended to Winstanley's classical texts in the hope of setting fire to them. He retaliated by fumigating our rooms with smouldering aromatic twigs from Egypt, which he tended like a devotee of some Eastern sect.

Higgins took his precautions straight out of the bottle, his habitual prophylactic against plague, pox, shipwreck, boredom, overwork and life. For my part I did nothing but trusted in luck and put myself under the protection of my Lady of the Foam.

"Let's see if the morality of the upper town reaches down into the lower. Tomorrow we'll inspect the breast cloths, what do you say Higgins?"

"Sir, I beg you, curb your lust. Drive out pagan *erotas* with Christian *agape*, the charitable love for fellow men and women."

"Don't make an enemy of Venus, Winstanley. She may take her revenge. Your smoky twigs are a poor defence against the plague of love."

I prayed that Winstanley's defence of his duelling partner derived from more than Christian charity. If *agape* turned to *erotas* there would be sport indeed.

ROXALANA

There are books which start at the beginning and go on to the end. I don't have the stamina to read such a book, much less write one. I like my literature prepared like a dinner of various tasty dishes brought in one after the other, not thrown all together in some *kazan*, the great cauldron of the Turks, and stewed up into an interminable soup that tastes the same from the first spoonful to the last and when you are full you look in the pot and there is still more left than you can imagine finishing. Would you sit through a Shakespeare play without a hornpipe between the acts? A Mozart symphony without a sprightly intermezzo between the movements? Our minds are not equipped to give attention to anything for more than fifteen minutes. Our conversations are made of digression, interpolation, aside, notation, interruption, witticism, repetition. I shall make my book like this - not to try your patience but to reward it with variety. It is said that the Great North Road is a single road but that the Great West road is a number of roads put end to end. Our road is like the latter. Our itinerary is composed mainly of diversions and intervals and interpolations.

The story of Roxalana is such a diversion. Skip over it if you wish and stick to the straight and narrow of our journey.

Roxalana is the heroine of the Covent Garden perennial, *The Sultan: or a Peep into the Seraglio*, a farce in two acts. And an enticing seraglio it is, far different from Ali Veri's nunnery, with half-clad houris, opulent furnishings and lascivious men. Into this royal bawdy house comes a new slave, an Englishwoman, the ungovernable Roxalana. She is wilful, obstinate, and impudent, and refuses to accept the dominance of men. She contrasts the oppression of the harem with dear old England, *"where reigns ease, content and liberty"*, where women are free and independent. With English forthrightness she overturns the subservient manners of the seraglio, throws open the doors for those who want to leave, and humiliates Osmeyn the chief eunuch. She is not a puritan. She does not want to abolish the pleasures of the harem, only to make them voluntary: *"let inclination alone keep your women within it."* Osmeyn wants her punished but Sultan Soleyman falls in love with her. He wants a friend who will tell him the truth as an equal. She consents to marry him if she shares the throne.

Roxalana invites them all to dinner but when cushions and low tables are brought in, sends them away. *"What, do they mean to make me squat like a baboon and tear meat with my fingers. Take away all this trumpery and let us have tables and chairs, knives and forks, and dishes and plates, like Christians. And, lest the best part of the entertainment should be wanting, get us some wine."*

Here is the superiority of English society and the duty to reform the repressed and dissolute Orientals: when they treat men and women as equals, drink wine and eat with a knife and fork, then they will be civilised like us.

Josh Reynolds made a picture of the lovely Roxalana, opening the forbidden curtain to the Sultan's sanctum. He captured the mix of allure and determination that Mrs. Abington brought to the part at the Theatre Royal. A whore before she was an actress, she brought an extra frisson to the sensuousness of her portrait. For it is not Christian charity, nor Platonic affinity that breaks down the prison walls of the Seraglio but erotic love based on reciprocity of desire and the freedom of both parties to exercise it. *Eros* frees women from oppression and arranged marriage. Women in the audience admire Roxalana's allure, capricious opinions, and dominance of her master, confident that her manners are as successful in a London drawing room as in a Turkish harem. "*Let men say whate'er they will, - Woman, woman, rules them still.*"

The piece is by poor Isaac Bickerstaffe, bosom friend of Mr. Garrick and fugitive to France from the laws of Sodomy. He invented the musical comedy - this is a drama interrupted by music, unlike an opera which is music interrupted by drama. His first musical comedy, 'Love in a Village', is forgotten but for the character of the Jolly Miller of Dee. I can sing you, *affetuoso*, the final couplet, an anthem for our egotistical age.

"*I care for nobody, not I - If no one cares for me,*"

Mrs. Abington as Roxalana
Josh. Reynolds

DR. ACHMET

My antipathy towards collective bathing dates from school. In winter new bugs were first in the water to break the ice and in summer last to wallow in the scum. The amorous possibilities of Bath and Cheltenham, where the health and sin are equally sulphurous, took the edge off my aversion but the furthest I willingly go in the direction of hot water is a two-person tub in front of the fire with a charming companion to test the temperature with her delicate parts. So it was only as a result of a misunderstanding that I accepted an invitation to take a Turkish bath.

"Hey ho, my lads, they humbugged us! They are civilised after all! We are invited by Pericles to the bagnio!"

Higgins joined in the general huzzahs but Winstanley preserved his sanctimonious sang-froid, when I had expected a sermon on the evils of the flesh.

"I think you will find that Pericles means bagnio in the sense of public baths and not a house of ill-fame." And so it was.

While we dressed, Higgins regaled us with the true story of Dublin's first hamam and the Turk who went with it. I will spare you the Oirishman's *well nows* and *he was afters* and other Celtic locutions, which you can reinsert for yourself if you wish.

Dr. Achmet appeared on the scene at the beginning of the seventies and instantly became one of the sights of the city with his turban, his robes, and his great black beard, strolling the streets and wishing a good day to all, by the mercy of Allah. He was tall, handsome, well built, pale skinned, and had such an excellent command of English that he imitated the brogue of the natives to perfection. "My God, if all the Turks are like him, no wonder they're at the gates of Vienna" was the general opinion. Producers of Oriental plays and pantomimes revised their casting and several swarthy villains resented the stately Dr. Achmet for the loss of their roles.

What was the reason for Dr. Achmet's migration from the Bosporus to the Liffey? To introduce the Turkish bath to the people of Ireland for their health and his profit, and in this he was supported by the medical faculty. Who better than a Turk to promote the first Hibernian Hamam? A subscription was launched, containing a full description of the project and endorsed with the signatures of all the medical men of the town. The city coffers coughed up and in 1772 Dr. Achmet opened the doors of his new establishment. It was a wonderful success and Dublin's own Turk prospered, not least in the affections of a pretty young actress by the name of Miss Egan. They were married and she took the stage name Mrs. Achmet. The couple lived in style and were lionized, if not by the *haut monde,* then certainly the *beau.*

In 1775 a new play was brought to the Dublin Theatre, the two act afterpiece called *The Sultan: or a Peep into the Seraglio,* with its tale of the English slave Roxalana. Mrs. Achmet was cast as one of the lovely concubines but who was to play the Sultan? What better casting than a genuine Turk? Enter Dr. Achmet in his début on the stage. His race, his celebrity, his pretty wife raised all expectations. "Now we shall see how a genuine Turk behaves in his harem." There was not a seat to be had on the first night; the house made a terrible hullabaloo when Sultan Suleyman made his grand entrance; and from this pinnacle of dramatic success it was downhill all the way to the final curtain. It was very strange: on the street and in the baths Doctor Achmet was Turkish to the bone but on the stage he completely lacked conviction: a Turk playing a Turk who was more unlike a Turk than an Irishman playing a Turk. His beard looked stuck-on, his robes made of a curtain, his turban a tea-cosy and his manners those of a farmer at a fancy dress ball. He was the talk of the town but in less flattering terms than before. People who had accepted him in good faith began to question his *bona fides.* They remembered his replies when they asked about his homeland - with a tear in his eye and a sob in his throat he pleaded that his nostalgia was too painful. In the more indelicate conversations of the ladies in the Green Room - and remember that the paths to the playhouse and the bawdy house overlap – when Mrs. Achmet was asked whether it was indeed true that Muslims shared with Jews a ritual mutilation, she was uncharacteristically modest.

Rumour circled, with ever decreasing radius, around the medical fraternity and perched finally on the head of Dr. Jebb, who had introduced Dr. Achmet to his colleagues. He confessed that a certain Mr. Cairns of Belfast, one time apothecary of Dublin, surgeon in the French navy and attendant at the Hummums bath house in Covent Garden, had come to him with a scheme for a Turkish Bath in Dublin. He was enthusiastic but thought that the proposal would carry more weight from a Turk. But where to find a Turk in Dublin? This was the moment for Mr. Cairns to grow a beard and assemble a costume.

The Dublin crowd is not vindictive. It took the imposture in good part. But Dr. Achmet was henceforth held in amusement rather than respect and although he continued to preside over his baths in full pantomime rig and his waters were no less efficacious than before, his custom dwindled to the lame and the scrofulous. His marriage too went up in steam. Mrs. Achmet kept his name but abandoned the rest of him. Dublin forgot the affable and stately Doctor and went back to its previous conception of the Turk - swarthy, voluptuous, and cruel.

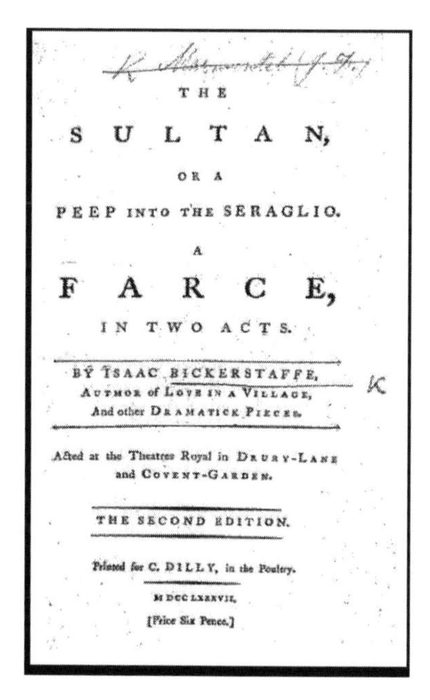

THE

SULTAN,

OR A

PEEP INTO THE SERAGLIO.

A

FARCE,

IN TWO ACTS.

BY ISAAC BICKERSTAFFE,
AUTHOR of LOVE IN A VILLAGE,
And other DRAMATICK PIECES.

Acted at the Theatres Royal in DRURY-LANE
and COVENT-GARDEN.

THE SECOND EDITION.

Printed for C. DILLY, in the Poultry.

M DCC LXXXVII.

[Price Six Pence.]

Dramatis Personæ.

MEN.

SOLYMAN the Great, Emperor of the Turks,	Doctor ACHMET.
OSMYN, chief of the Eunuchs,	Mr. WILDER.

WOMEN.

ELMIRA,	Miss SCARCE.
ISMENA,	Mrs. JOHNSON.
ROXALANA, an English Slave,	Mrs. DALY.

The Dublin Cast

BAGNIO

Pericles took us to the hamam beside the mosque, which it resembled with its cupola and tall chimney. He handed us over to an attendant and made excuses for himself. It was an unpretentious whitewashed building without windows. The first room was large and airy, lit by a glassed dome in the ceiling, and pleasantly warm. Around the walls were sofas and tables and in the middle a simple fountain bubbling into a marble basin. It was staffed by two shaven gentlemen, whose boiled appearance hinted at frequent patronage of their own establishment. They invited us to undress and gave us large white towels, much laundered and worn. Winstanley hitched his primly under the armpits, Higgins tied his over the belly and I dashingly girded the loins. Winstanley and I sported the alabaster English skin of subterranean creatures who never see the light of day but our Irishman was a painted savage with his masses of brown freckles, red hair, white scars and blue veins.

We were given thick wooden clogs, called *nalin* on which to clump and clack through a heavy red curtain into the next room. This was considerably warmer and more humid, but not unpleasant. It too was lit by a glassed dome that let in a greenish undersea light. Around the walls were set low marble seats and in the centre was a marble table, like an altar. Through a narrow archway in one wall was a room swirling with steam. Winstanley and I squatted on seats while Higgins, pleading fatigue, stretched himself face down on the altar, a sacrificial victim, as he was soon to prove. We perspired gently and listened to the soothing drip of water into some unseen basin.

"More tedious than I hoped but less unpleasant than I feared," I said.

"Yet another oriental pretext for indolence." said Winstanley.

Higgins began to snore and missed the entrance through the red curtain of a genie from the Arabian Nights. A bang and a puff of smoke could not have given us more of a fright. He was a mountain of swarthy Turk, naked but for a loin cloth slung under his powerful belly. His legs were bowed and his arms hung permanently akimbo, so swollen were they with muscle and fat. His cannonball head was hairless but for a continuous bushy black brow over glowering eyes. Winstanley shrank against the wall, clutching his sheet, and I regretted the swordstick I had left with our clothes.

The monster ignored us and padded over to Higgins as if to annihilate him first before dealing with the lesser fry. I called out and Higgins opened his eyes as the evil genie bent over him. I expected him to rise up, resist, grapple with his attacker and was astonished to see his face crumple in fear, eyes and lips tight shut, like a child expecting a slap. The genie raised a basin over our companion's head and doused him with warm water. The spluttering was silenced by a cupped handful of soap that instantly covered his head in lather. The ogre vigorously rubbed his victim's hair and beard, thrust his little finger in his ears, delved into the creases round his neck. It was a dreadful parody of a nursery scene, with hairy Higgins as the babe. The indignities did not stop there. The villainous nurse pulled off Higgins' towel, turned him on his back and soaped him all over right down to his fingers and toes, not neglecting his most intimate parts. Then it was the turn of his back and when it came to soapy fingers in the crack I did not know whom to pity more. When he was thoroughly enveloped in foam the nurse washed it off with basins of water. But it was not yet over. He took a big square glove of coarse material and scrubbed his victim all over, whipping up a black scum from our companion's skin, which he rinsed off from time to time. Lastly he twisted and pulled the limbs and fingers and toes, finishing with a wrestling hold about the neck and a quick jerk upwards. The crack of a dry stick echoed round the chamber. Higgins fell limp on the table, a rabbit dispatched for one of Mr. Reynolds' still-life pictures. His tormentor revived him with some basins of water, tapped him on the shoulder to show that he was finished, and pointed to the steaming arch. I pushed Winstanley to the torture table.

"Sir, I washed yesterday. My limbs are frail."

"Offer it up to the Lord. Wash away your sins. My mother will know if you accepted to be purified."

His look was venomous and he trudged to his fate like a boy to the birch.

I left Winstanley to his gasping, gagging and gurgles and went with Higgins to the steam room. His usual truculence had been washed away, and more. He seemed unmanned, unstuffed, unspirited, relieved from a terrible terror or in the grip of it. Despite the heat he trembled. I have seen such moods at the gaming table when a man has lost his fortune, his father's fortune, his wife's fortune, and all their chattels, properties and estates. At such times his friends rally round to keep him from killing himself before they can establish title to their winnings.

"What's the matter, Higgins? Buck up, it's only soap and water."

He paid no attention and slumped on the bench against the wall, his chin on his chest, impervious to the suffocating steam. I feel the same way about a hot room as I do about an Indian curry, for the same reasons: sweating forehead, stinging eyes, burning throat and a pervading sense of pointlessness. I believe pleasure should be pleasurable.

"Come on, man, you will have an apoplexy in here," I said, but he looked at me as if the advice was already too late.

"A brandy is what we need. I have a flask in my coat for emergencies."

I knew he was really out of sorts when even this had no effect. I shook his porky shoulder but he was obdurate.

I was thinking of fetching the evil genie to carry him out when in came Winstanley, strutting like a turkey-cock; a plucked and boiled turkey-cock but a turkey-cock nevertheless. As a sign of his transformation he wore his cloth loosely about the waist, showing off his scraggy torso. Those who fear what is not fearsome and endure it, often mistake the innocuousness of the experience for their own courage. They congratulate themselves on conquering their fear of the dark or of spiders, when the dark or spiders are not to be feared in the first place. Winstanley thought himself the bravest of bucks when all he had endured was a thorough wash.

"Don't hold back, Sir, it is very invigorating," he had the nerve to say.

"Our companion is poorly. Help me take him out."

Winstanley crouched down and looked Higgins in the eye. What he saw in there I cannot say but it inspired him to take the other's limp hand in his.

"Come on, my friend," he said.

After a moment's reflection Higgins stood up and allowed himself to be led like a child into the undressing room. Amazed at their mutual tenderness I let them go and subjected myself to the genie and his vigorous ablutions.

When I rejoined them, in a state of lethargy and elation, they were stretched on beds and wrapped in dry towels. Winstanley was asleep. Higgins lay on his back, ruddy cheeked, pink lipped, his hair combed flat with a little curl on his forehead. He would have melted any mother's heart, but for the red beard and yellow teeth. He clutched our little treasure box of opium pastilles. A handsome boy in a kaftan and skull cap gave me dry towels and a glass of sweet tea and I lay down on the next bed. I closed my eyes and prepared for sleep by conjuring up the Aphrodite of the waves to visit me in my dreams. She was gliding to my bedside when Higgins rudely scared her off.

"Da, he said, Da", not to me but to some unseen person.

"Da?"

"Da don't come. Da won't come..."

"Higgins, are you feverish? What's this Da?"

"Murther. Murther..."

"Pull yourself together, Sir."

"Ma...won't find me, won't find me..."

We carried on like this, sotto voce, as I called him to his senses from some daylight, living dream. From his ramblings I deduced a terrible but not uncommon story. It seems his father would beat the mother and, in his words, 'come soft' on the son. The sins of the fathers shall be visited on their children, in Higgins' case too literally. At the hands of our tyrannical Turk Higgins relived the sordid intimacies. For once I blessed my own bullying, boozy, indolent father who, other than for purposes of legitimate chastisement, never laid a hand on me.

At last Higgins fell into a deep sleep, from which he awoke his normal truculent self. Purged of the dust of travel and the contents of our purses we dressed and left. The boiled attendants cried "saddle her old son!"* to which I replied "If I find her I will!", the lameness of which shows the debilitating effect of a Turkish bagnio.

* *Sıhhatler olsun: good health!*

HIGGINS

I cannot vouch for the accuracy of Higgins' rambling monologue set off in the bagnio by the delusional encounter with his father and sustained by an opium pastille but I set it down as best as I can remember. In order to spare the reader its repetitions and meanderings I have made a narrative out of his confession and, once again removed his Irish barbarisms.

The boy was eleven years old when one evening he came home to find his mother murdered and his father dead drunk beside her. He fled from the house to Dublin and sneaked on a ship to Liverpool. From there he walked to London, begging for food, sleeping in ditches and avoiding fellow travellers. He arrived without friends or relations and determined to leave no trace that a father could follow. Such young innocents are easy prey to criminals, who turn them into commodities for sale in the street, the girls to the Gomorrah of Piccadilly, the boys to the Sodom of Birdcage Walk, or, if they are lucky enough to find indoor work, the bawdy-houses and molly-houses that enliven our city. As he entered on foot and not via the coaching stations, where child-stealers prowl, he came as far as Covent Garden before he was accosted by a man, who saw him steal an apple, and asked him if he would like to work for his dinner instead. He was middle-aged with a parson's sober clothes and demeanour. He spoke with a hoarse whisper and made play with a large scented handkerchief with which he dabbed his mouth and patted his cheeks. Higgins asked what kind of work to which he replied that his name was Ephraim and could be trusted. He stopped a pie man and bought a pasty and handed it to the boy.

I expected the banal little tale, rehearsed every day in our city, of his initiation into the ways of Birdcage Walk from the fluttering of the handkerchief through the coat-tails, the patting of the back of one's hand with the palm of another, the thumbs stuck into the armpit of the waistcoat with fingers drumming on the chest, to hasty work on Cockpit Steps or the rituals of the bedroom, in which his father had initiated him. Ephraim said there would be another pie if he would come with him. Higgins was snared, although he kept a hand on the knife in his pocket, and followed Ephraim into Saint Bartholomew's churchyard.

"Are you frightened here?"

"No", answered Higgins.

Ephraim led him to a corner of the churchyard, where a grave had been opened to receive a new occupant. At the bottom of the pit were scraps of wood and bone, and things that wriggled.

"Are you frightened?"

"Why should I be?"

"The spirits of the restless dead walk here," said Ephraim and waved his perfumed handkerchief as a charm to keep them away.

"The dead don't frighten me."

He had seen his mother lying dead and his father lying alive beside her. He knew which one to fear.

An officious person, armed with a stick and armoured with a leather hat, came towards them. Ephraim waved his handkerchief, the sexton waved his stick and went away, from which Higgins guessed that they knew each other.

"He thought we were here to spy out a grave to rob," said Ephraim, putting a hand on the boy's knee. "What do think of that?"

"If they are stupid enough to bury themselves with treasure, they deserve to be robbed."

"Isn't theft a sin?"

"It's not thieving. The dead can own nothing."

"The dead don't own treasure. They are the treasure."

This sounded ominous to the boy and he tightened his grip on the knife, although Ephraim looked too foppish and sickly to turn anyone into treasure.

"Do you have an appetite for another meat pie?"

Ephraim took his arm and steered him past the sexton at the lych-gate, who nodded as they passed, and through a warren of narrow streets. They came to Smithfield meat market and watched a lowing cow dispatched by a slaughterer in the yard and hoisted by the hind feet on a scaffold for skinning and butchering.

"Are you frightened to see this?"

"I've killed pigs with my Da."

"They do this with hanged men. The surgeons take them to cut up and pickle. What do you think of that."

"Meat is meat."

"And all the better for being in a pie."

If you have read this far without throwing the book on the dung-heap, I ask you to stand in the place of a country boy in the metropolis, hungry, alone, fleeing a murdered mother and a bestial father. There is a fine line between cynical cold-heartedness and the courage to face ordeals to which a child should not be exposed.

They strolled for a while about the market. The boy's indifference to the squeal and bellow of the massacred animals, the shouts and banter of the butchers, the stink of dung and blood and offal, was less to do with callousness than the combination of hot food and exhaustion. He must have fallen asleep on his feet for the next thing he knew he woke up in a bed on a pillow of hay. He had been undressed and put in a night-shirt but as far as he could tell this was the extent of interference with him. His own clothes were nowhere to be seen but at the foot of the bed was a smock and breeches of much washed calico and a pair of clogs. His first thought was for a chamber pot and he found a pail in the corner, whose contents left its use in no doubt.

He was in an attic with sloping ceilings and a low window whose bottle glass and grime revealed nothing but a gleam of daylight. He stepped out into the darkness of the landing. He could have been in a butcher's house from the reek of hanging game; or an apothecary's from the whiff of bitter herbs on charcoal that rose from the stairwell. He went down the creaking staircase into the gloom of the floor below, where the doors were all closed, and to the light of the floor below that. Through the proscenium of open double doors was a tableau from a Gothic novel: another boy in calico smock and breeches stood at the foot of a table; Ephraim stood at the side; other men gathered around and peered as he plucked the heart from a gaping corpse on the table and held it up for them to inspect.

"Ah," said Ephraim, turning to young Higgins, "the fearless boy. Do you fancy a meat pie?"

This was the Anatomy School of Doctor Ephraim Livingstone, who made a living from dissection, to which the hanged, the destitute and the resurrected were subject. The heart of the school was the theatre, which young Higgins now entered, like a sleepwalker into a nightmare. The dissecting table, with its drain holes and buckets underneath, was in the middle. When he had exhausted the educational possibilities of a limb or an organ Ephraim tossed it into one of the pickling bins of body parts behind him; the walls were lined with shelves of specimens, floating in vinegar, with pride of place to the freakish and diseased. The theatre was built over a courtyard, sealed from the street with high gates, opened only for deliveries by Sheriff's men, resurrectionists and impecunious relatives.

Higgins was employed as Second Boy. His first job of the day was to empty the buckets and pots of the house into vats in the cellar, starting with the chamber pots and ending with the buckets in the theatre. He trimmed lamps and candles and put fresh leaves on the charcoal burners and cleaned all the living rooms. The cook and the scullery maid stayed in the kitchen, a separate building in the courtyard. Their range was the only source of heat in the house, so the bodies kept longer. He then helped Jeremiah the First Boy with his chores in the theatre – cleaning and sharpening instruments, packing up specimens for customers, putting fresh vinegar in the bins and jars, preparing a cadaver for the day's demonstrations. There was night work when new bodies were delivered, laying out and draining and washing in Ephraim's patent embalming liquor.

Ephraim was distant but kind enough so long as the work was carried out to his satisfaction. Higgins did not especially take to the life but it was tolerable. He was well fed and sure his father would never find him. He discovered a talent for drawing, which Ephraim encouraged, giving him materials and examples to copy. 'Anatomy is but Observation,' was his motto.

Jeremiah was thirteen years old. He was pale and delicate and smaller than Higgins although the same age. Ephraim had bought him in a package with his dead mother and still-born sister. Out of compassion for the boy he sold the mother on, but the sister lived in a jar in the theatre. The boys shared the bed in the attic and soon developed a lively affection for each other. It was the first time either had given or received human warmth. In each other's arms they consoled each other for their past and encouraged each other for the future.

Jeremiah hated the place. One night he confided to Higgins that Mr. Smollett, a gentleman who attended the school, had offered him a position in his house in Mayfair. He was not a surgeon but one of the 'ghouls', as Ephraim called them, a coterie of dilettanti who visited the anatomy schools as others went to lunatic hospitals or the studios of artists. Jeremiah would have livery and shoes and not have to see and smell corpses all day. Mr. Smollett told him not to mention this to Ephraim but to slip away quietly on the next night a body was delivered. Jeremiah asked about Higgins and was assured there would be a place for him too before long. He promised he would come back for him as soon as he was settled. Higgins was dismayed but could offer no objection other than a general warning that persons with necrophiliac tastes were not to be trusted.

A corpse was delivered a few days later. Higgins saw Jeremiah in a black cloak, improvised out of a funeral drape, slip out when Ephraim's back was turned, his sister under his arm. Ephraim noticed he was missing only when the body was being washed and prepared. Higgins joined in the fruitless search of the house and denied all knowledge of the escape. He took on the duties of First as well as Second Boy until Ephraim brought home a new recruit, a gawky lad from Kent abandoned by his family. Mr. Smollett no longer came to the school. Ephraim said that, ghoul or not, it was pity to lose his money, not making a connection with the disappearance of Jeremiah.

Higgins pined for his friend but had no means of contacting him. About two months later Ephraim bought from the Coroner the body of a child drowned in the Thames. He was pleased because he was investigating how the brain matured and children, compared with infants and adults, were hard to come by. As usual it was delivered at night. When they opened the shroud upstairs they discovered, to their horror, Jeremiah. He had bruises on his mouth, his arms and his belly; his thighs and buttocks were covered in welts; his private parts were torn and bleeding. Higgins took up the knife and tube to drain the veins but Ephraim put a hand on his shaking arm. He told the boys just to wash the body. He himself sewed the eyes and bound up the jaw. They put Jeremiah in a coffin and next day took it to Bunhill Fields where Ephraim owned a plot protected from resurrectionists by an iron cage. He read the burial service himself. Higgins was touched that the anatomist gave the boy a proper burial, especially as he had been paid for at resurrectionist's rates.

Higgins sank into depression. He was haunted by nightmares that his bed-mate used to drive away. Chimeras made of body parts lurked in the corners of the theatre. The grotesque contents of the pickle jars winked at him. His diligence suffered, which neither whipping nor cajoling restored. He made elaborate plans to track down Mr. Smollett in Mayfair and rehearsed in his mind how to murder him, using his knowledge of anatomy to prolong the agony. One night, when a corpse was delivered, he slipped away when Ephraim's back was turned, taking a dissecting knife with him. He lurked in Mayfair for a week but no-one had heard of a Mr. Smollett, not even the boys who trawled for custom in Grosvenor Square.

One day he was collared by another patron of the anatomy school, a bona fide surgeon, who was lucky not to be at the sharp end of a dissecting knife. Higgins, worn down by depression, hunger and sleeplessness, broke into sobbing for the first time since his mother died and confessed everything. The surgeon took him back to Ephraim, negotiated his release and took him on as his assistant: he was an army surgeon and about to leave for the war in the American Colonies.

Higgins fell into a deep sleep. What most intrigued me was why he had chosen to confess this particular episode in his eventful life. Why not describe the death of his mother, misuse by his father, the origins of any one of the innumerable scars that covered his body? I knew from my father that he had lived enough adventures in America for three men. I can only conclude that his washing by the bath attendant had recalled the first and perhaps the only time in his life that he had experienced innocent, tender, uncorrupted love for and from a fellow human being.

Dissection
Wm. Hogarth

PANEGYRIS

The day after our bath was a holiday, which the Greeks call a *panegyris,* in honour of Saint John, the patron saint of the town. It was Winstanley's idea to invite Amelia to the festivities.

"It is our duty as gentlemen to escort her," was his pretext.

"She is brazen enough to come by herself," said Higgins

"It is common courtesy. I am not thinking of her reputation."

"What little of it remains," said Higgins.

Sucking his smoke too hard, Winstanley had a providential fit of coughing, which sent him from our room in search of fresh air and cut short the conversation.

Amelia was happy to be invited. She took her time to get ready. In contrast with her previous mannishness she wore a more feminine dress, with a ribbon in her hair and lace at her wrists. She took my arm and Winstanley's with the self-conscious gaiety of a belle off to a ball. The wilderness had not quenched the natural coquetry of her sex.

It is Turkish policy to tolerate the customs and institutions of their subjects For all the talk of oppression the Greeks enjoy plenty of freedom, especially in religion. The priests conduct their liturgies in all their finery and walk about the streets in their habits. The country abounds with churches and there is no restriction on celebrations of holy days. The icon of the saint was paraded through the streets with solemn chanting and I was astonished to see Turks as well as Greeks pressing up to kiss the bier on which it rode. The people of each religion venerate relics, mementos and holy places of the others, like a sportsman backing his favourite but placing side bets on the other runners. The Turks did not join in the revelry that followed but went back to their houses, as they disapproved of wine and the mingling of the sexes, of which others among us had high hopes.

While the common folk sat on the ground around large platters and ate with their fingers, Consul Pericles took us to a place of honour in the shade, an improvised high table from which we could observe and be observed, as much sources of entertainment to the merrymakers as they were to us. They brought barrels of wine into the square and set animals to roast on spits. The other main dish was a salad made of cheese, which they simply call *fat*, mixed with onion and cucumber and olives, all dressed with oil and wild herbs. Unlike the Italians they have not taken to the tomato either out of conservatism or taste. I am entirely in sympathy; the insipid fruit is only good for boiling down into a ketchup. The wine was adulterated with pine resin and I asked Pericles why.

"To make untasteworthy for our Turkish masters. Otherwise they ship it all to Constantinople."

"Surely the addition of resin and spices predates the Turks," chipped in my tutor. "The resin makes it keep better."

"Whatever the reason, nothing demonstrates more clearly the triumph of necessity over taste than our consumption of it. Pass the jug, Higgins."

At the end of his tour of inspection the Saint was set down in the portico of the church to supervise the bacchanal in his honour. He carried a kid on his shoulders.

"That goat ain't a Christian thing," said Higgins.

"What of it?" asked Amelia.

"By convention saints carry lambs, the animal of Christ, notably Saint John the Evangelist" said Winstanley.

"Are you a devotee of the Lamb and Flag Winstanley?"

An Oxford man, he would have known the notorious public house, built into the walls of Saint John's, where many an applauded graduate gets a clap from a saucy serving wench.

We were distracted from theology by the daughters of the town fluttering around the square like summer butterflies. Musicians started up and they danced prettily in a circle. They invited us to join them, which we did, except for blushing Winstanley, who remained resolutely seated despite the coaxing of Pericles' prettiest daughter Eleni. Amelia was no stranger to the steps while Higgins and I stumbled around, paying more attention to the transparency of breast cloths than our feet.

Since their watchful fathers and brothers prevented us from getting to know these beauties better, their inviting glances and sinuous movements only inflamed our natural desires. Nevertheless we did not give up all hope of sport, I because I believe that human nature will always assert itself over the restrictions of morality and Higgins because he was a Catholic and believed in the Fall of Man and the opportunities for pleasure it provides.

The music was truly dreadful. The musicians assaulted our ears with drums and tambourines and lyres and flutes. The worst offenders puffed out their cheeks like bladders and blew thick pipes with reeds in the mouthpiece to make a shrill and raucous racket. When they started up Higgins clapped his hands over his ears. Amelia had the idea of slipping a few coins to a pair of musicians to serenade him. They did their work too well, chasing him through the crowd like a dog whose tail they had set alight until he turned and chased them back. The business cost me six ducats before we were forgiven, two for the drum that Higgins smashed over the head of the drummer, two for the pipe that he snapped over his knee and two for a barrel of wine to pacify the scandalized merry makers.

Amelia's joke was at odds with her spinsterish soberness. Her gaiety affected even Winstanley, who allowed her to lead him off to join the dancing: he reminded me of the baboon in Vauxhall Gardens, who earns his crust by jigging to the music.

Amelia treated him with the embarrassed considerateness one shows in public to half-witted relations. Their cavorting put the idea of more mischief into our heads.

"Let's marry them off, Higgins. Picture them by the matrimonial fireside."

"Picture them in the matrimonial bed."

"She is pressing me to take her with us on our ship. They will keep us entertained and Winstanley off our backs."

"And him on his. I know who'd be the rider if they had a gallop."

The couple came back perspiring and downed cups of wine. Soon we were all merry, especially Amelia, who looked flushed by exertion and drink. Her vivacity, her laughter, the burning glances, which briefly caught mine, betrayed a ferment of emotion not grapes. I made a solemn prayer to the Goat Saint John that our stay on the island would be enlivened by a love affair. As if in reply a gang of mummers dressed in goat skins gambolled into the square with lighted torches and capered around us. We joined in the dancing again and ate and drank and left the feast not a little fuddled.

Officiating Habit of a Greek Papa or Priest

PARADISE MISPLACED

Higgins carried Winstanley to our apartments in a stupor leaving me to escort Miss Burbage to Pericles' house. If I tell you that I took advantage of a lady's high spirits, her liberal consumption of new wine, and a moonlit night, then you would think me no more of a buck than you already knew. As so often happens it was not my intention. Seated under a mulberry tree in the courtyard. serenaded by nightingales, scented with flowers, I unwittingly enticed her to bare all.

"What is that scent?"

"Jasmine. She is early. All my life is in that scent."

"Isn't Damascus called the City of Jasmine?"

"Bravo. Jasmine is one of my earliest memories. With Mama in her silk trousers and embroidered slippers. But you don't want to listen to childhood reminiscences."

This was true. As a rule the wine-sodden recollections of others fascinate only the teller. But I was too heavy-lidded to agree with her, which she took as encouragement. Like many who live in solitude, her pent-up conversation became an unstoppable monologue when her tongue was loosened.

"I remember being in a garden by the river and a band is playing. It is hot, the sun sets the water on fire, and the sky is Persian blue. The air is heavy with the scent of grass and flowers and tobacco. The ladies have parasols but they cover their faces with gossamer veils, even my sister Leonora, who is only two years older than me. They stroll with peacock gentlemen among the trees or sit on the grass and their laughting syncopates the music from the band. I hide my face in Mama's perfumed trousers until I am snatched away by a maid and taken indoors."

"Was this in Damascus?"

"Brentford. The garden of our villa ran down to the Thames and our visitors came as often by boat as by road. Our life was idyllic. Our little villa was small but exquisitely decorated in the oriental style, so that it seemed like a palace and our mother a fairy princess. She was a striking beauty so that even in dishabille she looked more elegant than any ladies I knew. She dressed the maids and us children to match our surroundings so we were like so many butterflies in an enchanted garden. My sister took more readily to this than I. In ringlets and powder she looked like a replica of Mama, which I could never achieve. When we were alone Leonora made me dress like a man and escort her round the drawing room and take the gentlemen's part in the quadrille and parrot the compliments we heard them make, which she parried with ripostes she overheard from Mama.

We did not go to school and rarely went outside the house. Mama taught us our letters and the elements of arithmetic. When we did venture out it was in a smart chocolate brown carriage and pair. I remember once a woman covered the eyes of her two children as we passed and I assumed it was to protect them from our brilliance.

In the season Mama was gone for long periods and came back with stories of London or Bath or some grand house she had visited. In the summer she stayed at home and gentlemen came to us. There were pavilions on the lawn, kiosks among the trees, arbours in the shrubbery. Chinese lanterns were lit at dusk. I suppose it must have rained but I only remember long summer evenings as magical as a Midsummer Night's Dream. It was presided over by our most frequent guest, a distinguished gentleman whom I thought very old. He was probably about forty. He arrived by river in his personal barge painted the same colour as our carriage and with a crest on the bow. He sat my sister and me on his knees and tested us on our lessons."

"Did you take him for your father?"

"It didn't cross our minds. Mama never referred to her admirers as anything but friends."

"When did you realise what her profession was?"

"Much later. Mama didn't pretend to be what she wasn't, nor did she explain it in so many words. We knew no other way of things. We were as innocent as cherubs. Until one Thursday morning in July. On the previous evening Mama and her special friend were sitting by the river. We kissed them good night and went to bed. When we came down next morning they were dead on the bank."

"Murdered!"

"Cudgelled by waterpads come to rob the house. They died in each other's arms."

"Was there a scandal?"

"The death of his Lordship at his pleasure pavilion was reported in the newspapers without mentioning the circumstances. His body and his boat and his chocolate carriage were fetched away before dinner time. The sheriff's men took Mama and we never saw her again."

"Didn't she have a Christian burial?"

"Who would give her that? Certainly not the Vicar of Brentford. Her only entrée to his church was as the subject of a sermon."

"A heavy blow. Two orphan girls."

"We were young. We didn't understand. We behaved as if Mama had gone away on one of her journeys. The only indication of the seriousness of our position was the despondency of the maids. Their fears were realised a week later when the house was invaded by rough men in black, who didn't take off their hats, not like any man we had seen in the house before. They stripped the house of all Mama's things, her gowns and drapes and caskets and boxes, and loaded them in a cart, never to be seen again. We heard wailing and shouting as the maids were thrown out in the clothes they stood up in.

A stern woman came with them and told us that she was our Aunt Sarah and that we would live with her now in Dulwich. She packed our things herself, tossing out our prettiest clothes as if they were infected with the plague. She confiscated my sister's box with all her frippery and shook her when she kicked and screamed. We were dragged into a shabby hackney and drove past the maids huddled like lost sheep in the road clutching bundles and weeping."

"Cast out of Paradise into Dulwich: the City Merchants' Kensington - without the Ton."

My shaft of wit went well wide. I took my leave, slightly piqued that she did not try to stop me, but seemed content to be left in the moonlight with her memories.

Earrings
J. Flaxman

SAINT JOHN

Our ship was still not ready. To pass the time and further our plans for Winstanley I encouraged him to call on Miss Burbage, with a flower or a sprig of olive. He was not to know this was the first step of their courtship. We marched him to Pericles' house and found that she had left for a walk outside the town.

I insisted that we all needed fresh air, so we followed her footsteps along a meandering path beside a stream through orchards of almond and olive trees. The air was crystal and the sky a brilliant blue, washed by a gentle breeze, perfumed with the scent of flowers and pine. The hillsides were humming with newly woken bees and vivid with wild flowers woven in a Turkey carpet of colours. Higgins grumbled as usual, his red beard sunk into his chest, indifferent to the bucolic scene around him, of which he was a reluctant part, like some liverish satyr. Winstanley was under the influence of the Bey's tobacco and what I hoped was Love. He sighed and quoted from the poets and for once I was in sympathy.

"*Genius of Ancient Greece! Nurse divine*
Of all heroic deeds and fair desires."

"Fair desires. We need nymphs, skipping naked between the trees, seducing travellers to enjoy their loveliness," I mused.

"I would settle for an unwashed shepherdess," said our satyr.

We came across a flock of devilish black goats led by a ram with gilded horns and festoons of ribbons, herded by a pretty boy, whose badge of office was a pipe made of reeds bound together. Higgins loathed their asthmatical trilling.

"Sure, boys don't learn the pipe because they are herdsmen. They are compelled to be herdsmen if they play the pipe. In the mountains they can tootle all day without aggravating the rest of us."

"Tell me, Winstanley," I said, "why the island has no ancient sites to speak of. I understand why temples and so on are in beautiful locations. But why are there many beautiful locations without monuments?"

"Some beliefs are better concealed than given a marble shrine," said Higgins.

"Faith is in men's souls not in their temples. It is a gift of God in the struggle for salvation."

"The more we struggle, the more we sink into the dunghill. There is nothing you can do except learn to like the taste of shite," replied Higgins.

"You are too cynical. Look at the loveliness around you. Faced with such beauty every warm and generous feeling we possess grows stronger and, while the heart swells with gratitude to God, it beats with goodwill towards everything on earth."

He was high or in love.

After a time we came to the source of the stream, a spring bubbling out of the hillside. Frogs plumped into the water among hovering dragonflies. We followed a narrow path above the stream between stone walls and the fields at eye level on either side until we stepped out onto a flat meadow. Behind us was the mountain. Below us was the town and the plain and the sea. It was like an amphitheatre and said as much to Winstanley, which was a mistake, since it set him off on the prologue to some ancient tragedy and spoiled the natural beauty.

Nestled in a hollow was a small chapel, whitewashed and planted round with olive trees. It was a simple, rectangular, unplastered building with a roof of split stone slabs. I left Higgins grumbling and Winstanley burbling love poetry and climbed down to look at it. I pushed open the wooden door and went inside. It was chill and dank. The roof was supported by a timber frame overlaid with reeds, like all the squalid houses of the island. In the shadows of the far end was a stone rood screen which the Byzantians call the iconostasis. In shadow and coated with candle soot, it boasted an extraordinary icon. The saint wore a purple cassock under a white tunic, hemmed and cuffed with jewels, under a long scarlet cloak secured round his neck with a collar also of jewels. His torso faced the front but his legs and feet and head were pointed towards his right side. His left hand was raised in blessing. His right hand held a white cross. What astonished me was this: on the body of the saint was the head of a goat. It had a goat's muzzle and a goat's mouth and a goat's beard. The horns were buds on his forehead, in the way that Higgins drew cuckolds. It was not a man made up as a goat or a goat made to look like a man but a natural creature. It was not a terrifying head; indeed the expression in his eyes was seductive. I am not affected by horrible fantasies - I sneer at tales of ghosts and hobgoblins, at least in daylight - but I felt the most peculiar thrill at the sight of this goat-headed man. I conquered the urge to run outside into the warmth and light of the spring morning. Instead I peered closer and deciphered above his left shoulder the words in quaint, Greek lettering *Agios Ioannes O Tragocephalos*, Saint John the Goat-headed.

I came out of the chapel. Its presence permeated the place where we stood, as any chapel or ruined temple sanctifies its site. The grass and trees and twittering birds were transformed. Yet nothing had changed. Winstanley was communing with his volume of Pope, Higgins with a bottle of arak. I corked his bottle and led him protesting into the chapel. When his eyes were accustomed to the shadows he ambled over to the iconostasis, tugging at his beard. I was not disappointed: he gazed at the icon and although he had his back to me I could tell that he was gripped by emotion.

"Will you draw it?"

He said nothing. I went out of the chapel to fetch Winstanley and when we came back our artist was on his knees. He scrabbled to his feet when my shadow crossed the door. His face was alight. I had never seen such radiance on him, even in his cups; his eyes were shining; the puffy flesh had melted from his cheeks and jowls.

"Seek and you will find," he whispered, more to himself than to us.

"Find what?" I asked.

"A new perspective. I have a new perspective."

He brushed dust from his breeches, took pencil and paper out of his his satchel and began to sketch, wildly and impetuously. Now it was the tutor's turn to examine the icon and he also blushed in the dim light. His voice trembled as much as Higgins' but with a different emotion.

"It is blasphemy. Thank the Lord for the light of learning and reason that has shrivelled such unwholesome flowers of ignorance and superstition."

"Not here it ain't."

"This is degeneracy, Sir, moral and spiritual degeneracy."

"It has regenerated Higgins. Look at him draw. I have to bribe him a shilling to work so fast."

"Sir, choose a more wholesome subject."

"The devil I will," growled Higgins.

"I'd like to know who made this image. And who worships it now?" I said.

"We all do."

It was a woman's voice that startled us and none more than Winstanley. He turned and blanched at the sight of his sparring partner framed in the doorway, a silhouette against the light.

"Forgive my intrusion."

"Madam, this pagan grotto is not for decent souls," said Winstanley.

Amelia ignored him and stood beside Higgins. She too was moved but in a different way: her breast heaved and her eyes glowed in the candlelight but for no deeper reason than amusement.

"This is unseemly," hissed her self-appointed moral guardian.

"You danced for him two days ago and ate his kids. He is the Saint John whose feast we celebrated."

"This is a travesty of sainthood. It is worse than Popery."

"This John is famous for his miracles. He was a priest on the island until he was summoned to Constantinople to be ordained a bishop. No sooner had he arrived when Papists sacked the city and massacred their fellow Christians."

"The gallant knights of the fourth crusade," I said.

"John escaped from the Patriarch's palace by tying a goatskin round himself and clinging to the underside of a billy goat. They ran through the burning streets to the port."

"An unoriginal ploy."

"Like Ulysses he was blown about the Mediterranean and had many adventures and shipwrecks. It must have taken him several hundred years to get home because when he landed the Turks occupied the island. He antagonised the other priests because his miracles were better than theirs. Whenever a Christian girl was in danger of being violated by a Turk, she had only to call out John's name and she turned into a dove and flew away. The Bey ordered him killed but he escaped into the mountains and lived in a cave. He preached to the goats and people dressed up in goatskins and went up to listen and to pray for miracles. The priests spread rumours about liturgies after dark and strange happenings at full moon so the Bey sent up his army to arrest him. They captured him and he was imprisoned in the castle tower. The night before his execution a young girl and an old woman came to visit him. When the guards opened John's cell in the morning they found a goat in his place. Everyone claimed it was a miracle, especially the guards who had let the hairy old woman in and out. The governor was not to be cheated of his execution so he had the goat beheaded in the square."

"A scapegoat!"

"John went back into the mountains. He still lives there. Pericles' mother says that when she was a child people dressed up in goatskins on the eve of his feast and spent the night in his cave."

"Do they do it now?"

"She says not. She says it is not a Christian thing to do."

"Amen."

"But I don't believe her."

During this recitation the saint smiled down on us, pleased that we were keeping his memory alive before his altar. We left him to Higgins and went back out into to the fresh spring air, where Amelia was sprightly and mocking.

"What would you pray Saint John to turn you into, Mr. Winstanley? A goat like him?"

I answered for him.

"We have one of those in Higgins. You would like to be a camel, I dare say. Kneel and be mounted? And beaten by your mistress now and then?"

"And you, Lord Exford, what would you become?"

"A stallion."

"The only transformation in your story is the story," said Winstanley. "They have taken Pan and nymphs and satyrs and poured them into other moulds and called them Christian saints. They are no less pagan for that."

"I think we should make an expedition to his cave up in the mountain. Miss Burbage will show off her rocky crags and tumbling waters and Winstanley will be self-righteous and preach Pope and Higgins will be goatish and I shall be capricious."

Enervated by exercise and the Bey's tobacco, I took a siesta after dinner. I dreamed of saints with animal heads and animals with human heads, men with the wings of birds, birds with the face of women, the parts of snakes and lions and bulls and cats and dogs all mixed up with the parts of human bodies. Several times I woke up to see them gathered about my bed and tried to cry out but no sound came. They danced around the room wreathed in incense, holding candles and blessing me with strange crosses, their wings and claws and horns and scales brushing my face and in the middle of these bestial phantasms was the Goat Saint, John.

Satyrs

DEVILS

I woke up haunted by goatish phantasms, of whom Winstanley was the most insistent, shaking my shoulder and gibbering from his mealy mouth.

"Sir, Higgins has suffered an apoplexy."

"What? He's pop-eyed? Red-faced? That is his normal complexion."

Higgins lay sprawled on his bed, heavy lidded, slack-jawed, as pale as his poxy, veiny face would allow. He stared unblinking at the ceiling, or rather through it, to some bewitching and terrible place. I was afraid that Winstanley had made a correct diagnosis. Yet he breathed and I shook his shoulder. He cutty-eyed me for a moment and returned to his hidden realm beyond the ceiling. We shook him some more and cursed him and wheedled with no result. He appeared to me not to be ill but dazed by shock. I had seen this before in a man whose credit was refused at White's: he pulled himself together sufficiently to shoot himself. But what had caused it in Higgins?

When he pushed away the brandy bottle I offered him and turned his head away from a pipe I knew we needed the services of a piss-prophet. I called for Pericles and asked if there was a medical man to hand. We were fortunate that the celebrated Rabbi Koen of Egripos was in town. I said ordered him to be summoned.

I was pleasantly surprised by the Rabbi Koen: he looked more like my banker than the snivelling creatures caricatured by previous travellers to the East. Only a Jew's blue slippers distinguished him from his fellow citizens. His turban, kaftan, sash, wide sleeve coat and pantaloons were unremarkable. On closer inspection he wore charms and phylacteries about his neck and woven into the locks about his temples, which were for the most part hidden under his turban.

He was accompanied by his son, a youth of some sixteen years, similarly dressed with a felt cap instead of a turban. He seemed old beyond his years with the pallor of study, not to speak of the solitary vice to which youths of every race and religion are partial. I was surprised to hear them speaking Greek to each other and not a Jewish language. To our further surprise their pronunciation, enunciation and grammar were closer to the classical Greek bum-brushed into us at school than to the mongrel dialect of the Christians. For example their b's were b's not v's, so barbarian was said barbarian not varvarian.

The rabbi and his son watched their patient in silence for a quarter of an hour; they demanded no turd to sniff or piss to taste; they proposed no lancet, no cups, no leeches, no poultices; he asked no questions; if I made a suggestion he put his finger on his lips. Meanwhile the object of their attention lay on the bed, seemingly aware of us and his surroundings but uninterested in them. At last, after a muttered conversation, with a gesture like shooing chickens, the rabbi pushed his son forwards to the patient. I asked if he had made his diagnosis. Pericles, not wishing to distract the physicians, whispered for them.

"Your companion taken by devils."

"Tell us something new."

"They will throw them out."

"What ho, an exorcism. Winstanley, how are you with bell, book, and candle? Will they capture the devils in a bottle and throw it in the sea? I saw it in a pantomime once. I only hope that when the devils are gone there's something left of our friend."

Our learned cleric could only gawp and stammer.

"Cast out devils? This is Popish."

I put a hand on my tutor's arm.

"Let them be. Either it is harmless, in which case there is no danger, or it succeeds, in which case our draughtsman revives and we have a wonderful anecdote."

The languid Higgins took no interest. The boy shuffled round him three times while muttering an incantation. His father explained.

"He is chasing away the devils born of your companion's night emissions. They gather round when a person is weak or dying."

The boy stopped and sat down on floor. Still Higgins affected not to notice him. In a piping voice the boy addressed him in Greek, which Pericles translated.

"He ask if he have met with hairless woman since you came."

I answered for him: "Since the modest ladies of Egripos keep their heads covered how can we say?"

"No, he means has he had pleasure with a hairless woman?"

"Come on, Higgins, confess. "

The patient said 'nothing and I answered for him. The precocious boy persevered.

"Has he had pleasure with hairless woman when sleeping?"

Higgins was again not to be drawn, for which we were grateful. I shuddered to think of his taste in erotic dreams.

"Why the preoccupation with bald strumpets?" I asked.

"Woman devils have no hair on heads."

"Is that a fact, Sir?"

"It is written," said the son, as if this was all the proof that was needed. Despite his revulsion at the proceedings, Winstanley could not resist a commentary.

"Boas laid his hand on the head of Ruth in order to know if he lay with a female devil."

"And how do we know a he-devil? A hairy head? Horns?"

"Devils assume any shape they please. We know them by their deeds not their looks," said the Rabbi.

"So how do we detect the impostor?"

"They cannot disguise their bestial voices. A woman should always get a man to speak to her before they have sexual relations."

"So that's why they insist on it. I knew there must be a reason. But tell me, Rabbi, if an old goat speaks like an old goat, how will we know he is a devil not a cantankerous Irishman?"

The rabbi treated my question as rhetorical and with a nod of his head gave the floor to his son, who rocked back and forth and continued the exorcism. In rapid Greek he chanted a prayer, pausing at the end of every phrase for his father to intone *Ameen* in the Greek way. There was no reaction from Higgins.

"Idolater," said the boy and they both sighed. The father was so kind as to explain.

"It is not a Jewish devil. No Jew would remain silent at that prayer."

"Are devils devout? But they are enemies of God."

"In no way. They are enemies of Man but not of their Creator. There have been many pious and learned devils."

"What kind of devil has got into Higgins? A lethargic one to be sure. I always assumed that demonic possession made a man more interesting, not less. Come on, Sir, fly around and speak in tongues."

The father and son took turns to instruct us, one topping the other with increasing absurdity.

"The souls of Devils, Spirits and Night Apparitions inhabit a sphere of heaven under the moon."

"Devils are like angels in two ways: they know what will happen in the future and can fly from one end of the world to the other. They are like men in three ways: they eat and drink, reproduce like men and die."

"Other devils are the children of man. When God created Adam He also created the first woman, Lilith, out of earth. But she refused to be subservient to him as they were created equal, and flew away. When he was banished from Paradise, Adam slept with Lilith and she gave birth to many devils."

"This is preposterous," said Winstanley.

"This Lilith is a spirited creature," I said.

"She has power to kill children conceived when a husband and wife enjoy each other by the light of a candle, when she is naked or when it is forbidden to sleep with her."

"Walking alone is dangerous, especially at night. Never greet another man at night in case he is a devil."

"The lowest degree of devils are the Bands of Fools who have no power to do harm but frighten travellers and get them lost."

"The next in order of malevolence are the mischievous devils who lurk in nut trees, on dung heaps and under water spouts."

"It is dangerous to go to the privy. When you go in you should say prayers for protection from snakes, scorpions and devils."

"You should not enjoy your wife afterwards for as long as it takes to walk half a mile for the privy devil follows you."

"A famous rabbi had a little window made in his privy so his daughter could protect him by putting her hand on his head when he sat down."

This devilish catalogue was interrupted by a faint but disconcerting noise: the growing rumble of an earthquake or the murmur of a mighty wind coming. With growing alarm we looked about us for the cause until Winstanley pointed to our companion. His eyes glowed bright, a ghastly rictus spread across his lips, his body trembled. He shook more and more violently while the rumbling from his chest grew into a roar. The Jews fingered their phylacteries, Winstanley his crucifix, I the pistol in my belt. He sat up, swung his feet on the floor and put his hands on his knees. An explosion like a burst bladder made us jump and there was a stink of sulphur and rotten eggs, the breath of Beelzebub himself. The roaring, rumbling gale now came in spasms as if Gadarene demons were struggling to escape. Only then did I realise what it was: an almighty guffaw.

"All your scriptures come to this," he roared and let rip another infernal fart.

"He is possessed," cried Winstanley, holding a kerchief to his nose.

"The Devil I am," said Higgins and guffawed again. "For the love of God won't someone bring me a jug of wine?"

Nargileh

Jean Brindesi

CLOCKWORK

Like rhymesters enraptured by babbling brooks, drifting clouds and blossomy scent, we reclined on cushions, entranced by the bubbling water and drifting smoke of our aromatic hookahs. Although he puffed like one of Mr. Boulton's steam machines, Winstanley did not find peace. He alternately praised and criticised Miss Burbage's independence of spirit. It was pleasing to see him wriggling on the hook of unruly emotions. He had fenced his life around with *must* and *should* and *ought*, so that *want* and *yearn* and *desire* threw him into confusion. The repression of natural feelings makes them so much more violent when they burst out in freedom.

Gradually he subsided like us into a more cheerful mood, finding things to laugh at, which in sober moments we did not find at all entertaining. Even Higgins lost his belligerence and re-discovered the joviality that he no longer found in strong spirits. The kindly herb cracked open the shell of reticence that clothes the kernel of Self, as when we teased Winstanley about the women in his life.

"I didn't know any women until I went to school. I didn't know what they were for. When I was a child I believed I was the son of a clock," he said in a matter-of-fact tone that set us off giggling.

This is the last time I shall mention our giggling, gaggling, gurgling: hear it yourself as the constant background of our conversation.

"Yes, a clock. I never knew my real mother. Father was a bookseller, a miserable trade, and we lived above the shop. Uncle cooked and kept house. He was not a relative but a friend, who shared our domestic life as an equal. He was frightened of the dark, which is why he shared my father's bed. He was a kind soul and very affectionate to me but couldn't take a mother's place, although I only knew of mothers from books and hearsay. In my child's universe her place was taken by the long-case clock in the hall.

It was a fine clock and our only noteworthy chattel. My natural mother had brought the clock into the house as her dowry. She came from a family of judges and bishops, who had cut her off when she married my father. It wasn't a gift of charity. Her father gave it to her because the maker's name that was written in copperplate on the face was Winstanley, my father's name. He didn't want his daughter's misalliance to taunt him whenever he wanted to know the time. As soon as I was of an age to recognise it, the name on the face was more proof of my origins.

Above the hands was a semicircular dial that showed the phases of the moon. A round face with pink cheeks, big dark eyes and a rosy mouth puckered in a smile migrated in an arc across a starry sky. It was meant to be the man in the moon but I thought it was my mother's face, stern but kind. As the weeks passed she waxed and waned, slipping away down to the right, leaving behind a starry sky for a few days before a sliver of pink came up again as on the left, coming and going out of my life, leaving me to grieve for her in the dark but always coming back to smile on me. She was my confidant and friend. When the mechanism wheezed and whirred before striking it was my mother talking to me in our secret language. I learned the phrases, consoling myself with them and greeting other clocks I came across.

When I began to question the mysteries of birth with scraps of evidence from hatching eggs, whelping dogs, boys' gossip, adults' obfuscations, I came to the conclusion I had sprung from the womb of the clock. On Saturday night my father opened the case to wind up the pendulum and I saw her entrails laid bare. The slow tick-tock echoed the pulse in my wrist. I asked my father where I came from. He chose to treat this as a question about the nature of the universe and the existence of God. He asked me to imagine I am out for a walk on the heath through grass and trees and stones. Then I find a watch on the ground. Do I think that it grew there like the plants or that it has being lying there since time began like the stones? No, I can't believe that all those wheels and springs and levers and their assembly into a mechanism could be anything other than the creation of a watchmaker. And so we and every animate and inanimate thing and the universe around us are the creation of the Supreme Horologist. Little did my father know that he had answered my original question: he had confirmed my conviction that I was a clockwork born from my mother in the hall.

This mis-conception evaporated as I grew older. I was not one of the Bedlamites, who think they are teapots or hat-stands. True, I am affected by the phases of the moon, elated at its waxing and despondent on the wane. The theology that the Universe is a mechanism built by the Divine Watchmaker was not news to me - it was how I had always seen the world. But a person whose mother was a clock cannot see the Universe as some heartless machine driven by a distant God, a cosmological steel spring: the divine clock is a person with warmth and feeling.

In his youth my father was touched by the divine muse of poetry. Alas he had no education or encouragement. For reasons he never disclosed, his father had turned him out without a penny and he went to London. He consorted with Horace Walpole, Thomas Gray and other like-minded poets and met Uncle among them. Finding no patron or publisher for his own work, he found employment as a servant in my mother's family. She was evidently taken by the young poet."

"As taken she most certainly was," said Higgins.

"For a second time he was thrown out, this time with a wife and a clock..."

"And a Winstanley to be."

"They went back to his parents' house, who had died, and that's where I was born. To keep his family he turned the ground floor into a book shop, at first promoting his own works and then more saleable volumes. When he died I found a case of his manuscripts. A bundle in red ribbon were odes to love, that I suppose were written to my mother, as they sing of forbidden bliss. Before I can remember she abandoned us, I don't know why.

I was taught at the village school but educated on the contents of my father's shop and primarily the works of Pope and Milton, which, so my father said, contain all the knowledge anyone needs in life. My ability to construe and declaim it got me into the grammar school as a Poor Scholar, where I learned my Latin and Greek."

"And on to Oxford. Your father must have put something by."

"I had a benefactor."

"Another Uncle?"

"It was shortly after my seventeenth birthday. I was about to leave the grammar school. I had plenty of book learning but was too shy for schoolmastering and unsuited for other forms of occupation. My father said he would take me into the business as the books that filled my head could now fill my pocket. He wanted me to take a travelling stall to the markets of the county, which filled me with dread.

I left the school one afternoon and went to sit in the church-yard to read and meditate. A lady sat down on the same bench, dressed in dark clothes and with a veil, so I deduced she was a mourner. Without any introduction she asked if I had relatives buried there, a father perhaps or a mother. I said I had left my father in good health that morning but couldn't answer for my mother."

"What? Didn't you say she was well-wound and striking?"

"She asked my name and then interrogated me about my accomplishments and prospects. I poured out my hopes from the past and dread of the future."

"To a strange female? This is not shyness."

"I felt I was talking with an old friend."

"How did she respond?"

"With tears, from which I deduced that she mourned a son. She wished me courage and a change of fortune and left in a carriage waiting for her at the lych-gate."

"Did you see her again?"

"Never. Several weeks later a letter arrived by messenger from Oxford. It contained a summons from the Dean of Christ Church to an interview and a banker's order settling on me a sufficient income to keep me at Oxford on condition I was accepted."

"What did your father say?"

"Only one thing: *the bishops have spoken.* He never mentioned it again. He gave me his blessing when I left for my first term and I never saw him again. He died of an apoplexy and his creditors took the stock and the premises. Uncle took himself to the workhouse and died soon after."

"And your benefactor?"

"I haven't seen the lady since. I tried to contact my mother's family when I was at Christ Church, if only to thank them if they were responsible. They wouldn't see me and denied any knowledge of my mother. Later, one old Canon in his cups told me he thought she had gone to Jamaica or some other wicked place."

"What about the clock?"

"I didn't have the money to buy it from the creditors. I hope to find it one day."

What I found arresting about Winstanley's tale was how his clockwork parent concealed a darker story. The Winstanley long-case embodied his mother's illicit passion, her flight from his father's proclivities, the abandonment of her child, her remorse, her atonement, and transformed it into a harmless anecdote. Perhaps all our stories conceal more than they reveal.

Meanwhile Higgins, who had been looking at him with the incredulous amusement of a spectator at a freak show, applauded with a belch and a cheeser, which eventually succumbed to our smoke.

Winstanley's Mother

CAVALCADE

We had the unwelcome news that the necessary sticks and ropes and other nautical things for our little ship were to be found only in Egripos, the capital of the island of the same name, some thirty miles to the north. Our captain was given permission to sail there under jury rig while we were to follow by land. Our annoyance that this had been decided for us without consulting us was relieved by not having to put to sea for some days. Moreover, from Egripos we would take the sheltered waters of the Gulf northwards to Constantinople instead of running the risks of the open Aegean.

Winstanley was delighted with the news.

"We'll see the famous Euripos," he said.

"Bigod, what's famous about it?"

"It's the channel between the island and the mainland of Beotia. At certain times of the month the tides flow both ways at once. Since classical times scientists have tried to explain the phenomenon. Aristotle was famous for it.

"Arithtotle?" I said. "He had a lithp. Did you know thith, Higginth? Arithtotle wath a thkoolmathter to Alekthander the Great."

"Sir, he was the greatest of all philosophers," said Winstanley

"Did he tholve the mythtery of the Euripoth?

"No. He threw himself into the water in despair and drowned."

"Couldn't we have told you that? Come on Higgins, you must know the Tippling Philosophers."

And we broke into song.

"*Arithtotle that master of arts*
had been but a dunce without wine
and what we ascribe to his parts
is due to the juice of the vine
Thirsty for knowledge his philosophy
was to booze his way through the cosmos
He fancied the wine-dark sea
So jumped in for a swig of the Euripoth."

"Serves him right," I added.

"Well now, what's Aristotle done to you?" said Higgins.

"Never mind. A pox on him."

"A Euripox," said Higgins.

"Good man. Hey ho, we're on the Grand Euro-poxy Tour."

We were a hotchpotch of a cavalcade. Higgins, Winstanley and I were given worn-out Rosinantes. Miss Burbage also swapped the camel for a nag, so she could make conversation. Her ludicrous beast insisted on leading us, forcing us to admire the luxuriant fartleberries on his moulting rump. Consul Pericles was mounted on his mule. The Rabbi Koen, who was going home to Egripos, rode on an ass, led by his son on foot. Chorbaji Two-Face was in command on a handsome black mule, considerately riding on the flank with his good side towards us. A dozen surly foot-wobblers brought up the rear with their muskets and accoutrements. As we left the town we were pursued as usual by a tag-rag and bobtail of stray dogs and ragamuffins.

We managed to pair off Miss Burbage and Winstanley but they could not have been more indifferent to each other if they had been married twenty years. They avoided each other's glances, and were engrossed in their books, she in botany and he in Pope's Iliad. I hoped this was a masquerade for our benefit.

I asked Rabbi Koen if he had found enough diseases and demons in Aliveri to make his journey worthwhile. He said that healing was not his business: his trade was linen. In the low-lying areas of the island the peasantry grew flax and from this span coarse linen thread, which he bought up and exported to the Sultan's shipyards in Constantinople for the manufacture of sails. I complimented him on the excellence of his Greek.

"Why shouldn't we speak the language of our fathers?" said the Rabbi. We are Greek and we speak the Greek language."

Like all the Greeks he referred to himself and his language as Roman but for the sake of clarity I shall persevere with the inaccuracy, which you may correct yourself, if you wish. I should also point out that his words were translated for us by Pericles, with asides and repetitions and interjections from the Rabbi's son. Indeed this conversation, like all the others, is so far removed from its original that I barely recognise it myself.

"But you speak Hebrew in the temple," said Winstanley.

"No Sir, God speaks to us in Greek and our scriptures are in Greek."

"How is it you speak the language of the Christians?" asked Winstanley, retreating to firmer if not higher ground.

"We don't. It is Christians who speak the language of Jews. We have first claim on the Greek language. Your Saint Paul was a Greek-speaking Jew from a Greek-speaking city."

"We were told that the language of the Jews here is Spanish," said Winstanley in an attempt to retrieve his self-appointed position as fount of all wisdom.

"Bah. Those Sephardim came from Spain yesterday. They are not true Jews like us, with their fancy ways and barbarous Ladino language. They give us Greeks a bad name."

"Are you Jewish or Greek?"

"Both. Greeks were Jews before they were Christians. And the first Greek Jews were on this island. Alexander the Great brought us here. In his conquest of the world he arrived with his armies at the gates of Jerusalem and was about to sack the Holy City. The High Priest went to meet him: before he could prostrate himself before the conqueror to plead for mercy, the conqueror bowed low to him. Alexander explained to his generals that he had seen man dressed like him in his dreams, who had prophecied victory. This was on the 25th day of Tevet in 3448 and is a holiday for us. My son is named Alexander as was my father.

Alexander not only spared the city but was so delighted with the industry of its inhabitants that he brought a number of families here to Chalcis to improve its prosperity. From here Jews spread to Athens, Thebes, Corinth, Thessalonica and other cities. They converted many pagans. For centuries the most important religion of the Greeks was Jewish."

"This cannot be right. There are only a few Greek cities mentioned in the Acts of the Apostles."

"They were the cities that made Paul welcome. Most of them, like Chalcis, did not let him in. They did not want their world turned upside down."

"You know the Acts of the Apostles?"

"Of course. They are the doings of our people."

These revelations shocked Winstanley to silence.

At midday we rested the horses and ourselves at an inn called the Three Khans. The inns of England could not have surpassed it for dirt and decay and the surliness of the keeper. His food was execrable and his arak like the worst medicine, so we stuck to our brandy and ship's biscuit.

I should like to record that the landscape kept us entertained, but I have to disappoint you, as we were disappointed. There was nothing in the scenery but a blue sea on the left and some unremarkable hills to the right. Our ride was neither pleasant nor arduous, relaxing nor enervating, eventful nor calamitous, so we had to make our own entertainment.

I shall not insult your intelligence by pretending that we told each other stories to while away the journey. You know the form - The Canterbury Tales for example. Have you ever done this in real life? My experience is that after some banter about this and that, the travellers soon get lost in their own thoughts. Story-telling is as fictitious as most of the other conversations and encounters recounted in travel books. How strange it is that once across the Channel the travel book scribbler is besieged by natives anxious to recount the history of their lives, while you and I are lucky to find someone to give you the time of day.

But how else would we while away the tedium of the road from Aliveri to Egripos? I don't mean our tedium but yours. We have to pass your time as well as ours - you clearly have nothing better to do, otherwise why would you be reading this? Have you no journeys of your own to make? Or are you abroad and finding it less enthralling and your companions more tiresome than you hoped?

So I will pretend we told each other stories; but while you read them, as I hope you will, spare a thought for us, their pretext, ambling at the slowest pace a hack can go, bored out of our minds, daydreaming of dalliances and dinner, inventing adventures to impress the stay-at-homes, wishing we had brought along an entertaining book of travellers' tales.

"Madam, where did you get your passion for botany?" I asked.

"From a clergyman. A Cambridge man and a fellow of Dulwich College."

PARADISE REPLACED

"**O**n the death of our mother my sister Leonora and I were taken in by her sister Aunt Sarah, who had a dame school."

"She was a mother to you," said Winstanley.

"A mother. But not our mother. It was amazing that the offspring of the same parents could be so different. It was as if the qualities they inherited from their parents had not been shared but divided whole between them. Even the way they sat in a carriage was different. Mama let herself be taken by the movement as if she were dancing but Aunt Sarah sat stiff and upright, as if the jolting and swaying were an affront. The foundation of Aunt Sarah's educational system was decorum. It was the basis of a good position and a good marriage."

"Was she a Tartar then?"

"Her natural feelings were suppressed by principles."

"So you think that children should grow up wild like the Emile of Monsieur Rousseau?" asked Winstanley.

"I think that we should all be guided at any age by our natural conscience tempered by experience and common sense and not by the rules laid down by old men living or dead."

"Yet your Aunt had the Christian charity to take you in."

"As she never ceased to remind us. In exercising it she saved her own soul. Is that charity or self-interest, Mister Winstanley?"

"It requires goodness of heart to follow our Lord's word."

"Not to speak of the five hundred pounds a year settled on each of us at birth. For the good of our souls Aunt Sarah kept this from us until she died, when her executors told us."

"The path to salvation can be stony and steep," retrieved Winstanley from his boundless store of platitudes, like the moralising chorus from a Greek tragedy, slowing down the action and not trusting it to speak for itself.

"We spent interminable Sundays in church or studying Scripture. Our only holiday was a Wednesday afternoon when we went for a walk with the Reverend Flower, aptly named since he took us for Botany. This was the only branch of Natural Philosophy that Aunt Sarah thought seemly for young ladies; it was the scientific extension of flower arranging and embroidery. She might have thought differently if she had read Reverend Flower's book on Linnaeus and his Sexual System."

"Madam, tell us more!"

"Linnaeus recognised that plants like animals consist of males and females who copulate to reproduce themselves."

"See Winstanley, the vegetables have their Aphrodite too."

"He divides plants into *classes* according to the number, size and location of their male parts. The *classes* are divided into *orders* based on their female parts. The *orders* are divided into *genera* on the points of fructification."

"Now there's an idea for you, a class system based on our sexual organs. It would shake up society, what?"

"Mr. Pitt would still be the biggest prick," muttered Higgins. In the presence of a lady even as worldly as Amelia we refrained from mining this entertaining vein of conversation.

"You can imagine how fascinating the subject was to a dozen little girls. Wednesday was the high point of the week. We walked hand in hand to Dulwich Common or the Vale or the Woods where we gathered round a plant and listened to the Reverend Flower reveal its most intimate secrets – for example, how the male genital swells and bursts to impregnates the female with its pollen on the nuptial bed of the calyx. We learned about male and female and also hermaphrodite and androgynous and polygamous behaviour."

"Did he enjoy his salacious little lectures?"

"He was so engrossed in the subject that he was quite impervious to the prurience of his little harem. In spite of our blushes and giggles he was a model of scientific detachment. He didn't realise that the Scientific Method is infinitely more corrupting to young minds than mechanisms of reproduction."

"But not as enthralling."

"We loved the old English names - Bishop's Weed - Stinking Bean Trefoil - Bird's Eye - Enchanter's Nightshade - Lady's Slipper. These became nick-names we called each other. Leonora was Love-In-A-Mist."

"What were you?"

"Adder's Tongue."

"Surely not."

"The Reverend Flower we called Stinkhorn because of his breath. Later the Latin names were a revelation to me, beautiful and mysterious. Adder's Tongue is *Ophioglossum vulgatum*. Love-In-A-Mist is *Passiflora,* the flower of passion. I learned them by heart from the Reverend Flower's book while the others picked them to press or weave into their hair."

"You were teacher's pet."

"Until I asked him to explain the Latin name for Stinkhorn, *phallus impudicus.* He did so objectively but that was the end of my tuition. Instead he gave me a copy of Thornton's book about the Sexual System of Linnaeus and said he had no more to teach me. By my thirteenth birthday I knew it all by heart and could draw from memory every plant in it. It was an open sesame into a cave of treasures and made my life tolerable."

"Did Leonora share your passion?"

"She was the replica of our mother. Like flowers that bloom in secret she hid a passionate nature beneath a seemly exterior. In the privacy of our room she used to spend an hour on forbidden curls and rings and then brush them out to go downstairs; she hid ribbons and cosmetics under a floorboard.

She gleaned the current fashions from passers-by and glimpses of pattern books in the Village Drapers. Like an actress she rehearsed smiles and glances in the looking glass; her principal topic of conversation was the males we met, from the parson to the butcher's boy.

One Wednesday afternoon the Reverend Flower was approached on the Common by a gentleman, who claimed a similar interest in Botany. He was very handsome in the Mediterranean way; fine boned and slim, with dark eyes and black curls. He introduced himself as Colonel Dumont La Peyerie of the Regiment of Cuirassiers of the King of France: he was a prisoner of war, the guest of a retired General of Horse in Sydenham and on parole d'honneur.

He made us laugh with the old-fashioned botanical classifications of Monsieur Tournefort, which he stuck to more out of national pride than common sense. But the names of the plants in French had an aphrodisiac effect upon us. The feelings he roused in me surprised me. I refused to behave like the other silly girls but kept my *sang-froid:* I avoided his looks and his conversation but I could not control my sudden physical urges and emotions. Have you ever been caught by a great wave when sea-bathing: lifted off your feet by an elemental force?"

"No but I once saw a bathing machine swamped at Brightlingsea. Devil of a mess. Thank God no-one was in it. Only a maid fetching the clothes, what?"

I lied about the maid. I put her in for effect but it did not impede Amelia's flow.

"Reverend Flower introduced him to Aunt Sarah. His charm worked even on her, to the extent that she engaged him to give us French conversation practice for no more remuneration than a cup of tea. I was so tongue-tied and stammering when it was my turn to read that I'm sure he thought I had a speech impediment. Leonora was the opposite. She was almost seventeen and very beautiful. She flirted without knowing it, every glance, every gesture straight from

Cupid's bow. Inevitably she attracted the dashing Frenchman's interest but, other than innocent questions about the pronunciation of the more poutful botanic names, such as *gueule de loup* and *nénuphar*, she did not respond. Her indifference to him was so extreme that I suspected it was a blind, that the two of them were conducting a secret *affaire de coeur*. My feelings towards him turned into raging jealousy of my sister. I spied on her day and night. I lay awake listening to her while she slept, waiting for her to breathe his name, knowing she was dreaming of him. In casual conversation I brought up the progress of the war with France, the unsavouriness of frogs' legs, the time the coach took to Gretna Green. She would not be drawn. I blushed then and I blush now to think of it.

One afternoon, while we were at class, the crier came past with news from Aix that the war was over. Aunt Sarah declared a half day holiday, although few of our pupils knew what a war was, let alone that we were fighting one. I didn't join in the merriment because Dumont would now be able to leave and my sister might elope with him. That night, as I got ready for bed, Leonora came into our room. Her cheeks were flushed and her eyes were bright and I feared the worst. When she said she was going to be married I swooned for the first time in my life. She said not to take on as she wouldn't be far away and I visit them as often as I liked. When I said it was a long way across the water she replied it was only a little pond. Geography was not her *forte* but I was too sick with despair to put her right.

"You have no dowry, no money, no property. He's toying with you."

She said that he had enough income for two and that he wanted her for herself and not her fortune. A terrible rage came over me. I hated them both.

"You know nothing about him, A man may like him has lovers and mistresses and a wife at home."

The silly goose clapped her hands to her mouth, not at the insult to her future husband but to stifle her laughter.

"What?" The Reverend Flower?"

For the last time in my life I swooned again.

Once I had recovered my composure we went down, full of merriment, to the parlour where the Reverend Flower had asked my aunt for her niece's hand. Aunt Sarah seemed put out, as if it was her own hand he should have asked for; indeed they would have made a more appropriate couple than a flighty and vivacious beauty with a solemn clergyman, who was twice her age and acted twice his own. Later I asked if she loved him. She said he was the most loveable of men.

"That's not the answer to my question."

"I look in the glass and see our mother. Am I condemned to live her life? You're right. I have no dowry, no prospects, no family. My face is my only fortune. Should I prostitute it to get on, like our mother did?"

I was determined to take my fate into my hands. At first light I slipped out of the house and walked to Sydenham. I knocked at the door of the house where Dumont lodged. I did not know what I was going to say to him, what I was going to do, I was standing on the edge of an abyss into which I was determined to plunge."

"You had taken leave of your senses."

"On the contrary - my senses and I had never been so close. It was only when the maid told me that Dumont had left that morning to take the stage to Dover that my senses took leave of me. They were replaced by a compulsion that possessed me, a divine possession. I was transformed into a force of nature. I flew home, collected some possessions and the few shillings I had scrimped, and in an hour was on the coach from the Crown to Southwark and the Dover Road."

"Were you afraid?"

"Fear and elation were one and the same."

Although he was half a day ahead of me Dumont's ship was still at the quayside, waiting for a favourable wind. I saw him on the deck. I convinced myself he had thoughts only for me and regretted his abrupt departure but I was afraid of being arrested and sent home if I showed myself. I waited in the crowd until the very moment the gangplank was taken up. I ran on and jumped on board.

"An old trick."

"I said I was the wife of Colonel Dumont. They brought me to him."

"I bet he was pleased. I would have sent you packing."

"We were under way. I stood on the rail and said I would jump unless he took me with him. I made him promise to marry me, which he did not keep, although his wife was very understanding when I introduced myself as her rival. She told me I was not the first but certainly the youngest."

"She was sure of her position, then."

"With her beauty and her fortune she could afford to be. She gave me to her sister as a governess for her children. I was penniless. I had no choice."

"Did you pine for Dumont?"

"I was enraged by being disposed of as a chattel. My passion turned into hatred."

"Love spurned. A volatile substance."

"I never saw him again. My master was appointed to a position in Damascus and I went with them. It was the start of my oriental adventures. I made a solemn vow that I would never be given away as property again."

"Don't you hanker for a more settled life?"

"Why should I? My way in life is not the result of jilting, rape, incest, failed marriage, or any other betrayal. I don't regret not having a good match, a good husband, a good income. There is more to life than marriage and money. I am not an exile. I am not a rebel, a revolutionist. I have not cast off shackles, thrown off chains, ripped off the straight jacket, because I have never acknowledged them. I am what I am because it is my will and my pleasure."

"Oh Roxalana."

"Sir?"

"Nothing."

"Do you disapprove of my impetuosity?"

"On the contrary. A passionate nature is not a weakness but a strength, if there is the courage to go with it."

One reason that men prefer young women is that they are so much less complicated than their older sisters. An affaire with an experienced woman carries the risk of entanglement in a web of previous desires and disappointments. I had no doubt that this was only the beginning of an epic of an eventful love life. We would leave that for Winstanley to enjoy.

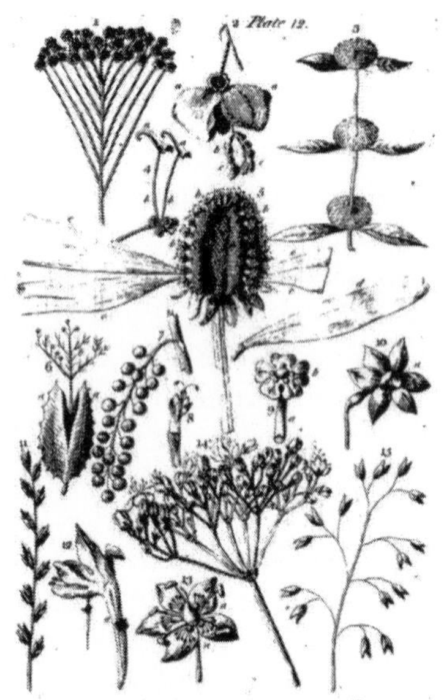

from An Introduction to Botany
by James Lee 1765

GREEK LIBERTY

Beside the road we came across fly-blown, rat-gnawed, crow-pecked half-corpses of executed criminals, some poor devils strung up on trees and others impaled on stakes. They do not waste the iron to fix them on the gibbet, as we do when we hang them in chains, so parts drop to the ground and are carried off by dogs. Imprisonment is unknown on the island; flogging, strangulation and impalement are the main punishments. Pericles described to us how executions are carried out.

Strangulation is the milder of the penalties, reserved for crimes of property such as adultery and burglary and highway robbery. Two executioners put the culprit's neck in the middle of a double strand of rope. They take an end each and twist until the wretch loses consciousness. They loosen the rope and bring him round with a punch in the ribs. This process is repeated twice. The third time they add a new torture. One of the executioners kicks the victim in the genitals and the other crushes them in his hands. They then finish wringing his neck. without interruption. When life is extinct the corpse is hung up on a tree outside the town.

If the criminal is a *raya,* that is a Christian or a Jewish subject, the body is hung only a foot from the ground so that dogs can feed on the remains. The Faithful have the privilege of being strung up higher so only the crows can get them.

For more serious crimes the convict is tied face down on a pack saddle and a stake, somewhat thicker than a hop-pole, with the end sharpened to a point, is banged up his body with a mallet. If necessary they use a razor to widen the orifice. The victim, still alive, is then set upright in the ground. Alternatively he is suspended by his wrists over a stake planted beneath him. His breeches are removed and he is lowered upon the stake so it penetrates the intestines by the weight of the body. The length of the torture is determined by the rate at which it is lowered – a skilled executioner can make the agony last for days. It is said that a long drink of water will accelerate the end.

Relatives can reclaim the bodies for burial only on the eve of their Sabbath - Friday, Saturday or Sunday depending on the faith - so it is thought a particular misfortune to be dealt with at the beginning of the week. Poor souls, with nobody to bury them, vagrants perhaps, or orphans – or foreign travellers, as Higgins pointed out - are left for the scavengers.

The victims by the road were in various states of repair. Some were skeletons held together by their clothes. Others were more recent, their lower parts gnawed by animals and their eyes pecked out by crows, but still recognisable as our fellow men. What they all had in common was their silent laughter, wide-eyed and open-mouthed, as if there was comedy in their fates, in all our fates. Look, they seemed to say, at the heart of terror is laughter.

A ride in the English countryside offers such sights at a crossroads gibbet, but not in such proliferation, since demand by our anatomists reduces the supply for display. Higgins was active with his pencil and sketch book as he rode past the gruesome sights. He claimed his interest was purely anatomical, although he refused to show us the fruit of his labours. Each of us had some comment to make:

"Well now, the cruelty of man to man is the way of the world. The devil is in our nature"

"Through their suffering those poor sinners surely achieved the bliss of salvation promised by Our Lord."

"Hurrah for England and her humane gallows."

"Do these sights frighten people into obedience to the law? Does a gamekeeper truly expect the vermin he nails on the fence to deter others? If so, more fool him. They are no more than trophies. An executed criminal is a symbol of authority not a deterrent, a reminder to the passer-by of the power of the master not the guilt of the servant."

I took the opportunity to rag Pericles.

"Tell me, Consul, why you put up with the cruelty and injustice of the Turks. Isn't this the Greece of heroes? And yet you Christians allow yourselves to be tortured and eaten by dogs."

"Our heads are down but hearts are proud."

"So your salaams to your masters are ironical. Yet you yourself profit from them, do you not."

"We must live in world. One day God willing." He looked uneasily over his shoulder at our Muslim escort and changed the subject. "Esteemed Lordos, what is the opinion in England of the Greek race?"

I had to avoid a truthful answer if we wanted to stay on good terms. Our well-being was in his hands. I thought it better not to quote from Winstanley's copy of The Grecian History by the garrulous grubstreetian Oliver Goldsmith - oh I beg his pardon, *Doctor* Goldsmith. (How did that ha'penny-a-line earn his Doctorate? By doctoring the works of others and putting his own name on the title page?) This is how the good Doctor He-tups-to-conquer summarises the English view of the Greeks.

The modern Greeks, without the least political importance, and sunk in slavery to a military government, retain but little of their original character...A quickness of invention, an acuteness of judgement, a subtlety in argumentation, have survived the extinction of virtue... These are still to be found in the dishonourable artifices of the Grecian merchants.

"Oh we admire of the Greeks," I said.

"Do you approbate our strivings for liberty from Turkish oppression?"

"The English support any man's desire for freedom, so long as it is not from the English. But surely you are not on the side of the libertarians. You have too much to lose."

"I am poor seaman."

"How did you become a hojabasha then?"

I bit my tongue but too late. The words were out. Might as well try to cork a genie back in a bottle as stopper Pericles' story.

Hojabasha

PERICLES

You are wishing to know how I came to my humble position, Lordos? I will tell you. Virgin Mother Star of Morning, Star of Sea cast me out on the ocean and brings me safe to harbour.

(I shall now transcribe his tortured lingo into something approximating the elegant language that is the envy of the world.)

I was married not far from here, in a village called Petries on the other side of the mountain behind Aliveri. My little brother passed the bridle wreaths over our heads and her little sister danced with us round the fire. My bride was a child of Alexander with yellow hair down to her waist and blue eyes and a skin like snow. Her name was Sirena and she said she was a mermaid. I was six years old and she was five.

My Sirena was the eldest daughter of the priest and I was the eldest son of the richest man in the village. We had over fifty sheep and as many olive trees. We were the beautiful princess and the handsome prince of our little kingdom. Our lives were peaceful enough. We rarely saw a Turk and the hojabashi of the time was easily deceived since our wealth was all in sheep and scattered in the hills. We had to keep an eye open for the pirates of Skyros who came looking for sheep and slaves but it was a steep road from the sea to our village.

The princess and the prince were together morning to night. We herded our flocks together, we learned the dances hand in hand, we hunted eggs and berries and little birds in the hills, according to the season. We were not discouraged by our parents until we reached the age when boys and girls go their separate ways. She put on long skirts and a scarf and spent her time in the women's quarters. I saw her in church and at feasts or what passed with us for the evening *volta*, but always with other women of her family to guard her. Not that this troubled me. I was more interested in wrestling with the other boys and shooting my father's guns. I had a gift for letters and numbers and at the age of thirteen I was sent away to school at the Moni Lefkon, the White Monastery, half way between here and Kimi as the crow flies.

We read the ancient pagans and the church fathers and despised the Turks, who had none of this great learning, and dreamed of Constantinople, which we would surely reconquer one day. But what was I to do with this knowledge? I had no inclination to be a monk or a scholar or a secretary to a pasha. Other boys talked of Constantinople and Vienna and Odessa and of seeing the world and doing great deeds. I thought of my ageing father and our flocks and playing the pipes under the plane tree by the spring. Was I a dull boy? At sixteen you burn with a passion for everything and nothing, you are a pod waiting to burst. No, I was not dull. I had not been given my calling.

On the Easter after I was seventeen years old I left the school for the last time and came back to Petries. Eros did his arrow work that day. In church and when we roasted the lambs in the street and at the dancing afterwards I had eyes only for Sirena and she for me. It was clear why I had not left on a ship to see the world. All my world was in her. And all hers in me. Despite our childhood together we were like strangers, averting our eyes, stumbling over our words, only our blushes betraying the fire inside us. What was our astonishment when the priest her father asked my father if she could take their little flock down to take a bath in the sea with ours? Was he so blind that he did not see our burning glances?

Early on Monday after Bright Week, I collected our flock from the field and drove them down to the little bay called Klimaki. Sirena waited with her score of animals and we drove them on together as if it was an everyday occurrence, although our limbs trembled and our hearts thumped in unison. The words of her father echoed in our ears, that I should be a guardian and protector and that she should be virtuous and watchful.

I will take the memory of that day with me into Hades. We said nothing at first, then we sang the songs we sang as children and remembered our wedding. On my travels since I have seen pictures they call pastorals of shepherd boys and girls in meadows of flowers under a blue sky. They are a dim reflection of the scene that day. The world seemed new-minted to us. We held hands as if for the first time, as no other creature in the world had held hands before. Have you ever felt like this Lordos?

"Get on with it Pericles."

We pledged ourselves to each other for the rest of time. We called on the Virgin Mother Star of Morning to seal our promise. We kissed and I still feel her lips on mine.

The other flocks arrived with their shepherds and we got on with our business. On one horn of Klimaki there is a cliff that overhangs the water. It was our custom to drive the animals over it so they fell into the sea to wash the wool for shearing and to drown the lice and ticks and other insects. Some of us went down on the beach while the rest drove the animals over the cliff. We herded them with our sticks while they cried to heaven like lost souls until they plunged into the sea and swam for dear life. The water was black with filth and vermin. They swam for the beach and when all were baptised we penned them on the sand while we made our dinner. Usually boys and their dogs tended sheep but on these days our sisters came with us.

We had lyres and pipes and soon we were dancing. For Sirena and me, with the secret of our promise to the Virgin Mother in our hearts, they were wedding dances. We resolved to broach the subject to our parents that very evening and could see no reason why they would not favour our match. If they did not, then we would run away to Kimi and take a ship across the sea.

The heat of the day was gone when we sorted our flocks and set off up the mountain track to the village. Sirena and I contrived to be the last so that our day together would last as long as possible. For my part there were thoughts of more kisses and, despite our promises to parents, perhaps more.

Have you ever seen a kite fall on a brood of chickens? Or an eagle on school of fish? Out of nowhere it comes on the unsuspecting victims and suddenly there is noise and confusion and terror. One moment we are feeding on each other's tender glances and the next we are thrown to the ground. Our bleating sheep mill and scatter. Sirena's screams pierce my head. I feel brawny arms around my chest and my face pushed into the sand. For a brief moment his hold is relaxed. I turn and kick and my knee finds his tender parts. He falls off me with a curse. I am on my feet and running for the trees. I dive into the spiny undergrowth. Only then do I look back.

A row-boat is beached in shallow water. A giant has Sirena trussed and kicking over his shoulder. A second man has a score of sheep huddled against the cliff beside the water. A third man clutching between his legs, hobbles to help him. The giant bundles Sirena into the stern of the row-boat and ties her hands and goes back to the sheep which the other two have penned. One by one he grabs them by the wool and heaves them into the boat. What can I do? What chance do I have against three?

You may say I should have risked everything. They may have killed me. Or they may have taken me captive with Sirena and I would have found a way to help the woman whom I had pledged that morning to love and protect for the rest of my life. I did not and from this you may judge what sort of man I am. But not too harshly, I beg you, until you have heard the end of my tale.

The three pirates loaded the boat to the gunwales with sheep and pushed her off, low in the water. Two men stood among the sheep amidships, pushing like the devil on their oars to make headway. The giant stood in the stern sculling the long oar. He pulled Sirena up and sat her on the thwart beside him. She screamed and shouted but her cries were lost in the bleating of the sheep and the cursing of the men. Then I finally had the courage to run out, shouting to Sirena 'I am here, I am here,' and much good it did either of us. The giant laughed at me and gave me the evil eye. I could do nothing but run back to the village to give the bad news.

Men went down to Klimaki with guns but what was the use? Night fell and despite the commands of my father I stayed on the cliff top, as you do when a person drowns, waiting for the sea to spit them back. Indeed I did see a body in the water drifting back in the moonlight to Klimaki. I believed it was my Sirena and waded as far out as I dared to meet her. The salt tears from my eyes mingled with the sea until I saw it was not her but the giant who had carried her off, eyeless and bloated. In the morning my father and other men came down. They buried the giant and watched with me for the next day but we saw no sign of boat or sheep or pirates or Sirena. How the giant had met his end was a mystery for there were no marks on him.

At last, after three days watching, I went back to the village. I did not give up. I had been given my task in life, to find Sirena. Knowing that my father would not give me permission I left for Kimi in the middle of the night with a dagger and a handful of coins. Why Kimi? Because I could only think that the pirates were from Skyros. Skyros lies across the narrow straits from Kimi. You can see it clearly. But how to get over there? The port was guarded by Turkish men at arms and crossing was forbidden. I enquired in taverns and cafés and after two days found a boatman who said he would ferry me over for a handsome fare. He was as good as his word. We left in the middle of the night, as if we were going fishing.

We arrived at Skyros at dawn. Their town is built inland on an acropolis for fear of pirates like themselves and of those commissioned to hunt them down. The port is nothing but a rocky inlet and a beach. A galliot was anchored there and a felucca or two. Pulled up on the shingle I recognised the row-boat that had abducted my beloved and my heart leapt. A group of men in Frankish costume lounged on the shore smoking hookahs. My ferryman took me up to a grizzled old fellow, better dressed than the others, greeted him as Kapitanos and muttered something in their argot. The Kapitanos looked hard at me and I stood firm.

"You're a brave lad to come here. We can always use good young lads. Especially so pretty as you." He winked at me and the others snickered. "So you are looking for your love. What makes you think she is here?"

"She was taken with my sheep by three men in that boat," I said, pointing to the row-boat.

"That is my boat," he said and laughed in my face. He suddenly looked fierce. "Are you accusing me?"

"Do you have news of her?"

"News of girls? We have plenty."

"News of Sirena. She has pale skin and golden hair and her eyes ..."

"...are blue as sapphires."

"You've seen her!"

"I have read your Greek romances. Come with us. We'll search for your Sirena. We'll call at every port. We'll ask every passing ship. We're a crewman short. You'll do."

"No thank you. I'll ask round the town first."

The Kapitanos looked over my shoulder and nodded. I turned and came face to face with the man I had kneed on the beach of Klimaki. He returned the favour with interest and added a kick or two for good measure while I lay doubled up on the shingle. I was picked up by the arms and dragged to the row-boat. They threw me in, and held the painter for the Kapitanos and a few of his fellows to climb aboard. Still dizzy and in pain I was barely conscious of being hoisted onto the deck of the galliot.

I was dragged by the hair to the rowing deck and made to sit on a bench where my ankles were shackled. There were fifteen oars a side and two men to an oar. My rowing mate was an Italian, bald all over, even the pubes and the eyebrows. He later told me he was hairy as a gorilla when he was captured five years before. He was not pleased to be paired with a stripling who moaned and threw up over his oar from the pain in his belly and the pain in his heart.

The men were naked, using any scrap of cloth they had to make a cushion. Their arses were leather but still they were afraid of sores and boils. We lived on those benches. We slept lolled over the shipped oars. We pissed where we sat. When we needed the other we shat on the feet of the man behind. He called out *kaka* and a boy came with a bucket of water to sluice it into the bilges. If you stood there was no headroom to stand upright. Men who had been at the oars for a few years had iron muscles on their chests and arms and legs but they walked bent over like apes. We never left the benches from Easter to Christmas. If the ship sank we went down with her. Such is the lot of a galley slave.

We heard a commotion on the shore. On my side we could see through the portholes what was going on. The whole town was in procession down to the shore. It looked like the Holy Thursday Epitaphios when the effigy of our Lord is paraded on his bier or the Dormition when the Virgin Mother makes her final round. Except that instead of a statue they were parading my Sirena. She wore only blue trousers. Her nakedness was covered by the golden hair that tumbled over her breasts and down her back to her thighs. She walked as erect and proud as she could on the stony path. But despite the crowd nobody came near her, as if she had some terrible pestilence. The procession was led by the usual raggle taggle of boys and priests with censers and monks chanting some litany or other. The crowd behind yelled and shouted like a mob at an execution.

When they reached the shore a felucca was waiting. My beloved was made to board and prodded to the prow where she stood like a figurehead. With many signs of the cross and cornutos and clenched fists and palms and all the other signs we have to avert or give the evil eye, the baying crowd bade her farewell. The rowers bent to the task and she sped out to sea. For my cries and shouts and raging at my chains I earned an cuff on the head from my oar mate and collapsed into a swoon. All I could think of was that she was a sacrifice to the monsters of the ocean, an Andromeda to be chained to a rock. And if you think this was too barbarous a suspicion in our scientific century you should know that on Skyros they keep alive ancient customs. To this day they dance in goat skins and honour Dionysos and carry out his rituals.

Word was passed round the crew and below decks to us that she was a self-confessed mermaid who turned any person who touched her into an animal. She had already turned a man into a sheep and another into a hoopoe. They were carrying her away from the island to an uninhabited rock where she would be thrown into the sea. They believed that when she hit the water her legs would turn into the two pronged fishy tail that was her true nature.

Why did I not die then? I had lost father, mother, family and friends, liberty and love. Where does the tiny glimmer of hope come from that lights up our darkest hour? For me it came from the love that I had lost. It is blasphemous but whenever I called on the Virgin Mother for help I saw Sirena of the Golden Hair and prayed to her. I promised to keep our love alive and never cease searching for her. And so it was.

I never saw her face again. For the next quarter of a century I looked for her. In all that time I was never long with the same ship. I was freed and captured, freed and captured by

Turk and English and French and Venetian and Barbary ships. I was a slave or a free man in Algiers and Cyprus and Ancona and Ephesus and Constantinople and Rhodes and Alexandria. I was shipwrecked on Malta and on Crete. I sailed with a British admiral of the Russian fleet and a French captain of a Turkish galley and a Genoese captain of a Barbary pirate. This is how I learned your Frankish languages.

Everywhere I went I asked the same question 'Have you news of Sirena the mermaid with the golden hair?' I asked this in markets and castles and palaces and whorehouses. I would not accept that she was dead, I would not accept that she had broken her pledge to the Virgin Mother. Of course I was no monk. You do not scour the brothels of the Mediterranean without getting dirty but it was only for need or pleasure or consolation and never for love.

Some fifteen years ago I was navigator on a Turkish galley. We put into Egripos for repairs. Near the Emir Zade mosque I was set on from behind. They put a sack over my head and bound me tight. I was no weakling but they were expert and I was helpless. I was lifted by the elbows and bundled down twisting streets to a door and down some stone stairs. I was sat down on a bench and untied. By the time I took off the sack my captors had left and locked the door behind them. I was in a stone-walled room, like a crypt or a dungeon, without windows. A table in front of me was set with wine and food. I was in no immediate danger but the strangeness of my predicament made me afraid as well as curious.

After a time the door opened again and two black eunuchs came in. Behind them came a woman covered in a dark blue veil embroidered with little gold stars. In spite of the disguise I knew straight away who it was. I leaped to my feet and rushed towards her. The eunuchs lifted me up and sat me back on the bench.

"Don't mind them, Pericles. It is for the best," she said.

My mind was spinning with terror and joy. She was alive but what had she become? Who had she become?

"I have searched for you."

"I have waited for you," she said, her voice drowning in tears, "and then today I saw you through the window of my balcony."

"Can I see you?"

"That is haram. Do you have a wife?"

"No. Do you have a husband?"

"I am the first wife of the Vizir of Egripos."

At this I swooned. I came to in the arms of one of the eunuchs while the other held a beaker of wine to my lips. I spat it out.

"Let me go. I want to leave."

"Stay and I will tell you what has happened to me. Then you can judge me."

The eunuchs pressed me down on the bench and she told me her story.

Pericles interrupted his story for breakfast. It was provided by some fishermen on the shore who were mending their nets after a night's work. They live on a strange type of fish, which they call ktapodi. It has several tails and no bones. It can change its colour to that of the seabed on which it lies and to grow again when cut, the smallest pieces sprouting the entire fish. We ate some and found it fairly tasty and as firm when boiled as flabby when it was alive. The fishermen showed us the little cups with which, so they say, it fastens itself to the tails of mermaids by which it is transported through the water.

a galley

SIRENA

On the beach at Klimaki Sirena was loaded onto the pirate's row-boat with as many sheep as they could stow. When she saw Pericles had run away her feelings were a mixture of relief and abandonment. She sat at the stern with the giant who sculled a single oar, while the other two stood amidships to row facing forward. She screamed for help but her cries were drowned by those of sheep for their lambs or mothers. When they reached open water the giant left the hard work to the others and pawed Sirena's breasts and described what he would do to her when they landed. Sirena butted his knees with her head. He teetered, swung on his oar and fell back over the stern of the boat. He floundered and spluttered and cried for help but the sheep drowned his shouts and the water drowned him. He sank out of sight.

The two rowers noticed nothing until Sirena pushed the oar over so they steered back to shore. One of them clambered back through the flock, wild-eyed and tried to grab Sirena. She said that if he touched her she would turn him into a sheep too. With signs of the cross and cornutos and open palms and any other defence against the evil eye he could remember from his travels he went back to his oar. They bent to the task and were soon at their galliot anchored out of sight behind a little island in the middle of the bay.

The Kapitanos was sceptical. He suspected they were spinning a yarn but could not fathom why. He interrogated Sirena but she said nothing. He put her in his cabin and the sheep on deck. They weighed anchor and rowed along the shore looking for their shipmate on sea and land. When they saw the villagers coming down to the beach and taking pot shots at them, they gave up the search and set sail for Skyros. Not a man on board slept that night for the bleating of the sheep and fear of witchcraft.

The next morning they led Sirena up to the St George monastery in Chora, the city. The pirate chiefs stood with the monks on the steps of the church and townspeople pressed into the courtyard. In front was the mother of the giant who had drowned.

"What have you done with my son," she screamed at Sirena and "which one is he?" she screamed at the flock of sheep. She ran to the biggest, a young ram, and threw her arms round its neck.

"Oh my Yannaki, don't be afraid, I'm here."

Like any son in this situation the ram tried to shake her off, which only confirmed the crowd's suspicions. The cry went up.

"How many others are there?"

The inquest turned to chaos. Monks hurried inside and came out with icons and holy water to brandish over the flock. Yannaki's mother tied her sash around her putative son and tugged him away. Other women elbowed into the flock and looked for signs of relatives lost at sea. Men surged forward to seize Sirena, and then held back, just in case, jostling those behind.

One of the pirate chiefs plucked up courage to take Sirena by the arm and drag her back into the church. He threw his cloak over her head and hustled her out of a side door into a narrow street. She let herself be led through a warren of alleys and steps until they came to a door. He unlocked it and pushed her inside. On Skyros wealthy men have parlours separate from the family house. It was furnished with a low divan built around a brazier for winter days and carpets and fretwork around the walls

"You are safe here," he said.

He was a handsome man, about fifty, dressed in fine wool and silk, with silver ornaments woven into his hair and braided moustaches. Tenderly he took off her cloak. She stood in her shift, barefoot, her golden hair tumbling to her thighs, her blue eyes aflame with defiance. He smiled.

"Will you turn me into a sheep?"

"No."

"Good."

"Because you are not a sheep. You are a pig."

"Oink. And what are you?"

"I am Sirena."

"A mermaid? Do you have a fishy tail" He looked hard at her thighs and licked his lips. "I must go back. I will tell them you have swum away. This afternoon we shall see what kind of fish you are and what kind of animal I am. I will send clothes and food and drink and everything you need."

He left. Sirena went to the window. It was large enough to climb through but below it the city wall and the cliff on which it was built plunged down to the sea. In a little while an old woman brought food and a change of clothes. The intentions of her captor were clear from her new wardrobe - a bodice and trousers made of flimsy silk. Sirena could see only one way out of her predicament, death. Praying to the Virgin Mother, Star of the Sea, she opened the window, keeping her eyes on the horizon. Before she could climb on the sill, in flew a hoopoe. She slammed the window shut. It fluttered round the room and perched on the divan.

Her divine protectress had clearly sent the bird. But for what? The thieving hoopoe with his stiletto beak and his showy crest was certainly appropriate. The ancient myth is that King

Tereus raped his wife's sister and cut her tongue out so she would not tell, for which the gods turned him into a hoopoe. No wonder he was the patron bird of pirate Skyros. Sirena racked her brains.

That evening, the little evening as Greeks say, when the sun has set and before it gets dark, the chief strutted back to his parlour, bathed and perfumed. His hair glistened with oil and his eyes glistened with tsipouro. He had told nobody except his old nurse that he had the girl. Rumours were rife about where she had gone. She had turned herself into one of the doves that flew away from the monastery roof; she had a cloak of invisibility and prowled among them, selecting her next victim; she disappeared in a puff of steam when holy water landed on her.

The chief laughed at these stories. In all his travels he had never witnessed sorcery. He guessed that somehow the giant had fallen overboard without the others noticing. However, he made sure he took he was wearing his grandmother's blue eye on his wrist and an icon of St Dionysos under his tunic. With the thrill of anticipation he unlocked the door of his parlour.

Sirena lay sprawled on the divan naked from the waist up, the silken bodice torn on the floor. With a snarl she threw something at him that took flight, thrashed round the room, beat his head with its wings. He ducked, flailed to defend himself and, before it flew away, saw the unmistakeable shape of a hoopoe. He followed it out into the street and half ran, half staggered up the street towards the monastery. He heard Sirena shout behind him.

"Come back my Prince. One hoopoe does not make a spring. We need another."

The general consensus was that one of the chief's men tried to take her and was turned into a hoopoe. What was to be done with her? The chiefs summoned the most wise of the wise women and the most learned of the monks. They concluded that they should not burn her or throw her off a cliff, which was the conventional treatment of witches, in case her victims stayed metamorphosed. They decided to take her at her word as a mermaid and throw her back in the sea in the hope that this would lift her spells. In case she stayed to haunt Skyros they would take her far away to an uninhabited island they knew as the home of seals and turtles and sea birds. So it was decided and at sunrise a squad of sailors with weapons drawn came to fetch Sirena.

The crew of the felucca was polite. They gave her a cloak to wear and food and drink. The wind was against them so it was noon before they came in sight of the island. At the same time they spied a sail bearing down on them from windward. It was unmistakeably a Turkish xebec, flying the pennant of the Captain Pasha, mandated to eliminate pirates. The captain ordered the crew to turn about and hoist the lateen. He himself made his way to the bow and in an act of great courage grabbed hold of Sirena. The crew held their breath. What would he turn into? He threw her in the sea.

"Row for your lives," he shouted, still his old tyrannical self.

The mermaid floated on her back, the cloak spread out like the wings of a ray. It stayed buoyant long enough for the xebec to reach her, ship oars and bring her on board. It had a crew of Greek sailors, Russian slaves and Turkish officers. Ignorant of her metamorphosing exploits and seeing only a lovely girl with a normal pair of legs beneath her transparent clothes they congratulated her on her good fortune to be a prize of the Captain Pasha. Whether he kept her or gave her away or sold her on, such a beautiful creature would be sure of a good home.

Sirena said nothing. She was exhausted in body and spirit. She resigned herself to her fate, clinging only to her faith in the Virgin Mother Star of Evening. She was well cared for, ogled but not molested. She was not won over by this, believing correctly that it was to maintain her market value, but was grateful for the respite from her trials.

After a month of uneventful cruising she was delivered to the Captain Pasha's harem in Constantinople. Once she had undergone confirmation that she was a virgin, she was given to the Bazoglou family as token thanks for their financing of cannon for the latest brig. They in turn presented her to one of their favoured slaves.

On the night of her wedding Sirena is bathed and perfumed and dressed and led by a eunuch into a rose garden by the Bosporus. The moon is full. A distant nightingale, lapping water, a plaintive flute, her beating heart is her bridal music. Her bridegroom waits for her on a silk covered divan. He is tall, handsome, beardless because he is a slave. He gestures for her to sit beside him but she remains standing and glowers at him

"What is your name."

"Sirena."

"Where are you from?"

"The sea."

He senses which way the wind is blowing and tries a different tack.

"My name is Hassan. I was christened Nikolas. I was born in Belgrade. I am the son of a schoolmaster and his best pupil. I was captured when I was sixteen and sold to the Bazoglou family. I am secretary to a Pasha. One day I hope to become a Pasha myself, inshallah."

"I wish you a happy and fruitful life and a peaceful death in old age. Without me."

"Alas the lives of Pashas don't always end on a peaceful deathbed. They often end on the bowstring. This is why families risk us slaves and not their sons in the service of the Shah Padisha, may Allah protect him. But why without you? I have no plans to divorce you. Yet."

He has a charming smile and warm eyes.

"You should know that I am under the protection of the Virgin Mother Star of the Sea. Men who violate me violate her. She transforms them into the beasts they are in their souls. I have a good record so far. A stupid sheep, a thieving hoopoe, a dirty pig. I have sworn to remain faithful to my true love until death."

He stares at her. A tear forms in the corner of an eye and trickles down his cheek. He jumps to his feet and walks out of the garden. At a loss, in truth disappointed at an easy victory, she sits on the divan among the moonlit roses until a eunuch takes her back to her apartment.

The next evening she is bathed and perfumed and dressed as before. She is led into the rose garden under a less full moon. Hassan waits on the divan. He gestures to the ottoman before him and she remains standing.

"Mermaid, frighten me. Tell me about the animals your violators were turned into."

She tells him about the boat and the sheep and the oarsman turned into a ram. Hassan claps his hands and chuckles and despite herself she can't help smiling. His chuckle is endearing, like a child's.

"Now tell me what really happened."

She cannot bring herself to lie to this man on a gentle perfumed night. She tells him how she butted the steersman overboard and how the other two didn't hear his cries because of the bleating of the sheep. This time his chuckle turns into laugh and she laughs too.

"You are ingenious in your own protection," he says.

"I don't do it for myself. I do it for my love, Pericles," she says.

He looks at her, tears trickling down his face, stands up and without another word hurries out of the garden in a rustle of silk.

The next night she is bathed and so on, just as before. She tells him about the hoopoe that flew in the window. Again she says it was for love of Pericles not for herself and he walks out of the garden weeping.

The next night she confesses that she lied about the pig.

For thirty days it goes on like this. The moon wanes and disappears and the garden is lit by flaming torches. They tell each other their life stories, piece by piece, episode by episode. Their conversations last sometimes ten minutes, sometimes an hour and they end with Hassan leaving her without a word and tears in his eyes. Not once does he try to touch her.

Then one evening under the full moon curiosity overcomes her and she asks him why he weeps. He tells her that when he was a Christian in Belgrade he was betrothed to Nikoleta, a neighbour's daughter he had known since they were infants. She was a star of the earth, a rose of the sky. They swore to each other by the Virgin Mother that they would remain always true to each other. When the Ottomans took Belgrade he was taken prisoner and never saw her again.

By now the tears are streaming down his face but he does not stand up and walk away as he usually does. For the first time since they met, for the first time since she was captured on Klimaki, Sirena feels tears well up in her own eyes. They reach out and touch each other's faces, wiping away the salty moisture with their fingers. Their hands grow bolder, caress each other, they kiss the tears away, they hold each other's heads, they hold each other's bodies and finally melt into each others' arms, oblivious to the sighs of relief from the eunuchs hiding in the roses. The spasm of pain in her hymen and the spasm of pain in her heart are replaced by growing pleasure. All the terror of the past year, all the grief for her Pericles surge and fade. The Pericles of Egripos merges with the Nikolas of Belgrade and she gives herself to him without restraint.

All night long they take pleasure in each other. In the brothels of Pera he learned his lessons well. He gives her the Butterfly Fluttering, the Parthian Archer (the side-saddle version), the Trabzon Knot, the ancient Lion on The Cheese Grater, the Hünkar Begendi (the Sultan's Delight, a famous aubergine dish and an in-joke of Sultan Murad IV) the Sword Swallower and its cousin the Whirling Dervish, and the no-nonsense straightforward tally-ho English Gentleman.

Dawn comes. The eunuchs snore among the roses. Hassan lies sprawled like a fallen hero on the battlefield. The nightingales are submerged in the growing chorus of songbirds in cages hung about the trellises of the garden. Sirena pulls her silks around her. Her body is tender inside and out, her lips and nipples bruised, her skin tattooed with wounds of love. The open roses are her sisters, each tender and perfumed and with a pearl of glittering dew in their hearts. Except that she harbours bitter gall. Her oath is broken. She has betrayed her guardian the Virgin Mother Star of the Sea, Morning Star, Help of Sailors and Mermaids.

As the sun rises she falls asleep. And then wakes up, or dreams she wakes up. She is still in the garden. But in place of sprawling Hassan stands a woman completely covered in a dark blue veil sprinkled with stars. Sirena immediately knows who she is and throws herself at her feet.

"Do whatever you want with me. I have been unfaithful, I have broken my sacred oath."

"Get up, Sirena, you are my faithful servant."

"But I have betrayed my love for Pericles and loved Hassan with my body and my heart."

"Your love for Hassan is in the everyday world. The love you swore to me is in a different place."

"But how can this be? How can I be true to my first love and yet give myself to this other person? This is a paradox."

"You call me Virgin Mother. How can I be both? Yet I am. Isn't this a paradox? Here. Take this."

She holds out her hand from inside the chador. Nestling in her palm is a perfect pearl.

"When you have troubles with the world or your husband or your children you will know that the one immutable and imperishable thing in your life is deep inside you." And with this she disappears.

"Lordos, can you imagine what I felt when she told me this?" said Pericles with a little sob. "What could I say?"

"Get on with it, Pericles. What did you say?"

"I asked if she was happy."

"What did she say?"

"Yes, I have been happy, Pericles. Hassan is a wise and just ruler in the divan and at home. He is a good husband and a good father. I have given him four sons. When he marries his daughters he consults them. When he takes a new wife he consults me. I lack for nothing. But there is not a day goes past when I don't think of you. This is part of my happiness. You Pericles, have you been happy?"

"I have no wife or family or home or fortune. I have loved some women and misused others. I have broken my pledge to the Virgin Mother. Today is the best and the worst day of my life."

"Have you ever stopped searching for me?"

"No. Not one day."

"Do you love me now? After what you know?"

"More than ever."

"Then you have not broken your vow. The Star of the Sea has tested you and found you true to her. She is not angry, Pericles. Has she not kept us safe on our journeys for all these years? Has she not brought us together at last? Our transgressions are forgiven. You were and always will be my first love. I love my husband and my children as much as it is possible to love them. Yet in my deepest soul I stay true to you, Pericles. You have shown me how love transcends this world."

"So what will we do now that we have found each other?"

"As we have always done. We will grow old and die in eternal love. But meanwhile it is my most fervent wish that you are happy, that you find a loving wife and have many children and cherish them until you die. Only then will you keep alive your vow of unconditional love to me."

"This is a paradox."

"Is not life a paradox? Here, take this."

Her hand came out from the chador and she dropped into my palm a perfect pearl set in a pendant.

"Keep this next to your heart. When you have troubles with the world or your wife or your children you will know that one immutable and imperishable thing in your life is always with you."

She stood up and nodded to the eunuchs. I tried to stand but was pushed down on my seat. Next thing I knew the sack was pulled over me and my arms were tied. I was dragged up stairs and outside and through narrow streets and dumped on a stone bench and untied. When I took the sack off they were gone. I was by the fountain of Halil Pasha and dawn was breaking.

"I thought you said you never saw her again after Skyros."

"I said I never saw her face again. That's as true as I'm sitting on this mule. I saw only her hand. It was scarred with the pox. For all I know it was vanity not modesty that kept her veil on. No matter. I want to remember her as the Sirena I first loved."

"So what did you do then?"

"Nothing. I was emptied. Sucked dry. Gutted. My life had no meaning any more. For twenty five years the purpose of my existence was to search for my love. Now I had found her what was I to do? I felt revulsion at going back to sea. There was no point. For two days I sat there at that fountain with the beggars. Then I decided what to do. I would go down to the bridge over the Egripos and wait until it was in full flood and jump in. Well, I had hardly stood up to leave the fountain when I was set upon from behind. This time it was two janissaries and they didn't use a sack. They hauled me through the streets and everybody looked at me like a criminal. They took me to the palace and through the courtyard and up the steps and through the anterooms and straight into the Vizir's divan. They threw me on the floor in front of him. I believed my end had come and I was glad of it although it didn't stop me quaking all over. I just hoped it was beheading not impaling.

"Get up," he said.

I knelt up and had my first look at Hassan. He looked like all the other pashas I'd seen. Well fed and mean. A few others in their finery sat on either side of him. There was a window high up on the side, like a balcony with trellising so people could look down without being seen.

"You are Pericles of Petries?"

He didn't wait for me to answer but held out a scroll to me. I shuffled forwards on my knees. All I could think was that they handed you your death sentence.

"This is your appointment as hojabasha of Aliveri. The terms are in the document. You will deliver to us twice a year the amount specified in the document. Your predecessor was found wanting. Now he wants his head."

"Effendi."

"Are you married? Do you have a family?"

"No Effendi."

"You should marry. That is my order. Be prosperous and serve me well."

He signalled to the janissaries who lift me up by the elbows and backed me out of the divan. I looked up to the window grille and saw a shadow behind.

What has become of her? Hassan Pasha did not die at the bowstring. He was recalled from Egripos and appointed to an embassy to the Tsar of Russia. He caught a fever and died a good death surrounded by his wives and concubines and children. Sirena is a fat hanımefendi somewhere playing with her grandchildren. Or she is bones in her grave. I don't know. No matter.

Why did I tell you this story? You asked how I can be a faithful servant to the Turk and dream of liberty? Do you understand now? We live in the head and the heart and they are different places. Life is paradox."

"It is and it isn't," I said.

SCRUMPY JOE

Our party stretched over half a league, with the four of us in front behind Ali and the camel. We stopped for refreshment at a neat little house with stone walls and a reed thatched roof, making three sides of a courtyard, with a fourth open to the road and hedged with mulberry trees. It looked like the house of a prosperous farmer in our own county.

The owner came out to welcome us in the Turkish way with courtesy but an unsmiling face, one of the many ways in which they differ from the cheerful Greeks. He introduced himself as Yussuf. He was middle-aged with shaven head and hennaed moustaches. He wore a simple brown kaftan, yellow slippers, and a blue felt cap. He sat us down us in the shade of a mulberry and went indoors, coming back a few minutes later with coffee, which he served with good wishes for our health and the blessing of Allah. After the usual banalities about our origins and destination we lapsed into silence to enjoy the pleasant surroundings on what, in England, would be a warm summer day, complete with bees, flowers and new-mown hay. So I was not immediately surprised to hear someone say in a West Country accent:

"Wha' would'n you gen'mun give fur a point a goodole scrumpy?"

"Mmm," I said, then, when the incongruity struck, "What ho?"

We looked around us for a yokel in a smock. Winstanley peered into the mulberry branches above us. Yussuf could restrain himself no longer.

"Woy, gen'mun, don' take on. Scrumpy Joe at yourn zurvice," he roared, and slapped his knees.

"Now don't look on zo. Stranger things happen at zea. And Scrumpy Joe should know."

I shall now leave his Zedland dialect to your imagination, since I find it as aggravating to write as to listen to.

Higgins was the first to recover his composure.

"Well, how did a Turk come to England?"

"Through my mother. As we all came into the world. From my father I got nothing but my name, Joseph Carter, before he drowned at sea."

"You are born and bred an Englishman?"

"I hope an Irishman doesn't hold it against me."

"An Englishman by God."

"Aye, by God, praise to His name. He found me through love, which I'll tell you all about if you wish to join me in a mug of my namesake. I'll bring a lemonade for the lady."

"Scrumpy will do fine thank you," said the lady.

Yussuf alias Joe went into the near wing of his house and came back with a big tin jug and five wooden mugs. He poured and it was cider good enough.

"Good wallop, eh gentlemen?" he said and wiped his mouth on the sleeve of his kaftan. "It was the only thing I missed. See, I was born in Minehead near on fifty years ago. I scarce knew my father, he went down with the Bountiful out of Brixham. This left our mother bringing us all up as best she could in the service of Mr. Eton of Watchet."

I knew Eton, a good man, a good horseman and a good shot until the brandy and the bailiffs got to him. He shook so much at the end it was a miracle he could get the muzzle of a pistol in his mouth.

"A right devil he was too. Worked his people to death. No more than slaves we were. Used the women as he wanted though I'll allow no-one to impugn my mother. What could she do? No point in changing master. All the squires are devils."

"I say, hold on," said Winstanley, leaping to the defence of my class, but I waved him to be quiet. We ignore the whingeing of the working class; it is the price we pay for our superiority.

"As soon as I was old enough I went to sea, fishing out of Minehead. It was hard work and dangerous but I took to it. There was good money and bad but I always had a few pints of scrumpy in the pocket and something to send my mother. Until the press gang got me and I woke up in His Germanic Majesty's Navy."

"What? Do the Prussians have a navy?" asked Winstanley.

"He means the British Navy," growled Higgins, looking hard into his empty mug. "Farmer George of Hanover."

"Enough sedition gentlemen, on with the story. We don't have all day," I said.

Yussuf filled our mugs and continued.

"To cut a long story, it was the worst five years of my life. We called our Captain Animal Jack but never in his hearing or he'd prove it. We lived like cattle and worked like monkeys and ate worse than pigs. We was posted to the White Sea."

"The White Sea?"

"It's the Turkish name. The Med to you. We were to keep the Frenchies at bay but it wasn't them as did for us. It was the Algerian slavers. Animal Jack took us too near the Barbary Coast."

"What? A ship of the line beaten by pirates?"

"We could outsail and outgun a rowing galley but only in a breeze. In a dead calm we were a sitting duck. A galley has its cannon in the bow. It rows up behind a ship and rakes it stern to stem. Nothing we could do. We surrendered for our lives."

"Jack was not so Animal then."

"He was all for dying for German George. He mustered us before the quarterdeck for a Rule Britannia speech. You should have heard the cheer when the bosun ran him through. Best thing that happened all voyage. We did for a couple more officers and the rest saw it our way."

"Britons never never never shall be slaves," I sang in perfect tune.

"That's as maybe but there were plenty of us in Algiers. We thought to be thrown in chains but they put us in a barracks by the fort. It was easy enough to get out and a few lads did but where would you go without the lingo? There was all sorts, Dagos, Frenchies, Maltesers, take your pick. They called us Christian slaves *kaffirs*. The better sort, like officers, were taken off for ransom but us common folk waited around to be sold off."

"Like cattle," said Winstanley.

"No worse than the old English press-gang. It's their livelihood. We didn't have to wait too long. The Turkish fleet came in. Me and three lads were sold off to an old kadirga, that's twenty six oars and two lateen sails, not much of a draught to her, handy inshore but a devil in a lumpy sea, for one thing the way the stem's raked..."

"You may skip the nautical details Joe. All we look for in a ship is where to throw up," I said.

"We thought we were in for it. The skipper was an evil-looking Turk, his nose sharp as his yatagan. He clapped us in the chain locker for a day to soften us up and then hauled us up before a big mulatto with an axe. He said we'd be chopped in pieces and fed to the fishes if we didn't turn Muslim on the spot. What would you gentlemen have done?"

"Taken Mohammed's shilling. It's all the same," said our brave Catholic.

"Damned if I wouldn't too, but I'd cross my fingers," I said.

"I pray I would stand steadfast in Jesus Christ and the faith of the martyrs," said Winstanley.

"That's just what we did," said Scrumpy Joe, slapping his knees. "Strange what gets into a man. It were being bullied put our backs up. Anyways we reckoned he'd spent good money on us and he weren't about to chuck it away. He threw us back in the locker to think about it for another day. The same thing happened the second time, made us sniff the axe blade. We cursed him and he threw us back. By now we were half dead with thirst, but it made us even more pigheaded. When we denied him the third time what did he do? Nothing. Shrugged his shoulders."

"You remained true to Christ? Praise be. And a curse on his enemies," said Winstanley.

"It weren't his fault. It's the duty of a Muslim to convert his slaves. He gets a ticket to Paradise for it. But if he can't, he'd rather own a live infidel than a dead one. Turned out he was an easy-going fellow. He left the skippering to a Genoese while he got on with his star-gazing. Half the crew started life Christians; some had gone over, some hadn't. Didn't make any difference. At prayer time when the Muslims got out their mats the rest of us had to kneel down at an altar in the foc's'l. No crucifixes allowed, mind, but they gave us a statue of Mary. They call Christians *purpurest*, idol worshippers. I'd never known prayers, hardly never been in a church, and here I was praying five times a day."

"Surely prayer was a relief from the torment of slavery," said Winstanley.

"A Turkish ship is a holiday after the Royal Nay-vee. We all took a turn on the oars but we weren't chained to them like the songs say. The food was better than hard tack and weevils. Your Turk never goes far without decent grub. No grog mind, they're dry ships, but funny tobacco they call *kif*. It don't have the kick of a good pint but the world looks rosier after a few pulls. Anyways when we get to Constantinople the star-gazing captain sells me on to a merchantman making the Egripos run. Us English have a good name for seamanship and I'm down as sailing master. Handy little brig she was, two master, narrower beam than usual and the strake's on th...

"Thank you Joe."

"The owner's getting on in years, his sons are running the business, he's married his daughters, he's made the Haj to Mecca and lived to tell the tale, so what more does he want? His ticket to Paradise by converting me. Only this time he don't use threats but promises. He offers me half share in his ship. I'll get a share in the voyages, more gold than I've ever seen in my life, and on top of all that, my freedom. All I have to do is swear on the Koran that I'll not leave his service. Weren't bad for a raggedy-arsed boy from Minehead not twenty-five years old. What would you gentlemen have done?"

"Taken Mohammed's shilling. Better a rich Muslim than a poor slave" said our brave Catholic.

"Damned if I wouldn't too. Then I'd pocket the cash and steer my half boat to Italy first chance I had," I said.

"I pray I would stand steadfast in Jesus Christ and bear witness to his faith," said Winstanley.

"That's just what I did," said Scrumpy Joe, slapping his knees. "Strange what gets into a man. I didn't want to swear an oath on the sacred book. They have powerful spells. I've seen a man wither and die when they put the evil eye on him."

"You remained true to Christ? Praise be," said Winstanley.

"The old man kept trying until he lost his patience and sold me on to a dye merchant in Egripos. I was sorry because I'd been my own man and it was an easy billet. My new master was a different sort. He went by the book. He thought being a good Muslim was looking in the Koran for every finicky thing he should do or shouldn't do instead of dealing from the heart. He had this little pinnace, lateen sail, six oars only, handy in the bay but a devil on a lee shore, not enough keel and the mast stepped..."

"Thank you Joe," I said.

"He used it to pick up the acorns and roots for his trade all round the islands here. He put me in charge but a lot of the time I was helping out in the manufactory. He had a wife and two sons and three daughters, each one prettier than the next. Of course we weren't supposed to know this as they wore the veil when they weren't shut in the women's quarters. But things being how they are with young girls when young men are around. Anyway, the youngest took a shine to me and me to her. Never touched her mind and didn't need to. A look were enough. But what could we do? She was watched by her family all the time and I was a poor kaffir. I tell you I was near crazy. The times I stood by the Egripos channel at a full moon when it's going this way and that and near jumped in."

"Is it so dangerous?" I asked.

"It is if you can't swim. I'm a sailor remember. She was doing spells and praying for miracles and such but we got nowhere. Then I got friendly with this dervish monk called Hadji Latif, lives in a tomb in the city walls. He'd seen me out by the Egripos at night and took me in because of the curfew. He told me summat as got me thinking."

Whether out of hospitality or narrative artifice Scrumpy Joe interrupted himself to refill our mugs.

"My little Ayesha took some persuading but she came round in the end. I won't deny I was in a funk, I was risking my head, but unless I found a magic lamp or a ring in a fish's belly I couldn't see no other way to win her. We planned it for Friday when he came back to the manufactory from the morning mosque. He always gave the Muslims the rest of the morning off to go to the coffee house so I was the only one there. Only that morning Ayesha was waiting with me. Her father found us in a lover's embrace."

"Out with the horsewhip, what?"

"His dagger. We skipped out of his way and without anyone to help he couldn't catch us. That's why we'd made sure he was on his own. By the time the rest of the family and the neighbours come running with his yells it were too late. The heat of the moment had gone and he weren't allowed by the law to kill us right off. He had to take us to the *kadi* first, that's the judge. So they gave us a few cuffs and did just that. They wanted me on a stake and his daughter put in a sack and thrown in the Egripos."

"And you had relied on a Turkish father's compassion?" said Winstanley.

"While Christian fathers are sweetness and light," I muttered.

"I didn't trust his compassion but the law. He was in his rights with a kaffir and his daughter. But if I converted to Islam we could be married on the spot."

"You surrendered the love of Jesus Christ!" gasped Winstanley.

"You surrendered your foreskin," chuckled Higgins.

"I'd have willingly put my best part on the chopping block for her but they didn't want it, bless them. We're not fanatics, they said. All I had to do was go to the mosque and tell the priest that there's only one God and Mohammed is his prophet. In half a minute I was a Muslim. Death could not sway me; gold could not sway me; only love could bring me to the truth and its Prophet. We was married next day."

"With her father's curse."

"Oh no. I told the mullah it were Father's example that made me see the light and he got his ticket stamped to Paradise. He gave us this farm as a dowry and the pinnace thrown in."

"You got your life and gold too. Well played," said Higgins.

"But a hard life. Seafaring and farming."

" I swallowed the anchor a couple years back. I bought myself an Essex man to skipper her."

"You bought a slave? A Christian countryman?"

"He likes it better than steering coal up the Thames on a winter's day. He'll earn his freedom bye and bye."

While Scrumpy Joe went back to the house to refill the jug, we meditated his story, each in our respective ways. When he came back I was first to air my thoughts.

"Is a Turkish girl worth the wedding, Joe?"

"Let me tell you. Before the marriage her mother and the married women of the family instruct the bride in what to expect on her wedding night and how to make the most of it. They give her perfumes and potions and unguents to slow a man down or keep him going all night. They bring out wooden models of a man's and a woman's parts and show her how best to use them. So when the great night comes the blushing bride puts a Somerset milkmaid to shame. Later on, when there's a new bride to be educated she shares her experience and comes home with her appetite and her skills refreshed. There isn't a husband doesn't look forward to a wedding in the family."

"I cannot believe you do not keep a love of Jesus Christ in your heart," said Winstanley, harping on when clearly the man was a renegade through and through.

"I give him his due, like all Believers. We hold he's the greatest prophet after Mohammed."

"And what of Christ's miracles? Do you deny them?" asked Winstanley in his preacher voice.

"By no means. When Mary gave birth in the desert under a palm tree, water came up from the ground and dates fell out of the tree so she didn't go hungry."

"This is not written."

"It's God's truth in the gospel of Saint Barnabas, the only gospel written by a man who knew Jesus."

"Preposterous!"

Our poor cleric was uncertain what to do with the lost sheep, pray for him or roast him on a spit.

"The Christian creed is too mystifying for a plain man. Word made flesh, body and blood into bread and wine, sacrifice for sins. Islam is plain and simple. But don't listen to me."

"We won't, don't worry," I said.

"Now what would you gentlemen say to a nice meat pasty? Settle the stomach for another mug of scrumpy."

The renegade went inside and came back with a round little lady in tow, dressed in black, a tight scarf around her head but unveiled, from which I deduced, if the scrumpy was not already proof, that they were of the tolerant Bektashi persuasion. She carried a tray loaded with food. Yussuf introduced her as his wife and clearly regarded her with affection. She was plump and plain and without any obvious quality that would cause a man to abandon creed and country. The mysteries of Eros are impenetrable to those who have never been initiated. But she made a fine meat pasty in the West Country way, which I supposed to be the sustenance of their enduring love.

Mosque
Tewfik Beşiktaş

ANNA

Scrumpy Joe rode with us to the next village. He put on a brown turban and joined us on a donkey so small that even seated side saddle his toes trailed on the ground. He was a ludicrous sight and I pitied a lusty Zumerzet man reduced to a pantomime clown. Then I considered our own Lady Lacemutton, Corporal Killdevil, Parson Pettifogger, and Lord Crackbuck, and thought we should all be in a farce. *

By now the rest of our party had caught up and we were delayed another quarter of an hour while Scrumpy Joe shared embraces and salaams with them all. At last we continued along the shore between sullen sea and scrubby groves. To our left, on the other side of the gulf, rose the mountains of Attica, to our right the gentler hills of Euboea. Our spirits flickered when Scrumpy Joe asked if we should like to visit a Temple of Venus. Alas the Temple of Venus was not a euphemism but a literal description of what I rightly feared would be a pile of old stones.

The site lay a quarter of a mile inland from a miserable collection of hovels, all that remained of ancient Amarynthos.

* *Loose woman - West Indian rum - Charlatan - Dandy*

The terrain was thickly wooded until it rose up to a hill on which stood a small church in the Byzantine square cruciform style. It looked down on an ancient temple of which no more remained than a broken column, about four feet high, standing upright among some half buried stones. Scrumpy Joe said that the pillar was a sacred object for childless couples both Muslim and Christian. Man and wife stood opposite each other, holding hands, with the pillar between them, pressing their bellies and their private parts against it. They pulled each other hard until one or other, usually the woman, cried out or swooned. They then went into the woods to fructify in the conventional manner. On their return they went up the hill to the church to offer a pair of doves to the priest in return for a blessing.

The church was dedicated to Aghia Anna, Saint Anne, the mother of Mary and the grandmother of our Saviour. As Winstanley reminded us at length she was desparate for a child. At the age of fifty seven she took doves to the Temple and was rewarded with the prophecy that she would give birth. I reminded him that doves were also sacred to Aphrodite, the goddess of childbirth as well as its enjoyable prelude and that she had simply changed her name. I pointed to the walls of the church and the marble carvings from the old pagan temple among the Byzantine brick.

Scrumpy Joe told us about a famous incident that had taken place forty years before. A Christian couple and a Muslim couple, both childless, came to the shrine on the same day. The pillar did its work and gave a daughter to the Christians, who baptised her Anna, and a son to the Muslims, who named him Selim. Both families came back every year on the feast of Saint Anne with gifts of doves. The children flourished and grew exceedingly handsome, as was to be expected from the intervention of the goddess. They also received the gift of music - Anna sang like a nightingale and Selim played the *saz*, the lute. As was also to be expected, the son of the goddess, naughty Eros, took an interest in the young people. In their seventeenth year they made their customary pilgrimage on the feast of Saint Anne. Struck by the golden arrows of first love they took advantage of the crowd milling about the place and, without the benefit of pillar or church, went together into the sacred wood. Dusk fell and they had not returned. A search party discovered them entwined beneath a myrtle tree.

As neither mullahs nor priests would approve their union and she was no longer marriageable, Anna and her dowry were handed over to the nuns of Aghios Dimitris, a fortress nunnery on the mainland road to Thebes. As they crossed the bridge over the Euripos Anna jumped out of the carriage and into the channel, calling for Selim to follow her. Her body was found three weeks later washed up on the shore close to the shrine of Anna-Aphrodite. Miraculously it was not bloated and eyeless but perfectly preserved, as if she had been alive at the bottom of the sea, waiting for her lover to join her. Her grieving parents gave her to the priests of Saint Anne, who took her although she was a suicide. Her gravestone, which Scrumpy Joe pointed out to us, became a shrine for young virgins who decorated it with ribbons and prayed for a successful outcome to their own loves. I was a little surprised to catch the not-so-young virgin Winstanley mooning and sighing at the grave side, where I had expected a homily on chastity. When I challenged him he said that earthly love was the reflection of divine love and she had found salvation in self-sacrifice. This was further proof that Winstanley had been unhinged by a secret love.

Selim never joined her, as she had asked. He now earned his living as a minstrel in a coffee house in Eretria, where Scrumpy Joe offered to take us.

SELIM

I do not need to explain that to interpolate a text is to insert new material that creates a false impression of the character of the original work. Like most travellers, we skimmed across foreign countries like water boatmen on a pond. That I should be interested in the story of Selim the Minstrel would stretch your credulity to the limit. So the following is a fine example of interpolation. I find it dull so skip over it if you like.

Selim did not follow Anna into the Euripos but drowned himself in music. The saz was his lover; they were inseparable night and day. He did not sit or eat or pray with his family but remained in his room, sitting on the floor with the saz on his lap, often silent, sometimes improvising in one of the mournful modes, sometimes singing a plaintive love song. His parents bribed and threatened and cajoled him to put away the instrument and his grief but to no avail. They took it away by force but he sank into depression until they gave it back. They made a secret peephole into his room to watch if he did himself harm but he either lay or sat eyes closed with the saz beside him.

For those of you not familiar with the saz, the sound box was mulberry, the top was spruce; the narrow neck, a yard long, was beech, with ebony for the finger-board, set with three double strings of Toledo steel. The movable frets were gut, tied round the neck. The plectrum was a quill from a hawk, filled with its blood and hung for thirteen days, then washed, flattened and folded in half.

On the advice of the Dervish who lived in the *turbe* of Hadji Murad built into the wall of the city of Egripos, Selim's parents stopped opposing his music and instead encouraged it by offering him as a pupil to Hadji Akbar, a venerable *Ashiq*, or minstrel. Selim agreed to meet the master.

Hadji Akbar lived within the city walls, in a modest house whose main amenity was a rose garden. He sat here on a carpet with the boy and listened to him play. He gave him a *tambur*, a flat drum held vertical, and asked him to play a rhythm. He had him sing a verse of the Koran and sight read a poem of the great Sufi mystic Yunus Emre. Finally he asked why Selim wanted to become an Ashik, expecting his reply to be connected with his lost love Anna, which were grounds for rejecting him, since, although Ashik means 'someone in love', mere earthly love can never be the wellspring of the deep spiritual passion necessary to the Ashik. Selim had rehearsed his tale, thinking that Hadji Akbar would be moved by the tragedy and its potential for inspiration. Face to face with the old man, whose milky cataracts seemed to see into his soul, he had to tell the truth, certain that Hadji Akbar would sigh and send him on his way.

"Master, some three years ago, I had a dream. I am in a desert the colour of marigolds. Before me stand two great white pillars topped with a lintel, like a massive Greek Π written on the cobalt blue sky. Beside it is a beautiful young man in a white robe. He smiles at me and I am filled with such joy. I go up to him and he offers me a cup. I take it and drink. It is wine so full of love that I want to embrace the world and the sky and God Himself. He takes back the cup and gives me a saz, not made of mulberry and brass like this one but crystal and gold so light and living that it sings by itself at the touch of a breath. He takes me by the hand and leads me to the pillars. I am so full of ecstasy…as we pass through I wake up."

"Have you told anyone about this dream?"

Selim shook his head. He had woken up bathed in semen and ashamed. He covered his eyes and waited to be dismissed. Hadji Akbar picked up the saz and played an opening in the Ushak mode before breathing a song in an old and cracked and still sweet voice

I opened the gate of the garden
I felt I was in heaven
The nightingale sang within
A rose bloomed. Oh my love.

He put down the saz and told Selim to learn the Ushak mode in all its variations before he came back next week. He allowed Selim to kiss his hand before waving him away.

If Selim's parents thought that by indulging his obsession he would be restored to normal life they were disappointed. If anything, channelling his passion into study made it more intense: he lived only for the saz. They did not even have the consolation of a tune to listen to. All they heard from his room throughout the day was scales as he perfected the *makkam,* the scales of oriental music. Only when he played all the makkam would he be ready to learn the art of the Ashik.

His parents indulged other foibles or, as parents do, ignored them. The biggest one was his abhorrence of water. It was to be expected that he never went near the Euripos, but he could not bear water in any form, in a fountain or a basin or a cup. He left the table if there was a water jug on it. He drank only tea. Rain was torture. He stopped his ears against the sound and stayed in his room until every puddle had dried. He refused to wash. He wiped himself with a rag dampened with vinegar and in the privy used a mulberry leaf to clean his hand. But God is merciful and revealed in the Koran that it is permissible to wash with sand when water is scarce, which Selim interpreted liberally and used sand from the shore of the Bay of Aulis to wash like a Bedouin. He did not allow his clothes to be washed either so he smelt like a beggar, sweetened by the perfume his mother sprinkled on him when she caught him unawares.

Another foible was that Selim could not bear any talk of girls. He hummed a makkam or unceremoniously left the room if the conversation came round to marriageable cousins and daughters of friends. Nor did he enjoy the company of young men. One night his mother, unable to sleep, saw a light in his room and heard the unmistakeable groans of pleasure. Through the secret peephole she saw him passionately embracing the saz between his legs. She said nothing to anyone and took it, as mothers often do, as a personal slight.

Time passed. Selim learned by heart three hundred makkams. He learned the rhythms of classical music - the 2/4 and 4/4 of the nomads and their horses of the plains of Anatolia; the 3/4 and 6/8 of the Black Sea coast and the rhythms of its waves; the 7/8 and 9/8 and 21/16 of the Balkans and all its varied topography and peoples. Then his musical education began in earnest. He learned how to sing 'from the head', using his diaphragm, and not 'from the throat', as the Greeks do. He learned how to breathe, to modulate his voice with the nose and the mouth and the larynx, to add vibrato and tremolo and trills and other ornamentation - and when to add nothing but let the voice sound clear.

He was sent to the Dervish Hadji Latif to learn the seven steps of meditation. He began a lifelong journey with the Sufi poets and mystics who would shape his art. He dedicated himself to the great Hadji Bektash Veli, the saint who preached love and tolerance and the enjoyment of the god-given things of this world, including wine and music. He used the Bektashi greeting '*ashkolsun*', let there be love, to the unease of his parents who preferred the traditional '*salaam alaikum*' and thought that love had already caused enough trouble in their son's life.

At last Hadji Akbar introduced him to the Ashik repertoire. He was admitted into the band of musicians who played in the *tekke*, or lodge, that was the old Venetian church of Saint Mark outside the walls - the murals were whitewashed and the Pantocrator painted over with flowery arabesques and stars. The faithful gathered on Friday evening for *Zikr*, the ritual of remembrance. They sat under the cupola in a circle while Hadji Akbar began a long slow improvisation in the meditative Sarat mode, which has no natural conclusion, or rather can end on any note of the scale, and so expresses the infinite nature of God.

One by one the other musicians joined in on flute and saz and tambur. A singer began to sing a poem about the oneness of God and how all of creation comes from Him and goes back to Him. At the end of each verse listeners intoned *Allah,* the first syllable rising, the second falling. As the mood took them the worshippers stood up and moved to the slowly accelerating rhythm. Men and women danced together, because God's creation is made equally of male and female, never touching, moving sinuously around each other, imitating the grace of the *serah*, the crane, sacred to Bektash and to countless other worshippers for generations before him and before the Prophet, peace be with him.

The music became faster and modulated into less plaintive modes. The dancers turned faster and faster arms out, eyes half closed. The singers and flautists ceased, leaving only the relentless rhythm of saz and tambur to transport the dancers and musicians through the whirling spheres of the universe to the perfect stillness of Allah. As the music slowed they drifted back to earth like dandelion seeds. Drunk on ecstasy they sat or lay on the floor until, alone or in little groups, they went silently into the night under stars immeasurably distant.

ERETRIA

As Grub Street well knows, we have a prurient fascination with the calamities of others. We were keen to see the love-struck minstrel performing in the coffee house, as Scrumpy Joe had promised. Pericles puffed Eretria as full of antiquities and I hoped that Selim would compensate for their tedium. Winstanley lectured us that in classical days it had been a powerful city state that sent ships and men to fight Trojans and Persians and Spartans. There was a pretty harbour and an acropolis with some stones but the modern traveller requires considerable imagination to recreate past glories.

All that survived was an amphitheatre, which now served as a khan for travellers. It was built into a hillside at the foot of the acropolis, rows of stone that would have accommodated more than five thousand bottoms. The semicircular 'orchestra', or arena, now penned our animals and the stage building behind it was for the travellers. As the quarters were filthy and the evening was fine, we made camp in the orchestra beside the marble seats of honour. Consul Pericles and Scrumpy Joe put up with acquaintances in town and offered to find us lodgings too but Amelia and Winstanley insisted we stay with Captain Two-Face and his men. Her pretext was that it was a fine night to sleep under the stars and Winstanley's that there was less risk of plague. Oh devious lovers!

While the resourceful Ali rigged awnings, laid beds, prepared our camp, and lit a fire for our dinner, Scrumpy Joe took us to the coffee shop where Selim headed the playbill. With hints of ever decreasing subtlety he implied that Miss Burbage's sex excluded her but he might as well have talked to a post.

"Mr. Yussuf, I have never been refused entry to a coffee house. You should know the syllogism: a woman does not enter a coffee house - a Frankish woman enters a coffee house - ergo she is not a woman - ergo she may enter a coffee house."

Scrumpy Joe had no idea what a syllogism was but like a dog that understands the tone of his master's words rather then their sense, knew that arguing was pointless. He doubtless hoped that her masculine dress and swaggering gait, so different from the local women, would excuse her gender.

Turks and Christians are divided by church and by coffee house. The Christian bean follows in the steps of Saint Paul from Asia Minor, where the Smyrna merchant Dracoulis has the monopoly for Christian coffee houses. The Mohammedan bean follows the Caliphs from Arabia to Constantinople, where the merchant Hadji Emre has the monopoly for his co-religionists. Each believes his bean is the most fragrant, the most godly, the most uplifting. The sensible Jews do not have a coffee house but meet at home and brew whichever coffee is cheapest in the marketplace regardless of doctrine.

The 'house' element of the business is small, since in all but the worst weather the patrons sit outside on a sheltered veranda. We should have been hard pressed to tell the difference between the rival coffee houses, if one had not been situated near the mosque and the other near the church on opposite sides of the main square. The patrons dressed the same and looked the same, sitting cross legged on divans or reclining on an elbow before their cups and hookahs. The coffee was brewed in copper pans on coals and served in china cups on copper trays with a mug of cold water.

Early in the day the Greeks, as usual, were livelier but as the evening came on the tobacco had its effect and they fell into an stupor indistinguishable from their Turkish neighbours. This is yet another difference between Eastern and English manners: we all seek comfort in liquor and drugs but ours make us more quarrelsome, theirs more pacific.

As she had anticipated, there was no objection to Amelia.

"You see how fragile such conventions are: women enforce them as much as men..." She jabbered on, converting her triumph into a tedious homily. How well she and Winstanley would get along.

We were served coffees and hookahs, although to our great disappointment, and especially Winstanley's, the tobacco was ordinary sot weed and not the hashish we had come to enjoy. It was sweeter than Virginia tobacco but pleasant for all that. Higgins had a bottle of arak which we substituted for the water that came with the coffee.

The sun was going down over the purple Attic mountains when Selim the minstrel made his entrance. The mind's eye had imagined a lovelorn Orpheus in his hydrophobic prime, not the old strummer who shuffled onto the platform. It is said that people grow to look like their pets, and this is born out by my mother's resemblance to her spaniel. In Selim's case he had grown to look like his instrument, with a pear-shaped body and long stringy neck and a pointy flat face.

As with coffee, religionists of both camps insist that their players and their tunes are superior to the others', but to the cultivated ear of a patron of the Theatre Royal both sound equally dreadful. To add to the cacophony they seem incapable of hitting a note first time but waver round it, aiming first high then low then splitting the difference like a marksman with his sighting shots. The audience does not appear to admire the music either. They listen in a bored silence, without applause or whistles or interjections, but for a plaintive 'a-maan' from time to time or a whispered 'all-ah.'

And so it was with Selim. The arduous ritual of tuning-up slipped imperceptibly into random twanging without any decent melody. The mullahs forbid whistling, a redundant prohibition as I never heard an oriental tune you could whistle if you wanted to. It reminded Higgins of an anecdote:

"Well now, the band of an English ambassador at Constantinople once performed for the Sultan. At the end he was asked which piece he would like as an encore. He replied the first, which they started to play again, but were stopped, as it wasn't the right one. The band tried others with no success and they were in despair. Then they began to tune their instruments and his highness cried out, 'Heaven be praised, that's the one!'"

When we thought it could get no worse Selim began to warble. Scrumpy Joe said that he sang this song every evening and was kind enough to translate it for us.

Oh my saz where are you now? Where do the waters flow?
I never saw, I never knew, until they drank her.
Her hair is full of sand. Bring a comb and comb it.
Mother, bring henna for her hands The fishes want her for a bride.
She came from God To God she has returned.
The stars, the moon, all will go back to God
Even I, with the kohl of a sinner on my eyes.

After this excruciating performance we treated the company to more lively and tuneful music. Fortified by arak and tobacco we gave them the Lincolnshire Poacher, in honour of our dear Prince of Wales, God Bless him, whose favourite ditty it is. With Winstanley's piping tenor and Higgins' lusty bass and my manly baritone we made the rafters ring. Our audience greeted it with their customary silence. Amelia did not join in but sat with her hand over eyes and nor did Scrumpy Joe, saying he didn't know it. He also refused to translate the verses for our audience, on the grounds that the hare, which is hunted in the song, is sacred to Muslims, as Ali, brother-in-law of the Prophet, kept one as a pet, since when the animal is known as Ali's Cat. I replied that I thanked God I was still an Englishman and not expected to tiptoe around the sensibilities of foreigners.

Oh, 'tis my delight on a shiny night in the season of the year.

Now there's a tune.

Saz
Jean Brindesi

MEMET I

We went back to our camp in the theatre, where Ali was busy with a brace of fowl. Cupped in the palm of the theatre under a gloaming sky, bats a-flutter, owls a-hoot, flies a-bed and mosquitoes not yet a-buzz, we sat round the fire. We invited Chorbaji Two Face to share our spatchcocks and sat him on a throne of honour, his good side towards us. He surprised us with a smattering of French and passable Greek, acquired during a childhood in Constantinople, where his family kept a shop in the street of The Phoenix, the Mecca of sweetie lovers. While Ali spitted the birds and Amelia prepared accompaniments from the contents of her saddlebags and Higgins broke open the wine and Winstanley fiddled with his plaguey twigs and I made myself comfortable, the janissary entertained us with a 'candied' history of his confectionery family.

Well he did not, as you perfectly well know, no more than a few remarks and asides, swelled out later in the library, but this is a travel book, we have already discussed this, we have to pass the time before we eat, and fill up the pages, or the book will be too short, a list of places we went and discomforts we suffered. Rejoin me in this conceit, if you please…

The dynasty was founded by great-great-great-grandfather Memet. He was a Bulgarian Christian, baptized Konstantinos, from a poor family of basket makers in the capital Sofia. The children made extra money by plaiting and weaving dolls, birds, and animals to sell outside churches on feast days but it was not enough. Their parents, out of self-denying love for their youngest son and fear of not being able to feed their other children, scraped together whatever they could and paid a janissary recruiting officer to take him into the service of the Sultan. He was a sturdy lad of eight years old.

"This cannot be. Christian children were snatched from their mothers by brutal conquerors," protested Winstanley.

"In the beginning this was true. But then mothers learned that their children would have a good start in life and there would be one less mouth to feed."

Little Konstantinos was shipped off to Constantinople where he was circumcised, given the name Memet, and indentured to a farmer for seven years. He learned to be a Turk and a Muslim and to despise Christians. He learned the language and customs of his new family, their sports and songs, but however well he blended in with his new people, he could never be one of them. He was given the hardest labour and the least food and was known as 'the boy', a slave of the Sultan. He learned to answer the taunts and bullying of the other boys with his fists.

After seven years of apprenticeship in Turkish ways, Memet was sent back to Constantinople. He entered the *Acemi Oglan,* the 'School of Inexperienced Boys.' He spent seven years in the academy barracks, subject to severe discipline, military training and hard labour on state building works. He learned blind obedience to his superiors and fanatical loyalty to the Sultan. At Bayram, the two great Muslim feasts of the year, the Inexperienced Boys proved their submission to the will of Allah by rampaging through the city in search of Christians to torment. Only one trace of his past remained. If ever a scrap of straw came into his hands he wove it unthinkingly into a tiny basket or a doll.

Memet thrived. His farmyard scrapping turned into a talent for boxing. With a fine physique, good looks, and natural intelligence, he was graduated into the crack janissary regiment, the *Bostanji,* the Gardeners. They were stationed at the Topkapı Palace as personal bodyguards to the Sultan. They rowed his galley when he went out on the Bosporus and escorted him on the great procession to the mosque on Friday They also provided his torturers and executioners. When they were not on guard duty they tended the Imperial Gardens, where their apprenticeship in the countryside came in useful. The regiment was divided into the Flower Gardeners, whose skill with roses and tulips was famous throughout the Empire, and the still more prestigious Vegetable Gardeners, to which Memet was assigned.

There was still another upward step for the ambitious janissary, a unit recruited from the Vegetable Gardeners that was the most prestigious, the most coveted, the most distinguished in the Imperial Army. It was the hearth, the *Orta* of the Imperial Larder, the cooks of Topkapı. These elite troops were spared all other duties except the most ceremonial, when they escorted the Kazan of the Corps, the sacred cooking pot in parades and processions. They were divided into three hearths, of equal status: the meat cooks, the vegetable cooks and the pastry cooks. Memet proudly took the rank of *Baltaci,* Wood Carrier of the Pastry Cooks. Their kitchens fed the Topkapı palace and its outlying pavilions, altogether the population of a small town. The first responsibility of the Pastry Cooks was baking their bread, from unleavened rough-ground cartwheels for the slaves to delicate French brioches delivered three times a day to the harem.

"Cooks? The pride of the Ottoman army?"

"Your regimental colours are flags. Ours are cooking pots. The cap badge of a janissary is a rice spoon. I have seen your soldiers with onions on their hats."

"Leeks. A Welshman wears a leek in his cap. But not because he knows how to cook it."

"A man must be fit for peace as well as war. We live well to fight well and fight well to live well."

For the first few years Memet's tasks were menial - cleaning ovens, hauling flour, grinding sugar and taking his turn on the great two-man paddles that mixed the dough. When he was not baking bread he kept up his boxing skills in fierce bouts with the meat and vegetable cooks or played chess with his hearth mates. He took part in the great monthly procession after Friday Mosque when the entire Janissary Corps took the regimental pots to the Sultan's kitchens to be filled with *Chorbayi ichmek*, payday soup. This was not entirely ceremonial. The phrase 'tip over the cook-pot' meant to mutiny and the Sultan waited anxiously to see if the Corps ate hearty. After the parades Memet changed into civilian clothes and took his meagre pay across the Bosporus to Pera, the Christian quarter, and the little lanes beside the water near the abattoirs where low wooden houses accommodated accommodating girls from Armenia and Georgia, Moldavia and Walachia. He avoided Bulgarians.

Memet might have continued in this way for years, working his way up the ranks from Wood Carrier to Soup Stirrer, from Flat Bread to Brioche. He might have been given other duties, in the torture room perhaps or, given his strength from boxing, taught the secrets of strangling with a bowstring, the most honourable form of execution reserved for officers, vizirs, Imperial princes and other notables.

"Surely this is an ignoble way to dispatch eminent people. It is the weapon of footpads and hired killers."

"We don't make a public ceremony of our executions. It is done swiftly, at night. Three men, one for the arms, one for the legs, one for the bowstring. It is quick, it is private, it spills no blood."

"I have heard it is not a bowstring but a silk cord."

"For a child or a woman or a soft-necked Eunuch. With a man you must use strength and there is a danger of cutting the flesh so we use a leather strap."

"Dear God. The agony."

"Not if you wear gloves."

With excellent comic timing Memet let his remark float between us before landing it with a chuckle. Two of us did not think it a good joke - you can guess who they were.

But Memet's life was to change one afternoon when he was cleaning the tables of the Sweet Pastry Cooks. He was in a meditative mood, musing generally on love and in particular a girl in the city. Automatically, without thinking what he was doing, he picked up a scrap of raw pastry and made it into a duck; then another scrap into a cow; followed by a falcon and a horse.

"Wasting time, Soldier?" barked the unseen Chorbaji of the pastry cooks into Memet's ear. He snapped to attention. His belly knotted and his knees trembled. This meant the humiliation of a beating in front of his hearth mates, the double humiliation of thanking his beater, the triple humiliation of paying him for his efforts.

"Carry on," said the Chorbaji, "no, give those to me," and he took the little pastry menagerie away with him. Memet gave the area an especially thorough clean and awaited the summons to his punishment. He was not called to the Chorbajis' room until the following morning when he was informed of his honourable transfer to the Sweet Pastry Cooks.

So began his fame as the finest confectioner in Constantinople. He plaited and moulded sweet dough into the shapes and figures of his Christian childhood - except for the hated crucifix. He expanded his repertoire to the exotica of the Empire and fantastical creatures of myth, folklore and his own imagination. He perfected pastry mixes of different hardness and malleability and colour with dyes and oils and sugars. He learned to spin his creations in sugar and sweet chocolate. His feel for oven temperatures was infallible, enabling him to nest sweetmeat inside sweetmeat inside sweetmeat. His first successes were pastry farmyards and menageries for the little princes of the harem. He was soon producing sweetmeats for the third lady, the second lady, the first lady and finally the Sultan himself. The culmination of royal favour was the secret production of pornographic cakes for His Sublimity's private parties: to sugary copulation he added exaggeration, grotesquerie and humour, bringing comedy to the Ottoman confectionery tradition.

His new life brought changes. He was forbidden to box and excused bowstring duties in case he damaged his fingers. He had his own alcove in the kitchens. He moved from a forty man dormitory to a four man room and rose to the rank of Chorbaji. On his visits to Pera he could now afford a saucy Circassian or a sultry Jewess.

All should have been well with Memet and so it was, for most of the time. But he could not get out of his mind the girl he had been thinking about when the Chorbaji caught him playing with the dough. She was not a Pera Christian but a Turkish girl he glimpsed at a balcony window in the Street of the Flower Sellers. Bright blue eyes, the palest of sapphires, looked straight at him, until a hennaed hand snatched her inside and slammed the window. She offended decency by standing unveiled at an open window but her youth, her beauty, her radiance, dispelled any suspicion of immodesty. In defiance of cliché Memet felt an arrow pierce his heart.

In the months that followed, while his body and mind were dedicated to mastering patisserie, his wounded heart lived the secret life of a lover. He lingered over the flowers in the shops by her house, although far inferior to those which his comrades produced; he drank innumerable glasses of tea at a stall far enough away from her balcony not to give scandal. He did not know if she saw him for the window was always closed. On the murky, rippled glass he saw shadows move, perhaps a blur of white, a lamp at dusk. He discovered from the tea-seller that the house belonged to a dye merchant from Egripos but the only people he saw coming and going were two old women. Only by a stroke of good fortune would he see the girl again, let alone get an introduction, but this did not stop him plotting and dreaming: he would charm the old women with a spell or disguise himself as a lamp seller or have himself delivered to the door in a giant olive jar, and other Sheherezade solutions.

At last he hit on a more realistic plan. He packed a box of his finest pastries. In the centre he put a white dove pierced by an arrow. He tied the box with a silk ribbon, tucked it under his coat and hurried to the Street of the Flower Sellers. With trembling knees and thumping chest he knocked on the door. Tak Tak. At the third time of knocking one of the old women opened the grille.

"A wealthy person of good reputation sends these for the lady of the house."

"Let me see," said the old woman. She stretched out a bony hand, snatched the box and slammed the grille shut.

A few days later he tried again. He packed a box of finest pastries, put in the centre a deer pierced by an arrow, tied it all up with a silk ribbon and tucked it under his coat. With trembling knees and thumping chest he knocked on the door. Tak Tak. At the third time of knocking the second old woman opened the grille.

"A wealthy person of good reputation, sends these for the lady of the house."

"Let me see," said the old woman. She opened the grille and stretched out a bony hand.

"My master would like a message from the lady."

"Tell him the dates stuffed with almonds are too hard on the teeth," she said, snatched the box and slammed the grille.

Memet puzzled over the meaning of the message, his spirits rising and falling with each new interpretation. But the third time he took no chances and left out the stuffed dates. He put a swan in the centre, pierced by an arrow, tied up the box with a silk ribbon and tucked it under his coat. With trembling knees and thumping chest he knocked on the door. Tak Tak. At the third time of knocking the first old woman opened the grille.

"A wealthy person of good reputation, sends these for the lady of the house."

"Let me see," said the old woman. She opened the grille and stretched out a bony hand.

"My instructions are to deliver them to no other than the lady of the house."

"I am the lady of the house."

"The young lady of the house."

"That's me," said the second old woman, who had been standing behind, "I'm younger than she is" and she stretched out a bony hand. This time Memet persisted.

"The daughter of the house then."

"There is no daughter of the house."

"But I...my customer has seen her at the window."

"He is mistaken. Only we live here."

"Who does the house belong to?"

"A dye merchant from Egripos and he has no daughters," they chorused. At this baffling news Memet lost his concentration allowing the first old woman to snatch the box and slam the grille. As he walked away he looked up at the window and thought he saw a flicker of white behind the glass but it might have been a trick of the light.

Fortune struck on a moonless night in winter. Memet was strolling back from Pera, scenting musk on his skin, desire for his unseen love temporarily assuaged, when he heard the fire tocsin. Although the Cooks and Gardeners did not have city fire fighting duties - this was the task of the Artillerymen assisted by Inexperienced Boys - his step instinctively quickened. When he realised that the glow came from the Street of the Flower Sellers he broke into a run. He arrived before the firemen. Three houses were in flames and in the middle the dye merchant's. Neighbours made a futile bucket chain from a fountain, while others huddled and wailed and got in the way. Smoke and sparks spiralled up from the roofs. Underneath the festive crackling began an ominous roar. A human silhouette beat its fists against the balcony window.

Memet ripped from the wall the flower seller's pot rack and used it as a ladder to reach the balcony. He hauled himself onto the sill and put his shoulder to the window bars. The frame gave way. His love, in a white gown, stared at him wide-eyed. Drawn by the open window, a wave of fire flooded into the room and broke over her. Her hair and robe burst into flames. She held out her blazing arms towards him. Hungry for air, smoke and flames tossed Memet back into the arms of firemen and unconsciousness, taking with him the vision of her dark eyes on fire with love.

From that day onwards, whenever he heard a fire tocsin, a black mood descended on him. His under-cooks knew to cut the talk and keep their heads down. The depression could last days or weeks. When he came out of it, he brought with him a new idea for a pastry but only he knew what drove him to creative despondency.

He was in the middle of a black mood, brought on by the burning of the apothecary's quarter, when Sultan Suleiman died of an apoplexy. He was succeeded by nineteen year old Murad, not the eldest son but the child of a lesser concubine, who had manoeuvred herself into the position of favourite. The Hearth of the Imperial Larder was busy. They had to prepare mourning banquets for court and harem, dignitaries and diplomats, mullahs, bishops and rabbis; take turn as guard of honour at the funeral in Sulemaniye and over the stone tomb in the mausoleum; take the bowstring to the new Sultan's twenty three brothers, from twenty year old Osman to an as yet unnamed three month old, and throw their weighted bodies in the Bosporus; send their mothers to follow them, alive and gagged, in weighted sacks; cut the throats of tutors and eunuchs; strangle three senior vizirs and behead a few minor ones; prepare the inauguration feast of the new Sultan.

"Those poor children!"

"Rivals, rebels, usurpers, egged on by jealous mothers. Let live, they would eke out their time in gilded prisons, a hope to malcontents and a threat to the throne. It was their *kismet.*

Whenever brothers have been allowed to live there has been calamity. What do you do with younger brothers of the monarch?"

"We let them live to entertain the mob with scandal."

Throughout the feverish preparations the Chorbaji-bashi of the pastry cooks worried about his head patissier. Memet refused to say what he was preparing. He was so withdrawn that it was not certain that he realised there was a new Sultan, let alone that he was charged with providing the centrepiece for his feast. But with three days to go he gathered his undercooks, announced his plan to gasps of approval and gave out orders and recipes.

On the Friday that the astrologers, muftis and mullahs decided was most auspicious, the new Caliph of the Faithful, Padishah of the Barbary States, Shadow of the Prophet on Earth, Allah's Vice-Regent made his first procession to the Great Mosque through a city in celebration. He came back to his feast in the biggest pavilion of Topkapı. His mother and sisters and concubines watched from a curtained balcony as the Grand Vizir, Governors of Provinces, Vaivodes, Agas, and Beys prostrated themselves at the feet of their monarch like so many gorgeous beetles before being invited to sit on the divans that lined the room. Other guests were led in to give their compliments and obeisances, Christian Bishops, foreign delegations, an African king. The feast began, dish after dish, delicacy after delicacy, while the janissary band played raucous marches on drums, horns and cymbals.

At last it was time for the cake. With a fanfare from the band, the Hearth of the Sweet Pastry Cooks, led by Chorbaji Memet marched in with their offering on a giant silver platter carried on the shoulders of four handsome Wood Carriers and carefully laid it down on the low table before their sovereign. The court waited in silence for a cue from the young Sultan. It was a giant effigy of a phoenix, half the height of a man, wings outstretched, sitting on a nest of fire, sculpted and coloured in intricate detail. Without stooping to anthropomorphism, the way the magical bird held her head and neck and wings expressed unbearable ecstasy and suffering. It sent such a chill through the atmosphere of festive self-congratulation that the Chorbaji-Bashi of the Larder, who was Master of Ceremonies, feared for his head.

It was not over yet. A Water Carrier handed Memet a lighted taper, who, with the deepest bow, handed it to the Sultan and invited him to touch the nest of sugar flames: it caught real fire. The Sultan and his guests gasped in unison. The bird blazed in a fierce blue light that suddenly flared and was gone, leaving her caramelised brown and black. Every man in the room, every woman behind the grille felt the breath of Asriel, the angel of death. With another bow, Memet handed his sovereign a long-handled silver spoon and with a gesture invited him to sink it into the breast of the phoenix. She resisted the first attempt but at the second collapsed into a heap of sugary crumbs. There was another gasp, louder than the first. The Sultan laughed and clapped his hands like the child he was when he first saw one of Memet's animals and the rest of the party joined in the applause. Rising out of the caramel cinders was a new phoenix, light and ethereal, holding her head and neck and wings in an expression of unbearable ecstasy and love, carrying in her beak a perfect purple tulip, the emblem of the new Sultan.

While the Pastry Cooks distributed purple sugar tulips to the guests, which only one minor dignitary dared to bite, for which he was subsequently introduced to the bowstring, the Sultan beckoned Memet to come forward. He prostrated himself and dared to kiss the carpet under the silk pouffe under the slipper of the sovereign.

"Chorbaji, ask me for a favour and I will grant it."

"Highness, I want for nothing. I have reached the pinnacle. I can do no more. Take my head. Give me peace." And with this he began to sob.

The Sultan called for the Chorbaji-Bashi, who prostrated himself next to Memet.

"What is the matter with this man?"

"Unrequited love, Highness."

The Sultan looked at the risen Phoenix and, as he was a sensitive soul who had grown up among women and wrote poetry, understood.

"Is he married?"

"No Highness," said the Chorbaji-Bashi.

"Chorbaji Memet, these are my orders. Tomorrow you will come to the Hall of the Maidens and there you will choose a wife from one of the concubines. She will have a dowry to fit her station and your genius. Make many children to delight with your creations."

As ordered by his sovereign, Memet chose a girl who most resembled his incinerated love. They were immediately married and allowed to live in one of the Sultan's pavilions on the Bosporus until they bought a pastry shop with the dowry. What began as a duty to his bride on their wedding night became a pleasure and then a passion. He recovered his spirits; the fire tocsin lost its power over him; he grew fat and happy and had many children who also grew fat from too much tasting. It was the beginning of the famous line of confectioners who kept a sweet factory and shop called The Phoenix.

By now the chickens were done. Ali lifted the spit from over the hot embers but it broke and the meat fell into them, spattering fat and flaring the fire back into life. Chorbaji Two Face stretched out his bad hand and picked them out of the flames as if his fleshless claw were made of metal.

"Chorbaji, I think there is more to your story," said Amelia, but we were all too hungry for more stories.

MEMET II

As Amelia suspected, there was more to Memet's tale than the founding of the Phoenix dynasty. Who was the girl consumed by fire? What was the connection with Egripos? How did our Memet become half man, half other thing? Where can we find good pastries?

Let us say that after spatchcocks and wine and pipes, we lay back under the stars and listened to Memet tell the rest of his story. Indeed he may have but we were already so fast asleep that his words would no more have impinged on us than the mosquitoes' hum and the chomp of camel cud; more likely it was scraped together from conversations in the saddle, the gossip of Scrumpy Joe, the indiscretions of the dervish Hadji Latif, the calumnies of Rabbi Koen; more likely yet, it took shape like a djinn from a cloud of hashish smoke; most likely it was all a confection. As are all our stories.

And so, satiated with arak, wine, brandy, tobacco, hashish, opium, dinner, travel, and each other, we reclined on our makeshift beds, wrapped in blankets against the night chill. On the stone seats around us flittered the shades of bygone spectators come to hear stories again. The Chorbaji sat, staring into the fire, his two faces flickering in its light, and continued his tale.

Years passed. Memets and Ahmeds alternately sired Ahmeds and Memets. The Phoenix gave its name to the street. It was joined by other confectioners from the Imperial Larder, adding another cartel to the janissaries' hold over trade in the city. The great Corps of Janissaries, whose military might had rolled over the armies of Christian kings as far as the gates of Vienna, became a guild of shopkeepers. They were allowed to marry, to live outside the barracks, to set up in business. They were immune from execution, exempt from taxes and still received a soldier's pay. This was raised a grade when a new Sultan took the throne, so there was an incentive to kick over the cook pots and install another, if they were not well rewarded. The recruitment of infidels declined in favour of the sons of janissaries. They were spared the hardship of the School of Inexperienced Boys: all they were good for was parading the cook pot through the streets. They still had civic responsibility for policing and fire fighting but hired others to carry them out. After the expansion of the empire ceased and before the incursion of new empires began - the Russian, the French, the British - there were no wars to speak of and the decadence of the janissaries went unnoticed.

Over the centuries the Phoenix lost its pre-eminence. In Pera the Greeks outdid them in patisserie and the Armenians in bread. A Turk from the provinces called Bekir invented a new sweet from starch and rosewater and sugar. He called it *rahat lokum*, 'we have eaten contentment'. It eclipsed the competition and its fame spread as far as London, where it was known as Turkish Delight.

In 1745 the first son of Ahmed of the Phoenix was born. By the will of Allah, or a helical twist of breeding, young Memet grew to be tall, lean, blonde, pale-cheeked, straight-nosed, unlike his parents. He was the darling of the street. Old ladies patted his hair and pinched his cheeks and spat to avert the evil eye. His mother hung blue beads about his neck. The boys on the street called him a dirty Frank and beat him up. He learned to answer back and fight them, two or three at a time.

Memet resembled his Bulgarian ancestor in another way. From the time he could toddle into the bakery he played with bits of cast-off pastry. With a concentration unusual in one so young he watched his uncles and cousins manipulate nuts and fruits, honeys and creams. He made his own sweets, letting his imagination run wild in defiance of tradition. He made fantastic shapes at first, which then took on the likeness of animals he saw in the street and in picture books. His family laughed at him: 'Memet, when you come into the business you will be the ruin of us.' In fact it was the opposite. One morning they put a few of Memet's animals on the counter and they were sold before Midday Prayer. The same thing happened the next day and the next. More customers came into the shop and bought other things, so that Ahmed had the unaccustomed satisfaction of begging them to buy from his neighbours too, as was the custom of the bazaar.

When he turned sixteen it was time for Memet to follow his father into the janissaries. In his new uniform he paraded with the rest of the intake in the Great Maidan before marching to Topkapı to take the oath and receive the badge of an Inexperienced Boy in the presence of the Sultan. After his first taste of the Sultan's *Chorbayi ichmek,* payday soup, from the Great Cook Pot, they marched back to the barracks. Then they went home. They would not be called again until they graduated, unless they paraded for the death of a Sultan or the birth of a prince.

A week after his induction Memet asked his father's permission to report for military training. His parents were appalled. It was only the sons of poor families who trained and became soldiers in an active hearth. It was no life for a gifted confectioner and scion of a merchant family. He would have to exercise, go outside in heat and cold and rain, expose himself to sharp things. If there was a war, Allah forbid, he might have to fight. His mother feared for his morals. She heard that the soldiers went over to the vice dens of Pera to defile themselves with Christian women and alcohol. Ahmed claimed ignorance of such things but urged his son to save himself for an arranged marriage, the pipe, and an occasional opium pastille.

But Memet was adamant so eventually, thinking he would come back to pastry after a taste of the hard life, his father gave him permission. Although they were surprised to see a 'soft-hands' reporting for duty, the officers were impressed by his boxing skills and added to them the cudgel and the scimitar, the pistol and the dagger, the musket and the pike. Memet enjoyed marching, bivouacs, camp fires and even the soldier's principal occupation of waiting around. He was anxious to see real action, for although there were no wars as such, there were operations on the borders against brigands and pirates. In Thrace for example, Greek mountain bandits, the *klephtes*, were becoming a nuisance. But whenever he volunteered for an active detachment, he was mysteriously refused and suspected his father of pulling strings. On the other hand he turned down invitations to join the Imperial Gardeners, as he had no desire to stand guard, prune roses and kill in cold blood. Eventually he found a compromise, the fire-fighters of the Artillerymen. It was not a popular calling, since the main tactic for fire-fighting, in a city built of wood, was pulling down the burning house and its neighbours with long metal hooks, which outraged the owners. But Memet enjoyed the action of a fire, the chaos and danger, the sense of importance. He lived at home and made sweets unless he was on duty, which he spent in the barracks practising martial arts and listening out for the fire tocsin.

One day, on his way back from delivering pastries to an important customer, Memet saw a girl in a white dress in the open window of a balcony of a house in the Street of the Flower Sellers. Bright blue eyes, the palest of sapphires, looked straight at him, until a hennaed hand snatched her inside and slammed the window. She offended decency by standing unveiled at an open window but her youth, her beauty, her radiance, dispelled any suspicion of immodesty. In defiance of cliché Memet felt an arrow pierce his heart.

There were no flower sellers in the street any more, only private houses and a tea stall with a convenient view of the house on the corner. He saw silhouettes against the dark glass and an occasional flicker of white but the window remained closed. He knew in his wounded heart that she was looking down on him but how could he get to see her? The only people he saw coming and going were two old women. Only by a stroke of good fortune would he see the girl again, let alone gain an introduction, but this did not stop him plotting and dreaming: he would charm the old women with a spell or disguise himself as a lamp seller or have himself delivered to the door in a giant olive jar, and other Sheherezade solutions.

Fortune struck on a moonless night in winter. Memet was on duty, playing chess with his Chief Ladderman, when they heard the tocsin. In the Street of the Flower Sellers three houses were in flames and in the middle the blue-eyed girl's. Neighbours made a futile bucket chain from a fountainwhile others huddled and wailed and got in the way. Smoke and sparks spiralled up from the roofs. Underneath the festive crackling began an ominous roar. A human silhouette flitted against the balcony window. Memet shouted at the ladder men and pointed at the balcony while he put on a hooded cape of fire-proof Carpasian flax. He climbed up to the window and smashed it with his axe. His love, dressed in a white gown, stared at him wide-eyed. Drawn by the open window, a wave of fire flooded into the room and broke over her. Her hair and robe burst into flames. He jumped into the room and threw his cape round her. He pulled her to the window and fell back into the arms of the firemen and unconsciousness.

Memet lay near death for many weeks, burnt on one side from head to heel. While he was unconscious he had the most voluptuous dreams. He was living in the countryside, on a hillside in a stone-roofed house with a well and a vine and a donkey and a cow. His love, the blue-eyed woman he had saved, was his wife, Ayesha. They walked over flower-covered fields, tended their orchard, tilled their garden, prayed when they heard the distant muezzin, and of course made love, after which she sang strange and beautiful melodies he had never heard before with words he did not understand. He felt he had always lived in this place and his previous life was a half-remembered nightmare. To which, one day, he awoke. His Chief Ladderman came to visit. Memet asked about the girl.

"What girl?"

"The girl I carried to the balcony window."

"There was no girl. There was no-one in the house."

"But I had her in my arms. In my cape."

"My friend, all you had in your cape was fire."

Memet's life as a confectioner was over. His right hand was useless as a bird's claw for delicate work and his appearance frightened the customers. But he could still hold a scimitar and a cudgel so he moved into the barracks and became a full-time soldier and fireman. He was content enough, although passed over for ceremonial duties and preferred for night watches. When not on duty he haunted the Street of the Flower Sellers. The house was being rebuilt but all the workmen could say was that it was paid for by a dye merchant from Egripos. He made enquiries in the dye-merchants' quarter but none of them knew anyone from the Street of the Flower Sellers.

A year passed. The Vizir of Egripos, who had over-enriched himself and built a house in Constantinople bigger than the Grand Pasha's, was deprived of his position and his head. His replacement was a Serb from Belgrade, who had been taken as a slave when a child and sold to the Bashoglu family. The Sultan presented him with three horse tails to hang on his standard, for Egripos earned the highest rank, and sent him on his way.

Before he left, the new Vizir selected a personal guard from volunteers among the full-time janissaries. Memet saw a chance to widen his investigations. Egripos was not a popular posting. Its great days were over, a provincial backwater with little opportunity for pleasure or profit for the soldier. So it was a sorry collection of disaffected, discredited, disenchanted, disgruntled and disreputable misfits, to whom Memet added disfigured, who paraded before the new Vizir.

"Allah be praised," he said when he saw Memet, "you'd frighten off a djinn let alone a klepht. You'll be my Chorbaji."

As soon as he stepped ashore in Egripos Memet felt ill. He had tingles in his burnt side and pains in his good, thumping in his chest, echoes in his ears, fiery flashes at the edge of his sight. He felt light-headed, disembodied, disconnected with the world. Sleep was tortured with chaotic dreams, looming demons, nightmares within nightmares. Wakefulness was haunted with nameless dread, shifting shapes on the edge of lamplight, distant cries and intimate whispers. The good side of his face grew gaunt and dull, the burnt side bright-eyed and inflamed. Analgesics, intoxicants, narcotics had no effect except to stupefy him. Pride and fear spurred him to carry on, more like an automaton than a man. He asked after the elusive dye merchant, more to remain connected with his old self than with any hope of success, so he was not disappointed when all he came up with was an old story of a family famous for the spontaneous combustion of a daughter on her wedding night.

The time came for the Vizir to make an inspection of his island. Memet rode at the head of the party on a black mule, inspiring admiration or fear, depending on which side of the road you stood. At every place they were welcomed with hospitality and gifts by beys and effendis, imams and priests, merchants and tax collectors. They nick-named Memet Half-and-Half and tried to gauge whether they had paid enough for the Vizir's favour from whether he turned his good side or his bad side towards them.

They headed south and held court at the castles of Vassilika, Pirgi and Panormia. At Protimo Ali Bey promised a dinner of the finest fresh-caught carp at his Serai beside Lake Dystos. They climbed a winding road to a plain ringed with mountains, that then dropped steeply to the lake. An icy coldness filled Memet's chest. He recognised this place. From a Frankish stone tower on their right a volley of muskets saluted them. Memet heard himself, as from a great distance, give his three Pot-Scourers the order to reciprocate. At the volley he groaned, fell from his horse like a sack of grain and lay motionless. Everyone looked at the Pot-Scourers but all the muskets pointed upwards. The Soup-Stirrer rolled Memet first on his stomach and then on his back but there was no sign of a wound. His eyes were closed and his breath was shallow, as if he was asleep.

"He who falls from a donkey dies but he who falls from a horse does not," said the Vizir, quoting an old proverb.

"He fell from a mule. Half-and-Half. He should be neither dead nor alive." said Ali Bey.

"An apoplexy," said the Vizir, making up for his previous whimsicality.

Ali ordered him to be carried over to the tower and put in charge of its little garrison of gendarmes. He lay on a straw mattress for a week. Between life and death he neither drank nor defecated. Several times the gendarmes thought he had died, seeing not even a breath's cloud on the dagger blade they held before his lips. At noon on the seventh day he sat up, stretched, yawned, and asked for a jug of water. He drained the jug, staggered outside to relieve himself, lay back down, and fell back into a deep sleep, saying nothing. He did the same on the next day. On the third day he woke at dawn, washed and joined the gendarmes at prayer. Over breakfast he chatted about this and that, as if nothing had happened, and set off on foot to Protimo to find a mule to take him back to Egripos.

His men were amazed to see him alive and doubly amazed to see how he had changed. Both sides of his face were alight with happiness. He was no longer brusque and distracted but amenable and attentive. He was still their Chorbaji, and kept his distance, but he was at ease in both his skins. He had told no-one about what had being going on inside his head, in case they thought he was possessed by a djinn, or driven mad by opium, or under a spell, so now he could not tell anyone that all his symptoms had disappeared.

Nor could he tell them where he went when he fell off the mule: to live with Ayesha his blue-eyed wife in their house on the plain above Lake Dystos. He resumed his life with her as if he had not been away. He got up at dawn and prayed; took sheep from his pen onto the hillside; ploughed a field; ate beans and cheese for dinner; planted seeds in the field; went down to the coffee house at sunset. The other men behaved as if he had always been one of them. At nightfall he went back home to his blue-eyed wife, sat with her to watch the moonrise and went to bed to make love.

Day followed day like this until Friday. He came home from the mosque at dinner time and sat under the vine. Ayesha brought him a cup of water and a spoonful of jam. He made her sit down beside him.

"Ayesha, who am I?"

She put her hands on his face, one on the left cheek and one on the right, both equally smooth.

"You are my husband Memet, Chorbaji of the Artillery, son of Ahmed the patissier of Istanbul, a man of flesh and blood."

"Who are you?"

"I am your wife Ayesha, daughter of a dye merchant of Egripos and a djinn of smokeless fire."

"Am I in paradise?"

She laughed and kissed his hands, which were normal.

"This is the world. Djinns live and die in the same time and place as men. Once in a while the power of love leaps across the void that separates them like lightning between the earth and sky."

"If you are made of smokeless fire, how can I see you? How can I touch you?"

"The proverb says that this world is a building with two doors. Allah has blessed us. He has shown us a third door."

That afternoon Memet went to sleep. He woke on a straw bed in the tower, drank water, went back to bed. He went to sleep and woke up next to Ayesha. And so his life continued in the world of men and the world of djinn. Both were equally real to him, although when he was in one, the other seemed like a dream. As he became more practised at living two lives he did not have to wait for sleep to pass from one to the other. It was like listening to a story-teller. You could be in the coffee house and in the story at the same time. The difference was that at any given moment he did not know which of his lives was the story.

One day he plucked up courage to seek out the dervish Hadji Latif in his *tekke* on the banks of the Egripos. It was a relief to pour out the story from his first sight of the blue-eyed girl to the present. Hadji Latif did not interrupt but sat with his eyes closed, rocking gently on his heels.

"*Allu akbar*, God is great" he said when Memet had finished. "Brother, why did you come to me?"

"To know if I am mad or cursed with the evil eye or damned by Allah."

"And if you are any of these things, what then?"

Memet had no answer to this, not for a holy man and servant of Allah and his Prophet. The true answer was he would do nothing. He would remain mad or cursed or damned rather than give up his love for Ayesha.

"I must consult my books. Come back tomorrow."

The following day Memet went back to Hadji Latif.

"Brother, you want to know if you are mad or cursed with the evil eye or damned by Allah. Set your mind at rest, you are none of these things, although I was first suspicious of her blue eyes. If ever there is an evil eye, it is Frankish blue."

Respectful of the divine wisdom he was about to impart, the dervish put his hands palm upwards on his knees.

"Everything that I will tell you comes from Allah's revelation to his prophet, peace be upon him. When Allah created the world He first made the angels out of his holy breath. Then He made men out of earth. Then He made the djinn out of smokeless fire but as He was about to clothe them in flesh the evening star rose for the beginning of His holy day and He rested according to His law. Do not confuse the djinn with the *afrit*, as ignorant people do. Afrit are monstrous spirits that wreak havoc in the world. The djinn eat and drink, procreate and die like men. As they are God's precious creatures they worship him, like us, and Mohammed is their prophet too. It is the duty of all Muslims in this world to acknowledge them as fellow believers."

"*Allu akbar,*" said Memet.

"Djinn and men live in the same time and place but different worlds," continued the dervish. "Usually they are separate and distinct but sometimes, if God wills, a favoured man or a favoured djinn can see into the other world. I believe that the djinn Ayesha saw you and was struck by love. As is her nature she burned with desire. You embraced her in this fiery state and your own desire joined with hers."

"Ayesha wants a child. Is this possible?" asked Memet.

"I cannot say. It would be born in the world of djinn so logic says it will be djinn. But as Aristotle says, a man's seed comes from his blood. Fire and blood united. He might be the Caliph unites the world and all its peoples under Allah."

"If it is a daughter?"

"Let us wait and see."

Memet put his head in his hands.

"Brother, what shall I do? How can I be in both places? If I die in one will I live in the other?"

"Only Allah knows your fate. Trust him."

"How can this all be? It is so hard to understand."

"Come with me, brother," said the dervish, stood up and took Memet by the hand. They went outside into the dusk. The beginning of a full moon, Allah's promise to the world, hung over the minarets of the town. The dervish led Memet to the Euripos and pointed to the citadel in the middle.

"In the time of the Franks Hadji Bektash was imprisoned in the dungeon of that citadel by Count Otto, the governor. There are no windows so night and day are the same. The only hole is in the floor, where prisoners relieve themselves into the waters. Hadji Bektash submitted to the will of Allah but one thing troubled him. Without sight of sun or stars he did not know when to pray. He asked Allah for a sign. In those days the Euripos flowed only one way. Allah in his goodness made it change direction when it is time for prayer. And so it has remained to this day a sign of Allah's power and Hadji Murad's piety. Allah made upstream meet downstream and downstream meet upstream, which is what he has done for you and Ayesha. Give thanks and submit, as a believer should."

Parading the Kazan
Jean Brindesi

TEDIUM VI(T)AE

Up betimes in the dawn and drizzle. Now, stories are all very well but, for a traveller, not worth a fig compared with a dry billet and a hearty breakfast. I once met a man who sailed with Cook to the other side of the world. I asked what were his most terrible and most wonderful sights, to which the explorer replied his warm hat blown away at Cape Horn and a roast turkey on Hawaii.

Everything was damp; our fire was out and everything else too; the sky, the stones, the animals, ourselves, were ash grey in the gloom; we were in no mood for more of the Chorbaji's orientalisms. For my part I believed his story to be a rationale of his disfigurement, rather than a reason for it: the poor fellow fell in the fire when he was little and had told tales about himself ever since: his injury came before his ancestry not after. So many of our histories are not genealogy but apology.

You may be sure that these thoughts were penned later beside a fireside with a glass of grog and not as we busied ourselves to resume our journey, each in our own way. Amelia got ready behind an improvised screen and reappeared an Amazon; Higgins used his fingers on his hair and his palms on his face - which was cleaning which is questionable - and was a

Satyr again; I yawned and farted and scratched my bugbites and beat my sides and slapped my thighs and generally acted the waking Hero; Winstanley dabbed himself with a sodden kerchief, wound his watch, examined his tongue, thanked God for surviving the night, and rejoined the Temple Virgins. After our respective stirrup cups to put us on our way (yaourt, arak, wine, patent cordial) we mounted our rain-greased saddles and, each immersed in our respective moods (resolution, resentment, resignation, restiveness), we abandoned Ali to his chores, the Chorbaji to his grumbling wobblers, and rode out of the theatre.

To the left of us, the sullen sea merged into a mist that veiled the mountains of Attica over the Gulf. To the right, the country was flat and featureless and likewise melted into grey. In this damp and dreary landscape I felt a sudden nostalgia for sodden England and its sodden folk, and wished I was there with a crew of boozy, brawling boys, chasing a fox in the rain. Instead I had to listen to Winstanley warbling on about the famous Lelantine plain, over which Eretria and Chalcis warred for generations in the days of heroes; famous, that is, to pedants like Winstanley, and of not the slightest interest to the rest of us.

Ancient history had as dampening effect on our spirits as the strengthening rain, so we took the first opportunity for shelter that offered itself, in the form of a ruined Papist monastery that now served as a khan for travellers. It was as filthy as we had come to expect but enough of the church roof was intact to give us shelter. The pointed arches and slender columns took us back to the time when Catholic knights of Italy, France and Spain divided up the island, the Bishop of Chalcis owed his see to Rome and Hellenes dreamed of a restored Byzantium.

At the price of a stand of olive trees, I bought wood for a bonfire from the keeper, a melancholic Greek with one eye, who treated his patrons more as intruders than guests. He still regarded the wood as his own and winced at every log we threw in the blaze, as if it were a piece of Chippendale. He insisted on using his ten words of Tuscan on us to show that he too was a man of the world and knew foreign places. I thought that he would tell us the story of how he lost his eye and gained his Italian, and his tale would relate to our themes of Aphrodite and Imagination and the Delusions of Religion, all anchored on our little island. But, to your relief and ours, he did not, because we were too cold and he was too surly and, like the majority of people in the world, had no tale to tell. Now I don't deny that every soul who ever lived has a story, only that most are as tedious as a tavern bore's and not worth the telling, much less the listening.

By the time the rest of our party rejoined us we had a roaring fire to welcome them and were almost dry ourselves. Ali busied himself over a sort of hasty pudding made with stale bread, curds and sugar, all boiled up with a seasoning of brandy. While it was offensive to the refined palate, it warmed us through and restored our spirits, so that it was a more cheerful band that lounged around the fire and waited for the rain to stop. It was time for booksellers' travellers to entertain each other and their readers with fictions in crafted prose, not spit into the fire and tell each other how wet it was or cold for the time of year, or close their eyes for a nap, or get out an interesting book: so, for the sake of the booksellers here is an interlude, a story of love and Egripos, a Middle Age romance.

MARTINO

Fourteen hundred years after the Incarnation of Our Saviour, when two Popes ruled Christendom and Plague stalked the world, the Fourteen Holy Helpers were considered the most efficacious of the saints. One of them, Saint Catherine of Alexandria, was especially venerated by Martino de Nicola, a lawyer, who lived in a little town in Campania, the crescent of fertile land around the bay of Naples.

One day Martino decided to make a pilgrimage to the relics of St Catherine in her Monastery on Mount Sinai. His wife was appalled. Martino had never travelled further than Naples. He was short-sighted and small, which, by the standards of Southern Italians in the fourteenth century, was small indeed. He took no exercise, did not hunt, could not swim, was never a soldier and had never been to sea. These days there is no impediment to little, pasty-faced, short-sighted, pot-bellied lawyers travelling abroad, and they do in numbers, but in those days he would have to weather summer gales in a little ship with rudimentary navigation, cross forests and deserts on horses and camels, run the gauntlet of Greek pirates, Albanian brigands, Arab marauders, Catalan adventurers, Turkic cavalry, Saracens of the Holy Land and, if he chose to go on the rampage again, Tamerlane and his Mongols. It was hardly safe travelling in Italy, what with the riff-raff of the Guelph and Ghibelline wars who terrorised the countryside.

Martino came from a family of lawyers and priests – his brother was a bishop - and hoped that his sons would follow in their learned footsteps. But Plague took them before they knew their Latin. Every day Martino went to the chapel of the family home, where they were buried, and remonstrated with Catherine for not taking him instead of them, as he had implored her when they fell sick. Although she was still of an age to do so, their mother had no desire to replace them, preferring to bring her sewing into the chapel and talk to them and placate the urges of the flesh with sweet pastry.

Martino had known Catherine longer than any other woman, since his mother had died giving birth to him. Born in Alexandria in about 290, she was a daughter of the governor of Egypt. When she was eighteen years old, during the persecutions of the Emperor Maximinus, she had an intense vision of the risen Christ and consummated a mystical marriage with Him. When the emperor ordered fifty pagan philosophers to convince her of her error, many were won over by her arguments and consequently put to death. The same fate befell the Empress and the commander-in-chief of the army.

The emperor ordered Catherine to be tied to the rim of a spiked wheel but it was smashed by a thunderbolt. She was beheaded instead. Her severed body poured out milk, before being whisked away by angels to Mount Sinai, the sacred mountain where Moses talked with the burning bush. Two hundred years later the location of her head and left hand, still wearing the wedding ring Christ gave her, was revealed to a hermit in a dream. Emperor Justinian built a monastery on Sinai to house them, which, by the order of the Prophet Mohammed, has been left unharmed by Muslims to this day.

So in June 1394 Martino set off for Gaeta, the nearest port. Five ships were bound for Alexandria with pilgrims to the Holy Land. Their first taste of danger was from Catalan warships besieging the fortress that guarded the Straits of Messina, between Sicily and the mainland, so they went round the west of the island. Two days out they saw a *Fata Morgana*, a mirage of palaces, turrets and towers, named after Morgan Le Fay, the half sister of King Arthur. Embellished over time and distance from their northern French origins, the legends of King Arthur had become fantastical tales of chivalry and magic. The Italian Morgana became a sorceress, temptress and seductress. Some pilgrims mistook the mirage of her palace for the Heavenly City of Jerusalem and fell down on their knees to give thanks for the miraculous transportation to their destination. The sailors mocked them and someone sang a *cantaro* about Morgana's magical castle on Mount Etna, where she imprisoned knights to seduce them.

Three weeks later they rounded Cape Matapan, at the southern tip of the Peloponnese, and were struck by a summer gale from the north – what the Italians call *borea*, from the Greek for north, and the Greeks call *melteme*, from the Italian for bad weather. Martino found a corner in which to cower and weep, to ask God for forgiveness and commend to Him his soul. He was not encouraged to see the sailors equally terrified.

After two days they headed eastwards across the Aegean and turned south for Alexandria, where they arrived on 25 July, five weeks after leaving Italy. Martino was anxious to find sites associated with Catherine - her house, the prison, the emperor's palace, the execution ground. There was no shortage of guides to show them, for a handsome fee, with a True Fragment Of Catherine's Wheel thrown in. They left the Hellenistic past and Coptic present of Alexandria and sailed up the Nile to Cairo. They toured the Ancient Egyptian sites of the city but did not venture to the 'granaries of Pharaoh' as the pyramids were known, since Arabs were raiding the outskirts of the city. Instead the pilgrims were occupied with assembling supplies, camels and armed escorts for their journey east across the desert to Sinai.

They travelled at night, fearful of Bedouin tribesmen and renegade Crusaders, kicking mules and biting camels, scorpions and snakes, sandstorms and quick sands, fever and thirst, dysentery and sunstroke. During sweltering days and sleepless nights of tedium and discomfort, punctuated by moments of terror, the pilgrims fortified themselves with prayer and hymns and lives of the saints. They also told jokes and stories and sang more poems about King Arturo and his knights and their devotion to a virtuous and beautiful lady.

After seven days they arrived at Saint Catherine's monastery. They kissed icons, touched relics, prayed, watched and fasted. They marvelled at lamps fed by oil from olives brought every year in their beaks by a pilgrimage of birds; the bush that burned for Moses and the stream that sprang out of the rock that he struck with his staff; the vine planted by John the Baptist; the head of Saint Catherine wrapped in the bloody cloth in which the angels carried it to Sinai. The abbot rubbed her arm bone with a silver stick to bring out sweet-smelling balm to anoint the pilgrims. At the end of their stay they were given a wooden ring as a memento of the Bride of Christ. Martino slipped it on his finger and dedicated himself to her for as long as he should live.

From Sinai they went north-east to Bethlehem and arrived in Jerusalem at the end of September. Martino visited the great sites of Christendom: the stone manger, the garden of Gethsemane, the Holy Sepulchre. At the end of October he left the Holy Land from the port of Jaffa in the hope of being home by Christmas. The best he could find was a passage to Greece.

In Athens Martino drank from the fountain that had given Aristotle his wisdom; he saw the sign of the cross traced by Saint Denis on the pillar to which he was manacled at the moment of Christ's death when the whole world shook; he touched the gates of Troy which were now the doors of the church of the Blessed Virgin inside the Parthenon; he prayed before the icon of the Virgin painted by Saint Luke and brought to Athens by an angel.

Did Martino *believe* these stories? If he could believe in the incarnation of God as man, the turning of water into wine, the healing of the blind, the raising of Lazarus, the Resurrection, it was a small step to believing in the miracles of Catherine and the other wonders, angels and demons of the Gospels, the Acts and the Lives of the Saints. If he accepted the miracles of the Bible he had no intellectual basis to reject the magic, wizards and dragons of myth and romance. Before the ages of discovery, reason and science he lived in the age of allegory. His world was explained in stories and poetry. If he denied them he denied his humanity and its part in the world.

Martino's plan was to travel west from Athens to Corinth but the way was blocked by the armies of the sons-in-law of the late Duke of Athens, who were at war over their inheritance. So travellers went east to the city of Negropont on the island of Euboea, where they hoped to find a ship to take them round the Peloponnese and up the Adriatic to Venice. They travelled by night from fortress to fortress until one morning, as the sun rose over the mountains, they looked down on the bay of Aulis, the Euripos strait and the walled city of ancient Chalcis, then known as Negropont. Which is where this story finally begins.

Chalcis
J. M. W. Turner

NEGROPONT

While we were not listening to Martino's tale, since it was inserted some time after our journey, the rain stopped. It was still overcast and misty and the road had turned into hasty pudding but we were anxious to continue on our way in the hope of better lodgings than the cyclops and his ruin could provide.

All our party was subdued by the dismal day, colouring it with their own private thoughts. Even the Greeks were quiet. Higgins resorted to the old soldier's facility of sleeping in the saddle. What dreams did he inhabit? The polluted house of his childhood? The charnel-house of war? The dissecting house, the bawdy house, the molly house? What night demons, incubi and succubi did he consort with? Or was it a gentler world, safe for the innocent child he once was? From the way he lolled and snored and dribbled it suited him, wherever he was.

My tutor continued to take refuge in the mists of his Lelantine plain. Poor Winstanley. He should have stayed at home. The Greece he inhabited in his scholarly mind, in which Homer flowed straight into Paul, was far different from the Greece, in whose mud he now floundered: where mosques and synagogues and monasteries shared space with temples and basilicas; where Jews claimed primacy of Greekness over Christians; where Muslims took Aristotle's Euripos Channel as their own; where peris and djinns took over the haunts of nymphs and dryads. Like the Chorbaji he lived in two different worlds that occupied the same space and time. I have no time for professors and preachers who harp on about heroic deeds and apostolic acts and other fairy fantasies but poor Winstanley struggled to accommodate them with the present.

For my own part, in harmony with our dreary surroundings, I slumped in the saddle and wallowed in the despondency of exile. It was at these times that I paid the price of rescue from the sharks of the gaming table and the vultures of the courts. I pictured my dear father, ruddy eyed with brandy, and my dear mother, milky-eyed with gin, and wondered how they thought I would be reformed by hardship, abstinence and Greek, when they saw it had not worked at school. My talent was for pleasure and society, for gambling and the sex.

"Why do you cover your ears, Lord Exford?" asked Amelia, yanking me into the present like a salmon from the water.

"What?" I replied, loading this little word with surprise at the impudence of the question, resentment at the intrusion into my meditations, incomprehension of what she was saying.

"When you are disturbed, or disconcerted, or distracted, you cover an ear."

Proving her point, I involuntarily put my right hand to my ear.

"You invariably do so when speaking to me. And you take great pains to hide your ears under your hair."

Blood runs down my skin, warm blood, my blood. I feel it pulsing from the vein; Barber Botcherby wipes his knife on his apron, the knife he uses to castrate our piglets and toss the balls to the boar to eat. He stands over me, wiping wiping, wiping; then the iron gimlet from the fire, red hot; Dr. Spidgeon and my father hold me down; a cotton gag between my teeth; the hiss of iron on blood; the smell of burning flesh. Then the same on the other side. A week later the fever breaks, the delusions, vanish, headache goes. Spidgeon is vindicated, his innovative intervention lauded. I am a specimen, a freak, fingered and flaunted to the piss prophets of the county

"Ear spiders, Madam. Crawl in at night, they nest, they make their young, they torment with their spinning and jiggling. Come out to catch mites and fleas for their dinner. Never block their passage: for they will go in, not out, and feed on brain juice; grow fat; murder their rivals; one giant spider left in your skull to rule your dreams ..."

This nonsense shut her up. She took a book from a saddlebag and began to read as comfortably as in a library armchair. If this was intended as a squib it misfired. When a lady brings out a book in mixed company it is an action of unequal effect: for her it is a snub, for the gentleman a favour. Her book was Italian and not a work of Natural Philosophy: the title included the word *Historia*, but I could not discover more without expressing an interest, and thereby giving value to her snub. But she had done her worst: I lapsed back into a bitter reverie, in which, with the most agonising slowness, Doctor Spidgeon and Barber Botcherby were impaled by Turkish mutes.

By narrative coincidence we arrived in sight of the city of Egripos, the former Negropont, at the same time as Martino's tale is due to resume. Our road took us uphill towards a castle looming out of the greyness. As we crested the rise the mist cleared and there was the ancient city illuminated with an effect I have not seen before or since. The sky above us remained covered in black thundercloud, while the horizon all round was clear. The westering sun appeared in this bright band and lit the scene with the colour of red gold.

"The lofty towers of wide-extended Troy," exclaimed Winstanley.

"The City of Midas," I countered, to show off the little classical learning I possessed, concerning the king, who turned whatever he touched into gold.

"Why, can you see his ears?" said Amelia, with malice. I struggled not to touch my own, while trying to remember the story of how Apollo gave him ass's ears for eavesdropping.

"It must be copper not gold," said Winstanley, and waited for us to beg an explanation from his fund of erudition. We did not give him the satisfaction, which unfortunately did not deter him.

"The ancient name of the city is Chalcis, which means copper. This place was a main source of the metal for Greeks and then Rome."

Why do we need to know these things? Why do we clutter our minds? Why do travellers let themselves be bombarded with miscellaneous facts; if they are indeed facts, and not worthless souvenirs of spurious knowledge invented by native guides and bought by foreigners to justify the inconvenience and expense of travel?

Under a leaden sky all the bright metals and their alloys were smithied together in a glowing panorama: the gilded city crowned a headland with a perfect ring of crenellated walls, punctuated with towers; it was divided by the narrow Euripos from the Beotian mainland and skirted on either side by the platinum waters of the Gulfs of Volos and Euboea. The landward side was further protected with a moat, bridged in three places. The fourth entrance was via the bridge across the Euripos from Beotia, interrupted by the citadel. Within its walls the town piling up to a palace in the middle was much as Martino saw it, except that campaniles and fluttering pennants were now replaced by pointed minarets and glittering crescents.

Outside the walls beyond the moat on the landward side spread the suburb, larger than the city, where Christians lived in white-painted houses around the cupolas of their churches. To the north were the shadows of distant mountains. On the Beotian side of the bay rose a steep hill dominated by the bronze fortress of Karababa, built by Turks after they took the city and therefore unknown to Martino. It looked down on the Euripos below and its Arthurian citadel. Beyond Karababa was Mount Messapo, a sharp pointed pyramid of rock. This was doubtless the mountain where, according to Ali Veri Bey, there was a cave of Pan with its vine and goat skulls. To the south was the bay of Aulis and the little inlet of Bourkos, where ships were moored or beached on the shore. We strained to see our own but to us one mast looked much like another.

We were anxious to reach the city but our Turkish companions told us that the gates were closed punctually at sunset and we would therefore have to look for accommodation in the Christian quarter, where we would be robbed. It was better to wait until morning. Our Christian companions told us that the city was ridden with plague and that we would be better in their quarter where the air was fresher. Rabbi Koen offered us his home but that was also within the walls. So we decided to pass the night in the place where we stood, which was called Kastri, after the ruined castle on the hill, where we were able to lay our beds.

Ali provided his usual services in the form of a dozen partridges skewered over the fire. We sat on the curtain wall of the castle to admire the panorama; fiery bats darted round us, the chatelaine owl abandoned us on burning wings; the city floated in a blaze of light, then foundered in the grey of night. From these lyrical observations you will conclude that we were enjoying the first heady puffs of the Bey's tobacco.

As to stories, here's the rest of Martino.

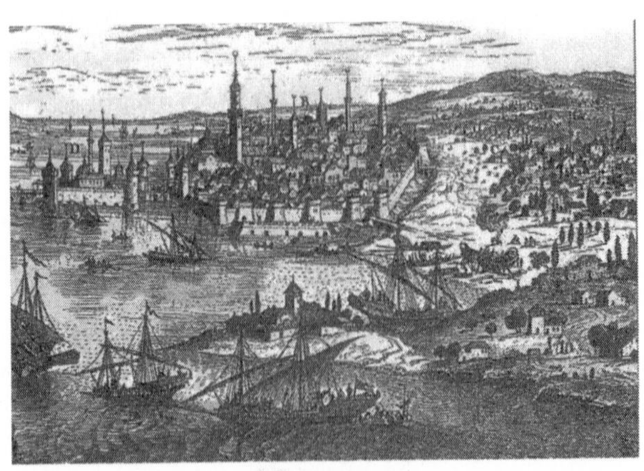

Negropont

GALVANO

Of all the places he visited Martino warmed to Negropont the most. Half the population was Latin, everyone spoke Italian of one kind or another, and the Roman church under the bishop of Chalcis was the main religion. He stayed at the house of Gianluca Sforzero, an Italian merchant, who had a beautiful wife and three children. They introduced him to the best society and for the first time in his life Martino tasted celebrity. He was no longer the pot-bellied, pasty-faced lawyer. He was lean and tanned and muscled and fit, his eyes still myopic but bright. His hair and beard were bleached by the rigours of the journey and cropped short, like those of a man of action. His lawyer's gown and schoolman's cap and velvet slippers had been exchanged for leather jerkin and breeches, wide-brimmed hat and traveller's cloak. He carried a dagger in his belt with the ease of a man prepared to use it and an iron-tipped staff instead of an ivory-handled cane. He had the easy manners of someone who has kept company with men of different classes, races and religions. He had the humility of someone who knows the limits of his courage and the self-assurance of one who has been tested to them.

Above all he had traveller's tales and a way of telling them that enthralled his audience. He had not forgotten his lawyer's rhetoric or his skill in pleading a case. He was precise, factual and credible. He looked instinctively for the salient point and the telling phrase and avoided the flamboyance and exaggeration of tavern raconteurs. At the same time, the company of travellers had stripped him of the long windedness, pedantry and waspishness of his profession. Above all, he had good stories to tell of danger and adventure. Accustomed to the lawyerly role of adviser, commentator, minute-taker, advocate, he was now the principal and enjoyed being the centre of attention. Ladies especially liked listening to Martino. They gasped, they sighed, they blanched at his exploits and, far from despising his confessions of weakness and terror, they warmed to him. He warmed to them too. He wrote in his journal that 'This town has notable and rich men and beautiful women. I believe that the women, successors of the nymphs who lived in the ancient castle, are in general of outstanding beauty and grace and dress beautifully, in the Italian fashion.'

The name of his host's wife was Flaminia. She took him to see the sights of Negropont. She showed him the footprint of Saint Paul in the rock where he landed on his flight from Thessalonica and the stone with strange carvings left behind by Marco Polo on his return home to Venice. The greatest curiosity was the narrow strait of the Euripos, whose waters changed direction without apparent cause and often ran both ways at once. A castle rose up from a small island in the middle of the channel. It was connected to the shore on either side by wooden drawbridges. The road from one shore to the other passed through a vaulted stone tunnel underneath the keep. Long swallow-tailed pennants streamed bravely from four turrets at each corner, tall and slender like minarets Martino had seen in the Holy Land, while the roof was pitched and steep, more typical of the Loire than the Euripos. It was a castle from a book of legends.

Flaminia's father was a *guardiano,* one of four honorary wardens of the castle, and entitled to a chamber at the top of one of the towers. In theory he was expected to keep watch for enemies, but the post was honorific and the real guarding work was done by sentries, whose quarters were in the body of the castle above the gate. He no longer had the legs to climb the tower and Flaminia kept the key to the room, which she had furnished with hangings and a couch. Her husband did not know about her secret boudoir.

From the turret room Martino and his charming guide looked out on the battlements of the castle, the walls and roofs, towers and belfries of the town, the gardens and orchards of the suburbs, the mountains of Beotia and Negropont, the gulfs of Euboea and Aulis that met in the turbulent channel of the Euripos. This had been the scene of many incidents of chivalry. On the plain to the south of the city the Dukes of Athens and Thebes had hosted a famous tournament in honour of Sir Lancelot. Further south still, in the Black Mountains, were still to be seen the lairs of dragons that Sir Galahad had slain. Most remarkable of all was the very castle in which they now stood. It had been built by King Arturo's sister, the witch Morgana, to imprison her lovers. The Euripos, which in those days was a gentle and regular current, made a natural moat. To make it more impregnable Morgana bewitched the water, making it rush this way and that so that when the drawbridges were raised it was impossible to cross by boat or by magic. As for swimming across, better try the Hellespont: no sooner had you made headway against the flood than it swept you in the opposite direction or, worse still, straight to the bottom and spat you out in the middle of the bay.

The window onto these marvels was narrow and Flaminia pressed close to Martino. Her warm breath on his cheek was perfumed with the mastic she tucked under her tongue to produce a fashionable lisp as she whispered old stories in his ear. She told him about Sir Galvano, or Gawain as he is known in the north. Hunting in the forest of Avlona to the west he fought a serpent with fiery breath that smelled of burning violets. Morgana's fairy army came to his rescue and whisked him off to this castle of the Black Bridge, the Negra Ponte. He became her prisoner, unwilling by day when he tried to escape and willing by night when Morgana came to him in the guise of any woman he chose - Helen of Troy, Guinevere of Camelot, the Queen of Sheba.

Flaminia ran a long fingernail down the back of Martino's hand from the wrist to his middle finger and he was lost. All the terror and exhilaration, wonder and exertion, longing and ecstasy of his pilgrimage condensed into her touch and, a few minutes later, erupted between them.

It was the first of many encounters. He was hasty at first and out of practice but she was patient and after a few days took equal pleasure. He asked her what they would do if they had a child. She replied that if it was a boy she would call him Galvano, if a girl Morgana. This was not what concerned him and she told him not to worry. On Sundays, before they went to mass, her husband dutifully knelt to his marital devotions. A child would cause no scandal. To soothe his jealousy she caressed his cheek and told him she would do anything he wished, without inhibition. Martino breathed deep and whispered his desire. She blenched and blushed. She said she had not done that for any man, not even her husband. He retracted, he apologized, he begged her not to think badly of him but she pressed a finger on his lips. Solemnly she unbuttoned her bodice and told him to help but his hands were trembling too much to be of use. Finally she stepped out of her undershift and stood in front of him, simply, her arms at her sides. He gazed at her unblinking and entranced. She was the first woman he had ever seen naked.

She said it was his turn to grant her the same request. He was as disconcerted as she had been. Since infancy no-one had seen him naked: mirrors were rare and he had never even seen himself. His fingers still trembled and she helped him unbutton. He stood naked and erect before her and hot tears poured down his face. He had never felt so vulnerable and so potent, so innocent and so knowing. He took St Catherine's precious wooden ring off his finger and slipped it on hers.

Martino's pilgrimage had come full circle. He had left home to seek salvation for his soul and peace for his mind from Our Lord and his mystical betrothed, Saint Catherine. The dangers and hardships he endured on his journey were as necessary part of his pilgrimage as the goal. They gave him self-knowledge, humility and faith. But there is a third element of pilgrimage that he had neglected: departure. A journey *to* is also a journey *from*. In Islam the first step in the haj is to free yourself from the world you are leaving. You should settle your affairs, pay off your debts, make peace with enemies, apologise to anyone you have offended, say good bye to loved ones as though you will never see them again. Finally, you throw off all your clothes and dress in two white sheets.

In Negropont Martino finally made the departure he should have made when he left home: he broke with his past. Stripped of inhibition, modesty, loyalty to marriage, religious obligation, the morality of his class, devotion to Saint Catherine, entirely stripped of allegory, he surrendered to the moment. He asked for nothing. He wanted nothing. He stood naked in mind and body and soul. It was the beginning of his pilgrimage and the end.

The unmystical betrothal of Flaminia and Martino was the culmination of the affair. They still took pleasure in love but there was nothing more to know. Flaminia told tales of courtly love when they were together but as an incitement, not an enhancement to their lovemaking. Two months after his arrival in Negropont a Venetian ship arrived from Constantinople bound for home. The agony of parting, the pledges of undying faith, the tears and passionate kisses could not disguise his willingness to leave and her willingness to let him go. As the little ship coasted down the Gulf of Euboea he was released from the spell of Morgana's Castle: he was filled with such lightness that it seemed like emptiness.

The journey home had its share of adventures. A storm took away the mast and they put into Zea for repairs. In a calm off Syros they were accosted by a Turkish galley and were saved only by a freshening wind. Anchored in a bay at Kythnos a landing party looking for water had to fight its way back through a band of Skyros pirates. In all these adventures Martino encouraged the other passengers and crew with his calm. He was not so much brave as indifferent. He no longer had anyone to call on for help or anyone to thank for deliverance.

After a month at sea they arrived in Venice. He was fortunate to find a Bishop returning to Naples and joined the party for the dangerous three week journey south. He sent word ahead, rather than arrive unannounced, and looked eagerly for his family among the citizens who came to welcome him home outside the town gates. They broke the news that his brother had been taken by Plague soon after he left and his wife had abandoned hope of seeing him again and died of worry. They were buried in the family chapel. His welcome became a wake. He placed chips off the marble of the Holy Sepulchre in their tombs and, without a glance at the picture of the learned Saint Catherine, locked the chapel and put away the key for good. It was generally assumed that he did so out of grief, which was true, but also out of shame.

The years passed by. He became an old, pasty-faced, pot-bellied lawyer again, living alone, all his family dead. He neglected his friends, his civic responsibilities, his religious duties. His household consisted of Lucia, his sons' old nurse, who looked after the few rooms he lived in, and her husband Franco, who grew vegetables in the otherwise neglected garden. His clients died off or deserted him for more dynamic counsel. He was left with a few lingering cases and some petty property transactions which he did pro bono, or old friends gave him out of sympathy. When he was not dozing in his study he drafted and redrafted his will. He would leave enough to provide for Lucia and Franco in their old age, and money for masses to be said for his wife and sons, but what to do with the rest? There was not enough money in the world to buy his own forgiveness.

One day Martino was nodding off over a bill of sale when Lucia announced a stranger. A young man came into his study, in Venetian dress and his blonde hair in fashionable ringlets. He asked if Martino had ever been to Negropont and, if so, if he had stayed at the house of Gianluca and Flaminia Sforzero. Stricken by memories, Martino could only nod. The young man said the whole family had been taken by Plague the year before. He was the only survivor because his father had sent him to Venice to learn the family trade. This would now be little use to him as his father had left nothing but debts. His mother Flaminia was last to die and, reconciled to her inevitable fate, had written a letter recommending him to Martino, if he was still alive, and enclosing a gift. He handed Martino a small but costly jeweller's box. The old man's hands were shaking, which he blamed on rheumatism, but he refused the young man's offer of help. At last he found the catch and opened the lid. On a velvet mount lay Saint Catherine's wooden ring. He took some moments to recover his composure and at last he told the young man, in a barely audible whisper, that he would give him any assistance he could and that he was welcome to stay for as long as he wished. He asked the boy's name. *Galvano* was the reply.

Martino blamed the rheuminess of age when he wiped his eyes, the pollen of summer when he blew his nose, the thinness of his blood when he called Lucia for wine. Nothing could explain away the light of joy in his face. After dinner, when the rest of the household were sleeping away the afternoon heat, he unearthed the key to the chapel. He prostrated himself in the dust before the painting of Saint Catherine and sobbed out his contrition and his gratitude. He put the wooden ring on his finger and pledged his life to her again.

Martino lived for five happy years. He sent Galvano to Caserte to train in law and took him on as his clerk and then partner. He became active again in the city and the cathedral and the management of his estate. When he died he left everything, except what had been promised to Lucia and Franco, to Galvano, who married and prospered and never went on pilgrimage, not even back to Negropont. Nor did he revert to the name given to him by his father but kept the one his mother told him to use if ever he sought the help of Martino de Nicola.

The Euripos Bridge

VIZIR

In the light of a bright morning the enchanted city we saw from a distance had been spirited away by an *afrit* and replaced with a crumbling relic of past glories. The shimmering walls proved to be clumsily whitewashed, stained and peeling and poorly repaired. We joined a throng flowing in through the narrows of the east gate, where we met a throng ebbing out, a Euripos of jostling travellers. The cause of this commotion was the impending visit of the Lord High Admiral the Captain Pasha. Accommodation was scarce and we were fortunate that the Vizir offered an apartment in the barracks of his residence to the gentlemen of our party. Generous Rabbi Koen invited Amelia to his gynaeceum. Ali and the camel were billeted in a stable in Kastri.

The streets were narrow, twisting and ill-paved. Since Venice relinquished responsibility for the cobbles three hundred years ago, no-one else had taken it up. Rubbish and other effluvia were tipped into open gutters in the middle of the street, providing a living for packs of stray dogs. The bazaar was a gloomy catacomb, reeking of incense and spices and damp, where lifeless men sat cross legged and heaped about with grave goods. The mosque of Emir Zade was a Turkish construction but the other six mosques of the walled city were Christian basilicas adorned with minarets. Next to the mosque was a cemetery, ringed with gloomy cypresses, that doubled as the city park. The houses were built in wood on whatever stone walls had survived the siege and sack of the city three centuries before; their balconies overhung the streets, shutting out the sun. Most windows were barred and shuttered, and those that were open were fenced with grilles to keep out fresh air and insolent glances. By all accounts it was an airless and fetid place in high summer and those who had them moved to houses at the seaside. Even on a late spring day a miasma of lifeless melancholy and decay hung over it.

Turkish gentlemen walked about these streets in the finest silks and furs like flies on a dunghill, born of it, feeding from it, ready to fly from it. They do not take care of public places but beautify the interiors of their houses for their own benefit. As we pressed through them they treated us foreigners with a combination of curiosity and contempt expressed in the catcalls and curses of the boys who followed us. We saw few women. They were deliberately ignored, veiled from head to toe, black ghosts flitting about their private business.

The Vizir's residence was the former Loggia of the Venetians. Like the rest of the city, the fabric was in disrepair. The main part of the building gave onto the square and contained the public apartments of the Vizir. In the centre of the facade was a portico, still adorned with the lion and standard of St Mark, topped by an arcade with five arches where the governor could show himself to the people in the square below. Through the archway was a paved courtyard formed by the other three wings of the Loggia, one of which was given over to the Vizir's harem. A second wing was for functionaries, servants and kitchens. The third was stables and quarters of the janissary guard, where we were lodged. Making the corner of the harem and the Vizir's apartments was a stone tower, intended as the last refuge of the inhabitants in times of war and a prison in times of peace. All round the first floor was a stone built gallery with a tile roof and round arches, enclosed on the harem wing with wooden grilles.

We had hardly dismounted when the Greek Grammaticos, or secretary, of the Vizir, invited us to pay our respects to his master. We demurred, being travel stained and needing a rest before the ordeal of a formal reception. The overruling of our objections by the Grammaticos and his bristling escort of janissaries was more like an arrest than an invitation. At the door to the audience chamber he told us to take off our shoes, make three bows and kneel to kiss the slipper of our host. I replied that we were English gentlemen and had no intention of sharing the daily humiliations of his own position but would greet his master as we would a distinguished minister at home. Which we did.

The Vizir was not at all put out by our lack of oriental ceremony. He sat on his divan surrounded by his Turks in office and waited on by a pretty boy in classic Greek dress, whose main function, I suspected, was not the most honourable. Behind him was his standard, with three horse tails hanging from the cross piece, the symbol of his rank. With a gesture he offered the sofa on his right. He wanted to know the reasons for our visit and seemed sceptical about our interest in ancient sites. Turks have no appreciation of Classical learning, with which I entirely sympathise. He asked if we had a firman from the Porte in Constantinople to inspect the fortifications. I replied that we had no interest in military matters and, if he provided us a guide, we would look at no more than he wished us to look at. I gave him a Brummagem silver pistol, the most decorative and the most inaccurate of our arsenal, for which he was duly grateful and reciprocated with a long embroidered towel. Then followed the tedious ceremonial of incense and rosewater and coffee and pipes.

So here was the latest in the line of Chalcidians and Macedonians, Romans and Byzantines, Franks and Venetians; the Muslim successor to pagans and Jews and Isis worshippers, Christians of Byzantium and Catholics of Venice; heir to the hoplites and legionaries, crusaders and condottieri, who had plundered the city; successor to the archons, tyrants, consuls, seigneurs, baillies, and pashas who had bled it. Who would be his heirs one day? Russians perhaps, or French? Or even loyal subjects of King George, God bless him? Certainly not Greeks, who had neither the means nor the spirit to take back what their ancient forebears had lost.

How then did a Turkish pasha come to be sitting in the palace of the Venetians? You can read about it while the rest of us settle into our lodgings and wash away the dust of travel.

Divan
Jean Brindesi

AITHERAS

In 1469 Senator Paolo Erizzo was appointed Governor, or Baillie, of Negropont. This honour was the culmination of his career. The island, known as 'the key to the empire', was wealthy and strategically positioned in the Aegean, between Venice and Crete and close to the mainland of Greece. The flag of Negropont flew in St. Mark's Square. At the banquet given for his departure Paolo was smugly self-deprecating while his daughter, who was going with him as the Lady Governor, was radiantly self-possessed.

She was as beautiful as her mother, who had died two years before, and as clever as her father. She was baptised Anna but thought this was an ordinary name and preferred to be called Ariela, after the heroine of one of her favourite romances. She was sixteen years old but her father treated her as a grown woman, indulging her to the limits of what was proper. They took the promenade together in the Piazza and she was his consort at public and social functions. He let her decide about proposals of marriage from even the best families, all of which she had so far declined, to his selfish satisfaction. He allowed her to read instead of embroider, learn Greek instead of sew. Had he known about her secret library of Alexander romances, Petrarch's love sonnets and Boccaccio's Decameron he might not have been so liberal. She was an expert in every aspect of love except the practicalities, for which she looked forward to a suitable opportunity.

The voyage was uneventful. The fleet of war galleys, well armed against the Turkish navy, Algerian slavers and Greek pirates, under the command of its new Captain-General Nicolo da Canal processed down the Adriatic. Paolo paid his respects to the Venetian cities of Dalmatia and Illyria, Corfu, the Cycladic islands, and Candia, the capital of the powerful island of Crete. There was more to these visits than pomp and ceremony. They demonstrated the resolve of Venice to defend its possessions against the Ottomans and gave Paolo first hand experience of the realities of governorship. He realised that the weakest links in the defence of the empire were its Greek subjects. Only in places like Tinos and Syros did their conversion to Rome seem whole-hearted. Elsewhere they paid lip-service to Holy Mother Church while hiding their priests and practising their liturgies behind closed doors. The Venetian bishops pleaded for more vigorous repression of Orthodoxy while the generals argued for more tolerance. They feared that, as had already happened elsewhere, Greeks would side with the Ottomans, who had reinstated the Orthodox Patriarch in Constantinople.

Meanwhile Latins and Greeks alike were won over by Ariela's innocent beauty, her vivacity, her intelligence. She declined proposals of marriage from the most distinguished knights in each place, not only Venetian but Burgundian, Catalan and Genoese, whose families had remained when Venice took over. Paolo was not unhappy. Although it could not go on forever it did his political position no harm to be courted by the best families in the Christian Aegean.

At the end of 1469 Paolo and his daughter arrived at their capital, also called Negropont like the island, to the congratulation of Venetians and the indifference of Greeks. The town was separated from the mainland of Beotia by a narrow strait called the Euripos. In the middle of the Euripos was a citadel. A wooden swing bridge crossed to the mainland.

A stone bridge crossed to the walled city, called the Kastro. The Venetians lived inside the walls with the Jews. The Greeks lived outside.

A few days after they had explored the Kastro and the palace, or Loggia as the Venetians called it, Ariela and her maid Beatrice, escorted by two Italian guards, ventured across the stone bridge, through the twin gate houses of the fort and across the swing bridge to the far shore of the Euripos. It was a fine autumn day. The girls skipped onto the narrow beach, slipped off their shoes and paddled in the water, squealing and laughing at the chill. They did not see a young man run down the bank towards them and nor, to their discredit, did the guards, until he was upon them.

"Ladies," he shouted in heavily accented Venetian, "don't go in the water. It's very dangerous."

The guards seized him, swords drawn. He did not resist but gazed into Ariela's dark eyes. He was a year or two older. With jet black hair curling around a pale face, straight Grecian nose, strong chin and girlish lips, he looked like the miniature of the handsome Adonis that she kept in her secret library. She gazed into his dark eyes.

"Don't be afraid. I am Aitheras the grandson of Pyrrhas, the fire artificer of the castle."

"We are Venetians. We know the dangers of water."

"Lady, this is no ordinary water. Once it was a natural stream. Then Dark Aphrodite – you call her Venus - waited here for her secret lover Ares – you call him Mars - while he helped Chalcis – you call it Negropont – make war on Eretria – you call it Panormia. "

"Venetians know all about your myths."

"Dark Aphrodite was walking where you are walking now. The passing water was so amazed at her beauty that it rushed back for another look. And forward. And back. Water piled on water, anxious to see her. That is why, without warning, the tides flow violently both ways at once. You must be careful here or you may be swept off your feet."

"Thank you for your advice. I shall not be swept off my feet. Why do you call her Dark Aphrodite?"

"Because she is honoured in the dark, out of sight of other people. Don't Venetians know all about this?"

For the first time their eyes broke contact as she turned her back on him to hide her blushes.

"My father is waiting for me," she said and "let him go," to her escort, and, over her shoulder, in heavily accented Greek, so they would not understand, "save me again tomorrow." Aitheras smiled and something stabbed her in the chest.

Delicious and agonising days followed; 'chance' meetings, glimpses, glances, coy smiles and blushes; poems and love letters crafted, re-crafted and torn up; troubled nights and restless daydreams. The maid Beatrice was first to see through them and became confidante, go-between and easy-going chaperone. She was twenty one years old and experienced in such things, especially the pitfalls lying in wait for young virgins, but her better judgement was clouded by her own growing affair with another handsome Greek called Proteas, an interpreter to the Governor's court. They progressed from the catch in the throat and the burning glance to more tangible pleasures faster than the first-time lovers.

Erizzo himself did not keep the fatherly eye on Ariela that he did in Venice. There was little time for private life. Venetian spies in Constantinople had sent back intelligence of war preparations, including the assembly of a large fleet. A sea-borne invasion could only mean an attack on the Venetian empire in the Aegean. Byzantium had already fallen with the taking of Constantinople seventeen years earlier, and with it the better part of the Greek mainland. Wealthy Negropont was a tempting prize, as was Candia and even Venice itself. There were many other islands still under Venetian rule but none that warranted an invasion fleet. Venice ordered its governors to prepare their defences and mustered a battle fleet of her own at Skiathos, to counter-attack wherever the Turks struck.

In March 1470, when the winter weather improved, Erizzo left his quartermaster to prepare for a siege of his capital and set off with his military commander, Captain Luigi Calvo, on a tour of the island's defences. He sailed south, calling on all his fortresses and towers, as far as the great castle of Karystos that commanded the Gulf of Euboea. His strategy was to leave them with skeleton garrisons and enough supplies for a month's siege and to order any surplus men and material to the capital. The main function of the outposts was to man the beacons that would signal an invasion and report its progress to the waiting fleet. As for defending his subjects, they would have to take their chances and pray the attack fell on Candia.

Meanwhile, with the collusion of Beatrice, whose head was spinning with love for Proteas, and took every opportunity to requite it, Ariela met Aitheras in her room overlooking the Euripos. At first they played like children, giggling and teasing and snatching kisses. Then less like children, gazing at each other in wonder and delight at each new discovery. At last they were man and woman. There were no mysteries any more. They no longer lived in the present like children but stood on the threshold between past and future, heirs of past generations and responsible for those to come.

In April the Turkish fleet set sail from the Dardanelles. Captain-General da Canal took his own fleet of fifty galleys to meet it off the east coast of Negropont. He was dismayed to count more than four hundred enemy ships and hid behind the island of Skyros. Instead of continuing due south to Candia, the Turks rounded Cape Oro into the Gulf of Euboea. Over the next four weeks they landed thirty thousand troops and captured all the coastal fortresses from Karystos in the south to Vassilika in the north, ten miles from the capital. The beacons announced their arrival and then went dark. The garrisons surrendered, or were betrayed, and were enslaved in the galleys or the field kitchens, according to their sex. As Paolo had feared, most of the Greeks sided with the Turkish liberators.

Worse was to come. News arrived that a second army of two hundred thousand men was marching from Thebes to join the invasion. It was led by none other than the Sultan himself, Mehmet the Conqueror. The moment of terror that gripped Paolo when he heard this turned to a craving for glory. He would be known in history as the man who conquered the Conqueror and saved the empire. He knew his enemy first hand. He was an ambassador to Constantinople when it fell to Mehmet and had himself led an unsuccessful sortie to disable the great siege gun, The Imperial, that eventually battered down the walls. He had no illusions about the challenge ahead of him, only about his ability to meet it.

His subjects were less keen to write his place in history with their blood. The Greeks of the capital melted away to join their compatriots in the Sultan's army or to tend the farms that fed the invaders. Jews were ordered to abandon their ghetto beside the south wall so the defences could be strengthened. Only those who had been compromised by serving the Venetians too well or converting to Rome or saw no point in exchanging one despot for another, remained inside the walls.

One evening after a council of war, Paolo called on his daughter in her apartment. He was surprised to find her undressed for bed so early.

"My dove, are you out of sorts?"

"No Papa, I am very well." But there was a catch in her voice and she looked flushed.

"You are not frightened, are you?"

"Of course not Papa, you are here." In fact she was terrified since a half naked Aitheras was behind the curtain.

"My dove, the last ship leaves for Venice tomorrow. By nightfall the Sultan's army will have closed the Gulf." The Ottoman fleet already occupied the bay of Aulis to the south of the bridge. North of the bridge the Gulf of Volos was unoccupied but land cannons on the Theban side could effectively close it.

"What is that to me?"

"You should be on it. Many women and children have already left."

"Are you afraid for me?"

He forced a laugh. "Not at all. Victory is our destiny. Still, this is no place for a young girl."

"I will shout to the sky that my love will keep me by your side, whatever may happen to us." For 'sky' she used the old word Aither, which her father assumed was to give poetic force to her declaration. He took her in his arms and kissed her on the mouth.

"Fame will be yours too," he whispered as gently she pushed him away.

The last galley left for Venice and the Sultan's army reached the shore of the Euripos. He ordered a pontoon bridge built across the narrowest part of the Gulf of Volos and a hundred thousand men crossed onto the island, surrounding the city from the north and meeting up with the sea-borne army at Vassilika. As he had done years ago at Constantinople he had a third of his fleet dragged on log rollers overland from the Gulf of Euboea to the Gulf of Volos. Three hundred thousand men and four hundred ships completely surrounded the city and its garrison of forty thousand.

Mehmet sent an ambassador to Paolo to guarantee the Venetians safe conduct in exchange for surrender. When the ambassador, a Florentine convert to Islam, was escorted into the Governor's hall he was surprised to find a beautiful young woman seated beside him. Distracted by her, he stumbled over the words of his ultimatum, so he sounded even more untrustworthy than a Florentine usually sounded to a Venetian.

"The Sultan and all his army and all his ships will let us leave unharmed, you say? What guarantee do we have of this?" asked Paolo.

"The promise of an Emperor needs no guarantee. His Highness keeps his word to the very letter," said the ambassador.

"And for this we have the word of a renegade. And a Florentine." The ambassador's hand instinctively went for the dagger in his belt. "Tell your master that my honour and the honour of Venice are one and indivisible. I will be sawn in half before I will surrender either. An Erizzo keeps his word. And his faith, Signor."

The ambassador gave a curt bow, turned on his heel and walked out without a word.

The siege began with skirmishes, cavalry attacks and sorties, more to test the defences than with any hope of a resolution. As the Sultan himself approached, fear whispered through the city. Paolo took to walking on the battlements and in the squares with his daughter, gossiping and laughing as cheerfully as though they were in Saint Mark's Square. Their insouciance was infectious and stiffened the resolve of the defenders. Still, it was an ominous day when the Sultan's standard was seen on the hill of Artemis barely out of gunshot range of the city.

Paolo was sure that the great siege gun, The Imperial, could not be far behind. It could fire a ball weighing a thousand pounds and had breached the massive walls of Constantinople. If Mehmet was allowed to fire it at the walls of Negropont the city was doomed. Paolo had to break the siege. The Turkish fleet was split between the Gulf of Euboea and the Gulf of Volos. Da Canal was still outnumbered in the Gulf of Volos but his galleys were better armed and their crews better trained than Turkish landlubbers and Christian slaves. Combined with a sortie from the city they could open up the Gulf for reinforcements and a counter invasion from Candia. Paolo gave orders for fire ships to be built - rafts loaded with straw - to attack from behind.

But there was still no sign of da Canal's galleys or any message from him. Three times Paolo sent messengers to him. Each one was brought back by his captors and impaled on the opposite bank of the Euripos, at night, when he could not be seen by sharp shooters from the battlements, and left to shriek and moan until a lucky shot delivered him. So Paolo was surprised when one of his interpreters, a Greek called Proteas, volunteered to try again. Paolo was sceptical. Never trust a Greek, he remembered.

"You saw what happened to the others. What makes you think you can succeed?"

"They were foreigners, Sir. Venetians. I am from Negropont. I have family and friends. If I am captured and questioned I will say I am a deserter who has left your service, like so many others."

"You are a Greek. Why are you doing this for Venice? Why not join your countrymen in the pay of the pashas?"

"I love a lady in your service, Sir."

Paolo made enquiries and learned that Proteas was intelligent and diligent and loyal and that his lover was his daughter's maid. "What have we got to lose, except an interpreter?" he said to his Captain. Proteas took a passionate farewell of Beatrice and slipped out of the city at midnight.

The next morning, after the dawn prayer and breakfast, an aga of the janissaries came to the Sultan's war tent and said that a Greek from the city wished to see him with important information. Despite every threat he refused to divulge it to anyone else.

"Where did you capture him?"

"He gave himself up, your Highness."

The Sultan and his retinue went outside where Proteas was prostrate on the ground between two janissaries. On the aga's signal they hoisted him to his feet.

"Your Highness, I wish to be of service. I am sent by Paolo Erizzo the Governor of the city to find Captain-General da Canal and order him to attack at once. He has prepared fire ships and artillery with fire-bombs. His men will sortie to the south and take Vassilika."

"Why have you disturbed me with this? We know it from the others. Deal with him as usual."

"Sir, that is not all. Let me go to Captain-General da Canal. Let me say that Erizzo orders him not to attack. That the walls are breached, hope is lost and he is about to surrender. That he should sail immediately to the defence of Candia."

"Why should the Captain-General believe you?"

"I have a seal and a password."

"Which is?"

"Ariela. The name of Erizzo's daughter."

"My ambassador told me about her. A most beautiful woman. And you? What do you want from your betrayal?"

"Ariela's maid Beatrice. Let her join me to prosper in your service."

The Sultan stroked his beard and looked at Proteas, weighing him and his words. The aga on his right whispered in his ear. 'It is a trick. This man wants safe passage through our lines so he can deliver the order to attack. I say we impale him like the others.' The aga on his left whispered in his ear. This man is a Greek. The Greeks hate the Catholics. His plan is good. It will buy us time while we bring the cannon. I say we risk it.' The Sultan looked at Proteas. Then he took a purse of gold from his sash.

"Proteas, your idea is excellent. We accept it. Here is your reward."

With a glance at the janissary by his side he tossed the purse on the ground. As Proteas bent over to pick it up the janissary whipped up his scimitar and with lightning speed cut his head off with a single slice. It rolled along the ground as the Sultan and his agas skipped out of the way of the spurts of blood from the trunk. The Sultan went over to the head and delicately rolled it over with the turned-up toe of his slipper. Proteas looked up at him, wide-eyed.

"Don't be surprised. You died rich in my service." The executioner prized the purse from Proteas's clenched fingers and handed it to the Sultan, who opened it and gave back a coin. Then he spoke to his agas.

"You are both right. It could have been a trick. But it is a good plan. Send a man with the message to the Captain-General with Erizzo's seal and the password Ariela."

The agas carried out his instructions, admiring once again their Sultan's ruthless guile.

As night fell Paolo and his officers waited for their latest messenger to re-appear on a stake. Beatrice was in church, on her knees before Our Lady, confessing her sin and bargaining her future chastity for the life of Proteas. Ariela and Aitheras watched from the window of her room. Below them was the ancient bay of Aulis, crowded with ships, and the Beotian shore covered in the camp fires and tents of the Sultan's army.

"It is the biggest fleet Aulis has seen since the Greeks sailed for Troy. Now Troy has come back for revenge," said Aitheras.

"It looks so festive."

"Why did your father not insist on sending you away?"

"My duty is here."

"Is that his idea or yours?"

"Mine. I am not a child. I am an Erizzo. We serve our republic."

"The leader of the Greeks, Agamemnon, sacrificed his daughter Iphigenia in that grove of pines on the hill, where the Sultan sits now."

"Why did he do such a thing?"

"The Greeks gathered here for Troy but the wind refused to take them. They were restless and threatened to go home. The priest told Agamemnon to sacrifice his daughter to Artemis at her shrine on the hill." As he told the story Ariela felt goose pimples of fear and clung closer to him.

"Agamemnon was torn between love of his daughter and love of glory. He chose glory."

"Surely love of his country, not himself."

"Whatever he loved, it was greater than his daughter."

He felt her stiffen and her hand left his thigh.

"It was my choice to stay here."

"Is it your choice to walk with him every morning on the battlements and every evening in the square?"

"What are you saying? That he is using me? For his own ambition?"

By now she stood in front of him, her eyes narrowed into points of fury, her lips spitting out the words.

"Greek," she hissed, "leave before I call the guards. You are not worthy of an Erizzo."

He was contrite but she refused to let him come to her. Her wound was all the more painful because there was a grain of truth in what he said. She poured her misery into writing sonnets in the Petrarchian style when she was not helping her father or consoling Beatrice.

Aitheras worked day and night with his grandfather Pyrrhas the artificer, making bullets and bombs and pouring into the explosive material the fury of his pent-up desires.

Mehmet the Conqueror
G. Bellini

EURIPOS

While the great Imperial lurched closer along the road from Thebes, Winstanley, Higgins and I left our apartments in the Loggia to see what had become of old Negropont. We were keen to see for ourselves the famous Euripos, which has given rise to so much anecdote, not least in this book. We collected Amelia from Rabbi Koen and passed through the western gate onto the bridge to the Beotian shore. We lined up on the parapet and gazed into waters as murky and motionless as the canal in St James's Park.

"So this is the wonder. The wonder is that it's so famous," I said.

"We are at a slack tide," said Amelia, with the naturalist's penchant for reporting the obvious.

"O dear Lord, O dear Lord," sighed Winstanley with his usual old-maidishness. It was no use asking the reason for his mooning and swooning, he would tell us anyway.

"Aristotle," he sighed.

"What?"

My hands didn't know whether to fly to my ears or his throat.

"Aristotle, I was musing on the death of Aristotle."

"Good riddance!"

"Why so heated, Sir?" asked Amelia

"A general aversion to philosophers. A good cook brings more happiness to our race than a score of philosophers. Let them all jump in the water, I say."

We followed steps down off the bridge to a narrow promenade between the water and the city wall. After a hundred paces or so it widened into a pebbled shore. At this place, set into the city wall was a kind of alcove, or cave. This was the *turbe,* the tomb of the holy man Hadji Murad, who had caused the tides to flow both ways, and the *tekke,* the lodge of its guardian, the dervish Hadji Latif, to whom we paid our respects.

He was a Bektashi, a follower of the saint Hadji Bektash Veli, who, in the thirteenth century, preached the love of Allah for all creation, including animals and infidels. Hadji Bektash was the patron of the janissaries, who wore a white cloth on their caps in his memory. His love of all Allah's creation extended to wine and arak, which endeared him to men. He allowed women to go about unveiled and have equal status to men in society, which was not so popular among the men but endeared him to their wives and daughters. His creed of love and tolerance and the Shiite tendencies of his teaching did not endear him to orthodox mullahs, especially in conservative places like Egripos, where they controlled the mosques and the ears of the kadis.

We were expected to remove our shoes to enter the tekke and I did not object: it is one thing to defer to petty potentates, another to respect a venerated place. I had put on silk hose that morning; Amelia was delicate in white cotton; Winstanley's grandmotherly black wool stockings had only a few holes; Higgins had the common decency to keep his unsavoury boots on and remain outside.

At the front was the tomb of Hadji Murad. It was a simple half tube of stone, worn smooth by the touch of countless devotees, polished by the wax of their candles, and otherwise unadorned. Behind it was a space for prayer with carpets on the floor. At the back, behind a wooden screen, was the cell of Hadji Latif. He wore a dirty white shirt, the brown homespun gown of a dervish and a conical red felt hat that came down to his eyebrows. A long hennaed beard covered the rest of his face in a hairy mask with holes for jaundiced dark eyes, blackened lips and yellow teeth. It was like sitting down with a goat in fancy dress.

"You are welcome. The blessings of et cetera, et cetera."

Now the sole purpose of our visit was to see a live dervish, like any other tourist sight. I summoned up all I knew about dervishes, from travellers who have visited the Tekke of Ibrahim in Athens. Amelia interpreted for us.

"Will you whirl for us, Sir?"

"He says they dance on Fridays, inshallah."

"Capital."

"He asks if we follow Aristotle. He saw us on the bridge."

Aristotle again. The cursed Aristotle.

"Good Lord, does he know Aristotle?" asked Winstanley.

"He says they venerate Aristotle. It is not true that he drowned in the Euripos. He did not study the tides because there were no tides before God gave them to Hadji Murad. Aristotle died in his bed of indigestion and was interred. The Greeks spread rumours about his being lost in the Euripos so his bones would not be stolen by the Franks. Sir, what is the matter?"

"I am tired of all this Aris-tattle. Good day."

I got up and left my companions to take proper leave of the old goat. I returned to our lodgings alone. It took two opium pastilles to drive damned Arithtotle out of my mind.

Chorbaji Two-face gave us dinner in his rooms. For all their great culinary traditions the janissaries of Negropont served up no better fare than the staple of mess cooks everywhere: boiled mutton and greens. The only piquancy came from the thought of the Erizzos in the very building where we now picked our teeth of mutton gristle, hoping and praying and striving for their deliverance while we knew, like the Almighty who sees everything that has passed and everything that is to come, that they were doomed.

ARIELA

With each day hope rose among the Venetians that Proteas had got through to Captain-General da Canal and that they would see their fleet arrive in battle formation. Instead, on the seventh day, they saw an ominous procession on the road from Thebes. Sixty oxen hauled a great bronze cannon. Behind it other teams pulled cartloads of cannonballs, specially hewn for the massive bore. Finally teams of mules dragged a covered wagon loaded with gunpowder.

"Canal must come tomorrow or it will be too late," said Paolo Erizzo to his captains.

"Or we must buy time by disabling the gun," said Captain Calvo.

"Let me have your best ideas by dinner time tomorrow," said Paolo and bravely thumped the table.

The next morning, as Paolo and his daughter and his officers and courtiers were glumly finishing breakfast, which they took together after walking back from mass with ostentatious cheerfulness, Captain Calvo's sergeant announced the artificer Pyrrhas. Paolo overlooked the lack of respect in his singed robes and unkempt hair. The Greek was known for his lack of interest in everything except guns and explosives. Behind him came his grandson, Aitheras, carrying what looked like a goatskin on his back. When Ariela saw him she blushed scarlet. When he saw her he turned white.

"Sir, the Sultan is bringing up The Imperial which is a serious threat."

"I know that."

"But he has a serious weakness. He hasn't built a proper store for the gunpowder. Nor has he taken the precaution of dividing it among several small wagons. It's a gigantic firework waiting for the fuse to ignite it."

"You have the fuse?"

"Here, Sir" and he pointed to the goatskin which Aitheras gently put down at his feet. "There is no doubt that the powder wagon is armoured. Their usual method is a wooden housing covered in hides to protect it from ball and fire arrows. It may also have a copper lining. Too often they neglect the underneath. My idea is to put the fuse underneath the wagon. I have invented an exploding device so powerful it will melt even metal."

His audience instinctively backed away, except Ariela, who was lost to everything but Aitheras.

"Inside this leather case are separate chambers filled with phosphor, saltpetre, other volatile elements and a naphtha I have distilled with oils so that it resembles the ancient Greek fire. It sticks to what it burns and gives off a greater heat than ordinary fire. I have named it *naphthalma*, the generous oil, from the ancient Greek."

"The etymology can wait. Will it blow up the powder wagon?"

"Yes, if it is under the wagon so the heat is concentrated."

"How is it ignited?" asked Calvo.

"When the top of the bag is pierced the phosphor meets the air. It spontaneously combusts and ignites the rest."

"Pyrrhas, even if your napalma does what you say I see one flaw. How does it get under the wagon?"

"I will put it there."

"You will leave the city, cross the Euripos, walk through the enemy camp and get through the guard with this on your back? You will push it under the wagon and blow yourself up?"

"Who else? It is the culmination of my pyrotechnical life."

"A blaze of glory," said Paolo.

"Yes Sir. Better than the scimitar. In any case there will be half a minute or so before the phosphor ignites the rest. There is time to escape."

Everyone in the room, even Ariela, looked at the old man in silence. Paolo broke it.

"Pyrrhas, pick up your bomb."

Aitheras went to help him but with a gesture Paolo forbad him. Pyrrhas heaved and struggled with the carrying straps and finally tottered under its weight.

"Come here," said Paolo.

Pyrrhas staggered a few steps until Aitheras caught him and helped him off with his load.

"Sir, I will take it," said Aitheras, swinging the bomb on his own back.

"No you will not! No!" shouted Pyrrhas and snatched at the straps. A nervous sergeant dragged him off and he collapsed on the floor, sobbing, hands over his face.

"I helped you make it, I know it, there is no-one better," said Aitheras.

"If you succeed Venice will be in your debt forever. No reward will be too great," said Paolo.

"Then promise me one, Sir. The hand of your daughter."

The collective intake of breath was followed by an ominous silence. Paolo chuckled although his eyes were gimlet sharp and his cheekbones scarlet.

"Are we in some fairy tale? The peasant boy kills the dragon and weds the princess?" he boomed, striding over to Aitheras, who held his ground. "She is an Erizzo!" He would have struck the boy if he hadn't been carrying a bomb.

"Yes, I am an Erizzo," said Ariela. "He is worthy of me and I shall try to be worthy of him. I accept his proposal."

She passed through the stunned spectators and stood beside Aitheras. Bomb or no bomb, Paolo would have struck them both down but his politician's brain overcame his father's heart.

"So be it," he said, and, turning to the spectators, "you have my blessing."

Everyone applauded, except the reunited lovers who saw only each other. Aitheras took her left hand and she twisted her arm awkwardly so he planted his lips below her left elbow. The others in the room smiled at the gaucherie of a first chaste kiss. They were not to know it was the only part of her that his lips had not yet touched.

Plans were made. At midnight there would be sorties from the north and south gates and fire ships set on the Euripos. Aitheras and a party of skirmishers would take advantage of the confusion to slip across the water. He would make the attempt on the powder wagon when the troops were distracted by the dawn prayer. If he lived he was to return to the north gate and get back in with the password Vulcan. His mission was kept secret for fear of spies but word was put about that the Governor would give his daughter to anyone who saved the city. Calvo put the finishing touch to the plan. He personally ordered the sentries at the north gate to kill immediately anyone who offered the password Vulcan and throw his body in the Euripos.

That night, when the alarums and sorties began, Ariela stood at her window dressed in the bridal gown from her trousseau. She watched the mayhem of battle and, in the dark hours before dawn, the soldiers returning, the fires flickering out, the wounded dispatched or carried way, depending whether it was enemy or friend who found them. Apart from its aim as a diversion the operation was a success in itself with many enemy killed and ships burnt.

When the sky lightened and a black thread could be distinguished from a white, muezzins called over the Beotian shore. Their echoes were dying away to the murmur of prayer when a different commotion was heard from the emplacement they were building for the great bronze cannon. Cries, clashes of steel, a brilliant white light. Ariela thought she saw a figure with a sword, silhouetted against the flare. The white light turned to a great blaze of yellow and crimson. She was sure she saw an angel soaring heavenwards on fiery wings before a booming roar and rush of wind and great black cloud obscured the vision.

Citizens rushed to the battlements. As the smoke and dust cleared they saw a crater surrounded by debris, fallen men and burning tents. The great bronze gun had disappeared. Countless different explanations of what had happened settled down to the approximate truth. Great cheers went up for the hero of the moment and his name was chanted "Erizzo...Erizzo...Erizzo" until he appeared in person at the door of his palace and led the way to church for a thanksgiving mass. Beatrice tried to keep up Ariela's hopes but there was no word from the north gate, and genuinely so, for the sentries were not called upon to carry out their orders concerning Vulcan.

If only da Canal's fleet had struck now. The besiegers were demoralised and the besieged spoiling for battle. But he did not come, ordered to stay away by the messenger sent by the Sultan with an authentic seal and the password Ariela.

Still, Erizzo exploited his moral advantage in the days to come. Pyrrhas's napalma bombs were lobbed by catapult if ever a target came in range; fire ships were launched against the fleet; cavalry sorties chased down patrols; night skirmishers overran forward posts. On the feast of Saints Peter and Paul, in honour of the Governor's name day, Captain Calvo led a sortie of his army in full battle order, engaged the enemy on the Lelantine plain, killed ten thousand at the cost of fifteen hundred and retreated to the city in good order. And still no fleet.

Mehmet the Conqueror grew angrier with every day's humiliation. He had six agas beheaded for incompetence and ran one through with his own dagger. The bronze cannon, undamaged thank God, was hauled out of its crater and five smaller brought from Athens and Thebes. More gunpowder was brought and this time stored in several secure places. Finally they were ready and the bombardment began. Day and night, with breaks only for prayer and to let the barrels cool, the great stone balls crashed into the walls. Smaller field guns and naval guns on the galleys pounded the breaches with smaller shot to stop them being repaired. Regiments of infantry protected the batteries from Venetian sorties, standing firm against muskets, bows, artillery and fire-bombs from the battlements. Ten days it lasted until the Imperial Flower Gardeners, led by Soup-Stirrer Ahmed, stormed the breach by the south gate and spilled down the Street of the Annunciation, drowning in blood anything that lived. The desperate citizens fought back the tide, street by street, building by building, until the whole city was flooded in crimson.

Only one part of Negropont now belonged to Venice, the citadel in the middle of the Euripos between the stone and wooden bridges. It was held by Captain Calvo and a few of his men with Paolo, Ariela and Beatrice. A familiar figure walked onto the stone bridge and asked to be let in.

"Will you surrender now, Signor? It is no disgrace to have fought well," said the Florentine renegade in his sing-song dialect. "The Sultan promises you will keep your heads."

"After all we have done to him?"

"Not a hair of your heads will be touched. His Highness keeps his word to the letter."

"And my daughter?"

"She will be treated as a noble lady."

"Then take me to your Sultan. I will surrender my sword only to him."

The Sultan received them on the banks of the Euripos on a throne surrounded by men of the Imperial Pastry Cooks, his fearsome bodyguard. Calvo and his men lined up, each with a janissary spear at his back. The two women, stood hand in hand. Paolo, battle stained and weary with failure, marched with as much pride as he could muster to the Sultan, bowed, handed over the sword of the Erizzos. Mehmet took its silver hilt, held the point in his other gloved hand and with the strength of unbridled fury broke it over the arm of his throne. Slowly and deliberately, so his chronicler could get it down word perfect, he addressed Erizzo, stunned by the desecration of his sword.

"If ever Venice is tempted to remember your resistance with pride, she will remember the consequences with bitterness. Mehmet the Conqueror will not be defied. All Venetians and Franks along with their women and children will be put to death; Greeks and Jews in their service will be sold in Constantinople."

"Your ambassador said we would keep our heads. I beg you to spare the other survivors too."

"You shall keep your heads."

He made a sign, as if he was flicking away a fly, to the janissaries guarding Calvo and his men. In one movement they thrust their spears into the prisoners, up into the heart.

"And you Signor Erizzo. You swore to my ambassador that you would be sawn in half before you would surrender your honour and the honour of Venice. So be it."

Again he flicked away an invisible fly. Men brought trestles and planks and a two-man saw. Paolo's legs failed him and two agas took his arms. Ariela ran to the Sultan and threw herself on her knees.

"My ambassador was right. Even in distress you are very beautiful."

"I beg you, for the sake of that beauty, for the sake of the beauty in yourself, spare me this sight. Your victory is complete."

"Lady, your tears are too much to bear. I will do as you ask," and then, to one of his agas, "spare her the sight. Take her to the palace. Guard her well. Let nothing happen to her."

The men had to carry Ariela, moaning and swooning. Beatrice made to follow but the Sultan had her brought back.

"Are you the lover of Proteas the Greek?"

She nodded. Paolo for a moment was distracted from his own predicament as misery was heaped on despair.

"He served me well. Thanks to him your Captain-General kept his fleet away until it was too late. I promised that you would join him. Do you wish to do so?"

He took a purse from his sash and tossed it on the ground for her to pick up. Relief and joy was still on her face as her head rolled to Paolo's feet. The agas and the executioner skipped away from her spurting blood. The Sultan flicked away another fly and Paolo was manhandled onto the trestle. Two janissaries held the saw over his midriff.

"Do not touch a hair of his head. Send the top to Venice. Send the tail to Crete."

And so it was done.

The work of hunting down Venetians lasted a week. The Sultan ordered them burned since corpses were choking the anchorages in the bay. A dark pall and the smell of kebab hung over the Euripos. Greek collaborators cleaned up the city before being herded on ships for the slave markets of Constantinople. Liberated Greeks, or so the Sultan called them, trickled back from the country to their houses outside the walls. The Jews were allowed to move back to their ghetto inside the south wall.

As soon as it was put in order the Sultan moved into the palace and received the submission of the priests, rabbis and other leaders of the community. He appointed *hojabashi* to collect the taxes that would pay for the siege and gave the second largest church back to the Christians. The largest church would be turned into mosque. He allocated land and houses to the agas and pashas who would remain to govern the island and appointed Mehmet Bey, who had been born in Constantinople with the name Christopheros, as Vizir.

When all this and many other things had been done, and the worst of the smoke and smell had dispersed, the Sultan looked to his own pleasure. On a warm summer evening, well fed and rested and pleased with himself, he dismissed his courtiers and guards from his bedroom, and summoned the beautiful Ariela, the last Venetian of Negropont. The Sultan had expected to see her cowed and surly in mourning clothes. Instead she was radiant and perfumed and dressed as a bride. Her beauty stunned even Mehmet, whose harem in Constantinople recruited from every part of the Empire. She came up to him and genuflected.

"At last I have come to meet my betrothed."

He was acutely self-satisfied that his majesty and power had overcome the feelings of a daughter. He was truly a conqueror.

"You should know that it is impossible to be the betrothed of a Sultan, as no-one is worthy to marry a Sultan. I promised to treat you as a noble lady. And I shall. Instead of a slave of the harem you will have the rank of concubine.

She genuflected again and his desire hardened into lust. He reached out and seized her by the waist. He sighed.

"Ariela, we are man and woman. Eros's arrow has shot us both."

"Eros has two arrows in his quiver. One is tipped with gold and fills its target with desire. The other is tipped with lead and poisons its target with loathing. An arrow like this."

She twisted from his embrace as she took from the folds of her dress a dagger which she thrust at his heart. She was not to know that, following a prophecy at Delphi the year he took Constantinople, he wore fine silver chain mail under his tunic. The dagger drew blood but only from his upper arm after it glanced off his chest and buried itself in his armpit. Inexperienced in such things she thought she had succeeded and her face flushed with triumph.

"I am an Erizzo. You are a pig, a donkey, a hook-nosed Tartar, a blood-soaked lecher."

Mehmet's first emotion was astonishment. He had not been spoken to like this since his little brothers were alive. She rounded off her tirade by spitting in his face. He drew his scimitar and with one sweep sliced off her head. With a ferocious backhand he cut her body in half at the slender waist while it still stood. Again and again he chopped and hacked. At last he stopped, paddling in blood, appalled at his own butchery. He called for his guards, who were equally dismayed. They had raped and butchered in the streets of Negropont but not in cold blood and not in so many pieces. The horror and guilt they felt for their own inhuman deeds was condensed in the shame they felt for their master.

He ordered them to fetch a sack and collect up the pieces. With his own hands he dropped in the head, staring at him with malevolent blue eyes. He tied the neck of the sack himself and dragged it through the blood to the window, whose balcony looked over the Euripos. With a growl he threw it into the water. It splashed but did not sink, bobbed to defy him, and at last floated south on the current. He watched it disappear, taking with it his rage and humiliation. Just as it grew too small to see, it stopped in midstream. It grew larger again. He looked on in horror as the sack came back. It floated past him. Again it stopped and floated back south, mocking him, and twice more. The two janissaries who stood beside him muttered prayers. 'Get it out,' he roared, 'burn it!'

He watched his men commandeer a boat and tow the sack to the shore, fighting the conflicting currents. They made a pyre of sticks, put the sack on top and set fire to it. The fire leaped and roared but the sack did not burn, perhaps a miracle or perhaps because it was a Negropontian munition sack woven out of fire-proof Carpasian flax. It glowed white among the cinders until a distraught Mehmet ordered his men to drag it out with hooks and bury it. They dug a pit but just as they dragged the sack to the edge there was the noise of a herd of galloping wild horses, the ground began to shake, and the sides of the pit caved in. Hoarse and pale, Mehmet ordered a double charge for the great bronze Imperial. Artillerymen heaved the canon round so it faced over the Bay of Aulis and chocked it up to its highest elevation. They tamped cotton bags of gunpowder into the great brass barrel and then the terrible sack. They applied a taper to the firing hole and blasted Ariela into the heavens.

It was probably their imagination but many people thought they saw an angel soaring heavenwards on fiery wings from the mouth of the Imperial. Certainly nothing was seen to come down again. In stories, at least, she joined her Aitheras in the skies over Negropont to giggle and sigh together over the secret rendezvous of lovers.

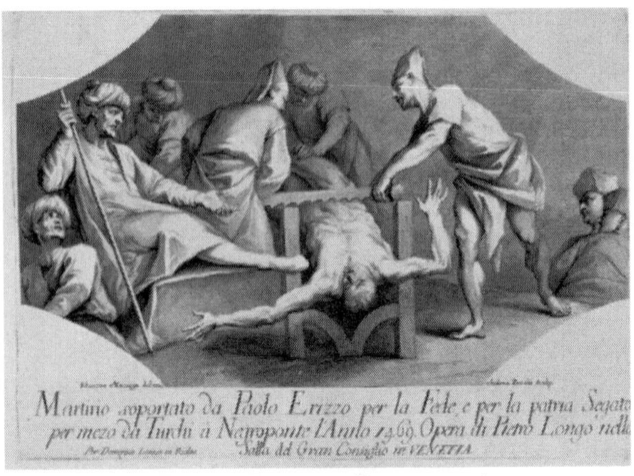

Paolo Erizzo Bisected
Pietro Longo

DRUSILLA

I was out of sorts after dinner, unsettled by the story of Aitheras and Ariela, the proximity of Aristotle and an excess of hookah mixture. On Winstanley's insistence we took a walk up to the hill where Iphigenia was put to death by her father as a sacrifice to Artemis. We did not try to enter the fortifications, to the probable disappointment of our janissary escort, who would have enjoyed preventing us. Instead we sat and admired the sunset over Beotia.

"What a pity for poor Iphigenia, What a waste," I said.

"Children came cheap. They still do," said Higgins.

"According to Euripides she went voluntarily for the good of all the Greeks. She is an example of noble sacrifice," said Winstanley.

"Why is it always women who are sacrificed?" asked Amelia. "All for men's ideas or wishes or conventions or ambitions or aspirations or money. We should not be a sacrifice to your sex. We should not be a sacrifice to ourselves."

"What about a sacrifice to each other?" I said, thinking of Aitheras and Ariela.

"Ah now, there's a sportsman changed his tune."

"Have you ever known true love, Sir?" asked Winstanley, impudently.

"Yes and it's none of your business."

Which makes a very poor story. For the sake of literature, this is what I might have said:

"That Gospel Shop you covet, Winstanley, and the parsonage across the courtyard, is where I first tasted innocent love. At school I had tasted the not-so-innocent variety - I was no stranger to a fluttering heart, a lovestruck eye and messy fumblings. But when it came to a hairless lip, a fuzzless cheek, an unbroken voice, I was still a virgin. As was my dewy-eyed Drusilla.

She was the only daughter of Parson Pompous, your intended predecessor. How such a peach was the fruit of such crab apples is a divine mystery. She was their antonym: gloomy-sunny, dark-fair, dull-lively, coarse-delicate, you get the drift. I remember the exact moment when I first noticed her. I had seen her often enough but paid her no more attention than the maids bobbing and curtseying around the place. The parson has a peculiar position in your Linnean order of society. He is ex-officio hanger-on to the gentry whenever some gravitas is called for but as a family man he ranks with the tenant farmer. His dependants are invited to the Christmas party and the Harvest Festival but otherwise we only meet them at the Gospel Shop.

I was dragged there one April morning when I was just sixteen, humouring my mother to touch her for a guinea. I was at that susceptible age when all one's energy and light is transferred to the world around. The air is heavy with youthful electricity and only needs the slightest spark to split the heavens. We processed to our pew and closed the door. When we stood for the hymn I looked over the side and was thunder-struck. An angel from the stained glass window sat with Mrs. Pompous and the churchwardens at the side of the sanctuary. She was bathed in a beam of light. She looked up at me and we were both transfixed. The raucous congregation was transformed into a celestial choir, the cherubs in the window took flight, the flowers exploded with intoxicating fragrance. If this patch is too purple for you then you have never been sixteen and smitten.

We were Romeo and Juliet, divided by rank not family. Our courting was secret. If you have a daughter I advise you not to have an apple tree outside her window. Or put bars on it Spanish style or a trellis like the Turks. By day she was the soul of charity, taking food baskets to the poor, especially those at the edge of the estate. In woods and hedges I waited for her, my heart in my mouth. Those warm spring days and budding leaves, those moonlit nights with the fields knee deep in mist, our world was butterflies and stars and we were at one with the beating heart of nature. For once I took up my books. Shakespeare and Virgil were no longer Greek to me but spoke crystal clear straight to the heart. We loved the world and we loved each other and we loved ourselves. First love is so powerful because you fall in love with the other and also with yourself as lover. I was Romeo and Narcissus combined in one. I had never before met a young man so handsome and full of spunk.

I had to go back to school. I postponed the dreadful day with pretended injuries and ailments that miraculously cured themselves as soon as Doctor Piss-prophet drove up the drive. I was bled for my bright eyes and pallor and agitated nerves. The quack confused moonstruck with lovestruck. But I couldn't put it off any longer. How I pined! My schoolmasters saw a change in me and hoped it was for the better. I was more tractable if more dreamy, more bookish if more distracted, more tolerant towards them. Ah, they said, he is over his rebelliousness. We can mould him into a gentleman. Little did they know.

At last I posted home with the prospect of a glorious summer with my Drusilla. Under a June moon I ran through the dewy fields to the parsonage. It was in darkness. I climbed the tree. I found the window open. My heart pounded. I put a foot on the sill. In the moonlight I saw an old crone in my lover's bed with a mob cap and no teeth. She opened her eyes and screamed, wild eyed and gums agape. I was winded by my crash through the branches but nothing was broken. I limped into the shadows as candles were lit and windows opened. In the agony of frustrated desire an

d thwarted expectations I went back to my solitary bed and tossed until dawn.

The next day marked the end of my youth. Scarcely awake I was summoned to the library. Father sat in the seat of judgement. My brain churned for words to butter him up. There was no point. My Drusilla was banished. I didn't see her at our place again. She wasn't spoken of. It was as if she had never existed.

I didn't see her again for nearly five years. She is the reason why we are all here in Allah-forsaken Negropont. I was sauntering in the Park when a phaeton drew up beside me. The crest on the door was a skinny legged eagle with a stripy shield. Inside was a woman with a veil. A footman hopped down and opened the door. Nothing venture nothing gain I hopped in. She lifted the veil and I was sixteen again, breathless and erect. She ordered the driver to circulate and she told me her tale.

Parson Pompous exercised his Christian charity by packing her off to distant relatives in Yorkshire. When she reached sixteen they threw her out of the house. She followed the well-trodden path of fallen women to London and from a sister in a similar position, whom she met on the way, got the address of Miss Kitty in Grosvenor Square. Miss Kitty is kind and considerate towards pretty young women who have fallen on hard times and who wish to make their way in the world. Her customers are all bucks of quality, as I can bear witness. So one bright Monday afternoon, straight off the Barnet stage, Drusilla knocked on the door of a house in Grosvenor Square. It was opened by a flunkey, who made no ribald remarks about applying for positions and ushered her into the presence of Mrs. Abigail Adams, wife of the Minister Plenipotentiary of the United States of America and their daughter Miss Abigail Adams. Drusilla had knocked on the wrong door.

The Adams family had been in London for a week and His Excellency had yet to present his credentials at the Court of St James. They were looking to employ a maid and companion for Miss Abigail, who was nineteen years old. They asked Drusilla what her qualifications were for the post and for answer Drusilla went to a piano forte in the room and sang a hymn. It was the first time she had done so since she was ejected from the parsonage and the Adams ladies mistook her tears for pious emotion. Mrs. Adams was also the daughter of a clergyman and they went through their repertoires until tea time, when a formal offer of employment was made.

Although Americans, the Adams were civilised and generous. Drusilla was a bridesmaid at Miss Abigail's wedding to the Secretary to the Embassy, Colonel William Smith, and was kept on after the marriage. A short time before I met her in the park Minister Adams was recalled to Washington and the Smiths would take Drusilla with them. She is in America by now, God help her. There is nothing more to say."

"You said she is the reason you are here," one of my companions might have said.

"I had half a case of port after dinner. I cut my swathe through Piccadilly and into the magistrate's court. From that bench to this one."

Of course this was by no means the full story. But how many stories are?

TRIBUTE

In spring, at the beginning of the sailing season, a fleet of a dozen warships of the Imperial Navy sets sail from Constantinople under command of Captain Gazi Hassan Pasha, the Lord High Admiral. The Sultan and his court see them off from the gardens of the Topkapı palace, for they are on a mission of national importance. What is this mission? Suppressing pirates? Resisting Russian incursion? Putting down revolution? Much more important than these: the most exalted mariner in the land is gathering in the harvest of taxes farmed from the Archipelago, the islands of Greece.

The Turks are so fond of the exchequer that they have two. The larger is the personal purse of the Sultan from which he funds the pomp of the court, the luxury of the harem, the splendour of his entertainments. In times of war or other national expense he may make a loan to the state but he expects to be repaid. He fills his purse from the sale of offices, gifts from foreign states and visitors, fines, inheritance taxes and the confiscation of the wealth of executed Vizirs and others, who have been too keen to display it. The gold and silver mines of the empire are his personal possession, although, like the ice for his sherbet, their treasures melt on the way from the mountains to his cellars.

The smaller exchequer belongs to the state. It is supported by taxes levied on households and on cotton, tobacco, and other trade goods. The most notorious tax is the tax on every non-Muslim male over the age of fifteen. Woe betide the subject who pretends to be a Muslim for if he is found out he will lose his head as well as his fortune. For some reason there is a poll tax on sheep but not on goats.

Egripos contributes some £250,000 sterling to the annual harvest, compared with a mere £45,000 from Athens. The total for all Greece, Anatolia and Cairo is £20,000,000, which is about the same as the revenue of our British government. Added to this, tribute in kind swells the rivers of revenue that pour into the Bosporus. While we groan at the pounds of flesh exacted from us by a rapacious government, our sense is figurative. Among the Ottomans, it is all too literal. There is human treasure in the revenue and none more precious than women for the harems of Constantinople.

So we were invited by the Vizir to a remarkable ceremony: the tribute of a virgin. It took place in the square in front of the Loggia. The Vizir sat in his portico on a low chair covered with a carpet, surrounded by his retainers and janissaries with scimitars drawn. On his right hand sat the chief *imam* and on his left the *kadi*, or judge of the town. Around them stood various other petty officials, dressed in their brightest foppery with silk and satin and fur and sashes and turbans and feathers, so that from a distance they were a splendid flock of cockatoos; we perched above them in the upper arcade like three dowdy sparrows.

The arrival of the procession was announced by the pipes and drums of a janissary band reverberating through the narrow streets. A great bass drum and several kettle drums beat out a brisk march time; bell-trees and cymbals and triangles were the jangly instruments; strident trumpets and raucous double reed pipes carried the tune. There were singers too, barrel-chested Stentors bellowing out their war chants in the voice of roisterers, not choristers. The leader of the band and the singers wore red robes, red drawers and red boxy turbans; the musicians wore green robes, red trousers and green turbans. The colours as well as the rumpety-tumpety music reminded me of Christmas mummers and indeed their march seemed more theatrical than martial: after each three paces they stopped and glared fiercely from side to side. As usual in oriental music there was no harmony other than that accidentally produced by the incompetence of the musicians. The melodies however were immediately accessible to the western ear, simple little tunes that a cloth-eared wobbler from the shires could march to. Powerful, rousing and shrill, it was a conquering, intimidating, triumphalist music. None of us could resist tapping our feet.

Behind them came a different sort of party, unmoved by the hectoring rhythm, but shuffling to the music of groans and ululations that had more in common with a funeral than a wedding party. Indeed they carried a flower-strewn bier among them, the sacrificial lamb upon it, the difference to a corpse being that she was sitting not lying. She was veiled from head to toe in fine white muslin sprinkled with sequins and embroidered flowers with a narrow slit for her eyes. And such eyes they were! Large and dark and as round below as above, the eyes of a goddess on a vase or on the prow of an ancient Greek ship.

The mourners' procession was led by the chief priest of the island who competed with the Turks in the splendour of his vestments. He wore a purple cassock under a white tunic, hemmed and cuffed with precious stones, under a long, scarlet cope fastened round his neck with a gold collar. The traditional tall hat of his profession and an ebony staff topped with a gold cross completed his outfit. Behind him walked the notables of the town, led by our consul and tax-collector Pericles, who had put on a bulbous, lop-sided turban for the occasion

"Oh dear Lord, oh Heavens, Pericles is giving his daughter Eleni," gasped Winstanley.

Pericles beat his breast and sighed with the enthusiasm of a father who is getting shot of a daughter without the expense of a dowry and digs deep for the finer feelings expected of him. Behind the bier came the mother and other women of the family, who made up the chorus of tragedical weeping and groaning. We were astonished to see Amelia walking with them and consoling them. Bringing up the rear was a rabble of Turkish boys, whose jeers and insults were barely contained by a platoon of dilatory gendarmes.

With a thump and a shout the band ceased its din and lined up in a guard of honour for the cortège. They halted in front of us and the bier was lowered to the ground. The priest and the father each took an arm of the girl and led her slowly to the Vizir's throne.

"She is a tasty little thing!"

"Sure you can't see a thing under that veil," said Higgins

"Which lets the imagination loose on the delights underneath it. There's a lesson for you Master Draughtsman. Shroud your landscapes in romantical mist."

The priest then made a speech, which managed the necessary combination of dignity and subservience. The Vizir acknowledged his sermon with a nod. Two women of the Vizir's household bustled out from behind his throne and took Eleni into their care. The poor girl gave one pitiful glance over her shoulder to the family and friends she was leaving for ever and was led away beneath us. It would have been a hard heart that did not feel for her as she began her long journey to an uncertain fate. It was a pitiful and moving scene, belonging more to ancient times than ours: I thought of Iphigenia sacrificed by her father on the wooded hill not far from where we sat - hard as it was to imagine Pericles as a Greek of the age of heroes.

I turned to Winstanley expecting a similarly pedantic comment. What was my astonishment to see him in the throes of a seizure, staring and trembling. His skin was even whiter than usual, his mouth wide open, his nostrils flared. I was afraid he had been stricken by apoplexy or an epileptic fit. I elbowed him in the ribs, I stamped on his toe, all to no effect. With a little cry he slumped forward in a faint. I shook his arm until he recovered. He put a hand to his forehead and blamed himself for missing breakfast.

The Vizir stood up and followed the booty indoors with his retinue, while the janissaries closed ranks on the portico, not that the precaution was necessary. The musicians did not take up their racket again nor the women their caterwauling; the mother left on Amelia's arm, while her other companions quickly recovered their composure, smiling and chatting as if they were going home from market. Pericles and his cronies went a different way with the sense of purpose of men on their way to an ale-house after a job well done. An ass was led forward for the priest and the rest of the townsfolk melted away as if nothing had happened. The little lamb might have been whisked away on a magic carpet.

We followed the Vizir inside to his divanand were offered cushions on his right. The Vizir noticed Winstanley's pale and sweaty face.

"I hope it is not the plague," he said, which sent a tremor around the room.

"Stick out your tongue, Winstanley," said Higgins.

The booby stuck out his tongue and it was not black.

"It is the sun, your Excellency."

Coffee and sherbet and hookahs were served. When we were settled with our pipes our host clapped his hands and announced it was time to inspect the tribute. This was an improvement on the usual entertainment. Revived by coffee and hashish Winstanley recovered his composure and questioned the Vizir with uncharacteristic vigour.

"Sir, why do the Christians meekly hand over their daughters into slavery? Why don't they resist?"

"It is a gesture of affection to their protector, the gift of a grateful child to a loving father."

"Sir, you tax our credulity as well as the good will of your subjects."

"On the contrary, the girl is accepted in lieu of taxes. Despite your Utopian theologians and our Koranic lawyers money does not breed. Daughters are easier to come by."

"It's the same in England," I said, trying to lighten the tone. "The virginity of daughters is also sacrificed on the altar of profit. My mother receives a proposal every week from parents hoping to advance themselves by giving me their daughters."

"The girl you are about to see is very fortunate. She is destined for the harem of the Sultan's chief eunuch, the Grand Kislaragasi. Athens and the islands are part of his personal estate."

The Lord of the Aegean was an African. White eunuchs have only their stones cut off while black eunuchs, who are allowed into the harem, say farewell to Old Roger as well. The Grand Kislaragasi was said to be rapacious, cruel, vindictive and treacherous. Although mutilation had left him without the slightest capability he had a harem full of lovely virgins, whom he could no more service than piss standing up.

Eleni was led in by the two women who had collected her from the castle steps. Wafting around her was the fragrance of roses and musk. Her white veil had been removed but she wore a yashmak over the bottom part of her face. Through it we could see the outline of her lips, which did more to arouse me than any rouge or kohl or beauty spot. Around her lovely eyes was painted blue and inside the sockets was tinged with black. Wide and glistening and deliciously timid, they looked down at the carpet beneath her feet. On her head was a green skull cap sewn with pearls and a yellow band around her forehead. Curls tumbled down her cheeks and ornate braids, powdered with little bits of silver, cascaded over her shoulders and down her back to the waist. Around her slender neck were strings of pearls and gold sequins. She had fine gold bracelets and like Dawn was rosy fingered, the tips being stained and the nails painted red. The toes on her dainty bare feet were also stained and painted. Trousers of fine gauze, embroidered with flowers, hung from hip to ankle. Over them she wore a silk shirt with wide sleeves and embroidered seams. A light blue silk coat, lined with yellow satin, shorter than the shirt, was cleverly tailored to fit her bosom and her hips so it enhanced rather than concealed them. A richly ornamented girdle was fastened round her waist with gold clasps set with precious stones.

Winstanley leaned back against the wall, mouth open, wig askew, a cloud of smoke billowing round him

"*What winning graces! What majestic mien*
She moves a goddess and she looks a queen."

She was delectable. She stood bewildered on the Vizir's carpet as if she had been snatched by a djinn from some oriental paradise. For the first time in her life she was being ogled by men who were not her family.

"The poor creature. It is not right. We are sizing her up like a horse. She is terrified," said Winstanley.

"Well, in my experience of women, she is enjoying the attention," said Higgins.

"She will become ill and depressed locked up in your castle," said Winstanley.

"We expect the fleet of the Captain Pasha any day. We will hand her over and soon she will be in Constantinople where she will have many companions like herself."

"Slaves and eunuchs!"

"If her fate is of such interest and you would like to enter the service of the Sultan to accompany her, you could be accommodated. At a stroke."

The Vizir fixed Winstanley with his piercing black eyes and made slicing gestures in his lap. The threat was humorous but real and Winstanley wisely returned to silent contemplation of the beauty of women and the furious bubbling of his hookah. Meanwhile I diverted my own turbulent feelings into curiosity.

"What could a eunuch want with such a plaything?"

"Not *a* eunuch - the *Chief* Eunuch. He has the ear of the Sultan and indirectly governs the whole empire. The combination of physical impotence and worldly power attracts beautiful women to great men in your country too."

"We don't lock our women away. In the Turkish empire one half of the human species is cut off from society. It is against their natural rights. And what can one man do with so many wives?"

"Sir, our customs are ours. If you wish to criticise, criticise your own."

"As I do. But I prefer the Christian practice in which a man can take his pick of several wives but need not be married to any of them."

The girl was led away by her chaperones and after a few moments of idle talk, such as might be heard around the auction ring on market day we paid our respects and left.

HELEN

That evening we called on Amelia at the house of Rabbi Koen. The Jewish quarter of the town was piled up higgledy piggledy among the buttresses of the Venetian walls. I knocked my stick on the Rabbi's door expecting the squalor of a cottage on our estates and was pleasantly surprised to be taken by a servant into a delightful courtyard garden, where the Rabbi's wife served us mint tea. Unlike the Muslims, the Jews let their women show their faces to strangers, although in the case of Mistress Koen this was not much of a privilege. The Rabbi and his son were away on some errand, driving out devils perhaps.

Our conversation with Amelia was dominated by the events of the morning. My tutor, for once, led for the revolutionists.

"Where is the Theseus, who will rescue this maiden from the monster? Where are the heroes who will overthrow tyranny?"

"Sitting on stakes," said Higgins.

"For once I agree with my tutor. It is a scandal." I said.

"I thought all men dreamed of a harem of beautiful women," said Amelia.

"I am not cross because a pretty girl is made the toy of a heathen tyrant. Who are we to criticise? Every day a new Fanny Hill comes fresh from the country to London and lucky the man who gets first go. It is a woman's vocation to give us pleasure..."

"Sir ..."

"...which, in my experience of women, is mutually enjoyed. It has always been the prerogative of the rich and powerful to look for pleasure wherever they find it and there is no lack of women prepared to give it to them, in Great Britain no less than in the East.

Men, some to Business, some to Pleasure take,

But every Woman is, at heart, a Rake.

See Winstanley I can spout Pope too."

"If you have no more sympathy for her than the lamb in the flock marked out for your dinner, why are you cross?" asked Amelia.

"It's not for the use she will be put to, but the use she will not. I'm sorry to see a good horse unexercised. Winstanley would serve her better than a eunuch."

"Sir, Sir," susurrated Winstanley.

"She would be better with the Sultan himself than his gelding."

"Don't be so sure. She could wait months or years before being taken into the royal presence, depending on the whim of his chief concubines and eunuchs. She may catch his eye as he parades round the Seraglio or while she dances for his titillation with fifty of her rivals. If fortune smiles she is bathed and dressed and delivered to the imperial bedchamber. This will be the most important event in her life, not for sentimental reasons associated with her maidenhead, her girlish longings, her feelings for the man who first possessed her, but for the practical reason that if she fails to please her master she will never be summoned again. One night may be her lot, the rest of her days frittered away with her rivals, embroidering and gossiping and growing fat and remembering the one night when it was her right to empty the Sultan's pockets. Who knows if she may ever rise so high? They may give her away like a horse or a parrot or traded for a pistol or simply forgotten in a backwater of the river of tribute that flows from all over the empire to the palaces on the Bosporus."

"Well now, the Muslims believe that women have no souls," said Higgins, in a tone which implied his agreement with the proposition.

"It is disgraceful. Women are treated no better than domestic animals," said Winstanley, ever anxious to stick his oar in. Amelia took up the gauntlet.

"This is not true. Muslim women are more free than their Christian sisters. They can own property and divorce their husbands. If a Christian woman wants a divorce and her dowry back she runs to the Muslim kadi and not the priest."

"So you approve of the Muslim's attitude to marriage."

"Marriage is a form of slavery for Muslim and Christian women alike."

"And how do you reform them? Isn't it in men's interest?" I asked.

"Women must be reformed before the men. Their education has no other purpose than to fit them for servitude. A woman who can read and write is considered a prodigy. She serves her husband his dinner and then eats with other women. The master feeds with his cronies or alone, like the greatest pasha."

"Yet another example of Turkish tyranny."

"It was like this in the Aegean before the Turks arrived. Your Helen of Troy was a chattel. That bully-fop Paris stole her like his neighbour's cattle."

Winstanley sprang to his feet.

"A chattel? She was Queen of Sparta."

"Married to a ruffian."

"Don't you know your Homer, Madam? How handsome Paris and lovely Helen fell in love and ran away from mighty King Menelaus? How they stood on the walls of Troy and watched the battle fleet of Agamemnon sweep down from the horizon? How ..."

I enjoyed watching the simpering bore driven to distraction by this opinionated woman. There are many ways to make a eunuch and immersion in the romances of the past is one.

Winstanley blabbed of love and women but the touch of a real woman's lips would turn him into Paris – Plaster of Paris. We carted him off to bed drunk on his own delusions and craving the Bey's tobacco.

For my own part, whether it was the events of the day or Winstanley's oratory or frustrated desire that caused it, I was also taken with romantical feelings. Unable to sleep I took my pipe to the balcony overlooking the inner courtyard and the tower of the Vizir's harem. I imagined Eleni sighing at the moon through the window, the dread of Turkish violation driving out her girlish daydreams of the hero she would marry, while her guardians relived their own youth and their entry into womanhood. If only I had a charger and a lance and a suit of silver armour and like a true knight rescued her, as my ancestors were said to have done, according to my mother when I was at her knee

The Slave Merchant
J. Cawse

EXERCISE

We went to fetch Winstanley for breakfast and surprised him lying on his back on the floor with his legs in the air, puffing and gasping. He reddened and excused himself with a quotation from Hippocrates about humours and the brain. I noticed that my scabbardless sword was leaning against the wall beside the window. He got to his feet and tried to leave the room but we would not let him pass.

"Well now, I am afraid for our friend. He is taking exercise," said Higgins.

"Exercise is punishment inflicted by vanity on an innocent body."

"Exercise is self-inflicted torture."

"Like flagellation, fasting, penance, purging, diet and other forms of self improvement."

"Exercise is self-harm."

"A bookman has no need of a firm body and the martial arts."

"Only the vain and the unhappy take exercise for its own sake."

"They want to become what they are not. They aspire to be a model of themselves, which is constantly out of reach."

"You would better learn to match your body to your true nature, Winstanley."

"But what is Winstanley's true nature?"

"Who knows? It is drowned under book learning."

"Unless there is another explanation."

"Insanity you mean."

"Very near Mister Higgins. I am told that love is a plague that affects the brain as well as the heart."

"Get out, Sirs, out," shouted Winstanley and drove us from his perspiring presence.

"Is our bookful nincompoop so lovestruck with Miss Burbage?" Higgins said, when we were alone again.

"I know the signs, Higgins. Saint John of the Goat has answered our prayers. Love shrinks the belly and swells the chest and encorages dreams of manly exploits."

"Even our dry scholar?"

"We would all be heroes in the bedroom."

"Is he gone so far?"

"Even our cleric. Yet there is something that troubles me. Did you hear him explain himself with a quotation from Hippocrates when I found him on the floor? For days now he has been quoting Homer and Virgil and others I don't recognise. He doesn't restrict himself to the classics. He talks Shakespeare and Bacon and Pope."

"Anyone who passes himself off as educated peppers his speech with quotations."

"In his case it is covered in pepper. His speech is entirely made up of quotations."

"We all learn speech from our mothers knee. We parrot them."

"So here is the character Winstanley on stage in Drury Lane, the love-sick pedant spouting someone else's lines. A figure of fun to while away a scene or two while the principal actors change their costume. But he is no stage character, he is a man like us, Higgins."

"Me like him? God help us."

"Is this borrowed speech a costume or is it or the essence of him? If his words are borrowed then what about the feelings behind them? Are they borrowed too? If his passion is borrowed, where is the true Winstanley?"

"And if we are all automata, what of it? That is what we are and to fret about it is pointless, like touching toes and running on the spot. My actions may be borrowed but I can take pleasure in them none the less."

"You're right. Let us take pleasure in Winstanley's. We must help him hit the target of his gymnastics. Some human beings, like some animals, need help to couple."

"Does Miss Burbage share his feelings?"

"She is past her prime. She has no expectations. She has unfulfilled desires. She will accept his overtures with gratitude, if nothing else."

A glimmer of envy tinged my glee with its sickly light. It was I who should be struck by Eros, not Parson Sapscull, it was I who should find love in the erotical wilderness of the Vizir's puritanical domain; it was I who should be riding in the candle light. My consolation was that Aphrodite made the mannish Amelia arouse Winstanley's desire. But I do the goddess of love an injustice. There is a lovely Helen in the heart and skirts of every woman for those who find her.

GANYMEDE

In separate lodgings inside the city, pandering our two lovers was well-nigh impossible. We should also benefit from more sensible exercise than Winstanley's contortions. So I sent word to the Vizir that we should be grateful for his permission for an expedition into the mountains. It would give us the opportunity, if the lovely goddess was kind, to couple our lovers before we took ship. Higgins was keen to visit the goat-skull cave, which Ali Veri had told us about in his serai.

As we left the Loggia for our evening constitutional, Chorbaji Two-Face invited me to follow him past a sentry box and its indolent occupant and through a narrow archway to the rear of the Vizir's quarters. I was surprised to find a secret garden, in the middle of which was a delightful summer house. Flowers tumbled over Moorish patterns inlaid in the brightly coloured tiles of the walls and floor. The Vizir was waiting for me. At his feet was a prayer carpet that mimicked the profusion of flowers around us. He invited me to sit next to him and Captain Two-Face slipped away behind a vegetable arras.

The Vizir flicked his fingers to summon a delicate boy scarcely ten years old, clad in nothing but a diaphanous tunic, with a tray of sherbet. While we sipped he put a hand on my thigh. I was reminded of visits to my housemaster's rooms: I waited for the simper and the 'how are you getting on dear boy' and the squeeze of the knee. In many ways is an English education preparation for encounters with Levantines.

"How do you like our humble garden?"

"I have heard that the Muslim paradise is a garden. Such a replica is surely blasphemy."

I wanted to flatter him before I rebuffed him. He crooked his finger to bring the delicate boy to my side.

"And how do you like our Ganymede?"

"Well enough, Sir."

"Only well enough?"

"If he were of the other sex I would like him more."

"Speak honestly, you are my guest. This is my private sanctum. We are not on ceremony now."

"You have the word of an English gentleman."

"Forgive me. It was a supposition based on ignorance. In Constantinople, as in France, we speak of the English vice."

"In England we whisper of the Italian vice. Perhaps the Italians talk of the Ottoman vice, who knows?"

"Who knows?" He took his hand off my leg on the pretext of brushing away a fallen flower petal. "And yet, in this ancient city of Chalcis, it is incorrect to call it vice. The ancient Chalcidians regarded it as a virtue. The ancient Athenian word for male love was 'chalcidize'. They honoured a pederastic hero with a statue in the square. Kastri, where you stayed the night, was ancient Arpagio, the site where Zeus snatched the boy Ganymede, or catamite as you English say."

"We can respect the traditions of a place but not be bound by them."

We sipped our sherbet and he changed the subject.

"May I ask if your compatriot. Miss Burbage, is a typical Englishwoman?"

"If she were, more of us would have a taste for Ganymedes. We encourage those like her to go abroad. Some of our women would not be out of place in one of your harems and we keep them at home."

"We are not used to women such as Miss Burbage."

"She is a bird of passage."

"Birds are shot by hunters."

"Under your protection what has she to fear?"

"My protection cannot extend to the isolated places where she wanders. I have received reports of conduct which creates scandal in the eyes of my subjects. She rides a camel, which is blasphemous for a woman. She keeps company with men who are not her family."

"You find this shocking?"

"Not I. My subjects."

"Is she in danger?"

The Vizir made no comment; his warning was real. The sooner she was off the island the better.

"Sir, do you know when our ship will be ready?"

"In two days. But first you will have the chance to review the fleet of the Lord High Admiral, the Captain Pasha."

"Meanwhile, would you give us your permission to go into the mountains?"

"Why?"

"To visit the goat-skull cave of Pan."

"That might further antagonise some of my subjects. They regard the place with perverted reverence."

"But Sir..."

"However, I have no objection to a hunting expedition. I will supply you with a guide. If you stumble across some wild beast's lair, that is God's will."

I admired his diplomacy: in few words he gave us permission, denied responsibility and implied that we would be watched. We made further desultory conversation until the sun tipped the horizon and I left him in his earthly paradise to make his gymnastics, whether on the prayer mat or the boy I dare not say.

PARIS

We set out before sunrise and crossed the Euripos into Beotia. We foreigners had horses while Amelia's Ali and a quartet of guards made do with mules. Our hunting master, a surly rogue with a lance, a horn and a spaniel, went on foot. He was the only native islander among us, dressed in homespun tunic and un-dyed woollen trousers and a red cap with a tassel, a more practical garb than the janissaries' riding coats and turbans. The sun rose behind us and lit up the pointy mountain ahead. It flooded the eastern sky with all shades of red and yellow and orange, while behind us the town and the bay of Aulis were bathed in blood.

The sun was high when olive gave way to pine. Greek mountain pine is not the stuff of ship's masts but a stunted crabby thing with feathery foliage. Yet its perfume is pleasantly sweet and lemony, unlike the medicinal astringent of its northern cousins. By now the path was steep and difficult, narrow, twisted and littered with stones. Only Amelia and I remained mounted, she because she was an accomplished horsewoman and I because I wished to stick with her and further Winstanley's cause.

After the pines came gorse and bushes and stunted holm-oaks, dense with dark green prickles and nutty little acorns.

The path was steeper still and we had to dismount. Beneath the appearance of feminine frailty Amelia had an iron constitution and I had difficulty keeping up. We reached a flat spot covered with all kinds of grasses, flowers and asphodels. I saw hare and red partridge and woodcock and above us soared a pair of eagles. If our hunting expedition had been more than a pretext we would have had good sport.

The view behind us opened up and we could see the two gulfs of Euboea, the bay of Aulis, and the walled city of Egripos, restored in the light and distance to a *Fata Morgana.* The sky contributed to the dramatic scene with a brilliant blue over the sea and towering black clouds above the mountain. I wished I had some mechanical device that would instantly capture the view for posterity. While we admired the scene and waited for the rest of the party I puffed my tutor.

"Madam, I have something to discuss with you."

I gave her the burning glance and frank expression I have so often practised in the mirror. She returned it with a frankness that if she were not a spinster, past her prime, I would have described as brazen. She was intrigued. Curiosity is a woman's most instant emotion and opens the door to the others.

"Speak plainly. We are alone here."

"You know the story Winstanley tells about Paris and Helen consumed by love. All lovers are touched by the gods. All men are handsome, all women are the most beautiful on earth for a moment in their lives."

She gave me another brazen look that would have brought a blush to the innocent lilies and orchids on which she usually fixed her attentions. She started off across the meadow.

"Someone we know is struck with a passion so deep-rooted, so all consuming, that it threatens his sanity."

She walked more quickly, her breast heaving. Had I been too bold? I pressed on.

"Would you take pity on our friend?"

"We should envy him not pity him."

"So you would be well disposed towards him."

"I am well disposed to anyone touched by love."

"And if it concerned yourself? What should he do?"

"He should follow his heart and conscience. Love is the force of Nature."

On cue from the stage manager of the universe, the sky was split from mountain top to sea by a flash of lightning accompanied by a crack of thunder above us. The horses reared and we struggled to control them. Not a minute before there had been blue sky behind us, now it was a curtain of black. Another blinding flash and a bolt of lightning ran along the ground not fifty yards from where we stood and exploded on a stunted oak. Amelia's horse bucked and kicked and she let it go, for fear of being pulled over. It turned dark as night, the burning tree was doused by sudden rain, then brilliant lightning struck again. I shouted that we had to find shelter and started in the direction we had come. By the time we reached the path it was a raging torrent, impassable up or down, and we turned uphill again.

An English storm is an April shower by comparison with the downpour in which we struggled more like swimmers than ramblers. Amelia breasted the deluge like a ship's figurehead, serene against the spray. We blundered blindly, taking our bearings by lightning flash. All our senses were assaulted by the constant roar of thunder, the beating of the rain, the reek of wetted earth and ozone. Amelia took the lead, for I was at a loss, and led us to the right, where there was some vegetation. We discovered too late that they weren't bushes but the tops of trees and we slipped and fell together. I held on to the horse's reins but he dug in his heels and the bridle snapped.

There is a child's game in which the victim is blindfolded and pushed over what is supposed to be a precipice but the drop is a foot or less. So it was with us. Thinking we were launched into the void we tumbled all of a heap about four feet below on a wide sandy space before a cave. Our relief was mingled with amazement. The cave mouth was some ten paces wide and five high and was protected from rain and wind by the overhanging cliff. In the most sheltered part of this proscenium grew an ancient vine, whose trunk, made up of many twisted smaller trunks, was as thick as an English oak. From it the plaited branches spread out and up to make a canopy above us and, between the strands of branch and trunk were the horns of animals. We saw all this by lightning flash so fear and imagination added a riot of mythological creatures entwined with tendrils and capering round us in the dark.

We peered into the cave. I drew my dagger, in case of wild animals, and tiptoed inside. On either side were heaps of animal skulls, like the ossuaries of catacombs, and in the centre under a natural vault was a fireplace ringed with stones. Charred wood and fresh-gathered kindling showed evidence of recent use. I looked with longing at the ashes while Amelia took more practical measures. She unfastened from her waist an oilcloth bag and produced those feminine necessaries essential to a woman of the world - tinderbox and matches and half a candle and a sharp knife and strips of jerked mutton and a ship's biscuit. I smiled at the idea of introducing this Mohican to the women in my family whose only shields against adversity were fans and smelling salts.

Under her skilful hands and my bellowing breath we had a fire that raised our sodden spirits and set our clothes steaming. I rigged a branch or two to spread our riding coats before the fire but she was not satisfied with this. She stood with her back to me and raised the hair bun from her nape.

"Please unbutton me."

"Madam?"

"Haven't you ever seen a woman in her drawers? I won't catch pneumonia for the sake of modesty."

I did as I was told. She stepped out of her dress and I was surprised by the lace and ribbons in her bodice and petticoat as I expected more nunnish undergarments. She undid the bun and ran her fingers through her hair to dry it and laughed at me.

"If you had any sense you would do the same."

I undressed down to undershirt and drawers. By now the fire was blazing, there was no shortage of wood, and our clothes were cooking nicely. The flames threw flickering shadows on the wall and I tried to remember Plato's allegory but got it jumbled. In any case I could never remember the damned point of it.

"We should exercise to fend off the rheumatics."

She raised her arms and danced a few mincing Greek steps and then broke into the new-fangled waltz to the tune of the British Grenadiers.

"You can't dance a waltz to a march. Try *The Bold Dragoon*".

I tra-la'd it for her and beat time with my hands until I couldn't sit out any longer and took her waist. To this day I smile at the vision of us whirligigging in a smoky fire-lit cave in our underwear, our shadows spinning on the walls, singing *The Bold Dragoon* in triple time at the tops of our voices, watched by heaps of skulls. She was an excellent dancer, light on her feet despite her boots. She out-danced me until I was out of breath. I tried to let go but she pressed herself against me and through the linen I felt her heart pound against my breast.

"Follow heart and conscience," she hissed.

Her face remains imprinted on my mind. I had never in my life seen eyes bum so bright. Her hands gripped my head from behind, her lips were on mine, and they were no spinster's kisses, no virgin's, no maiden aunt's. Her body clung to mine. I struggled free, staggered, tripped and fell, hitting my head on the earth floor. She was on me like a harpy, plucking and tearing at my clothing and at hers, attacking my face and chest with bites and kisses. Even if I had not been dazed by my fall I would have had difficulty resisting her. You will think I was a willing victim, as women who are raped are said to have brought it on themselves. Man or woman, let them fall into the clutches of a succubus like Amelia.

I thought that the monsters of the poets were fantasies but in that cave I met Medusa. She had twenty hands and twenty legs and twenty mouths that devoured me until she sat astride me and there was one of her again, riding me, grinding me, swallowing me like a snake does a frog with sighs and moans until I cried out and spurted to join her. Her hair was over her face and I would not have been surprised if it hid the head of a lion or a cat or a goat, nor if my own body sprouted wings or talons or a mule's mane. Her hair lashed my face and my body, her fingers stroked and scratched until I was hard and we began again. This time I was a willing partner, thrust with parry, parry with thrust, not deliberate and calculating like a seasoned lover but like a youth, going at it headlong until I was lost again, outside myself.

I came to my senses. I saw and heard things with unusual clarity. Fear and longing and curiosity were gone and in their place swelled from deep within me, from a place I had never before thought existed, a mortal terror so overwhelming and so sweet. She leaned over me and whispered 'Paris.' I parted her hair and gazed at the most beautiful face I had ever seen or imagined. I shuddered and she held me in her arms but it would not stop me trembling.

She let me stand up and I walked to the cave mouth, dazed by the light. The storm had abated as quickly as it came. The lightning moved out to Beotia and the intervals increased between the flashes and the thunder. The clouds had gone, the sky was a perfect blue, the sun was overhead. The sea below and the mountains beyond were clear as a Canaletto. There was no sound, neither of insect nor animal nor bird, no breeze rustling the leaves. A great stillness settled over the earth and I was alone, the last creature alive at the end of time. The terror reached my mouth, my limbs, I wanted to run and scream and leap and howl, but I was paralysed, as in a nightmare. She touched my shoulder. I clutched her, knowing that her beauty would protect us both.

"Helen," I whispered.

She led me to the fire, spread my greatcoat on the floor and we played the final movement, adagio.

We helped each other to dress like parents with children and she pinned her hair demurely back behind her head again. We sat under the vine hand in hand and filled the stage below us with scenes from our future life together.

"We shall be free in the forests and the mountain," I began.

"We shall follow only our natural impulses."

"Reject the trivial preoccupations that rule the lives of other men."

"We shall travel the world."

"China and Africa and India."

"We shall learn from the natural goodness of simple savages."

"They will teach us genuine human wisdom."

"Based on feelings and above all love."

"We shall be an example to the world."

"Our children will grow unconstrained by ignorance, superstition, and artificial morality."

At this I clapped my hands on my ears.

"No my love, I did not mean…"

But she did mean. And she knew that nothing is more chilling to a man in the hot flush of love than talk of babies, a subject more passion-quenching than marriage or her mother. In this case she was mistaken. Talk of children cast a shadow but not for the reason she believed.

"I am a eunuch."

She looked up at me with an expression that in happier circumstances would have been comical.

"Sir?"

"I am a eunuch. There will be no children."

"We have just…"

"You are looking at the last of my line. The dynasty stops with me."

"Nonsense. You are as virile a man as I have ever coupled with. If eunuchs were like you, women would beat down the doors of harems to be let in."

"The juice is no good."

"Not in my recent experience."

"It is infertile."

"How do you know this?"

I spat out the hated name.

"Aristotle."

"Our tête-à-tête was interrupted by hallooing from the meadow above us. I pressed my finger on her lips.

"I will prove it. Meet me tonight at Rousseau's stable. Until then, keep mum."

We found our horses grazing in the sunlit meadow. It was as if the storm had never been but for the black stump of the unfortunate oak. The rest of our party had found shelter of a sort beneath the pines and a makeshift canopy but were considerably more bedraggled than Amelia and I.

Winstanley and Higgins were amazed by the vine and the skulls. We took burning brands to explore inside. In a second grotto rock pillars grew from floor to ceiling, covered in animal skulls. Our artist needed no encouragement to start sketching.

They were all too engrossed in the mysteries of the cave to sniff out the erotic consummation of the storm. Despite the mask of indifference we put on, humming *The Bold Dragoon* together might have given us away.

Eros

Th. Rowlandson

ARISTOTLE

Back at our lodgings Winstanley, unused to serious exercise, fell asleep on his bed, Higgins retired to draw goat skulls, I slipped away to Rousseau's stable in Kastri. Amelia sent Ali away on an errand and we sat hand in hand on the straw like two rustic sweethearts. Rousseau ruminated over us, the disdainful chaperone. Amelia made light of my Aristotle.

"So my sweet bob-tail, my little capon."

I reached into the inside pocket above my heart for an oilskin wallet, about five inches by three and half an inch thick, and took out a scuffed leather-bound book the size of my hand. I gave it to her. The frontispiece was an engraving of Aristotle the philosopher prince in his library, sitting at his desk in a long scholar's gown, looking out at the reader. He had a scholar's dome and a bushy black beard. On his desk was a globe of the heavens and behind him a picture of a skeleton holding a scythe. Opposite was the title page that she read out loud.

"*Aristotle's Last Legacy. Unfolding the mystery of nature in the generation of man. Treating:*

One. Of Virginity, what it is, its Signs and Tokens, and how a Man may know whether he marries a Virgin or not.

Two. Of the Organs of Generation in Women, with a Description of the Fabric of a Womb.

Three. Of the Use and Action of the Genitals, in the Work of Generation.

Four. Of the Instruments or Organs of Generation in Man.

Five. Of Conception; and how a Woman may know whether she hath conceived or not; and whether a Male or Female.

Six. Of Barrenness, with Remedies against it, and the Signs of Insufficiency both in Men and Women.

Seven. Of the Pleasure and Advantage of Marriages, with the unhappy Consequences of unequal Matches; and the ruinous Effects of unlawful Love.

Eight. Directions to both Sexes, how to manage themselves in the Act of Coition, or Venereal Embraces."

The list brought a colour to even her experienced cheeks.

"Look on page fifty one. The corner is turned down."

There was only one dog-ear, not that it was necessary. The book fell open at a dampstained page. As she read I recited it by heart.

"*But among other causes of barrenness in men, this also is one that makes them barren, and almost of the nature of eunuchs, and that is the incision, or the cutting of the veins behind their ears: which in case of distempers is oftentimes done. For according to the opinion of most physicians and anatomists, the seed flow from the brain by those veins behind the ears, more than any other part of the body. From whence it is very probable, that the transmission of the seed is hindered by the cutting of the veins behind the ears, so that it cannot descend at all to the testicles or come thither very crude and raw.*"

"This is what was done to you?"

"Yes. I lied about the ear spiders. There is not an hour that passes without my touching the scars. They are my inheritance."

With one hand I grasped hers and with the other pulled back my hair and exposed the back of an ear. I made her fingertips trace the scar. I did the same with the other ear.

"But you have plenty of seed. And vigorously ejaculated. I can testify to that."

"Crude and raw. Infertile."

"And Aristotle is your only authority?"

"There isn't a physician or a surgeon or a midwife in the land who does not take this book as his bible. Do you think I haven't confirmed this with the most famous medical men of London? None of them denies Aristotle."

"When did you first know about your condition?"

"I told you how I came home from school and found my Drusilla turned into a hag. The next day I was summoned to the library. My father told me she was sent away away for more than kissing under the apple tree.

'The Parson what?...here a week since... daughter... with child... blame you... marriage... instanter... sent packing... flea in ear... boot up fundament... impossible... slut... not at my door... ten guineas... took it... knew all he would get... showed him this... should have told you... never round to it... late than never what?'

That's when he gave me this book. I have carried it since that morning. It is my legacy. My fate. My curse. The end of love.

'Ten years old... distemper... near death... bled you... nothing for it... had a spare... yerbrother what?'

They cut my veins to me to save my life. They didn't do it to my younger brother so I would have an heir. He died of the fever."

"Couldn't your mother have more children?"

"I asked that. '*Yerbrother... last of the litter... came out with half her entrails...*"

My father couldn't bear to look at me. His son and heir a eunuch, his fertile son dead, his wife barren, the end of our name and our heredity. I took Aristotle and left him with my head in a turmoil. I didn't know which news to dwell on. I was infertile, the last of my line, the despair of my parents, a traitor to our name. This should have been my greatest wound but it was nothing compared with Drusilla's treachery. Wasn't I good enough for her? While I was writing sonnets, who was she with? The ploughman's boy? A passing gypsy? Our caresses, our endearments, our oaths meant nothing to her. The poetry we had whispered turned to ashes. She taught me that true love is a sham and shame was the price of her infidelity. If a parson's daughter can't be faithful to her first love then who can? And if she of all people, my angel, could be so duplicitous then what of ordinary women? She was truly a Helen of Troy, a scheming adulteress."

"On this you base your lack of faith in women."

"Women use men as men use women - for pleasure and for profit. When a mistress professes her undying love I see Drusilla. When she grows a belly I know she has been unfaithful. It can't be mine."

"Have there been other Drusillas?"

"Word got round about the ten guineas. There has been a procession of babes claiming me for their father. Every three-penny upright in London knows to bring me her whelp and she might get a guinea. Some of their mothers I did bed. Evidently I was not the only one to do so."

"Did you bed Drusilla?"

"Of course. She said she abandoned all her upbringing, all her religion, all her modesty to give herself to me. Fool that I believed her."

"And you never saw the child?"

"Parson Pompous packed her off to Yorkshire, where she was delivered of a son. The babe was taken away and sold by the relatives to a childless couple. All Drusilla knew of them is that they were of good family. After her lying-in she was disowned and put out with the ten guineas of my father."

"What did she say when you met her in the Park?"

"I asked who the father was. She could tell me now she was going to live with savages. She said she'd known no other man but me, before or since. I showed her the book. She said it could not be true."

I lay my head on Amelia's breast and wept.

"My dear, my dear," she whispered and stroked my cursed ears until I was empty of tears, empty of feeling, empty of even pity for myself. When I was myself again, she took on a more practical tone.

"I have heard nothing from your lips but contempt for Greece past and present. And yet you carry the work of her greatest philosopher next to your heart and in your heart."
"A man can be a slave to what he detests."

"Are you sure that Aristotle is right?"

"Who am I to doubt him?"

"Do you believe that the earth goes round the sun?"

"No. What has that got to do with it?"

"Aristotle did. Do you believe that the fleas and lice that bite you in the khan are spontaneously generated from the dirt?"

"What is this nonsense?"

"Aristotle did. Do you believe that women are a lower form of life than men? That we have no souls? Aristotle did. He upheld these monsensical things and many more besides."

"If he is mistaken about semen, what is the truth?"

"It's not known for sure. One authority says that the female carries eggs that contain human beings already pre-formed and the sperm starts off their development. The second says it is the man's sperm that has the human being inside it and the mother provides a home and nutrient. The third says we all existed in the testes of Adam or the ovaries of Eve. A fourth looks in the microscope and sees little worms swimming in the sperm which he says are worms of putrefaction. A fifth says that our blood is condensed and refined in our genital organs to such potency that when it is mixed with another's a person is formed. A sixth says that the mere sniff of sperm is enough to engender us in a receptive womb. The truth is that no-one knows how we are conceived, not Aristotle nor Harvey nor Linnaeus nor anyone. It is a mystery. It is a miracle. There is no more reason to believe that sperm is created in the brain than it is in the liver or the heart or the spleen. Our blood and other fluids circulate through all our organs."

"This is all unproven twaddle."

"Your Last Legacy is convenient for you. You are sad that the line ends with you but you are happy that it makes you a free man. You can care for nobody for nobody cares for you. You can do what you please because there are no consequences."

"Aristotle's book."

"Fi on your old books. You must find your own answers through the evidence of your own senses and your own powers of reason. Aphrodite rules the world. This is your professed religion. Then live by it. Listen to your heart. And let it rule your head."

With that she lifted my head from her breast, kissed me tenderly on the lips, raised her skirts and lay back on the straw.

ARISTOTLE'S
LAST LEGACY
Unfolding the Mystery of NATURE
In the Generation of MAN:
TREATING

I. Of virginity, its signs and tokens, and how a man may know whether he married a virgin or not.
II. Of the organs of generation in women, with a description of the fabrick of the womb.
III. Of the use and action of genitals in the womb of generation.
IV. Of conception; and how to know whether a woman has conceived, and whether of a male or female.
V. Of the pleasure and advantage of marriage; with the unhappy consequences of unequal matches, and miseries of unlawful love.
VI. Of barrenness, with remedy against it; and the signs of insufficiency, both in men and women.
VII. Directions to both sexes how to manage themselves in the act of coition, or their venereal embraces.
VIII. A vade mecum for midwives and nurses, containing particular directions for the faithful discharge of their several employments.
IX. Excellent remedies against all diseases incident to virgins and child-bearing women: Fitted for the use of midwives, nurses, and all such persons only as are concerned in these matters.

LONDON:
Printed and Sold by the Booksellers, 1764.

this alſo is one that makes them barren, and almoſt of the nature of eunuchs, and that is, the inciſion or cutting off their veins behind their ears; which in caſe of diſtempers is oftentimes done; for according to the opinion of moſt phyſicians and anatomiſts, the ſeed flows from the brain by thoſe veins behind the ears, more than from any other parts of the body; from whence

POSSESSION

I went to bed without supper, pleading fatigue, whereas in truth my mind was a Euripos, swirling this way and that. What was I doing? What had I done? What was I to do? I was no stranger to protestations of love, of visions of eternity together, of ever true and undying passion, but always made before the consummation of desire and not after, when they served no purpose. I had never experienced ecstasy so intense as in that cave. This was different from *affaires* with ladies of society and fornications with women of the town. Was Amelia herself the source of passion or was it the romance of our surroundings, the adventure of the storm, the unstoppering of unaccustomed abstinence?

Then there was the matter of Aristotle. Why did she refuse to believe me? Why did she try to persuade me that proven science was wrong? If she was correct, what did that mean for my *liaison* with Drusilla? For the other babes who had been brought to me? For my father, for our family, for my future?

No matter. I believed in all sincerity that my future life would be ruled by heart and conscience, that I would ignore unnatural constaraints, that I would do great deeds for freedom with this strong, brave, passionate woman at my side.

With the help of the Bey's tobacco and a bottle of Monemvasia I fell into a fitful sleep in which I slew my father, ran with the brigands in the mountains, wrestled with Aristotle, and was distraught for lack of tooth powder. It turned into a nightmare of grinning goats and pointed stakes from which I mercifully awoke . I went to the balcony to take some air and heard a disturbance in Winstanley's room. The door was half open and I saw him furiously pulling on trousers over his night shirt.

"What's the matter?"

"Aphrodite has appeared to me in a dream."

"And told you put trousers *on*? She has changed her tune."

"The goddess of love will not be mocked."

"True. Did she also tell you to put both feet in one leg?"

"*He rushes to her bed, impatient for the joy*
Helen followed, slow with bashful charms
And clasped the blooming hero in her arms."

"Wait. Come back."

But he rushed out of the room and was gone. There was danger if he ran into the watch or made a commotion outside Rabbi Koen's house. Besides, he was too late, another cock was in the hen house. I dressed, lit a lantern, belted a brace of pistols and hurried outside across the courtyard to the gate. At the cost of a few piastres to the guard I went out into the moonlit street. It was a fine, fragrant night, the air soft and warm, the moon bright. Night creatures chirruped and sang and hooted and squealed when they met their end. The balmy air, the scent of honeysuckle, the lover's moon brought back heady memories of my own nocturnal escapades.

I hurried to Amelia's lodgings, expecting to find Winstanley languishing under her latticed balcony like Romeo. There was no sign of him. I looked up. There was a light behind the lattice and I saw shadows move. Could he have got in to her room so soon? Could their rendez-vous be pre-arranged? Fury filled my head to bursting at this thought. Not twelve hours since, she had sworn her love to me. What should I do? Heart whispered to climb up on the balcony, tie him up to watch me pleasure her, shoot them both, fly to our ship and become a pirate. Conscience told me to forgive her frailty, challenge Winstanley to a duel and bury him with honour. Reason told me the balcony was too high to reach and there was nothing to stand on. I blew a bitter kiss and left them to it, desolate and furious and amazed at such a transmogrification in Winstanley and such feminine treachery in Amelia.

By the time I reached our apartments the mistress of all emotions, depression, was getting the better of the rest. Having nothing to humour her in my room I went to find Higgins' brandy, expecting to find him in his usual snoring stupor. But he was not in bed. A trio of guttered candles on a low brass table flickered in the draught from the door that opened on to our balcony. Drawings were strewn over the table and the floor and a portfolio was open. But where was the artist? Was he too on the tiles? And if so with whom? A drawing caught my eye and I lost all interest in the whereabouts of its creator.

It was a picture of Saint John Goat come alive in his chapel, a demon leering down on the viewer. He belonged at the edge of dreams as they turn into nightmares. There were others. Here he loomed over the landscape of Egripos as a destroying angel. Here he sat on a throne to receive the tribute of a virgin. Here he cavorted beside the lake by the light of torches held by his acolytes. Here he loomed in his cave among the dismembered carcases of animals and men. And who were his acolytes? I and Winstanley and Amelia and Higgins himself, naked, deformed, horns sprouting from our heads. Other caricatures showed Winstanley impaled on a stake, Amelia tupped by a he-goat, a she-goat tupped by Higgins, all with the same expression of ecstatic pleasure. And where was I in this hellish gallery? A snotty coxcomb on a goat's hind quarters dancing a jig to pan pipes played by an ancient, pox-raddled version of myself.

I was at the same time drawn and repulsed by these monstrosities. They went beyond the bounds of art and taste yet they were fascinating in their intensity and power. What force inspired him, a brute in life and up to now a milksop on paper? The candles flared. Higgins stood in the doorway to the balcony, a black shadow against the moonlight, holding his pencil like an assassin's dagger.

"Higgins, you are possessed."

"We are all possessed."

"Not I."

"Even you."

"These are the work of a lunatic."

"Sure. I work by moonlight."

"Destroy them before they destroy you."

"You sound like that impotent blatherskite Winstanley."

"Impotent or not, he is on the tiles tonight, tomcatting with Miss Burbage."

"He is not after that pussy. Come and see."

He led me to the balcony that looked out on the courtyard of the Loggia and the brooding tower in the corner.

"The foot of the tower. Where the moonlight meets the shadow. What do you see?"

It was a man in a black cloak. Gazing up at the tower he slowly raised his arms until they were parallel with the ground and then dropped them to his side again in the most eloquent expression of despair. He sighed and groaned aloud and raised his arms again. Then he made a rush for the wall and clinging with toes and fingers to the crevices between the stones began to climb.

"Winstanley. What is he doing? Where is Amelia?"

"What has she to do with this? The Vizir keeps the Eleni girl in that tower."

"Dear Lord. Love has made a fool of him."

"And fools of you and me."

"Quick, Higgins, before he is discovered."

By the time we reached him our human fly was already three feet off the ground. We swatted him down just in time, for the guards were on us with scimitars drawn. A few more piastres and the universal gestures to signify intoxication saw them off and we dragged our love-sick companion indoors. His madness had given him the strength of three and it was with great difficulty that we wrestled him to his room and dosed him with sufficient laudanum to keep him asleep until the following day.

The Rape of Helen
Gavin Hamilton 178?

REMEDIES

My tutor did not love Amelia but had taken it into his head that he was Paris and the girl in the tower was Helen and it was his destiny to rescue her. He was in love, a victim of the plague of desire, the more afflicted since he had avoided its contagion for so long. He had worshipped at the altar of reason and now the gods of passion demanded their due, with interest. To sedate him we plied him with his favourite hashish. He spent the morning sitting on a cushion, looking out at the tower, his head wreathed in smoke, eyelids half closed and a smile on his lips. From time to time he jerked out of his lethargy, leaped to his feet, rubbed his legs to restore their circulation, pissed in the chamber pot, paced the floor while haranguing himself in Greek or quoting Alexander Pope, and went back to his cushion. By dinner time he was befuddled and unaware of us or his surroundings.

"*Fair Venus' neck her eyes that sparkled fire*
And breast, revealed the queen of soft desire."

"His head is stuffed with a lifetime's nonsense, a lifetime's airy fiddle-faddle. They say the burning of the library in Alexandria was the greatest calamity the world has ever known. I say there is one greater, that all the other libraries had not burned down in sympathy. What miseries that nonsense has caused. How many bums have smarted to keep alive those dead languages and the fairy tales they tell? How many brains have been worn out learning them? How many lives have been wasted ?"

"Isn't that a pretty speech. But what do we do?" said Higgins.

"We must not let him out of our sight. There is real danger to us all in this delusion. The little heifer in the tower now belongs to the Sultan's herd. I would rather be Hercules and steal the Sun's cattle than make cow eyes at her."

"Now you are babbling mythology. It must be catching."

"If he so much as hints that he fancies her we will all end up on pointed stakes. Is that plain enough?"

"*Let the business of our lives be love*
These softer moments let delights employ
And kind embraces snatch the hasty joy."

"He is safe as long as he feeds on dreams," said Higgins.

"We must have him away from the island."

"We'll reason with him."

"A waste of breath. Insanity is never amenable to reason."

"*Do not despise the charms*
With which a lover golden Venus arms."

"Isn't he the scholar? He'll listen to the reason of my fist," said Higgins.

"*No hostile hand can antedate my doom.*"

"That will drive him deeper into his infatuation. Madness has to be humoured not bullied."

"*Fond love, the gentle vow, the gay desire*
The kind deceit, the still-reviving fire
Persuasive speech and more persuasive sighs
Silence that speaks and eloquence of eyes."

"We'll drug him with hashish and opium. We'll carry him to the ship in a litter. We'll say he's caught a fever."

Once we were at sea it was to be hoped that fresh air, distance from his supposed love and the healing powers of nature would cure him. More important, the rest of us would be out of danger.

I sent for Pericles and asked him to make sure that our ship was ready for sailing the next day, as the Vizir had promised. He was surprised and perturbed that our departure immediately before the arrival of the Captain Pasha might be considered an insult. When we mentioned fever he became deeply concerned, furrowing his brow and wringing his hands. I was careful to describe the symptoms in such as way that the illness would be thought serious but in no way resembling the plague. We insisted that our patient needed sea air and a change of climate.

Pericles was not convinced. He knew no precedent for removing a sick man to a ship from a lodging on dry land, where he was sure of fresh water, wholesome food and a stationary bed. He was sure that we would not be allowed into the port: there was a general prohibition against transporting the sick from one place and another, as a precaution against the transmittal of diseases. The quarantine regulations would be particularly enforced in view of the Captain Pasha's visit. If it were known that the authorities of the island had exposed His Excellency The High Admiral to sickness then many sturdy stakes would be whittled to a point. If Winstanley's illness became known, we would be confined to our lodgings until the Admiral left and we were all free of symptoms. I thanked him for this information and, with furtive winks and gestures asked Higgins to see after my tutor's health. He soon returned.

"Well now, he has woken refreshed. The fever's gone, there's no sign of redness and he's calling for his breakfast."

Pericles and I greeted this cheerful news with exclamations of relief and thanks to the Almighty. No man ever had a more sudden illness nor a speedier recovery, passing from health to health via serious illness in a twinkling. Winstanley proved our point by emerging in his nightshirt, the very picture of robustness, only to be confused by the congratulations of the Consul and wishes for a continued recovery.

Our patient did indeed seem recovered over supper, talking of this and that and making no mention of his Helen. Yet several times I noticed a cunning glance at one or other of us.

"He is well again. Think no more about it," said Higgins.

"The fox isn't dead but gone to ground. I have experience of this. I'm of the Nobility, remember, half my family is mad. We must not let him out of our sight."

"Then what shall we do?"

"We must think of a stratagem."

Half my family is insane but the other half is damned quick-witted. We don't grow scholars and men of science on the family tree but many people of practical cleverness among whom I make bold to claim a place. It took three pipes to come up with a stratagem to humour Winstanley's delusion and yet get us away from Egripos with our honour and our bottom-holes intact. It would also give us an anecdote to trump the highest card in traveller's whist.

"First: Winstanley believes he is Paris. His destiny is to rescue his Helen imprisoned in the Tower. Second: we must get him off the island as soon as possible. Third: Miss Burbage is begging to sail with us. Ergo: we shall stage the Rape of Helen. Winstanley will play the Hero. Paris will rescue his love from the castle and take her to our ship."

"What kind of stratagem is that? Sure it's what we want to avoid."

"We shall persuade Miss Burbage, as the price of her passage, to disguise herself as Helen. She will remain veiled until we are hull down over the horizon."

I shall always treasure the incredulity and delight that swept across Higgins' face as I revealed my plan.

"But how do we persuade Miss Burbage to play her part? She is not easily led."

"I have charmed enough women in my life to give much more than this."

"But when we have him aboard he will unveil his Helen. He may murder us all."

"He will come to his senses before then. He is a scholar, not a man of action. If we make his adventure difficult and dangerous it will jerk him back to sense. Failing this, the consummation of his desire may bring about its extinction, a phenomenon to which many lovers can bear witness."

"But he won't have consummated his desire. He will not have his Helen."

"He goes on about death in battle, the pain of love, the sacrifice to arms and other heroic nonsense. I don't believe he is in love with Helen but with himself in the role of Paris."

"Arrah, it's too deep for me."

"If his madness is so deep rooted that it persists up to the moment he finds that his Helen has disappeared, we have an explanation. Euripides says that Helen never went to Troy. She was spirited away to Egypt while her phantom went away with Paris. Either Winstanley stays mad and accepts the fiction or sees through it and recover his wits. A beauty, eh Higgins?"

"Genius. I hope."

"The essence of genius is invention. Keep him under guard while I go and seduce Miss Burbage."

I left Higgins with Winstanley and went to find Amelia at her lodgings. We sat demurely in the little courtyard, watched by hidden eyes, yet exchanging such burning glances that I had to take off my hat and put it on my lap.

"Last night I waited at my window like a silly girl, gazing at the moon and praying for my knight to come and then you came. The kiss you blew me was as sweet as any."

Her eyes were moist with tears. I let my own eyes speak for me and then launched into the practical purpose of my visit.

"On the mountain I told you about my tutor eaten up with a passion that is driving him insane. He is deluded that he is Paris and it is his destiny to rescue Helen, the girl they gave to the Sultan."

"Winstanley thinks he is Paris? What you told me yesterday on the mountain was about him?"

"Of course. Who did you think it was? Me?"

We both laughed at this. I then explained my stratagem, that we would stage the abduction of Helen and that she herself, we hoped, would take the place of the girl until we were on the ship. She replied with a non-sequitur I would haveassociated with the less logical sex but which I didn't expect from practical Amelia.

"When did you love me?"

"I have loved you for ever."

"Yes, but when did you first know that you loved me?"

"Yesterday. In the cave."

"Ah."

"Listen. Will you do it?"

"What will he do when he discovers I am not the Helen of his dreams?"

"It doesn't matter. We shall be safe at sea."

"And if he takes me as his Helen, what then?"

Before I could reply she looked down at the sun-freckled backs of her hands and made another non-sequitur.

"What will you do when I am old?"

"You are my Helen. You will never grow old."

"I am twenty years older than you."

"That many? You could be …" I smothered the words 'my mother' but she guessed.

"Dear Oedipus."

I had no reply to this, as I was struggling to remember who Oedipus was. We sat in breast-heaving silence for a moment. At last she spoke.

"Why did you come to my window last night? Was it to do with Winstanley?" No. I will not force you to answer."

If you have ever been in an ironworks you will have seen in the swirling smoke a stream of molten metal, fluid and bright hot. In the mould it hardens to a more familiar colour, but retains its heat. Amelia tempered herself.

"Will you do it?"

"Yes."

"Capital!"

We agreed that until we were on board ship we would behave as though nothing had happened between us. As I outlined our plan and the preparations for it, the smile on her lips seemed less loving than mocking. As the Rabbi's wife served us mint tea I was piqued that she hid her true feelings with ease, as in my experience of illicit love, even if the cuckold himself is present, the lady can't resist little smiles, sidelong glances, and other signs of secret passion.

"My love, why are you suddenly so sad?"

She didn't reply. I put my hat back on and took my leave.

penny plain and twopence coloured

YOUR HERO

On the morning of our performance I woke before the others, dressed and went out of the Loggia. I had something to do in private. I headed downhill to the Euripos and against the crowd coming over the bridge into town. In the middle was a niche for a pedestrian to stand. I looked over the parapet. For once the waters swirled, making eddies and waves where the currents collided. I reached inside my shirt and took out Aristotle's Last Legacy in its oilskin wallet. I dropped it into the water. I had weighed it with pistol ball. It bobbed for a moment and sank.

"Good riddance."

Did our journey have a quest after all? Was it for this that I endured the discomfort of travel? Was I lighter without my burden? Of course. At the same time, like a bad tooth or a wart, when it was removed it was like losing an old friend.

There were other stories to finish. We spent the rest of the day preparing our pageant. By evening the play was written, the parts given out, the properties collected. In our travelling troupe I was playwright and director; Amelia was the heroine, a non-speaking but essential part; Higgins was villain, army, horses, noises off, and Winstanley was Hero and Audience, ready to be purged of pity and fear, delusion and madness, a catharsis of which Mr. Garrick would have been proud.

Three of us assembled in the stable outside the city walls where Rousseau watched us from his manger with a critic's disdain. First we were Winstanley's dressers. Over a thick wool shirt and under his thickest coat we strapped a heavy metal breastplate and back plate I had bought from Chorbaji Two-face. I told Winstanley they had belonged to a valiant knight of Athens who had fought the Turk at the Battle of Lepanto. We didn't have cuisses and greaves but the body armour was enough for a scholar used to carrying no more than the weight of his pedantry. He was already sweating before we tightened the straps.

Ceremoniously I presented him with my sword, telling him how it had passed through the family since the days of William the Conqueror, defended king and country at Cressy and Agincourt and fought for honour and love in the lists and duelling fields of a hundred castles of England. The truth is that my draper grandfather bought it off a bankrupt builder, who had it made by a cutler in the town on the day he paid Chatham for a knighthood in expectation of his profits from the South Sea scheme. Higgins gave him a pair of antique pistols he had acquired on our travels, primed and loaded with harmless cotton wads, which he said had belonged to a knight of Rhodes who was descended from the first Crusader to enter Acre.

The best was the helmet. Higgins bought it off a blacksmith, who was going to melt it down. It was made of iron in the Venetian style and very heavy. We polished it and fixed a neck strap and some goose feathers as a crest. We said it had been discovered in a pit in Aulis that was doubtless a grave of a Greek returning from Troy or an Argonaut bound for the Golden Fleece. It was too big for his head, coming down over his ears and obscuring his vision unless he held his head back.

The more far-fetched and extravagant our tales, the more eager Winstanley was to believe them. The fabrications of his imagination fed on themselves, swelling and growing with every swallow until they were eaten by one bigger. We should have feared them bursting, and his mind with them, but we were too carried away to restrain ourselves. He stood head erect, sword aloft, feet astride, knees trembling with the weight of armour, crowing in his magnificence like a Hercules, declaiming a battle hymn in the manner of Homer, sweating like a Turk in a hamam, the helmet slipping over his eyes and pushing out his ears. I helped him to a chair and lit his hashish pipe while Higgins mixed a tonic of sherbet and brandy.

Restored, we introduced him to the camel. It chewed the cud and looked down at his new drover with consummate arrogance. We explained that Ali did not have the courage for so dangerous a journey but that a camel was no more trouble than a donkey, except their bite was more severe.

The characters had their parts and the scene was set. The plot was simple. We told Winstanley that I had bribed the guards of the Loggia to hand over Helen to us. They would bring her to the stable after dark and it was his task to carry her off to the port and embark her on our ship. We told him that Miss Burbage had agreed to lend her camel and her firman, so that anyone they met on the road might believe it was her and not the lovely Helen. Meanwhile Higgins and I would follow the following morning with the real Miss Burbage disguised as a servant. On no account was he to unveil his prize before they were on board ship. The innocent girl would swoon at his manliness while he himself would be distracted by her beauty from the task in hand. I quoted Menander, who wrote that Paris had not gazed upon the face of Helen nor she on his until they were on the island of Githion where they spent the first night of their honeymoon. He remembered the quotation, although I had made it up, and promised by his sword to keep her covered up.

"*This day, this dreadful day, let each contend,*

No rest, no respite till the shades descend,
Till darkness or till death shall cover all"

"Give me your hand, my hero," I said, and slapped the side of his helmet to make his head ring.

"A fine warrior," said Higgins and slapped the other side.

"We commend you to Mars and Venus, war and love."

Inspired by divine madness he surprised us by standing unaided with drawn sword, to bid us farewell.

"*The beauteous warrior now arrays for fight*
In gilded arms magnificently bright."

We hurried outside to the shadow of a plane tree, doubled up with laughter.

"Will he last a hundred paces?" snorted Higgins.

"If he can heave that camel so far."

"And if he can't?"

"We will come to his aid. I have a bottle of laudanum. If necessary we shall put him to sleep, load him on the camel and describe his feats of bravery to him when he wakes up. Hush. Here comes his beloved."

The covered litter we had hired from town came along the road and stopped outside the stable door. Winstanley came out to meet it, resplendent in his helmet, opened the curtains and handed down Amelia, who played the hesitant damsel to perfection. The litter bearers left with ribald comments about what was to happen next. We crept to the stable and peered in through a crack in the wall. We saw the dim shape of Winstanley on his knees before Amelia, gazing up at her as she stood quite still, head bowed. He spoke to her in a mixture of modern and ancient Greek, punctuated by English. Had she been the girl he thought she was, she would have burst out laughing or run from the spot for fear she was in the clutches of a madman.

Amelia bowed graciously and in a gentle, girlish voice that mimicked the accent and intonation of the island, thanked him for his courage and hoped that she would be worthy of him.

Even though I knew she was acting I was irked to hear my mistress flirt with another man and for the first time felt remorse. I looked angrily at Higgins to stop his indecent gestures at her pretty speech.

Sentimentality was soon dispelled by Winstanley's attempts to mount his beloved on the camel. Amelia played her part as if she had never in her life climbed on such a thing. It was beyond Winstanley's skill to make it kneel so he put a ladder against the wall. He puffed and groaned and cursed until finally she was seated on the camel, facing the front, in the right place before the hump, holding tight with hands and knees and will power. We spied from the bushes as Winstanley, with many a heroic tug, urged the lumbering beast into motion and began the journey through the night to the port.

We followed at an easy pace. The streets of the towns were policed at all hours of the night but the watch did not extend to the country roads. We had nothing to fear from gendarmes, only from brigands and other predatory fish who swim in the dark, against whom Higgins and I were the hidden escort.

The hero strode in the bright moonlight with more swagger and liveliness than his puny frame, his scholarly stoop, and weight of armour should have allowed. His coat was open to reveal the gleaming breastplate; through the tail stuck his sword; over his right shoulder he held the camel's rein; in the crook of his left arm he held the helmet, the humble goose feathers transformed by moonlight into a brilliant panache. Behind him was the camel, no more the scrofulous, moulting stinking beast, yellow toothed and drooling, but a wonderful figment of the poet's imagination, like Pegasus or a Sphinx, implausible to common sense, carrying, before the hump, enveloped in the white mist of a veil, his Helen. With the moonlight and excitement and the romance of the scene I felt, to my surprise, a twinge of envy of the hero.

I had warned Amelia that we would stage our own little bits of business to test our hero's courage and embellish his story, in which her part was to scream a little and keep the camel calm. Moved by the sight of them I urged Higgins not to disturb their peace but he insisted. I suspected he was motivated more by malice than mirth.

With a forced march through an olive orchard we overtook them and lay in ambush on either side of the road. When they were twenty paces from us we called to each other in gruff voices and scraped our daggers on our swords and called ready lads and steady boys in mock Greek and generally stirred up a racket that would terrify any traveller in the dark. Our victim put on his helmet, which he must have padded at the top for although it sat on his head like a bucket no longer squashed his ears.

With a flourish that would have instantly got him a part in Drury Lane he drew my sword and defied his enemies to show themselves. Higgins choked back laughter and let go a cracking fart. Shouting the name of Helen as his war cry Winstanley rushed towards him. Afraid that Higgins would be unmasked I jumped up, my face hidden behind my cloak, to draw him off and was rewarded with a startling flash of flame, a crack and the whistle of shot past my ears. Winstanley must have given Amelia the old pistols. I feared more for her safety than ours, since the barrels had not been tried for many years, and thought her concern for realism had gone beyond common sense. I beat a retreat, pursued by the gallant Hero rushing towards me. I skipped back into the shadows of the olives and he gave up the chase, returning to defend his lover, who was now screaming at the camel turned skittish by the din.

Breathless with effort and laughter I saw Higgins standing on the wall bordering the road, waving a stick, ten paces from the restive camel. The moon was behind him and he towered over the scene. Even though I knew who it was, I shuddered at the apparition of this demon. Winstanley rushed towards him and he turned his back, gave another cracking fart, and crouched to jump back in the field. There was another flash of flame from Amelia, answered not by a fart but a cry of pain. He raised both hands and plummeted head first into the field.

I laughed to burst my breeches at this performance, capped by the sight of Amelia pretending to lose control of the camel, which she made to canter down the road at a loping trot, sticking its neck out like a flying duck. With no more thought for his attackers Winstanley capered after them, waving his sword and struggling to remove his helmet.

As the Grecian Knight galloped into the darkness I called gleefully to Higgins, but there was no answer. I scrambled over the wall and found him flat on the ground, not moving. I turned him over, cradling his head, and felt the wet and warmth of blood on my hand. I pressed my ear to his chest, to his mouth, and, fearing he was dead, cursed our fooling with the infatuation of our friend, and wondered how I would explain it to the Turks. Imagine my relief when Higgins groaned and sat up. He felt the back of his head and pulled out of his hair the cotton wad from the pistol. He felt his body for other injuries but thank God, the God of Carnival, Dionysius, who looks after his revellers and pranksters, the scalp wound was the only damage.

We decided against more ambushes, having had full value from the first. I bandaged Higgins' head and went to find Ali, who was minding the horses and baggage. The three of us continued to the port, where we arrived shortly before sunrise.

TRIUMPH

The Lord High Admiral's fleet filled the harbour. Our little ship was ordered to lie at anchor with some stinking fishing boats half a league along the coast, an indignity for which we would later be grateful. Two large men o'war, were anchored beneath the castle of Karababa. Inside the port crowded galleys festooned with flags, pennants and colours, a picturesque and festive sight. Between the galleys and the men o'war was a constant traffic of little boats. The Admiral's barge was an elaborate and top-heavy tub, adorned with tapestry and gold paint, suited more to the Bosporus than the fickle Aegean.

When the sun rose, the city was already a boy-poked ant-hill: a bustle of carts and mules carrying supplies to the hungry fleet, a flurry of worthies dressed in their finest clothes, a scurry of officers and messengers in peacock uniforms parading their men and standing them down and parading them again before the walls. Among them strolled the *leventis,* the sailors of the fleet, eyeing the taverns and the girls and agitating peaceable citizens with the prospect of the havoc they would wreak after nightfall.

Higgins and I hurried to the jetty and were rewarded by the sight of the camel, tied up in front of the customs house and looking no worse for wear. We were in time to see Winstanley and Amelia confront the guards and officials that lined the quayside. He walked with a grenadier's swagger, quite unlike his usual mincing shuffle, one hand on the hilt of my sword and the other cradling his ridiculous helmet. They had to present their firmans for examination three times and I imagined Winstanley's terror as he ran the gauntlet of authority in the mistaken belief that if the true identity of his companion were discovered they would suffer the most agonising torture. He seemed calm enough and Amelia played the modest part, although from her bearing she was unquestionably English.

Seeing them safely installed in the stern of a bumboat and casting off for our vessel, we turned our attention to our own preparations. These were mainly to do with the camel, which, since our vessel could not come alongside the quay, would have to be transported out by caique and winched aboard with derrick and span. Ali assured us that the camel was used to such treatment, as he himself was used to convincing the owners of small boats, and we left him to his negotiations while we engaged another boat to carry us aboard. Higgins stumbled as he boarded and almost fell into the sea.

Winstanley waited on deck for us. I looked for the black looks of reproach or fury or despair that would indicate he had discovered the trickery and was about to harm himself or us. He was in great spirits, exuding the self-righteous satisfaction of those whose deeds exceed their expectations. He greeted us with a courtly bow. I put on a serious tone and clapped the poor dupe on the shoulder and commended him to the captain of our ship as the bravest fellow I had met. I must confess that the irony in my words was only partial. By his lights he had braved the terrible penalty of discovery, crossed hostile territory in the night with a camel and a damsel, fought off a band of ruffians, bamboozled the Admiral's guards and was now within an anchor's weigh of success. For a man of action this was meat enough but for a scholar and a dreamer it was ambrosia. My speech to the brave macaroon was sincere.

"You have made words into deeds. You have brought poetry to life."

"The divine power of the muse, Sir."

"What do you say, Higgins? Did life imitate art or what?"

I expected the rude rebuff, the grumbling insult, the sneering joke. But Higgins was civil for once.

"Bigod, you have triumphed. I admit it."

"Sir, your words are linctus to the spirit."

"Where is the lovely Helen now?" I asked.

"In your stateroom."

He pointed to the heap of my belongings thrown out of my cabin onto the deck. I tried the door but it was locked. Winstanley showed me the key about his neck.

"Fear not, I shall defend it with my life."

"How goes it Madam?" I shouted through the door.

"She doesn't speak English. But where is Miss Burbage?"

"She is looking after the camel. She will be here shortly."

There was nothing more to do than stow our belongings and make fast for departure. An offshore wind was freshening and the sea was favourable. We could have slipped quietly away from the island if it had not been for the dammed camel. We rigged a tackle from the mizzen while Ali haggled with boatmen on the shore. The Captain was doubtful about stabling it on deck but his fears were assuaged with piastres. Higgins complained of fatigue and went below. I listened with admiration to Winstanley's account of the battle he had fought against a devilish band of brigands until my ribs hurt - there were ten of them and he killed three. I went below into the saloon and fell into a dreamless sleep.

CAPTAIN PASHA

I was woken up by a hubbub and a roaring. I came on deck to find the camel swinging in mid-air above the stem and voicing its displeasure, despite the blandishments of Ali in the rigging. They were watched by a Turkish officer in bulbous turban and court dress, flanked by a pair of imposing janissaries. Winstanley stood before my stateroom door, his hand on his sword like Horatio at the bridge. The officer presented himself as captain of the *Capitano*, the Captain Pasha's flagship. In tolerable English he said the Captain Pasha would be glad of the pleasure of our company on board his ship. I replied that we were greatly obliged and would call on His Excellency immediately and escorted the captain and his guards to their gondola. Winstanley became quite pale and shrilled orders to our Captain.

"We are discovered. Captain, take up anchor! Break sail! We must leave!"

"How far do you think we can get before those men o'war? They will be on us in a trice, not to speak of the battery on the castle," I said, biting back my amusement.

"We shall give them a run and then we shall stand and fight. Captain, prime the guns!" He puffed out his chest and eased the sword in its scabbard.

"We have come so far with stealth and cunning, let us put off brute force a while longer. If we are discovered we have no hope of escape and are best advised to negotiate our way out of our plight. If we have not been discovered, then we should act as though we were innocent in order not to draw suspicion on ourselves. Leave the Captain here to guard your lady and come with me to humour the Captain Pasha. We will set sail as soon as we get back. Trust me this time, Winstanley."

I weighed the risks of Winstanley's foolhardiness and judged him safer by my side inside the lion's den than dancing about outside it. I woke up Higgins with difficulty and helped him dress, since brandy and fatigue had dulled his ability to manage ties and buttons.

Having persuaded Winstanley to leave his sword and armour on the ship we were fetched by the Captain Pasha's barge, an imposing craft of twenty four oars and richly decorated, nearly as long and as broad as our ship. From a distance the Turkish man o'war was imposing but close up she did not bear comparison with an English ship of the line. The stern was very high with several ranges of decks and she was broad of beam. Her ungainliness was compounded by the ill-assorted rigging and the awkwardness of the *leventis,* hampered by the long dress they wore.

The Captain received us on the quarter deck and took us to the Captain Pasha's state room, a cabin with decorations and furnishings as fine as we had seen anywhere on land. Only the dappled reflections of the water on the ceiling revealed the nearness of the sea. The Captain Pasha sat on a sofa surrounded by his officers, including our Vizir. He was bulky but with thin face and hands, indicating that his corpulence was not inherited but cultivated over many years of extortion and indulgence. His lips were thin and cruel, and his nose like a hawk's beak between two close eyes: despite his courtesy he sent a chill about the room. The fear that pervaded the islands when he visited, and lingered when he left, had its origin in this icy man. He was polite enough, treating us with perfume and towels and sherbet and coffee and interrogating us about our travels. To the obvious satisfaction of the Vizir, I said our visit to the island was the crowning glory of our tour. Although masked in civility this was not an idle chat. It was an angling conversation, in which every question and every comment was a hook to catch information about his domain.

"I was told there were four travellers, that there was a gentlewoman among you, a learned botanist."

"She presents her compliments to your Excellency and begs you to excuse her. She is indisposed."

"I hope it is not serious," said the Vizir. "I spent a pleasant hour with her yesterday and she seemed in good health and spirits. I allowed her to visit the fortunate girl whose privilege it will be to travel with His Excellency to Constantinople."

The Captain Pasha asked the Vizir a question in Turkish and they rudely carried on talking and joking in their own language. It was obvious that the subject was the girl in the tower and Winstanley looked about to beshit himself.

"Sirs, may I invite you to take a tour of our ship and the others of the fleet? They do not compare with the ships of His Britannic Majesty's Navy but I hope they may be of interest."

Since nothing was done by this man without design I assumed that he wished intelligence of the strength and readiness of the Turkish navy to be carried back to Whitehall, little knowing that it was unlikely to get further than Vauxhall Gardens.

"When you have finished, it will be time to witness the presentation of the gifts I am privileged to carry to the Sultan."

This invitation, phrased in terms that did not contemplate refusal, almost brought on an apoplexy in my tutor. It would suit us all not to linger but I thought it best not to offend this little potentate.

"Your Excellency, nothing would give us greater pleasure than to inspect your command, which has already impressed us with its might."

I launched into my excuse, which rambled all the more as signs of dissatisfaction clouded the Captain Pasha's brow, when Higgins, with the greatest presence of mind, saved the day by pitching forwards on his face and lying motionless on the carpet. The sudden flurry drew a dozen daggers before fear of attack was replaced by fear of infection. My excuses were accepted without a murmur and slaves summoned to carry our companion to the boat. As we were bundled into the barge we saw censers brought to fumigate the room. When we reached the safety of our own deck I congratulated Higgins on his presence of mind but his fit was genuine and he was carried into the saloon.

"Where is Miss Burbage? You told me she was coming with us," asked Winstanley

"Safe on board."

"Then make sail quickly, Captain."

I was amused but also irritated that Winstanley's supposed exploits had given him the right to command us.

Captain Pasha
Jean Brindesi

FREEDOM OR DEATH

The breeze was slight but sufficient and short work was made of weighing anchor. Winstanley and I stood at the poop rail and, seeing a commotion at the harbour, borrowed the Captain's telescope. A troupe of horsemen galloped out of the city, followed by a crowd of citizens, whose yelling we could hear across the water. The sailors on the boats at the quayside caught up the shouts which spread from vessel to vessel. We heard the boom of cannon from one of the smaller warships, followed by two more. Winstanley clutched my sleeve in panic.

"All sail, Captain, we are found out."

"Calm yourself, it's a salute."

We replied with a salute from our bow cannon. What was my surprise then to see our own salute returned, this time from the battery on Karababa, and this time with shot. A column of water rose between us and the open gulf, followed by another. Their aim was bad but in such circumstances one thinks only of the lucky shot and not the calculated odds. Two more shots came from the castle but they came no closer and we decided that we were out of range. Our relief was tempered by the sight of sails being broken out and other activity on one of the men-of-war and two smaller galleys of the escort.

"It's all up. Now me have to run," said Winstanley.

"Heave to, Captain, it is foolish to run when we have done no harm," I said, tired of the charade.

"Done no harm? Captain your life is in danger too, you are an accomplice to our crime," said Winstanley.

The Captain asked what crime. For answer Winstanley took the stateroom key from around his neck, unlocked the door and went in. He came out leading his Helen by the hand, unveiled. I went to greet my Amelia and wondered why she was still oriental dress. Then I saw it was not Amelia. It was Eleni, daughter of Pericles, the maiden in the tower.

"Who is this? Is this your English Lady?" said the Captain.

I was speechless. I stared at the face of each man in turn to verify they were who their clothing claimed. I rushed into the cabin and willed so hard to see Amelia on the bunk, under the table, in the chest, that she appeared in all those places, like a ghost, and disappeared again. I ran out on deck and burst into all the cabins, even the Captain's, fighting off his attempts to restrain me.

"Where is Amelia, where is Amelia?"

"Not here, not here."

"By God she is on this ship and I will find her, if I have to tear it plank from plank."

I pushed him off and ran to the saloon. Higgins was lying on his bunk, looking up at the ceiling. Black rings had formed around his eyes and his teeth were bared in the mockery I had so often seen in him. I shook him by the shoulder .

"You know where she is, Higgins, tell me or I shall smash the grin off your face. The joke is over."

His head rolled on the pillow and he looked at me, staring through me with his goatish eyes, as though I were a phantom. I slapped his face and it was stiff and cold. Winstanley and the Captain and his men came up behind me. The sailors held my arms and the Captain put his ear to Higgins' lips.

"He is dead."

The ship was heeled only slightly and scarcely pitching as she crept before the skittish breeze but never in any storm or earthquake has the ground beneath my feet seemed so insubstantial. I was taken on deck in the practised grip of the sailors, while Winstanley closed the eyes of our companion and covered him with a blanket.

Helen came to meet me from her cabin and handed me a paper. The sailors let go my arms and let me read while they held my coat, although this became unnecessary .

"These lines must be brief as I embark on my next adventure as soon as the covered litter arrives. I have persuaded the Vizir to permit me to visit the girl and his firman is in my hand. If you are reading this you will know that I have executed your ingenious plan to the letter, not the spirit you intended. I have changed places with Helen and, if your stratagem has worked, she is with her Paris and I await my fate. You must believe that what I do is not done with despair or malice. I do not have the martyr's bent and my pain at not being loved by you is more than compensated by the memory of our brief happiness.

My life has been ruled by impetuousness of heart and word and deed, a quality which has excluded me from society. I do not regret this, since I have found inspiration and joy in the deserts and mountains, which few men or women have experienced. But I no longer want to be the plaything of my passions and you will be my last and therefore most enduring love. Who can explain the thunderbolt of love? Its consummation in the cave of Pan seemed to be the end of all my wanderings. How quickly was I disabused! Lightning illuminates the world and is gone in an instant. I believed that you too had succumbed when, unable to sleep with thoughts of you, I got up and saw you standing beneath my window, lit by moonlight. It was your tutor's love that drew you to my window, not your own. I thought, for a blessed moment, that you would join me in my world of wandering and adventure, free of the petty conventions and cares of society, but you showed me that this ideal realm exists only in the heart. Once we left this enchanted island our love, if it survived at all, would be transient and secret.

I am tired of wandering alone but where shall I go? Dulwich is as petty a world as any seraglio. You put the answer in my hands and I shall offer myself to the Sultan in exchange for Helen. No, I am not gone quite mad. He will not be attracted by my charms, although I believe you will agree that I have learned on my travels a few tricks, which would compare with those of his most skilful concubines. If I am spared I can make myself useful in his household with my botanical learning, painting and knowledge of the world.

I have no love for Turkish despotism but I feel a duty to my sisters, the other Helens of the harem, to enlighten their imprisonment. Most of all it will satisfy my most consistent passion, curiosity. No territory is more uncharted and exotic than the Sultan's courts and I have long wished to explore them. The paradox is amusing, is it not, that I hope to find new freedom in the harem? If the Sultan does not accept the exchange and takes my head, then I have still done you the service of disappearing from your life.

I hope that it will also render a service to Winstanley, who has come late to love, and no less ardently for that, and to his Helen. She is a spirited and intelligent girl, lacking only education, and will risk everything for freedom. She has the true Greek spirit of independence and swears she would rather be deflowered by a stake than a Turkish despot.

Please do not try to save me from the fate I have chosen for myself, either with a foolhardy gesture of your own or through British diplomats. I have little love or loyalty for that cold, grey island in the north and expect none of it for me. Some years ago, influenced by Ali's generous faith, I converted to the Muslim religion, rejecting the Hebrew, Greek and Heathen hotch-potch of Christianity with its strange beliefs and myths, in favour of the simpler, clearer faith of Islam. I do not think that the government of Great Britain cares for Muslims, even though many are its subjects.

I ask only one favour. Ali has been a devoted servant and a generous lover, tolerating my impetuous affairs. By the enclosed paper I bestow title to all my property upon him and I look to you to ensure this is executed.

This enterprise is a risk for us all, but so is life itself, however much we hedge it about with prudence and timidity. How else do we deserve reward? Your loving Amelia B."

I read this letter in a tumult of emotion. Mingled with the memory of the rapture I had experienced in the cave and the protestations I had sincerely made of undying love, was the knowledge that she was right. A love affair with a woman without youth or fortune was doomed to transience. I was not made to cut myself off from society and my inheritance. Honour and common sense, love and self-interest, remorse and relief struggled in my breast. For once the finer feelings triumphed over the base.

"Captain, I order you to go about and return to Egripos."

"Milord I will not. Better an hour as a free man than forty years a slave. Freedom or Death."

I protested all the louder to drown the inner voice that told me to be glad that I was shot of her. I cried out to my tutor.

"Winstanley, don't you condemn Aeneas, who abandoned lovely Dido to her death?"

"Sir, don't be deluded by old fables. They are only stories."

I allowed myself to be over-ruled, against my better nature but with my better judgement. Apart from abandoning Amelia this was not the way I would have wished to take leave of our Turkish hosts, from whom we encountered only hospitality, and which we repaid with incivility and rapine. Our captain seized the helm, threw his cloak back over his shoulders, thrust out his chest, tossed back his head, twirled his moustaches, and steered us through caiques and bumboats out of the port, coaxing every cat's-paw of wind. Taking advantage of what little wind there was he sailed close to shore, taunting the pursuing janissaries to catch us. They doubtless did their best but in that race it was wise to be flat-footed and fall behind, since those of our crew not engaged in nautical business lined the rail with blunderbusses and carbines.

In the middle of the defenders stood Winstanley and his Helen, my antique pistols in their hands. He had put on his ridiculous helmet and took up a hero's pose, shooting arm outstretched in front, balancing arm outstretched behind, like Jupiter about to unleash a thunderbolt. His paramour took a more practical position, two hands around the pistol butt, barrel on the rail. She had thrown off her veils and put on Winstanley's breastplate. Her eyes blazed, her hair flowed free, powder smudged her face not kohl, passion coloured her cheeks not rouge. She looked every inch a warrior princess and again I felt the pangs of jealousy. Why wasn't I the centrepiece of this pageant? I should be the hero defending liberty and love against the tyrant, not this half-baked scholar, this pompous cleric, this weed-fuddled fopdoodle. Instead I had abandoned my love in a tower to face her fate alone.

I then made the vow to which I have been faithful ever since - within the constraints of practicality and circumstance, human weakness and reasonable self-interest. I would let my life be ruled by heart and conscience.

We were abreast of the mosque when our captain judged that we were out of the lee of the fort and the cliffs behind. The breeze was stiffening. He ordered the foresail backed and helmed hard over to take us close to the wind and out to sea. We inched away from the shore but were in no less danger since the Turks had manned boarding galleys and were rowing in hot pursuit. The clumsy Turkish ships for all their lubberly crews would have soon outrun our little craft if we had not been saved by a *fortuna*. The wind picked up strong and gusty from the south. The sky was overcast and the horizon covered with black clouds streaked with a treacherous light. Neptune, who blew us to our fate on Egripos, blew us off again. The sky darkened, the sea rose, and we lost our pursuers in a cloud of mist and rain.

We had one casualty lost overboard. Roussseau burst three of his tethers and threatened to strangle himself on the others and kick down the side of the boat. The Captain ordered him cut loose and the last we saw of him was swimming with head and hump above the waves like some mythical sea monster. If ever he reached the shore alive and was found browsing by the water's edge he was surely the origin of more tales. Ali grieved for his camel and his mistress for a decent time and then, with the fatalism of his race and the promise of compensation, resumed his placid disposition.

When calm returned we buried Higgins, sewn in a canvas bag with a cannonball and his devilish sketches for company. I prayed that the waters would quench the hell fires in his breast and give him the oblivion he craved. Helen gave him such a piercing ululation, with those oriental intervals he detested, that I half expected to see him stir within his shroud. I did not tell her she had killed him with her pistol. Winstanley asked some pointed questions about our whereabouts on the night of his adventure but I was mum and he soon gave up. Besides, he had other things to think about. He stayed in their cabin with Helen and I had to clap my ears against their sighs and groans and giggles, morning, noon and night. When they appeared it was hand in hand, eyes only for each other, deaf to our ribaldry and envy. Consummation of his mad desire cured its cause, Aphrodite brought him back to his senses. His words were now his own and when he talked of Paris and his Helen, it was by way of metaphor .

We sailed west, avoiding land and other ships as long as our provisions would allow, in case the news of our crime had spread through all the Turkish empire. By dead reckoning and the grace of fortune the Captain steered us to Corfu, where we left Winstanley and Helen. They had no wish to leave Greece and with glowing references from me he entered the service of the governor as tutor to his sons. I gave them money and a letter of credit so that, before I took a fond farewell, they bought a dilapidated property on a promontory, built like a small castle, from the battlements of which they could stand in fond embrace and watch the horizon for the Sultan's ships sweeping down upon them like the vengeful fleet of Agamemnon.

Greece Liberated

POSTFACE

So there was a quest after all. Which was not revealed until it had been accomplished. Indeed there were several hidden quests, each with its consummation. Winstanley found enlightenment, love and a vocation - the rebirth of Greece. Higgins achieved endarkenment and the oblivion which he sought in the brandy bottle. Amelia found a new adventure and a use for her learning.

What was my hidden quest? Liberation from Aristotle's legacy? A better understanding of love? A decent hand of traveller's whist?.

ADDENDUM

Following is an extract from a document in the archives of the Turkish Academy of Sciences, Istanbul and kindly translated into English by Dr. Çelik Pasinlı, deputy archivist. It is dated Ramadan 1178 (October 1788) and signed by the Vizir of Egripos. It was addressed to Ahmed Baylat Bey, Constantinople.

In the name of God the Compassionate and Merciful to his esteemed and learned brother etc etc This letter should be delivered to you by the hand of its subject, a distinguished English natural philosopher by the name of Miss Amelia Burbage. Despite her sex she is a person of great learning and practical knowledge. I commend her to you in the hope that she may be of use to you in your great project for the Academy of Sciences, (may God smile on it).

Miss Burbage was our guest on Egripos for some months during which time she made an extensive study of the flora of the island. She has made a copy of her treatise and the more important sketches for your use. The originals, along with specimens, drawings and paintings I have presented to his Excellency the Grand Kislaragasi (may God protect and keep him as he protects us). May I suggest that you solicit the permanent loan of them for your new library. I hope that they will contribute a grain to the storehouse of knowledge that you are building for the honour and glory of his Magnificence the Sultan (God bless his name and keep him).

During her sojourn on Egripos I had often urged Miss Burbage to offer her services to the Sultan, knowing how he desires to improve the education of his court and the general knowledge of science. She is weary of constant travel in pursuit of her vocation and has little love for her native country, not least because her sex precludes her attending their scientific societies or publishing her work.

Towards the end of her stay three English travellers arrived on our island. They said they were making the Tour, as they call it. We are familiar with Tourists in Athens but what was my unpleasant surprise to find them washed up on our shores. They purport to be gentlemen of good family but if so, why do their parents allow them to go on such fruitless and expensive wandering to the detriment of their reputation and that of their native country? They claim an interest in antiquity but pass the days intoxicated and the nights with loose women.

Their ship wanted repair so I had no choice but to offer them the hospitality to which Tourists believe they are entitled. My plan was to keep them quiet with narcotics and wine until they could leave. In order that they should not offend my subjects with their customary lewdness I laid upon them stern strictures concerning relations with the fair sex.

As you may remember, the Christian population offers each year in lieu of taxes one of their refractory daughters to the Grand Kislaragasi (may God bless him and keep him). What good to us is another idle body fattening itself at our expense on the sofas of Topkapı, breeding dissatisfaction and discontent? It is my belief that we should curtail this privilege and insist on piastres.

One of the English gentlemen, a scholar priest despised by his companions, became infatuated with the girl, to the extent of climbing the walls of the tower in which she was kept. They would not confide in me and decided to flee the island in secrecy and haste. In order to amuse themselves at their companion's expense, they concocted a plan whereby Miss Burbage would pretend to be the girl and he would escort her to their ship at night. Such is the brotherhood of Christians.

Miss Burbage divulged the plan to me and asked that instead of a substitute I would permit the girl herself to be abducted. In return she offered to engage herself to the Sultan for a period of five years and to present our protector the Grand Kislaragasi with her entire library and portfolio of studies.

I discussed this proposition with his Excellency (God smile on him and help him). As you know, from his beneficence to your cause, he too has an interest in natural philosophy. We allowed the abduction of Helen to proceed. Once on board we teased them more by delaying them and then let them go with a few cannon shot to speed them on their way.

May merciful God keep Tourists from our peaceful shores.

EDITOR'S NOTE

On the evidence of the surviving draft of Exford's manuscript and associated papers, corroborative texts of contemporaries, and topographical research on Euboia, The Hero Of Negropont is based on an original diary written in the early summer of 1788.

It is likely that the first narrative version of the story was a private memoir of an incident which had a profound effect on the young author and was to influence the rest of his life. With the calamitous changes in his fortunes over the following years and the necessity to make a living it appears that he reworked the original manuscript with a view to publication or as a libretto for the musical theatre. Letters he wrote to the booksellers James Jordan of Holborn and S. Walters of Printing House Square refer to a 'literary property' and negotiations were opened with both, although with no result. Similarly he wrote to the manager of the Theatre Royal Covent Garden with a 'proposal for an entertainment in three acts on an English, Greek and Turkish theme', again with no success.

With an eye on publication he embellished the original narrative with literary conceits and motifs popular at the various times that he composed the successive drafts. There are borrowings from many European writers from Shakespeare to Chateaubriand. He plagiarised travel writers like Boswell, Sterne and Hobhouse. The verse quotations are from Alexander Pope's Iliad. There are also theatrical, operatic and artistic allusions. If one includes the work of lesser known writers of the day it is conceivable that, like Winstanley's speech, 'it is entirely made up of quotations'.

Three apples fell from the sky,
one for the teller of this tale,
one for the listener
and one for whoever will pass this tale along.

Traditional Turkish

ILLUSTRATIONS

(For illustrations in colour see fortunebooks.xyz)

Boufalo, Dystos, Klimaki, Aliveri, the Euripos.
What are they like now, two hundred years after Exford?

IT'S ALL GREEK TO ME!

by
John Mole

Sun, Sheep and Sea, Ruins, Retsina – and Real Greeks.
A love affair with Greece.

A little whitewashed house with a blue door and blue shutters on an unspoiled island in a picturesque village next to the beach with a taverna round the corner - in your dreams Moley. Welcome to a tumbledown ruin on a hillside with no road, no water, no electricity, no roof, no floor, no doors, no windows and twenty years of goat dung.

Come to our village on Evia. Meet Elpida, who cures bad backs with a raw egg and spells; Ajax the death-dealing butcher; Saint John the goat-headed saint; beautiful Eleni yearning for Düsseldorf; old man Christos, dug up on a sunny summer morning; sun-touched Dionysos dancing like an English tourist; the family saved from a watery grave and Hector their dog, a mutant specially bred to frighten little children.

Here is timeless, rural Greece - catch it before it goes.

Published by Nicholas Brealey (including Kindle)
www.fortunebooks.org
ISBN: 9 781857 883756

John Mole

Greece and Constantinople.
What were they like two hundred years before Exford?

THE SULTAN'S ORGAN

The diary of Thomas Dallam 1599
put into modern English by
John Mole

In 1598 merchants of the City of London paid for a Present to be given by Queen Elizabeth to Sultan Mehmet III of Turkey. In return they hoped to secure trading concessions and to turn the Sultan's military might on England's Spanish enemies. The Present was a carved, painted and gilded cabinet about sixteen feet high, six feet wide and five feet deep. It contained a chiming clock with jewel-encrusted moving figures combined with an automatic organ, which could play tunes on its own for six hours.

With it went Thomas Dallam, musician and organ builder. He encountered storms, volcanoes, exotic animals, foreign food, good wine, pirates, brigands, Moors, Turks, Greeks, Jews, beautiful women, barbarous men, kings and pashas, armies on the march, janissaries, eunuchs, slaves, dwarves and finally the most powerful man in the known world, the Great Turk himself.

Dallam was the first foreigner to record a glimpse into the Sultan's harem and the first to cross mainland Greece. His diary is a wonderful traveler's tale that will richly entertain and inform travellers to Greece and Turkey and fans of Elizabethan history.

Published by Fortune Books (including Kindle)
www.fortunebooks.org
ISBN: 9 780955 756924